*The Secret Adventures
of Charlotte Brontë*

❧❧

THE SECRET ADVENTURES OF CHARLOTTE BRONTË

Laura Joh Rowland

THE OVERLOOK PRESS

New York

This edition first published in paperback in the United States in 2009 by
The Overlook Press, Peter Mayer Publishers, Inc.
New York

NEW YORK:
141 Wooster Street
New York, NY 10012
www.overlookpress.com

Cataloging-in-Publication Data is available from the Library of Congress

Book design and type formatting by Bernard Schleifer
Manufactured in the United States of America
US ISBN 978-1-59020-154-1
2 4 6 8 10 9 8 7 5 3 1

To my agent, Pamela Ahearn,
for her loyalty and perseverance

The human heart has hidden treasures,
In secret kept, in silence sealed;
The thoughts, the hopes, the dreams, the pleasures,
Whose charms were broken if revealed.
                    —CHARLOTTE BRONTË
                        "Evening Solace," 1846

I hardly know what swelled in my throat . . . such
a vehement impatience of restraint and steady
work . . . such a strong wish for wings . . .
                    —CHARLOTTE BRONTË
                        Letter to Ellen Nussey, 7 August 1841

PROLOGUE

>‹‹

THERE ARE CERTAIN EVENTS THAT HAVE THE POWER TO RAVAGE LIVES and alter the fate of nations, yet they transpire unnoticed by the general public and leave no record, because their history is a secret locked within the souls and memories of the few mortals involved. Such were the events that I, Charlotte Brontë, witnessed in the year 1848.

I have sworn to take the secret to my grave, and to speak any word of it would bring censure, scandal, and disgrace upon myself and betray a sacred trust. Still, my knowledge burns inside me like a fire, a pressure that must find release or shatter the fragile vessel of my being. I cannot bear that the most singular episode of my own history should go untold.

It occurred at a time when my life held meaning and promise, and I had the companionship of persons most beloved to me. But now, as I write, a year has since passed, and my companions are gone. Thus stripped and bereaved, I spend night after night in terrible solitude, haunted by memories. I have decided that I must record the events of that summer—come what may—and although I know not whether anyone will ever read these words, they shall be my tribute to the valor of those whose loss I mourn. Let these pages survive them, that they shall not fade into obscurity as their mortal remains disintegrate into dust. The fantastic narrative which

I am about to commence is the truth as I know it, and I shall be as
candid as the truth requires. God is my ultimate witness, and I beg
His forgiveness if I say anything to offend.

My story does not begin with me, nor at the moment when I
stumbled into these events that would transform my life. It begins
on the other side of the world, in Canton, the port of foreign trade
in southern China. The date was 14 May 1841. Imagine a twilight
sky swollen with storm clouds hovering above British warships on
the river outside Canton. Their tall, square sails heave like dragon
wings in the tropical wind; cannons and guns on the decks thunder,
bombarding the waterfront. The Chinese Imperial Army returns
fire from war junks and from forts and watchtowers on the river-
bank. Flames consume docks and warehouses on shore. The turbulent water reflects the blaze, gleaming crimson as if layered with
blood. Smoke drifts towards the wall surrounding Canton's Old
City, inside which crowds of Chinese stampede through alleys in
desperate flight. Ruffians loot abandoned shops; renegade soldiers
brawl in the street outside an estate belonging to a high imperial
official.

The incident that precipitated everything which befell me
occurred within this estate, a complex of courtyards and gardens
surrounding a mansion. Precisely what happened there that
evening is known only to persons who are no longer able to speak,
but I shall recreate the terrible drama and hope that speculation
based on facts will not compromise the truth.

Inside the mansion, a woman named Beautiful Jade huddles
in her chamber on a carved bed draped with satin curtains. She
wears multicolored silk robes; tinsel ornaments sparkle in her
black hair. Her slim arms encircle her two daughters, small ver-
sions of herself. Their delicate faces pinched with fright, the
three listen to the gunfire and the rioting in the streets. The
bitter fumes of gunpowder mingle with the scent of jasmine
from the garden.

Beautiful Jade fears that the battle will rage until Canton lies in
ruins and everyone inside it is dead. The estate's guards and servants have all fled. She longs to follow suit and remove herself and

her beloved children from danger, but her husband has insisted that they remain inside until he returns.

A loud crash outside startles Beautiful Jade. She looks through the window. The night glows with the ruddy, fitful light of a sky reflecting fire. Beautiful Jade hears rapid footsteps in the courtyard; erelong, she sees shadows moving in the garden, where palm trees rustle. The footsteps mount the stairs to the veranda, and the door creaks open. An icy terror spreads through Beautiful Jade. The barbarians have invaded Canton. They have entered her house!

She scrambles off the bed, dragging her daughters with her. Five men burst through the doorway, one bearing a torch that splays flame light onto the chamber walls. They are not foreigners but Chinese ruffians dressed in ragged clothes and straw hats. Each carries a long knife. As her daughters scream in fright, she asks the men who they are and what they want. They command her to tell them where her husband is. When she replies that she doesn't know, they rampage around the chamber, hurling vases to the floor, overturning tables, smashing chairs, and ripping down tapestries. The terrified children cling to their mother. Again, the men demand to know her husband's whereabouts. Even had she known, Beautiful Jade could not have betrayed him.

Now two ruffians grab the girls. Aghast, Beautiful Jade holds tight to them, but the men drag the children away. The girls sob while she begs the men not to hurt her daughters. Another ruffian lashes out at her with his knife—she screams. The blade cuts through her robe. Faint with horror, mouth agape, she clasps her hands over the blood welling from her bosom. The knife slashes again. Beautiful Jade flings up her arms and feels the blade slicing open her flesh. Desperate, she tries to stumble away from her tormentor. Beyond him she sees her daughters helplessly flailing in their captors' grasp. They shrill in a high-pitched chorus that pierces her heart. She falls to her knees, bleeding from countless cuts, weeping in pain and terror, crying in vain for help.

Were the last sounds she heard the thunder of cannons from the attacking ships and her daughters' screams?

I shall never know the anguished last thoughts of these three innocent victims, but I do know that they were found with their throats cut, their bodies mutilated. As to why they were slain, and the consequences of their murder, those facts became apparent during my own part of the story, which begins seven years thence.

—CHARLOTTE BRONTË, *July 1849*

1

❖

WITH A TALE SPINNER'S SLEIGHT OF HAND I ADVANCE THE calendar—the date is now Friday, 7 July 1848. I rotate the globe and sight upon my home village of Haworth, in the North of England. Reader, I present for you a picture of Haworth on the morning of that fateful day when my adventures began. The sun, glinting from between cloud masses in the vast, cerulean Yorkshire sky, illuminates the ancient stone houses that line the steep, stone-paved main street. Shopkeepers scrub their doorsteps, a farmer herds a flock of sheep, and village women carry baskets past a horse-drawn cart piled high with raw wool. At the top of Church Lane, isolated at the highest point in the village, stands the parsonage, a two-storied house built of grey-brick, roofed with stone flags, and flanked by graveyards. Beyond the parsonage lie the moors—undulating hills cloaked in grey-green heather, shading into the far horizon.

Inside the parsonage, I was sweeping the hall when I heard a thud outside. Puzzled, I set aside the broom and opened the door. My younger brother Branwell toppled towards me and crashed at my feet, sprawling across the threshold.

"Branwell," I said, peering with consternation at him through my spectacles.

He pushed himself to his knees and smiled jauntily up at me. "Ah, my dear sister Charlotte," he said, slurring the words. "How convenient that you should be here just in time to welcome me home."

I regarded his bleary eyes and lurid complexion, his disheveled clothes and shaggy auburn hair. Rank fumes of whisky rose from his person. "You have been drinking again." I felt the anger, disgust, and helplessness that Branwell's inebriation always occasioned in me.

"It was just a little tipple down at the Black Bull Inn," Branwell protested, clambering to his feet. "Life gets unbearably dull hereabouts, and surely you wouldn't deny me a bit of amusement now and then?"

"Except that it isn't only now and then." I shut the door more firmly than was necessary. "And it's not just the drink. You've taken laudanum, haven't you?" Branwell had, alas, degenerated into a habitual user of that tincture of opium dissolved in spirits.

"I'm sorry, Charlotte," Branwell said, "but I was so in need of comfort." A coughing fit wracked his thin body. "Can you not see how miserable I am? Please forgive me."

Reluctant compassion quenched my anger as I observed my brother. He was only thirty-one but looked a decade older, his once handsome features haggard. Still, I could see in him a vestige of the robust, bright-eyed boy who had been my favorite childhood companion.

"You had better go upstairs before Papa sees you like this," I said.

The door of the study opened, and out stepped our father. Though in his seventies, Papa was still an imposing figure—over six feet tall, whitehaired, stern-featured, and proud of posture. Beneath his black clerical garb he wore a voluminous white silk cravat wound high around his neck to protect him from Yorkshire drafts and guard against bronchitis. He squinted at Branwell through the spectacles perched on his prominent nose, and a look of anxious confusion came over his face.

"I thought you were asleep upstairs," he said to Branwell. "Have you been gone all night?"

Branwell hung his head; his coughs subsided into wheezes. "Not all night. I just slipped out for a few hours. That's God's honest truth."

"It is a sin to deceive," Papa said, frowning in reproach, "and shameful of you to invoke God as your accomplice."

My younger sisters, Emily and Anne, appeared in the parlor doorway. Anne, neat and unobtrusive as always, held a cloth with which she'd been dusting furniture; when she saw Branwell, distress clouded her violet eyes and gentle features. "Oh, dear," she murmured.

Emily, tall and lanky, pushed up her leg-of-mutton sleeves. Always indifferent to her appearance, she stubbornly clung to that outmoded style of dress. She had been canning blackberry preserves, and purple stains blotched her apron. Heat had frizzed her brown hair and flushed her long face, and that day she looked even more wild and singular than usual. She glared at our brother. She had lost all tolerance for the sickness, the convulsive fits, and the unpredictable moods that Branwell inflicted upon our household.

"Well, have you all gotten a proper look at me?" Branwell said with sudden belligerence. "Then I believe I shall go to bed. I'm all done in."

Reeling towards the stairs, he stumbled. Emily grudgingly helped me assist him up the stairs. I couldn't help but regard with some sadness the family portrait in the stairwell. Branwell had painted that portrait. He had, when he was younger, possessed artistic talent, and Papa had sacrificed much in order to pay for painting lessons. All of us had hoped Branwell would attend the Royal Academy, but his ambitions and our dreams had come to naught. Now, awkwardly climbing the stairs, Branwell began to weep.

Emily and I dragged him into the bedroom he shared with Papa. Anne turned down the coverlet of his bed and pulled out the pillows he had rearranged to trick our father. Emily and I heaved Branwell onto the bed.

"Lydia, my distant, darling Lydia," he keened. "My love for you has ruined me!"

Six years ago, Branwell had become a tutor to the son of the Reverend and Mrs. Robinson at Thorpe Green Hall, near York. Lydia Robinson, a wanton woman of forty, had seduced Branwell. He had fallen madly in love with her, and they'd conducted a torrid affair until her husband had discovered it and dismissed Branwell. Ever since then, Branwell had pined for Lydia, drowning his woes in liquor. What a sorry waste he had allowed that terrible woman to make of his life!

"None of you understand how I suffer," he moaned as Emily tugged off his shoes. "You have never loved and lost as I have!"

With great self-restraint, I forbore to remind him that our father had many years ago lost his beloved wife, and we our mother. Emily, stern and unrelenting, went downstairs without a word, but Anne tenderly arranged the coverlet over Branwell.

"Oh, Anne, don't fuss so," Branwell cried. "Lord, I wish you would all go away!"

Chastened, Anne crept out of the room. Papa sat beside Branwell. "We must pray for God to forgive your sins and give you the strength to reform."

"I cannot bear another sermon now," Branwell said in a tone of rising hysteria, "and besides, there's no use moralizing, Father. It's too late; it's all over with me."

Stifling a sigh, I left the room. I knew I ought to finish sweeping and set out for my afternoon visits to parishioners suffering from the hard times that had fallen upon the country. Yet the tedious routine of my days oppressed me so that I succumbed to the powerful urge to escape to my other life, the secret existence known to but three other people besides myself.

Furtively, I slipped into the small room above the front hall. Near its window stood a battered desk. I took from my pocket a key, then unlocked and opened the desk drawer. I lifted out a book whose cover read "*Agnes Grey*, a novel by Acton Bell." Opening it to the title page, I read the handwritten inscription: "To my dear sister Charlotte, with much love, Anne Brontë."

In another book, "*Wuthering Heights*, by Ellis Bell," Emily had simply penned her signature. I then took up my own book, and pride swelled within me as I caressed the gilt lettering that read "*Jane Eyre*, by Currer Bell." Almost ten months had passed since its publication, but I felt the same ecstatic thrill as when I first held it in my hands. I could still hardly believe that Emily, Anne, and I had accomplished our dream of becoming authors. But the drawer contained further proof of this miracle. I perused book reviews cut out of newspapers. The one from the *Westminster Review* read, "Decidedly the best novel of the season."

There were also letters from my publisher, informing me that the first edition of my work had sold out, and notices of two subsequent editions. I smiled at a handbill for a play, *Jane Eyre, The Secrets of Thornfield Manor*, produced in London. Finally, I turned to the account book where I had recorded my income—one hundred pounds for the copyright of the novel, and an additional hundred pounds in royalties. This was no great fortune, but it represented ten times more than the annual salary I had earned in my former occupation as a governess. Yet uncertainty about the future and a nagging dissatisfaction with the present worsened as I paged through the notebooks that contained the manuscript of my next, as yet unfinished, novel, *Shirley*.

I had developed serious doubts about this novel and its reception by my publisher and, ultimately, my readers. I feared their high expectations of Currer Bell, whose identity was a subject of intense speculation among the literati. And I mourned that my present success had failed to bring me everything I craved.

As a young girl, scribbling stories and dreaming of a future as an author, I believed that publication would gain me passage into a world of art galleries, concerts, and the theatre, where people conversed brilliantly. I'd hoped to travel and to win the friendship of writers, artists, and intellectuals. Yet here I remained, hidden behind a nom de plume, my life as a parson's spinster daughter virtually unchanged. A wistful melancholy stole over me as I looked out the window and down the hill upon the grey rooftops of Haworth and the grey smoke from the textile mills in the wooded valley. Beyond these familiar environs lay the world of my dreams. I was thirty-two years old and, it seemed, destined to spend the rest of my days in torpid retirement.

Then I spied the postman coming up the road, and my spirits lifted. The post was a source of light and life to me. I carefully locked the desk drawer, because although Papa had been told the secret of Acton, Currer, and Ellis Bell, no one else must know—not even Branwell, who could not be trusted with the secret. I tucked the key in my pocket, hurried downstairs, and eagerly accepted a letter from the postman. I read the sender's address on the envelope: "Smith, Elder & Company, 65 Cornhill, London."

This was the letter that would launch me on a dangerous path through worlds beyond my imagination, but all I then understood was that the letter came from my publisher. As I scanned the two sheets, my anticipation of good news turned to dismay. I rushed downstairs and found Emily stirring a cauldron of preserves on the stove. Her bulldog, Keeper, lay beneath the table where Anne and our servant, Martha Brown, sealed jars. The kitchen was humid with fruity steam and hot from the coal fire.

"Emily. Anne," I said, "we must talk."

My face must have revealed my agitation, for they immediately followed me through the back door to the yard, out of Martha's hearing. Above and away from us spread the moors, their hilly expanses broken only by a few stunted trees and the distant black lines of stone walls. Blustering wind whipped our skirts.

"Currer Bell has just received a disturbing communication," I explained, then read aloud:

> My Dear Sir,
>
> As you will no doubt recall, Smith, Elder & Company has secured from you the exclusive right to publish your next novel and to grant secondary right of publication to our counterparts abroad. However, it has come to my attention that Mr. Thomas Cautley Newby, publisher of the works of Acton and Ellis Bell, has sold to an American publisher, for a high price, a book entitled *The Tenant of Wildfell Hall*, which he claims to be the new work by Currer Bell.
>
> We at Smith, Elder & Company were quite indignant to learn that a rival business has gained a property which is lawfully ours. Are we to believe that you have deliberately breached your contract with us? (It would appear so, judging by the enclosed document.)
>
> We respectfully request an explanation of this circumstance.
>
> Yours Sincerely,
> George Smith

Emily and Anne stared in astonishment. I cried, "Anne, my publisher believes your book to be mine. He suggests that I've cheated him!"

"There must be a mistake," Anne said hesitantly. "My publisher knows that Acton Bell and Currer Bell are two separate individuals. Surely Mr. Newby would not claim otherwise."

"But he has," I said, holding out the paper that had accompanied George Smith's letter. "This is an extract from a letter written by Mr. Newby to the American publisher: 'To the best of my belief, *Jane Eyre*, *Wuthering Heights*, *Agnes Grey*, and *The Tenant of Wildfell Hall* are all the production of one writer.'"

Emily shook her head, frowning. Anne, looking bewildered, ventured, "I cannot believe that Mr. Newby would intentionally misrepresent me."

"I can," I said, "because he has already treated you both in a shabby fashion. Remember that he charged the printing expenses for *Agnes Grey* and *Wuthering Heights* to you. Then he delayed publication of your books. And he hasn't yet sent you the royalties he owes you. Mr. Newby is an unscrupulous man who would do anything to profit himself."

"And he is doing so by capitalizing on the success of Currer Bell," Emily said. Her large, luminous eyes, ever a magical mixture of fire and ocean, were of a hue that changed with her moods; now anger darkened them to slate blue. "He seeks to elevate little known authors by confusing them with a celebrated one."

I winced: Emily was a person of few words, and those often too blunt for comfort. The differing degrees of success achieved by Currer, Acton, and Ellis Bell represented a sensitive issue that we avoided discussing. Though Emily and Anne were genuinely pleased by my good fortune, I knew that if our positions were reversed, I would envy them, in spite of our affection for one another. I also knew how badly they must feel about the reviews of their books.

"There is not in the entire *dramatis personae* a single character which is not utterly hateful or thoroughly contemptible," the *Atlas* had said of *Wuthering Heights*. *Agnes Grey* had fared no better. "It leaves no painful impression on the mind—some may think it leaves no impression at all." Worse, both Emily and Anne had suffered from comparison to me when the *Athenaeum* had proclaimed of *Jane Eyre*, *Wuthering Heights*, and *Agnes Grey*: "All three might be the work of one hand, but the first issued remains the best."

How much I regretted that my writing had set me apart from my sisters! Would that today's missive had not done further damage to our harmony!

"Dear Charlotte, I'm so sorry that my book has endangered your reputation," Anne said.

She was always too ready to accept blame and thereby restore peace. "The fault belongs to Mr. Newby," I said. "And I fear he has endangered more than my reputation." I paced the yard in a fever of anxiety. "I know little of the law, but enough to see that appearances suggest that I've broken it." I had a horrible vision of the authorities descending upon the parsonage, and myself arrested and thrown into prison. "What am I to do?"

"Write to Mr. Smith. Tell him that Currer Bell, Acton Bell, and Ellis Bell are three distinct individuals, and that anyone who says differently is a liar," said Emily.

"But I told him as much when the critics raised the question of our identities," I reminded her. "If he doubts me now, why should another letter convince him?"

"Perhaps I could order Mr. Newby to set matters right," Anne offered.

"Why would he, and put himself in the wrong?" I said, dismissing the notion that mild-natured Anne could force anyone to do anything. I halted my pacing and faced my sisters. "The only way to solve the problem is to dispense with pen names and reveal who we really are."

Anne gasped in alarm. "No!" Emily burst out. Vehemence harshened her normally quiet, melodious voice, and her eyes darkened to a stormy grey-green. "When you first suggested that we try to publish our works, we all agreed that we would always use pen names."

While Anne and I had adopted pen names because we enjoyed the secret and thought that male aliases would assure our work a more favorable reception, Emily had wished to avoid unwanted exposure. Neither my sisters nor I participated much in any society, but Emily was the most reclusive among us. She was like a wild creature—happiest when rambling the moors alone. She shot a pleading glance at Anne, who moved close to her.

"Dear Charlotte," said Anne, "I know your situation is grave, but surely there is a solution that doesn't require us to reveal our true identities."

Anne always took Emily's side, for they shared a special intimacy that excluded everyone else. They were like twins sharing one heart. A familiar pang of envy needled me, because Emily was my favorite sister as well as Anne's.

"But there is not another solution," I insisted. "Even if I manage to convince Mr. Smith that I didn't write *The Tenant of Wildfell Hall*, problems will continue to arise as long as there remains a mystery about who Acton, Ellis, and Currer Bell are. People will always confuse us."

"Let them," Emily declared, tossing her head. Her hair swirled in the wind; with her back to the clouded sky and sweeping moors, she seemed a wild force of nature. "I don't care."

"Well, I do," said I. Even as I admired Emily's independent spirit and hated to cause her pain, I suddenly felt a tremendous impatience to cast off the pen name that had obscured me like a suffocating shroud. "We must let Mr. Smith and everyone else know us at last."

"But . . . ," Anne wrung her hands. "If Mr. Smith doesn't believe there are three authors named Bell, why would he believe you if you write informing him that the authors are three Misses Brontë?"

"He probably would not," I said, encouraged by a sense that Anne shared my desire for recognition. "Therefore, I propose that we go to London, so that Mr. Smith may see us with his own eyes." As I spoke the words, my heart fluttered like wings inside my chest; the world of my dreams seemed suddenly within reach.

"London?" Emily said, as though I had suggested a trip to Hades. The color drained from her face, and she retreated from me. "I won't go. I can't!"

Here I must add a few more strokes to my portrait of Emily.

She had spent almost her entire life in Haworth. Each time away, however brief, she would become sickly and lifeless, like a plant torn from its native soil. She feared strangers and crowds, and hated noisy, dirty cities. She made me feel selfishly cruel for asking her to travel to London; however, I was determined for us to go.

"Please, Emily," I said. "It won't be so terrible. We needn't stay very long, and we won't reveal our identities to anyone outside Smith, Elder & Company."

"No!" Emily ran to the parsonage and pressed herself against its brick wall, looking more a frightened child than the woman of thirty years she then was.

Anne asked cautiously, "When would we leave?"

"Today," I said. "I must mend my relations with Smith, Elder & Company as soon as possible."

"Anne! You wish to go, too?" Emily gazed at Anne in disbelief. "You want to break your promise to me?"

"Oh, no," Anne hastened to say. "It's just that I think we must do what is right, and perhaps Charlotte knows best . . ." She quailed under the look of hurt and outrage that Emily gave her, then turned to me. "But we can't just arrive at Smith, Elder & Company without warning. What would they think of us?"

My determination wavered. We possessed among us no beauty to help us gain favor, and I considered myself the plainest—so small and thin am I, with a head too large for my body, irregular features, and a pallid complexion. Furthermore, my plan seemed audaciously forward, defying convention that required modesty of the female sex. But I put aside vanity and fear of social censure; I got a firmer grip on my resolve.

"Smith, Elder & Company can hardly think less of us than they do at this moment," I said. "We must risk a minor discourtesy for the sake of achieving a greater good."

"Well, I'm not going," Emily said. She was breathing hard, and her fingers kneaded her folded arms. "It's not my predicament. Mr. Smith's complaint regards only you and Anne. I've done nothing to warrant exposure. And I forbid you to tell anyone anything about me!"

It was clear that Emily would never be persuaded. "Very well;

you may stay home," I said reluctantly. "I won't reveal your identity. I suppose that two of us will be enough to prove ourselves separate individuals to Mr. Smith . . . if you'll come with me, Anne?"

Biting her lips, Anne looked from me to Emily, torn between her sense of duty to me and her loyalty to the person she loved best. When I became nurse, tutor, and disciplinarian to my younger siblings after the deaths of our mother and eldest sisters long ago, Anne was the only one never to disobey me. She had meekly accompanied me to the school where I taught, and she studied hard because she knew my salary paid her tuition. I knew she still felt indebted to me.

"Anne," Emily pleaded.

A small sigh issued from Anne. Bowing her head, she murmured, "We'll need Papa's permission."

Emily stood in stricken silence. Her eyes blazed with her fury and pain at Anne's betrayal. Uttering a cry of despair, she turned from us and ran towards the moors with the swift grace of a fleeing deer. Anne and I silently watched her figure recede; then, without looking at each other, we went into the parsonage.

Papa was in his study, writing a sermon. When I told him about George Smith's letter and our resolve to set things aright, he said, "Of course you must uphold your honor, and your proposal seems the only way." Though I always defer to his authority, his generous heart is loath to deny me anything. He went on, "However, the idea of your traveling two hundred miles to London disturbs me. These are dangerous times."

A cataclysm of revolution had convulsed Europe during the year. In France, radicals had rebelled against a corrupt, oppressive regime; strikes, riots, and warfare had beset Paris; the king had abdicated and gone into exile. In the Germanies, mobs had clashed with the army in the streets of Berlin. The Italian states had risen up against Austrian rule; in Vienna, the Hapsburg monarchy had battled its own citizens when they clamored for social reform. In Britain, Irish nationalists had revolted against English domination, while across England, radical Chartists had staged mass demonstrations. Their quest for voting rights for all men and equal representation in Parliament had incited violent disturbances. Queen Victoria had fled London. Yet I had no inkling that these events held any significance for me—they seemed but minor disturbances in distant domains.

"Things are somewhat quieted lately, Papa," I said. "Anne and I should be safe enough."

"Emily does not wish to go?"

"No, Papa." Guilt sickened me.

Papa said with reluctance, "I should escort you and Anne."

"Oh, no, Papa," I said, "you must not risk your health." He was susceptible to severe colds, and besides, I'd set my heart on our going unaccompanied. "We'll be fine by ourselves. I've visited London before, and I know my way around the city."

"Very well," Papa said with evident relief. "But do be careful."

"We shall, Papa." I hesitated, then asked, "May we stay a few days to see the sights?"

After some debate, Papa consented. Jubilant, I hurried Anne upstairs, where we began hastily packing. I was folding garments into a trunk when I noticed Anne standing at the bedroom window. Outside stretched the moors, like an empty sea. Emily had disappeared.

"She'll understand that we have no choice. She'll forgive us," I endeavored to reassure both Anne and myself.

Anne blinked away tears. I suffered a fresh onslaught of guilt, but resumed packing. The future beckoned.

➤✦◄

Now, as the hour grows late and the candles burn low, I wonder if I would have gone to London had I known that I was taking my first step towards a man who personified evil and madness. Would I have gone knowing what pleasure and pain, hope and despair, terror and glory, would be mine? But the fact is that I did go; and perhaps, when I have finished recording my tale, I will know whether I am more glad or sorry.

2

❧❧

ONCE, DURING A TRIP TO THE CONTINENT, I SAW A MEDIEVAL tapestry that depicted an everyday scene in an ancient town. Lords and ladies promenaded around the castle; merchants plied their trade in the street; peasants worked the fields while mounted hunters galloped through the forest and pilgrims entered a cathedral. Each tiny creature pursued his own business as if unaware of the folk in distant sections of the tapestry—yet all were joined by the underlying warp. I am struck by the resemblance of that tapestry to my story. On the morning I received George Smith's letter, I had no knowledge of events occurring a hundred miles away or of persons whose lives would soon be interwoven with mine.

Birmingham is a large industrial city south of Haworth; for my description of it and the happenings there, I elaborate upon an account given me by my sister Anne, who became closely acquainted with certain characters and environs. In a district known as the gun quarter is a courtyard surrounded by the brick buildings of Lock Gunworks. The noise of saws, hammers, and metal on grindstones emanated from neighboring businesses. Smoke from forges blackened the sky. Across the city resounded the Birmingham Roar: continuous gunshots from the test-firing of weapons. On this day the craftsmen of Lock Gunworks gathered in the courtyard around Joseph Lock, proprietor.

"I have interrupted your work to make an important announcement," Lock said. "As you are aware, Lock Gunworks has a long, illustrious history. My ancestors armed King William's troops against Louis the Fourteenth of France."

A portrait that hangs in the parlor of his house depicts Joseph Lock as a robust man with bold features and shrewd blue eyes. He appears quite the successful merchant and town leader. As to the thoughts in his mind at the time of this announcement, I must enter the realm of conjecture. I imagine him feeling an eerie sensation of being two selves divided—one the physical manifestation of Joseph Lock; the other, an ugly wretch cowering inside him, ridden by guilt.

"My father—may he rest in peace—manufactured guns for the Napoleonic Wars and the African trade," Lock continued. "It has been my birthright and my privilege to manage the firm and carry on the family tradition of loyal service to the Crown." Lock's voice cracked; tears of shame welled in his eyes, for he had dishonored his privilege and broken tradition through a secret, abominable crime.

He gathered himself. "However, I summoned you here not to speak of the past, but of present concerns. It is with great regret that I am today retiring from my post as head of Lock Gunworks and ceasing all involvement in the firm's operation."

An uneasy stir rippled his audience; Lock noted surprise on many faces, curiosity on others. He reviled himself for making his men accomplices to his crime. He looked upon the grimy, calloused hands that crafted the guns that bore his name, and he hated himself for lying.

"I do not make this decision lightly," Lock said. Indeed, he had agonized over what to do. But the chain of events that had begun with one small mistake brought his frantic search for alternatives to a single unavoidable conclusion.

"However, my advancing age and poor health leave me no choice but to retire." Another lie, that: he was only fifty, and in enviable health. "Therefore, I appoint my brother Henry as head of the firm." Lock gestured, and the young man stepped forward. He was twenty-nine years old, pale, handsome, and nervous.

"I ask you to work as loyally for Henry as you have for me," Lock told the workers, although he had no right to speak of loyalty after breaking all its bonds himself. "As a farewell token from me, you shall each receive an extra day's pay."

He hurried out of the courtyard, followed by the workers' murmurs of "Thank you, sir," and "God bless you." He strode through the gun quarter, past the workshops and public houses, to his home in the suburb of Edgbaston. Here lived Birmingham's important, wealthy citizens. The air was fresh, the smoke from the foundries a distant black smudge on the horizon, and the Birmingham Roar a muted echo. Birds sang in the trees that shaded the wide, sunny streets; mansions graced expansive lawns. The Lock residence was an elegant stone Italianate house. When Lock entered, his wife greeted him.

"You're home early," said she. "Is something wrong?"

"Not at all." Lock regarded her, blonde and rosy and innocent. Guilt and despair tainted his love for her. His betrayal of her was as grievous as his betrayal of his father and country. He said, "There's just something I need to do."

His two young sons raced into the hall, shouting and laughing. When they saw Lock, they halted, fell quiet, and stared at him. Lock mounted the stairs, consoling himself with the thought that his sons' heritage and livelihood would remain intact, and they would never learn the worst about him. He went into his study and locked the door.

Cabinets lining the walls displayed firearms produced by Lock Gunworks. He removed a pistol. The sinner in him directed his trembling hands to place powder and ball inside its chamber; he welcomed punishment, craved release from suffering. But the vestiges of Joseph Lock, pillar of the church and community, resisted compounding his previous sins. His breath rasped; nausea roiled his stomach as he cocked the pistol. He deplored the agony and shame awaiting his family.

Did he perceive the true nature of the villain responsible for all he suffered? Perhaps he thought about *her*, and the terrible heat of longing again enflamed him. He sat clutching the gun, torn by warring impulses, until his sinful, guilt-ridden self persuaded him that there was no other escape from the hell that he'd made of his life, and certain disaster lay ahead if he did not act. By yielding to temptation and cowardice, he had abetted forces powerful enough to ravage the whole kingdom, and this offered the only possible means by which to stop them. "God have mercy on my soul," he whispered, putting the pistol to his temple. He pulled the trigger.

The echo of that fatal shot quickly dissipated, but the inaudible reverberations traveled far beyond Birmingham, across time, and soon reached me.

3

❧❦

URING MY LIFETIME A MIRACLE HAS TRANSFORMED ENGLAND. Iron roads have spread fast and far, connecting every part of the kingdom. We now live in an age of steam engines and speed, and fortunes have been gained and lost on railway speculation. The rapid tide of progress merits awe, but on the evening when Anne and I set out for London, the miracle of train travel became a force hastening us towards doom.

That morning, Anne and I had sent our trunk to Keighley Station by wagon. Anne refused to leave without bidding Emily farewell, and Emily did not return from the moors— perhaps she hoped her absence would prevent our departure. Finally, after tea, I propelled a reluctant Anne out of the house. While we walked the four miles to Keighley, a thunderstorm drenched us, and I began to harbor serious doubts about our journey. Despite my earlier enthusiasm for the journey, and despite my assurances to Papa, I was far from confident about my ability to manage in the dazzling metropolis of London.

From Keighley we rode a local train to Leeds. It was dark by the time we arrived. Soldiers patrolled the platform—Leeds had been the site of recent Chartist demonstrations, and the threat of violence persisted. Soon Anne and I were boarding a first-class carriage for our nightlong journey. The carriage resembled an elongated stagecoach and contained three separate compartments. Anne and I occupied the center coach compartment, which had two upholstered seats facing one another, and a window on each side.

"Charlotte?" Anne said tentatively. "Where shall we stay in London?" This was the first expression of interest she had shown in the trip, as if she had only just accepted the reality of it.

"We'll go to the inn where Emily and I lodged with Papa on our way to school in Belgium." That trip had occurred more than six years ago, and I hoped the inn was still existent, because I knew nowhere else to go. Nausea born of apprehension churned my stomach.

"Do you think Mr. Smith will receive us?" Anne said.

"I daresay he will," I said, "if only out of curiosity." Surely Mr. Smith was as eager as the rest of the public to know the identity of Currer Bell.

"What shall we say to him?"

"We shall simply introduce ourselves and explain why we came." As my nausea worsened, I saw Anne's chin quiver with anxiety, and I hastened to reassure her. "The whole business should take but a moment, and we'll then be free to see the sights." I felt a duty to make Anne's first trip to the city a pleasant one. "Would you enjoy that?"

"I would." Anne smiled. "Dear Charlotte, you are so brave and capable."

The engine roared and the departure bell rang. Suddenly the coach door opened, and a woman stepped inside. She set a large bag on the floor. Before seating herself opposite Anne and me, she gave us a polite bow. I returned the bow; then a closer look at her arrested my attention.

She was tall and slender, with pale gold hair and a face so pure of line and complexion that it seemed modeled from rosy alabaster by a great artist. Dark lashes shaded eyes of deep, clear aquamarine. Her mouth was full yet sensitive, the lips a natural pink. Although she wasn't young—indeed, she appeared near my own age—her features constituted a striking beauty. A troubled air shadowed her aspect. She glanced out the windows, as if looking for someone.

The whistle sounded, and the engine chugged; the train moved forward with a laborious turning of wheels, through smoke and steam. The woman gave a sigh of relief. She and Anne soon fell asleep, despite the train's jolting, clamorous progress through the moonlit countryside. I cast furtive, envious glances at the stranger. My own plain, puny appearance has been a lifelong source of grief to me. As a young girl I wrote stories featuring heroines variously named Mary Percy, Zenobia Ellrington, or Augusta Romana di Segovia, all beautiful and much desired by their heroes; I created in fantasy what reality had denied me. As I now beheld all my heroines embodied in the stranger seated opposite me, awe gave way to curiosity.

Who was she? Her clothes appeared of decent quality but were neither new nor expensive. Her straw bonnet was unadorned; the grey pelisse hid whatever she wore beneath it. Was she married or a spinster? A gentlewoman of modest origins, or royalty in disguise? More speculation occupied me for many miles. On what business did she travel alone?

A sudden moan issued from the woman. Her eyelids fluttered; her head tossed from side to side, and she cried, "No! No!" Bolting to her feet, she lurched against me.

"Madam!" I exclaimed in alarm. "What is it?"

The woman's arms flailed; her eyes were blank with terror. I recoiled backwards in panic. Anne stirred but slept on. Was the woman having a fit? Trapped in the coach with her, miles from the next station, what should I do?

"Help, please, help!" the woman shrilled.

I considered waking Anne, then decided she would be of little use. Rising, I seized the woman by the wrists, pressed her into her seat, and sat beside her.

"Tell me what's wrong," I urged, "so I may assist you."

The woman was trembling, her breath a rapid wheezing. She lunged towards the door.

"No!" I held tight to the woman to prevent her jumping from the train. "Calm yourself: It was surely just a bad dream that frightened you."

"A dream." The woman's gaze cleared, and her voice conveyed grateful relief, but her complexion turned ashen in the moonlight. Her hand clutched her chest.

Quickly I rummaged through my satchel and brought out a vial of *sal volatile*. The woman inhaled the powerful fumes and coughed; her breathing slowed and deepened, and color returned to her cheeks. Lying back in her seat, she smiled weakly at me.

"Thank you," she murmured. "You are so kind. I must have disturbed you terribly." She spoke in a melodious, wellbred voice tinged with a North Country accent. "I do apologize."

"There's no need. I'm glad to be of service," I said. Conversation with strangers is contrary to my habit—I am usually tongue-tied in their presence—but the incident had fostered a sort of intimacy between the woman and myself. "What could have frightened you so?"

"I hardly know. Nightmares are so often forgotten upon waking." The woman's gaze darted, and I suspected that she, in fact, did recall but preferred not to say. Then, apparently feeling that she owed me some courtesy, she said, "Please allow me to introduce myself. I am Isabel White."

"It's an honor to make your acquaintance," I said. "I am Charlotte Brontë, and that is my sister Anne."

Isabel White regarded me with dawning interest. "Your surname is quite unusual. How is it spelled?"

I told her, adding, "It was originally 'Brunty,' but my father modified it when he left Ireland as a young man. He renamed himself for the Duke of Brontë—the title conferred upon Horatio Nelson in recognition of military services. He has been for many years the parson of St. Michael's Church in Haworth."

"Do you and your sister live with him?" Isabel asked, her aquamarine eyes intent on me.

"Yes. Anne and our sister Emily and our brother Branwell and I all make our home at the parsonage." I was flattered by Isabel's attention, as handsome people seldom paid me any. "Do you live in Yorkshire?"

Isabel's expression turned opaque, like a window when frost forms upon it. "Once I did, but no more."

The terse reply stung me, and I blushed because my innocent question had apparently offended Isabel. I was ready to excuse myself and return to my seat, when Isabel seemed to regret snubbing me and explained, "I have been working as a governess."

Though gratified to learn her social position, I was disappointed that she was but a humble governess. Now the lovely Isabel seemed an object of pity. There were advantages in being my plain self: Currer Bell had happily quit her former occupation. "I, too, have been a governess. How does the profession suit you?"

"I consider it less a matter of suitability than of necessity," Isabel said. "When circumstances require, a woman must support herself, regardless of her feelings about her position."

"I quite agree," I said. "I've always endeavored to earn my own livelihood."

"There are but few jobs open to women," Isabel said. Her manner seemed oddly defensive, and I wondered why she should need to justify herself to a comrade. "I should be thankful that I was given an education that won me pleasant, lucrative employment."

"As should I be," I said, further confused by Isabel's tone of bitter sarcasm. She might be making a joke about the hard labor that governesses performed for low wages; yet I sensed in her words a hidden meaning. I wondered why such a beauty had not acquired a husband who would have spared her the necessity of employment.

I myself had received no fewer than two marriage proposals, from eminently suitable clergymen. I had refused both, since I harbored no tender feelings for my suitors, nor they for me. They were merely eager to acquire wives to share their work, and I was unwilling to accept a man I could not love. I have become well convinced that I shall never marry at all—reason tells me so, although stubborn hope persists against all odds.

"Governessing might not have been so bad if I had any aptitude for disciplining children." Recalling my time with the Sidgwick family of Lothersdale, I shook my head ruefully. "I hope I never again meet such unmanageable cubs as those of my first employer. The eldest, a girl of seven, threw tantrums whenever I asked her to recite her lessons. Each day was a battle of wills, and I often the loser."

A pained, understanding smile curved Isabel's lips. "Children can be difficult."

"At my last post at Upperwood House in Rawdon," I said, "the little boy passed his water into my workbag."

We laughed, and our shared mirth warmed me. "Even worse than the children were the mistresses of the houses," I said. "They treated me as an inferior, and it was a sore trial to live as their dependent, at their command. It was no use complaining to them about their children's misbehavior. They scolded me for failing to maintain order and allowed the children to do as they liked. I shudder to think what ill-mannered adults those children have surely become."

Isabel nodded; a faraway look unfocused her eyes. "We are indeed products of our early training," she murmured.

Shyness barred me from asking what she meant by this cryptic comment. She baffled and fascinated me increasingly. "I often found the masters of the houses preferable to the mistresses," I said in an effort to keep the talk flowing. "Their presence caused the children to behave better. They made no demands on me; indeed, they made my lot easier."

"If that is the case, then you have been fortunate, Miss Brontë." Isabel gave me a queer smile in which self-pity blended with condescension.

Not knowing how to respond to this, I said, "Where are you currently employed?"

Isabel hesitated. "At the home of Mr. Joseph Lock. He is a gun maker in Birmingham."

"Is Mr. Lock a kind master?" I inquired politely.

"He is a good man," Isabel said, gazing out the window, "but kindness played little role in our association." A frown shadowed her profile as she mused in silence for a moment. Then she said in an almost inaudible voice, "I was brought up to believe that we should do unto others as we would have others do unto us, but I—I have broken that rule, as well as many others. Is it futile to hope that I may escape punishment?"

This sounded to me like a confession, but of what sins? I guessed that Isabel's troubles involved Mr. Lock, and I pondered what might happen between a man and a beautiful woman living in his house. I blushed again, ashamed of entertaining thoughts about subjects that were none of my business; yet my curiosity persisted.

"Are you going to Birmingham, then?" I asked, because that city lay on our route.

"No!" A shudder accompanied Isabel's violent negative. Then she turned to me and said, "I am on leave from my post and traveling to London." The frosty look had returned to her eyes. "Where do you and your sister go, Miss Brontë?" she said, abruptly steering the conversation away from herself.

"We are also traveling to London." I fervently hoped Isabel wouldn't ask why.

Isabel only asked, "And how long do you stay?"

"A few days," I said, glad that I need not fabricate a lie to conceal my private purpose.

"Will you be taking up employment soon?" Again, Isabel studied me with close scrutiny, as if genuinely curious.

Since I couldn't discuss my current occupation as a writer, lest I give away my identity as Currer Bell, I said, "At present, I'm between positions and living at home."

Isabel nodded, and I had the disconcerting sense that she was making note of this information for later reference. After a while, Anne awakened, and I introduced her to Isabel, and the three of us made trifling conversation. Whenever the train stopped at a station, Isabel cowered in her seat, seeming to avoid the window for fear that someone would see her. Anne and I left the carriage several times, but not she. Still, I doubted that Isabel could pass the whole night without leaving the train, and when we reached Nottingham just before midnight, she accepted my invitation to go into the station.

The platform was dimly lit by gas lamps; a few passengers and station officials awaited the train. Exiting the coach, Anne and I left our satchels inside, but Isabel lugged her carpetbag with her. This was large, bulky, and patterned with red roses. I wondered what was in the bag, and why Isabel would not let it out of her sight. Did it contain something valuable, perhaps stolen? Was it the law that she feared so?

As the three of us walked towards the privies, I watched Isabel dart wary glances at the other passengers. Her fright was contagious. I found myself peering across the dark train yard in search of pursuers, and seeing malevolence in the faces of the railway guards. Isabel stuck close by Anne and me as we entered the station's refreshment room. I bought tea to drink with the bread and cold meat we'd brought from home. I returned to Anne and found Isabel gone.

"She just turned and fled without a word," Anne said in bewilderment. "Why, I wonder?"

I watched the door swing shut. "I don't know."

"There's something about her that makes me quite uneasy," Anne said.

We ate our meal, then hurried back to the train. The window of our coach showed no sign of Isabel, but when I opened the coach door, a cry rang forth. Startled, we beheld Isabel lying curled on her seat, staring up at us.

"Oh. It's you." Relief erased the panic from Isabel's face.

"Whom did you think it would be?" I asked.

Isabel shook her head. "No one."

Anne and I exchanged glances as we took our seats. Soon after the train began moving, Anne dozed off. I tried to rest, but my mind seethed with questions about Isabel, who brooded in the seat opposite me. At last I slept, disturbed by dreams of unknown pursuers chasing me along railroad tracks, and of myself arriving naked at the offices of Smith, Elder & Company.

➤←

I awakened to sunshine on my face. Stretching my cramped muscles, I yawned. Through the window, beyond the railroad tracks, spread miles of dingy shops, warehouses, and tenements. Smoke cast a grey pall over the cityscape. During the six years since I'd last seen London, it had grown tremendously. This was the great capital of England, bursting with mansions and slums, pleasure gardens and markets, factories and monuments, and some three million inhabitants. I recalled how Emily had hated it. But I loved the sense that anything could happen in London. I sat up, alert, my nerves tingling with dread and excitement. Anne was awake, too. Isabel White looked as if she'd not slept all night, her lovely face wan and haunted.

"Good morning," I said.

My companions murmured in reply. Isabel said, "Miss Brontë, I must express my gratitude for your assistance and the pleasure of your company."

"The pleasure was mine." I was disappointed that our acquaintance must end and that I would never know more about the mysterious Miss White.

Soon the train drew into Euston Station and screeched to a halt beneath the iron roofs that sheltered multiple tracks. On one side stood inns, taverns, and a street filled with horse-drawn wagons, carriages, and omnibuses. Along the other extended the terminal building, fronted by the platform. There, a huge crowd milled. Gentlemen in tall black hats and ladies in fashionable gowns mingled with children and common tradesmen amidst piled trunks, bundles, and hampers. Vendors sold refreshments from trolleys; beggarboys roamed. The pandemonium daunted me, and I hesitated to leave the coach, but Isabel flung open the door, hefted her carpetbag, and quickly stepped onto the platform. Anne and I picked up our satchels and followed. Steam and smoke from chugging locomotive engines assailed us as we huddled together in the rushing crowds. Other passengers alit and greeted waiting friends; railway guards climbed on the train's roof and unloaded baggage. Whistles shrieked and voices clamored. Isabel stood near me, her worried gaze scanning the chaos.

"Have you a place to go?" I asked, feeling a certain responsibility towards her.

Clutching her bag, Isabel nodded vaguely, looking past me.

On impulse I said, "Anne and I will be staying at the Chapter

Coffee House in Paternoster Row. If you desire company, please do visit us there."

The guards pulled our trunk off the train and dropped it on the platform. Anne and I hurried over to claim our property, and when I again looked towards Isabel White, she had vanished.

4

>—<

B Y EIGHT O'CLOCK THAT MORNING,
ANNE AND I MADE OUR WAY TO
the Chapter Coffee House. We washed ourselves, breakfasted, then
set off for the premises of Smith, Elder & Company.

London engulfed us in its overwhelming turmoil. Horse-drawn
carriages manned by red-coated coachmen rattled through the
crammed streets. Costermongers hawked fruits and vegetables;
female peddlers sold matches and needles. Crude laborers trudged
along every thoroughfare; ragged children armed with brooms
begged to sweep our path clean for a penny. We walked rapidly,
clutching our pocketbooks, fearful of thieves. Sharp London
accents colored the voices around us. And everywhere was filth
even worse than I remembered. We sidestepped garbage and horse
droppings upon which flies swarmed; we forded streams of black,
malodorous water in open gutters. A foul stench of decay emanated
from the nearby Thames River. The air tasted of cholera.

Breathless and perspiring in the heat, our clothes grimy with
dust, we at last reached Cornhill, a broad avenue in London's financial district. Around us towered the Royal Exchange, the Bank of
England, and other examples of classical architecture. London is
the world's richest city, and we were in its mercantile heart. Foreign
languages buzzed through the district. Wealthy traders congregated
in coffeehouses and jostled humble black-coated clerks.

Number 65 Cornhill turned out to be a large bookseller's shop in an imposing row of four-story buildings. Above its display windows, the legend "Smith, Elder, & Company" was engraved in stone. I swallowed hard, looked at Anne, and said, "The sooner done, the better."

We entered the shop and found inside a spacious room with bookshelves lining the walls. Customers browsed while lads bustled about wrapping books in paper and string, hauling stacks in and out, calling remarks to one another. Everyone had an intimidating air of sophistication. After some hesitancy, Anne and I crept up to the counter.

"May I help you?" said a clerk.

He was a distinguished-looking gentleman with a brisk manner, and my nerve almost failed me. I cleared my throat and said, "May I see Mr. Smith?"

"Is Mr. Smith expecting you?"

"No," I said. "But it's quite important."

"Very well," said the clerk. "Please wait a moment."

He went through a door at the rear of the shop. Anne and I huddled together. I regretted that we, in our simple country frocks, looked not at all like famous authors. I wished I resembled Isabel White, and I momentarily wondered what had become of her. Just as I experienced an overwhelming impulse to run, the clerk returned, followed by a tall man.

"Did you wish to see me, ma'am?" the man said in a well bred, dubious tone.

Stricken by terror, I peered up at him through my spectacles. He was lithe and clean shaven with smooth brown hair and sideburns; he wore a dark grey summer coat, pale trousers, a crisp white shirt, and blue silk stock. "Is it Mr. Smith?" I quavered.

"It is." A touch of impatience colored his polite manner.

George Smith was younger than I had expected—not above twenty-five years of age—and quite handsome. He had dark, shrewd eyes, regular features, a dimple in his strong chin, and a fair complexion. I grew all the more flustered because I am uncomfortable in the presence of attractive men. That they care not for me was a painful lesson learned early in life. I fumbled in my handbag, took out the letter that had brought me to London, and handed it to Mr. Smith. He examined it, and I saw confusion on his face.

"Where did you get this?" he said, regarding Anne and me with sharp suspicion.

"You sent it to me," I blurted, then lowered my voice so that no one else in the shop would hear. "I am Currer Bell."

George Smith's jaw dropped. "You?" he exclaimed in amazement. "You are—"

"Charlotte Brontë," I said, suppressing a wild urge to laugh. "And this is my sister Anne Brontë, who writes under the name Acton Bell. We've come so that you might have ocular proof that there are at least two of us."

My forthrightness must have convinced Mr. Smith, because an incredulous smile lit up his face. "How wonderful to meet you at last!" He shook hands with me, then Anne. "This is an honor."

If he was disappointed by the sight of the notorious Bells in the flesh, it did not show. Light-headed with relief, I heard myself and Anne making polite replies. Mr. Smith escorted us to a small room. He entreated us to sit in chairs, while he perched on a desk cluttered with books, papers, pens, and inkwells. "You must have traveled here immediately upon receiving my letter," he said, still beaming with excitement.

"We—we left Haworth that very day and just arrived in London this morning." Blushing violently, almost too agitated to speak, I said, "We apologize for coming uninvited and without warning, but we wished you to know at the earliest possible time that Anne is the author of *The Tenant of Wildfell Hall* and that I have not breached my contract with you."

"Ah, yes. Well, now that you both are here, the misunderstanding is resolved." Mr. Smith added with sincere entreaty, "Please forgive me for doubting you, and let me express how splendid it is to make the acquaintance of a truly great author."

Wonderful praise, this—more recognition than I could have hoped for! Dazzled, I murmured, "Sir, you are too generous—I do thank you—yes, of course you're forgiven—"

"Tell me, Miss Brontë," said Mr. Smith. "Is Ellis Bell another of your sisters?"

Anne said in a nervous, strident tone, "Mr. Bell does not wish his identity revealed."

Mr. Smith's eyebrows rose, and I feared that Anne had offended him. However, he proved himself capable of tact and sympathy, for he shrugged, smiled, and said, "Perhaps it's best that some mystery remains. How long are you in town?"

"I thought we might stay until Tuesday," I replied.

"Splendid! I shall host a dinner at my house to introduce Currer and Acton Bell to literary society!"

I stared dumbstruck at him. Anne turned to me, face blanched, eyes terror-stricken.

George Smith rushed on, happily oblivious to our reaction. "Oh, how I look forward to settling the question of whether Currer Bell is a man or a woman!"

That question had been the subject of hot debate in the press. While my publisher named prospective guests, I had a dizzying sense of events carrying me further than I had intended to go. I yearned to meet distinguished persons I had admired from afar, but I was also terrified at the thought of exposure.

"Sir," I said, "you mustn't trouble yourself on our account, or present us in public. Anne and I are as resolved as ever to remain incognito—we confessed ourselves to you only in order to do away with the inconveniences that have arisen from the mystery of our identities."

Enthusiasm flushed Mr. Smith's face. "But this is a splendid opportunity for Currer Bell to increase her fame and astound the literary world." His winning smile flashed.

I saw Anne's pleading gaze fixed on me, and I knew I must resist Mr. Smith for the sake of Emily, whose privacy would be lost if the authors Bell became connected with the Brontës of Haworth. "I'm sorry that I must disappoint you," I said. "To the rest of the world we must remain the unseen Currer and Acton Bell."

George Smith looked chastened but said, "Of course I shall respect your wishes. I imagine this is all a bit overwhelming for you both, and you must be tired from traveling. Surely you would like a rest."

I thanked him for his solicitude. Too much excitement and too little sleep had rendered me faint and weak, and my head had begun to ache.

"You must come and stay at my house, with my family," Mr. Smith said.

Oh, the dismaying prospect of living on intimate terms with strangers! While working as a governess or even visiting friends, I had suffered much embarrassment when people had closer obser- vation of me than I wished. The human body is ever a potential source of disgust, and I lived in terror of offending. "We mustn't impose on you, and besides, we've already engaged lodgings at the Chapter Coffee House."

"Well, at least allow me to bring my sisters to call on you." Mr. Smith went on to suggest places he might take Anne and me dur- ing our stay.

His words blurred together in my aching head. Flattered by his attention, yet feeling fainter by the moment, I agreed to everything he suggested. At last he ushered us outside, summoned a hackney coach, helped Anne and me climb inside, and paid the driver. As we rode away, he called, "I look forward to seeing you tonight!"

➤◄

The coach left us at the entrance to Paternoster Row, a nar- row, flagged street. Paternoster Row had once contained shops where pilgrims and clergymen could buy rosaries and drink cof- fee, but now the street harbored the dingy warehouses and offices of printers, binders, and stationers. Above the roofs, the sun illu- minated the vast dome of St. Paul's Cathedral, but the street lay in shadow. As Anne and I walked along the hot, deserted lane, our footsteps sounded loud against the muted roar of the city outside. The distant bellows of livestock emanated from the slaughterhouses at Newgate Street, and I could smell the odor of rotting flesh.

"I am very glad that events transpired as happily as they did," I said, "but oh, so glad they are past!"

"I, too, am glad," Anne said.

"Thank you for coming with me," I said belatedly, again regretting how I'd coerced Anne. Our felicitous reception at Smith, Elder & Company mattered much less to her than to me, and the event had been an unpleasant ordeal for her. "Tonight's visit from Mr. Smith and his family should be far less unsettling than what we've already endured; and fortunately, we have time to refresh ourselves, because my head aches as if hammers are beating inside my skull."

We were on the verge of entering the Chapter Coffee House, an ancient inn, when a shriek rang out. "What was that?" I said, startled.

More screams followed, alternating with cries of "Help! Help!"

"Someone is in trouble," I said. I started down the row, seeking to discern the source of the cries.

"No, dear Charlotte!" Anne held me back. "It's too dangerous. You don't know what may happen."

However, I was a parson's eldest daughter, accustomed to serving when someone was in need. "Go inside the Chapter Coffee House and fetch help," I ordered Anne, ere I hurried away.

The cries, now incoherent and desperate, issued from an alley between two warehouses. Halting at its entrance, I peered inside. There, in the dimness that exuded a loathsome stench of sewers, two figures struggled. Alarmed, I squinted at them, but they appeared mere shadows to me. One was a woman clad in a bonnet and full skirt; the other, a man in a brimmed hat. The man slammed the woman against a wall, muttering to her in low, angry tones. Her hands beat at him, and he grappled with her. She sobbed.

"Let her go!" I cried.

The man thrust himself hard against the woman. A scream of agony burst from her; then she was silent. He glanced towards me, and I glimpsed his face, pale and indistinct above his dark garments. He sprang away from the woman. As she crumpled to the ground, he dashed to the alley's opposite end, where he vanished into a blur of sunshine.

I hurried into the alley. The brick walls gave off a dank coolness; my shoes splashed in filthy puddles between the rough cobblestones. I bent over the woman. "Are you all right, madam?" I said, breathless from excitement and fear.

She lay immobile. Blood in great, wet, crimson quantity stained the bodice of her grey frock, and a wooden-handled knife protruded from between her ribs. Gasping, I recoiled; I clasped my hand over my mouth and retched. My heart's thudding reverberated inside my aching head as my horrified gaze traveled to the woman's face. Framed by a bonnet and tousled blond hair, it was white as paper, the mouth open, the eyes staring sightlessly. The chill mask of death had fixed its terrified expression. Fresh shock assailed me as I recognized those features.

The dead woman was Isabel White.

5

I STUMBLED OUT OF THE ALLEY AND INTO ANNE'S EMBRACE. SHE HAD brought servants from the Chapter Coffee House, and they fetched a constable, who told me to wait while he examined the corpse of Isabel White. The activity drew a noisy crowd that filled Paternoster Row, and they gawked at me as I sat outside the alley upon a chair someone had brought. Waves of nausea, trembling, and faintness besieged me. I had never seen anyone murdered, and the experience inflicted upon me a severe distress. Anne stood beside me, offering silent comfort. I closed my eyes, yet could not expunge from my memory the images of the blood, the knife, and worst of all, Isabel White's lifeless stare. Desperately fighting the urge to vomit, I wished myself home in the peaceful isolation of Haworth.

The constable emerged from the alley and stood before me. Clad in indigo trousers and a matching coat with shiny buttons down the front, he had sharp blue eyes in a face that reminded me of a fox. Rusty sideburns protruded from beneath his tall black hat.

"I'm Police Constable Dixon," he said.

I'd had but one previous experience with the law, when a sheriff's officer had come to the parsonage to order that Branwell either pay his debts or go to prison. I feared the power of the law, and the Metropolitan Police seemed as menacing a breed as the London thieves, swindlers, and cutthroats they were sworn to apprehend.

"Your name and place of residence, please?" Constable Dixon penciled the information I gave him into a notebook. "Visitin' town, then, Miss Brontë? A pity you should witness a crime." His manner was sympathetic but businesslike. "Now I know as this's been a terrible shock for you, but we need your help catchin' the individual what killed that poor woman. Tell me everything as happened."

I nervously eyed the truncheon he wore at his waist. The crowd listened while I described what I'd seen, and the constable recorded it. He said, "Did you get a look at the perpetrator, miss?"

Reliving the incident, I trembled as I shook my head. "The alley was dim, and I am nearsighted. But he wore dark clothes and a dark hat." I suggested timidly, "Shouldn't someone go looking for him?"

"Well, now, miss, London's a big city, and there's plenty of men what fit that general description," the constable said. "Can you recall anything else about 'im?"

I exerted my memory, in vain. "No, sir. But I did know the murdered woman." Interest stirred the crowd. "Her name was Isabel White."

"A friend o' yours, then?" Constable Dixon said, writing.

"Not exactly," I said, although my sense of comradeship with Isabel made me feel that I had lost a friend. Tears and sour bile rose in my throat, and I gulped them down. "My sister and I rode on a train to London with her." I described Isabel's strange behavior, adding, "Perhaps the person she feared followed her here, then killed her."

"And would you know who that person might be?"

"Miss White didn't say."

"This is an interestin' theory, miss," Constable Dixon said, his polite tone laced with condescension. "But likely this was a robbery, and a thief killed the lady because she resisted when 'e tried to take 'er pocketbook. 'E must have got it anyway—there wasn't nothin' on 'er."

"But I cannot believe he was a common thief," I protested. "He looked to be dressed like a gentleman."

"Ah." Constable Dixon nodded sagely. "Then 'e must've been a swell mobsman." Seeing my puzzled expression, he explained, "Swell mobsmen is criminals who get themselves up fancy and loiter about the banks. When they sees someone take out lots of money, they follows the person and robs 'im. Likely, that's what happened to Miss White." The constable closed his notebook.

I was unconvinced. Although I knew nothing about solving crimes, and I recognized the audacity and danger of telling the law what to do, I felt compelled to say, "Miss White told me that she was governess in the house of a Mr. Joseph Lock of Birmingham. Perhaps he could help you identify her killer."

Irritation flushed Constable Dixon's face. "Perhaps he could, miss; then again, perhaps not." His expression deemed me a foolish, hysterical female. "The police 'ave enough to do without chasin' all over England."

"Then you won't investigate Miss White's death any further?" I said, alarmed by his apparent intention to dismiss the murder as the work of a stranger impossible to locate. Tremors wracked my body, Anne blotted perspiration from my forehead, and I feared I would be sick at any moment.

"I shall refer the matter to my superiors," Constable Dixon said pompously, "and if they think any investigatin' is in order, it shall be done. Now, if you'll excuse me, Miss Brontë?" He touched the brim of his hat in farewell, adding, "You'd best get yourself to bed. You're lookin' a bit poorly."

>✦<

I must interrupt my account of what happened to me after Isabel White's death and direct attention towards another segment in the tapestry of my story. Reader, look away from poor Charlotte Brontë huddled on her chair, and focus your mind's eye upon the crowd in Paternoster Row. Do you discern one man who observes the proceedings with particular interest? He is perhaps thirty-five years of age, his lean, strong figure clad in dark coat, trousers, and hat. The features of his lean, swarthy face have the proud sharpness of a falcon's; they are framed by unruly black hair. Do you see his eyes—a brilliant, crystalline grey in hue—fixed hard upon me?

I was too preoccupied to notice him and did not learn until later that he was there. His name is John Slade, although some people— including myself—knew him by various other names. Mr. Slade, having listened to the exchange, watched my sister lead me into the Chapter Coffee House. His countenance betrayed no reaction to what he had witnessed. He hurried from Paternoster Row, hailed a hansom cab, and rode along Fleet Street and the bustling Strand, through Covent Garden, and alit in Seven Dials. Along the narrow, tortuous cobbled streets, soot-blackened windows gazed like blind eyes from grimy, crumbling tenements. Deep open gutters reeked of excrement; rats and stray dogs foraged in rubbish tips. Seven Dials is a place of despair, and none live there but the desperate.

Mr. Slade cast his brilliant grey glance around him. Toothless old women sat on stoops; waifish children swarmed; beggars and vagrants wandered, and a man wheeled a cart full of bones and rags. After ascertaining that no one was watching him, Mr. Slade walked up the steps of a tenement and through the open door. A dim hall stank of urine and cabbage. Rude speech, babies' cries, and the clatter of crockery emanated from the many rooms. He climbed the rotting stairs to the attic and tried the door. When he found it locked, he took from his pocket a picklock, opened the door, and entered the room, shutting himself inside.

A sloped, bare-raftered ceiling and stained plaster walls enclosed a bed, a chair, and a dresser. Light seeped through a small, grimy window. Mr. Slade spied a carpetbag patterned with red roses standing on the worn floorboards. He dumped the contents on the bed. He briefly examined, then set aside, a woman's garments. Wrapped in a fringed, India silk shawl he found a ticket for a ship scheduled to sail for Marseilles the next day. He searched the dresser, then looked under the bed and the mattress and behind the furniture; he scanned the walls and the ceiling for cracks, and he tested the floor for loose boards.

He found nothing.

Mr. Slade cursed under his breath. Then he made the bed,

replaced the furniture, and repacked the carpetbag. He departed the room, locked the door, hurried outside, and caught another cab to a tavern near Exchange Alley.

The Five Coins Tavern is a haunt of minor bankers and merchants; it occupies an ancient brick and plaster building with crooked timbers. A sign over the window depicts a jester juggling coins. That day, a lone customer sat at a table, a glass of wine before him. As Mr. Slade approached him, the man looked up. He was of middle age, with high, square shoulders, colorless hair, arched eyebrows, and a nose as sharp as an accusation. He pulled a gold watch from his embroidered waistcoat, then looked at the timepiece and pointedly at Mr. Slade.

"Sorry for my tardiness, Lord Unwin," said Mr. Slade. He sat opposite the other man.

"You had better have a damned good excuse," Lord Unwin said in an affected, aristocratic drawl.

The publican came over, and Mr. Slade ordered whiskey. When he and Lord Unwin were once again alone, Mr. Slade said, "Isabel White has been killed."

Lord Unwin's eyebrows arched higher. "Well, you did suggest that such at thing might come to pass. How, precisely, did it happen?"

Mr. Slade described the stabbing in Paternoster Row. The publican brought Mr. Slade's whiskey and departed. Lord Unwin raised his wineglass and said, "May she rest in peace."

He and Mr. Slade drank. Lord Unwin sat silent for a moment, his manicured hands encircling his glass, his head bowed, then he fixed his shrewd, colorless gaze on Mr. Slade. "A case of murder means an official inquiry."

"Not this one," Mr. Slade said, and explained how the constable deemed Isabel White's stabbing a botched robbery not worth investigating.

"How fortunate that the law is so cooperative." Lord Unwin smirked. "It wouldn't do for anyone to connect us with Isabel White and draw the wrong conclusions."

"No one will," Mr. Slade said. "As far as I know, there's no evidence of any business between us and Isabel White."

Lord Unwin's eyes narrowed. "What about the book?"

"The police didn't find it on her. Nor was it in her room. It's gone."

"If it exists at all, and is more than just a figment of your imagination." Lord Unwin's thin lips twisted into a sneer.

"It exists." Mr. Slade took another drink.

"By the by," Lord Unwin drawled, "I have news for you. A message from Birmingham came this morning. Joseph Lock is dead."

"What?" Shock jolted the exclamation out of Mr. Slade. "When? How?"

"Steady, my good man, steady now." Lord Unwin made a calming gesture, but his eyes gleamed with spite. "Yesterday, Mr. Lock put a bullet into his head. It seems that your options are disappearing in rapid succession."

Mr. Slade clenched his jaws. With Joseph Lock and Isabel White dead and the book missing, he faced the ruin of the most important venture of his life.

"Just how do you plan to finish the job now?" Lord Unwin demanded, but a tinge of apprehension colored his authoritative bluster.

"There was a witness to Isabel White's murder," Mr. Slade said. "Her name is Charlotte Brontë. She and Isabel traveled together on the train from Yorkshire to London. Perhaps Isabel told Miss Brontë something of value to us."

"Then you had better pursue Miss Brontë, hadn't you?" Lord Unwin pushed aside his glass. He took from his pocket a thick envelope and flung it across the table to Mr. Slade.

Mr. Slade inspected the banknotes in the envelope, then rose. He and Lord Unwin exchanged a stare of mutual dislike and reluctant conspiracy. "I fully intend to," he replied.

6

WHO WAS JOHN SLADE? WHAT HAD HE BEEN TO ISABEL White, and what were his intentions regarding me? The answers to those questions will emerge in due course. For now I shall resume my own story.

In my room at the Chapter Coffee House, I vomited into a basin for the fourth time since Isabel's death. Anne held my head, which pounded with thunderous pain. Finally I lay back on the bed, exhausted from my violent reaction to the trials of the past two days.

"Poor Charlotte," Anne said, gently wiping my face with a damp cloth. "I'm sorry that you are suffering so badly."

Sallow dusk glowed through the windows. The room was hot and stuffy. The Chapter Coffee House had once been a haunt of booksellers, publishers, writers, and critics. Later it became an inn frequented by university men and country clerics who were up in London. My father, who had stayed there during his days as a divinity student, had brought Emily and me here when he took us to school in Belgium. But that morning, upon our arrival, the proprietor had informed us that the Chapter Coffee House seldom accommodated overnight guests at present. Seeing our distress, he had graciously allowed us to stay and given us this dingy room upstairs. The inn was an empty, desolate place.

"My suffering is nothing compared to that of Isabel White," I said, tossing feverishly. "That such a beautiful creature should be cut down in the prime of her life!"

"She is now at peace with God," Anne said.

Faith had sustained our family through many troubles, but I drew meager solace from it now. "Isabel White came to Paternoster Row to see me!"

When I returned to the inn after speaking to the constable, the proprietor told me that Isabel had called for me a short time earlier. She had seemed upset to learn that I was out, he said, and had hurried away. Her killer must have attacked her immediately afterward.

"I knew she was in trouble, and I told her where to find me if she needed my help." I winced at the agony of my headache. "It's my fault that she met her death here."

"Oh, Charlotte, you mustn't blame yourself," Anne said, bathing my face with cool water. "You were trying to do good. The blame belongs to the evil person who killed Miss White."

Although I recognized the wisdom of my sister's words, she could not dispel my guilt. "I'm certain that the police will do nothing to find the killer. Most probably, they consider it not worth their effort."

"Perhaps the killer was a swell mobsman, as the constable suggested," Anne said. "Perhaps he'll be caught by the police in the course of his subsequent crimes, and punished then."

"I cannot believe that the murder was but an accident of fate, and I cannot bear to simply wait and hope that another accident of fate will bring justice," I cried with a passion. "No! I must try to discover who killed Isabel White."

"You?" Anne was astonished. "My dear Charlotte!"

"It's the least I can do for Miss White."

"But it is police business, not yours. You've neither the right nor the means to investigate murder. What could you possibly do?"

"I don't know," I confessed. "But I must know the real story of what happened to Isabel. If I weren't so ill, perhaps I could devise a plan."

With uncharacteristic acerbity Anne said, "I begin to think that your illness has affected your mind."

"My mind is perfectly sound." I sat up, nettled by her suggestion.

"What other than mental aberration could explain these peculiar notions?" Rising, Anne twisted her hands in anxiety, but a rare defiant spark lit her eyes.

"You may be content to wait passively for matters to arrange themselves, but I am not," I snapped. While I knew that my wish to find Isabel White's killer sounded unreasonable, I resented my younger sister's challenging me. "Why, if I hadn't decided upon selling our writing, and persuaded you and Emily to join me in sending our work to publishers, we would have published nothing."

"Too much initiative is as bad as too little." Anne's voice was breathless; she grasped the chair for support, but her gaze held mine. "I daresay that the murder isn't the only thing that has impaired your judgment. Perhaps your literary success has rendered you foolishly bold."

Sputtering in astonished indignation, I said, "Perhaps you envy my success and wish me to do nothing more than spend my life in idle, dull obscurity; but remember this: If not for my foolish boldness, we wouldn't be where we are now!"

Tears shimmered in Anne's eyes. Averting her face, she said, "I wish we were not."

Now I was ashamed because I had hurt Anne. The murder must have been as upsetting to her as to me, but while I had collapsed, she had nursed me. She also had stood loyally by me during our expedition to Smith, Elder & Company. I felt guilty that I often gave Anne short shrift because she had never been my favorite sister. I loved Anne dearly, of course, but compared to Emily, brilliant and original of mind, Anne seemed dully inferior. I was suddenly horrified at how we had turned against each other. The rift between my sisters and me was growing. I climbed off the bed and hobbled over to Anne, who stood, head bowed, beside the window.

"I'm so sorry," I said, taking her hand. "I shouldn't have spoken as I did. Can you forgive me?"

Anne sniffed, managed a tremulous smile, and nodded. "If you will forgive me for speaking harshly to you."

We embraced in mutual relief. Still, I harbored a need to learn the truth about Isabel White's murder. A persistent curiosity gnawed at my mind, as though I'd been reading an engrossing book and had it snatched away from me before I could reach the end. I desired to obtain justice for this stranger who had engaged my interest and my sympathy. I could only hope that somehow an opportunity would present itself.

"Mr. Smith and his sisters will be coming to call soon," I said. "We'd better prepare ourselves."

After another hour's rest, we washed, then dressed in fresh clothes. My sickness abated, though I still felt very shaky. When I peered in the mirror, my face looked as though it had aged ten years. Turning away from my ghastly reflection, I went with Anne downstairs to meet George Smith and two young ladies, whom he introduced as his sisters. They were brown-haired, fair, and lively like himself. They were very elegantly dressed in white silk gowns.

"I am pleased to present Miss Charlotte Brown and Miss Anne Brown, my friends from Yorkshire," George Smith said, keeping his promise to conceal the our true identities.

He looked quite handsome and distinguished in tailcoat and white gloves, carrying a tall black hat. I experienced a stir of feelings long repressed. It had been years since I had permitted myself to admire a man.

"We should be on our way," Mr. Smith said. "The opera will begin soon."

"The opera?" I had by no means understood that we had agreed upon a trip to the opera, though it explained the Smiths' formal dress. Panic struck me, for Anne and I were inappropriately attired. But if we refused to go, we would disappoint and offend the Smiths. Forcing a smile, I said, "Yes, let us go."

In the carriage, I sat between Anne and Mr. Smith in the forward-facing seat, while the Misses Smith sat opposite us. As we clattered down the dark street, I experienced a thrill in spite of my

illness and my shame at my poor appearance. Was an evening out-
ing in London not the sort of adventure I had craved? The presence
of George Smith, so near that I could smell his clean, manly scent
of shaving soap, intensified my excitement. Inside me awakened,
against my will, an old yearning. Twice in the past I had fallen in
love. The first object of my affection had been William Weightman,
my father's curate nine years ago. Bonny and charming, he had
flirted with me, but I eventually realized that he flirted with all the
unattached ladies and preferred those prettier than I. As for my second love—how disgracefully I had humiliated myself! Now I willed
my heart to calm its quickening rhythm.

"How did you spend your afternoon in town?" Mr. Smith asked.

"I'm afraid I had a most disturbing experience," I said.

As I described Isabel White's murder, his sisters exclaimed in
shock. Mr. Smith said, "I wish I'd convinced you to stay with me,
so that you needn't have witnessed such a terrible crime. You and
Anne shouldn't return to Paternoster Row; you must come to my
house."

His concern touched me, and the invitation, which offered the
prospect of a better acquaintance with him, strongly tempted me,
despite my aversion to living among strangers. Yet I knew myself
vulnerable to inclinations that would cause me misery.

"You are very kind," I said at last, "but I must decline your invitation, as there's no need for you to protect me. I don't consider
myself to be in any danger."

I explained that I believed that the killer was someone who
had been known to Isabel and had followed her to London. After
giving my reasons, I added, "I fear I will never rest until I have
done everything in my power to find out who is responsible for
the murder."

"Your wish to exert yourself on behalf of a virtual stranger is
commendable," Mr. Smith said. Leaning closer, he whispered, "It
reflects the same wonderful, generous spirit that I perceived in the
author of *Jane Eyre* even before I met her."

His compliment warmed me; I was afraid to look at him. Were
the characteristics he'd mentioned those he valued in a woman?

Did I dare think he valued them more than youth, beauty, or charm? I said timidly, "Could you advise me on how I might persuade the authorities to investigate the murder?"

He pondered a moment, then said, "I have a slight acquaintance with the commissioner of police. If you like, I'll ask that he consider the facts you've provided."

"Yes. I do thank you." Gratitude increased my already favorable disposition towards George Smith.

Our carriage turned onto a noisy thoroughfare. Coaches rattled past strolling crowds, and street peddlers hawked playbills. Taverns filled with revelers, and gaudily dressed women loitered, shouting lewd invitations to men passing by. Gas streetlamps, their brightness veiled by smoke, lent the scene an unreal air that was at once frightening and intoxicating.

The Misses Smith were peering out the window, chattering to each other. "That carriage has been following ours since we left Paternoster Row."

"Yes, it stays so closely behind us."

Unease crept over me. I peered backwards out the window and saw an enclosed black coach drawn by a black horses, and the figure of a driver seated upon the box. A fearful notion constricted my heart: Could someone be following me? Was it the same man who had followed Isabel White?

I hastily recoiled from the window. Mr. Smith said to me, "You are shivering. Are you cold? Do you want the carriage blanket?"

"No, thank you, I am quite comfortable," I said, deciding that my imagination had gotten the best of me.

We entered Covent Garden and drove past elegant stucco row houses. Men clustered outside the song and supper rooms or escorted ladies along the streets. Although July was the end of the London season, the theatre district was jammed with carriages. Scrutinizing them, I was relieved that the strange black coach seemed to have gone. Traffic converged upon the glittering Royal Opera House.

When my party disembarked, Mr. Smith offered me his arm. His somber, direct gaze lent the polite gesture an intimacy that sped my pulse. I floated into the theatre with him, scarcely aware of Anne at his other side or the Misses Smith behind us. The foyer was filled with men in formal dress and women who wore gowns of brilliant hues, displaying naked shoulders and bejeweled bosoms. They cast critical glances at my plain country garments. Wellbred laughter pealed. My head still throbbed, and my stomach was queasy, but giddy anticipation masked my discomfort. I involuntarily clutched George Smith's arm, and he turned to me.

"You know, I am not accustomed to this sort of thing," I stammered.

He laughed as if we shared a joke. I savored our march up the crimson-carpeted staircase. Mr. Smith greeted acquaintances and introduced me as "My dear friend Miss Brown." He smiled at me as if our secret joined us in a daring conspiracy. I began to think he liked me, I blush to confess.

Erelong we were seated in a box in the first tier. Five more tiers—decorated with gold flowers, separated by gold columns, and filled with people—rose to a domed ceiling. An enormous crystal chandelier radiated sparkling gaslight. Ladies' fans fluttered in the heat, amidst a roar of conversation. The box afforded me a welcome measure of privacy, yet I had the prickling sensation of watchful gazes focused on me.

"The opera is *The Barber of Seville*," said Mr. Smith, at my side.

I noticed a man standing some fifty feet away, near the stalls in front of the stage. He was looking straight at me. My poor eyesight could barely discern that he had dark hair and wore dark clothing, and I perceived an air of menace about him. Then he abruptly turned away.

"Anne," I whispered, nudging my sister, "do you see that man?"

"Which one?" Anne sounded puzzled.

Alas, our view was at that moment obscured by other persons, and by the time they had passed, he was gone. "Never mind." I thought of the black coach: Had it brought that man here to watch me? Was he connected with Isabel White's murder? Anxiously I searched the audience for him. He seemed a disembodied, threatening presence spread throughout the crowd. People peered through opera glasses, and whenever I saw them pointed my way, I cringed.

The lights dimmed, and a hush descended upon the audience. The orchestra played the overture, and the stage curtain lifted, revealing a medieval street scene. An actor dressed in a cape and wide-brimmed hat strode onto the stage. A band of musicians assembled, and he sang a serenade. It was very grand, but because the opera was performed in Italian, I didn't understand a word. My sense of ominous, hidden watchers burgeoned. The warm air of the theatre was tainted with gas fumes that worsened my headache. As the drama unfolded, a female singer performed an aria; her high, piercing notes reminded me of Isabel White's screams. I swallowed an eruption of nausea.

"Please excuse me," I whispered to George Smith. I dreaded leaving the safety of the box alone, yet that seemed preferable to vomiting in front of him.

I clambered from my seat and stumbled out the door of the box. The long corridor was vacant. As I hurried along it, I heard stealthy footsteps following me. Too afraid to look back, I walked faster. Vivacious music emanated from inside the theatre. The footsteps quickened; they echoed the pounding of my heart. A stairwell appeared, and I ran down iron stairs. I heard the metallic racket of my pursuer descending after me. Desperate, gasping for breath, and direly ill, I burst through a doorway, into another corridor.

A door flew open right in front of me, releasing loud, uproarious singing. A group of ladies poured from their box. I followed them down the grand staircase, grateful for their unwitting protection. Outside I relieved my illness at last. My pursuer had disappeared.

When I returned to my box, I met George Smith outside its door. "I was looking for you," he said. "Are you all right?"

"Yes, I am, thank you," I said. We resumed our seats, but the opera was lost on me. I could neither forget my frightening experience nor cease to ponder its meaning.

><

It was past one o'clock of Sunday morning when Anne and I returned to the Chapter Coffee House. The inn was silent; Paternoster Row slumbered. As we trudged up the stairs to our room, I told Anne what had happened at the opera.

"Dear Charlotte, are you sure that someone was chasing you?" Anne said skeptically.

"Quite sure," I said.

"But even if it was the man who killed Isabel White, what could he want with you?"

"Perhaps he believes I can identify him to the police, and he wishes to stop me."

"But you didn't obtain a good look at his face."

"He cannot know that," I said.

"Why didn't you mention the incident to Mr. Smith? There was ample time during the interval, when he could have asked someone to look for the man who chased you."

I let out a sigh. "I was afraid he wouldn't believe me." I could tell from her expression that Anne didn't believe me, either. "But it was not just my imagination. There *was* someone chasing me."

Outside our room stood a table that held candles. I lit one and opened the door. Cool air rushed outward; the candle flame wavered. Entering the room, Anne and I both exclaimed in shock. Our trunk lay open, our belongings strewn about, and the dresser drawers were open. The covers had been flung off the bed, and the mattress dragged off the frame. Broken glass littered the floor under the window, where a jagged hole gaped. The curtains stirred in the breeze.

7

❄

SOMETIMES A DOOR TO THE FUTURE SEEMS TO OPEN, AND BEYOND THIS portal you can see a radiant blue sky, gardens blooming with flowers, and glorious sunshine. But when you draw nearer, the door is discovered to be an impenetrable wall with a bright, false vista painted upon it by your own folly. That is what happened to me the day after the opera.

Sunday afternoon lay like a golden mantle upon London. The Thames sparkled beneath a sky miraculously cleared by a freshening breeze; the city's spires, domes, and towers glittered. Church bells tolled across the rooftops of Bayswater, a respectable suburb. Its terraced Regency-era houses basked in the sunshine, their white stucco façades and black wrought-iron fences gleaming. Children rolled hoops, and nurses wheeled perambulators under leafy trees in the square near Westbourne Place, where George Smith resided.

He and I sat in his dining room with Anne, his mother, and his sisters. The house was splendid, with Turkey carpets, polished mahogany furniture, white table linens, and fine crystal, silver, and china. Flowers masked the odor of cesspits that permeates even the best homes of London. Yet Anne and I were so bashful that we could only pick at our portions of roasted joint. Neither of us contributed much to the conversation until I described my experience at the opera and what we had found upon returning to the Chapter Coffee House.

The company expressed shock and sympathy. George Smith said, "You didn't spend the night in your room after it was ransacked, I hope?"

"No," I said. "The proprietor of the inn was kind enough to give us other accommodations."

"Do I correctly understand that you believe the two incidents and the murder may be related?"

"The proprietor said a common thief must have climbed onto the roof and broken into our room. But I doubt that a murder, a chase in the theatre, and a burglary all on the same day of my life are mere coincidence."

"Was anything taken?" inquired Mrs. Smith. She was a handsome, portly woman with rich brunette hair. She had not been told the true connection between her son and his guests, and she eyed me with curiosity.

"No, madam," Anne murmured.

George Smith frowned, one hand clasping his chin while the other toyed with his glass. "Whether or not these experiences are connected and someone wishes you harm, I do not like this disturbance to your peace of mind."

Gratified by his concern, I expected him to reiterate his invitation for Anne and me to stay with him. Instead he said, "Perhaps you should return home immediately." His solicitude seemed as genuine as ever; yet I felt dismay at the suggestion that he wished me to leave.

"Last night you indicated that you would speak to the commissioner of police about investigating Isabel White's murder," I said. "Should I not remain available in case I am needed?"

"I shall go to the commissioner as I promised," said George Smith, "but should it be necessary for the police to communicate with you, a letter will surely suffice."

Mrs. Smith seconded this opinion; Anne nodded. I beheld my publisher with increasing perplexity. Yesterday he had seemed an ally in my quest for the truth about Isabel White; but now he appeared eager to dismiss me and handle matters himself. What had changed?

"I am most grateful for your assistance and concern, but I think that Anne and I should stay at least until Tuesday," I said, spurred to assert my independence.

"As you wish," George Smith conceded graciously, but I could tell he was displeased.

When dinner ended, the ladies retired to the parlor. The Smith sisters hurried to the piano, taking Anne with them, and Mrs. Smith joined arms with me.

"I welcome this chance for us to become better acquainted," she said in a friendly fashion. "Come, let us sit by the window, where we can smell the roses in my garden."

Seated beside Mrs. Smith on a divan, I nervously braced myself for questions about who I was and why I was there. I wouldn't like to lie, yet I dared not break my pledge to Emily.

The Smith sisters began playing and singing a gay tune for Anne. Mrs. Smith said, "My dear George is often at his business all twenty-four hours of a day." Her maternal tone was fond. "He works so hard."

"How admirable," I said, relieved that I was apparently not to be the subject of the discussion.

"Yet he is the most attentive son and brother anyone could wish," Mrs. Smith said. "No matter how busy he is, he always makes time for his family."

I had noticed the affection between my publisher and his family —particularly his mother.

"George and I have always been the closest of companions," Mrs. Smith said, as a maid served coffee to us. "I believe I know him better than does anyone else." Her smile was uncannily like her son's. "And I hope you will excuse a mother's boasting if I say that I'm tremendously proud of him?"

I nodded, trying to determine where the conversation was leading.

The Smith sisters commenced a new song. Mrs. Smith said, "Even though George is so busy, he must soon embark upon a most important phase of his life." Her manner turned conspiratorial. "You will understand that I refer to matrimony?"

Wariness stole over me as I sensed something unpleasant coming, although I couldn't imagine what.

"The choice of a mate is difficult for my George. Wherever he goes, the young ladies flock around him." Mrs. Smith's hands lifted and fell in a gesture of mock helplessness. "Ah, but you understand his appeal for the fair sex——do you not?"

Her smile persisted, but her eyes had turned hard as flints: She had noticed my admiration for her son, and her disapproval was evident. I felt mortified that I had been so transparent. I sat speechless.

Mrs. Smith laughed, and the sound had an undertone of scorn. "But I have no doubt that my dear George will make the right marriage when the time comes. His wife should be his equal in youth, beauty, charm, and fortune. After all, like deserves like, wouldn't you agree?"

Nodding automatically, I experienced the further embarrassment of realizing that Mrs. Smith, who didn't understand the relationship between George and myself, assumed that I wished to engage him as a suitor. She was warning me off because I was too old, too plain, too awkward, and too poor for her son! Although I had never presumed to dream of marrying him, I burned with humiliation. How I wished I could tell her that the good fortune of Smith, Elder & Company owed much to a famous book, of which I was the author! Instead, I lifted my cup and swallowed coffee that tasted bitter as poison. I could not reveal my secret.

"Mr. Smith has been most attentive to me," I said instead, desiring his mother to know I had cause to believe he cared for me.

Anger replaced the self-satisfaction on the face of Mrs. Smith; she gave me a mocking smile. "My dear George bestows his kindness upon everyone. Often, people misconstrue his motive as affection when he is merely giving sympathy to those who need it. And sometimes his business requires him to endure people outside his usual circle."

My heart contracted as if under the crushing pressure of a

giant fist. The scent of roses turned sickening. The sad truth was now clear—George Smith's attentions towards me stemmed from his interest in me as Currer Bell, not as Charlotte Brontë. At last I understood why he was so eager for me to leave London: He wanted Currer Bell safe from harm so that she could write more books for Smith, Elder & Company.

Mrs. Smith regarded me with an air of smug triumph. "Surely you understand me when I say that my dear George will neither disappoint his mother nor jeopardize his own prospects when he marries?"

When George Smith entered the parlor, I dared not even look his way.

>←

The next morning Anne and I called on Thomas Cautley Newby, the publisher whose fraud had brought us to town. After an unpleasant talk during which we chastised him and he insisted that the problem was but a misunderstanding, I took Anne to the National Gallery in Trafalgar Square. The firmament arched blue and cloudless above us as we walked by the monument to Admiral Horatio Nelson. The square impressed me as an apt symbol of England's military power. I bethought myself a citizen of the great kingdom that had defeated Napoleon and ruled the seas unrivaled ever since, commanding an empire that extended across India, Australia, New Zealand, and Africa. While insurrections had shaken Europe time and again during our century, Britain had so far held firm—the army had quelled the Chartist demonstrations that had taken place in London this spring. Now vendors sold trinkets to sightseers streaming in and out of the church of St. Martin-in-the-Fields; pigeons fluttered, chasing breadcrumbs tossed by children. All was tranquil.

Anne and I joined a throng heading into the gallery, whose massive Grecian façade dominated the square. The viewing of fine paintings has always given me great pleasure, and the gallery's cool, echoing chambers contained works by my favorite artists; yet they could neither distract me from my shame over George Smith nor soothe the pain of hope denied yet again.

"Dear Charlotte, you seem unhappy," Anne said as we strolled the gallery. "Is it Isabel White's death that troubles you?"

"It is." I would rather have died than admit how I had deluded myself about Mr. Smith, and Isabel White did still weigh heavily upon my mind. "I doubt that I can depend on Mr. Smith to help determine who killed Isabel. I fear that I can do nothing about the murder."

"Perhaps it's for the best." Anne added, "I shall be glad to be home. There, no one will chase you or invade our rooms."

The prospect of leaving London the next day depressed me all the more. Absently wandering the galleries, I lost Anne in the crowd and walked into a room of Italian paintings. In the deserted, shadowy chamber, medieval dukes, noblewomen, and Madonnas gazed down at me from their golden frames. Distant sounds echoed eerily like whispers from the past. A man appeared before me so suddenly that he seemed to have materialized from thin air.

"Miss Brontë?" he said.

The unexpected sound of my name halted me. Startled, I focused on the man's black frock coat at my eye level. My gaze moved upward to the white collar and white cravat that identified him as a clergyman, then alit on his face. He had keen, intense features and an olive complexion shaded by a cleanshaven beard. Wavy black hair tumbled above grey eyes of striking clarity and brilliance. Staring into these, I experienced a peculiar, electrifying sense of recognition; yet the man was a stranger.

"Please excuse my accosting you in this rude manner," he said. Fleeting confusion clouded his face, as if he noticed my reaction to him—or felt the same shock? "My name is Gilbert White. I'm the brother of Isabel White—I believe you've met her."

"Isabel's brother?" I felt dismay as I wondered whether the clergyman knew of his sister's death, for I did not wish to have to break such news. Noticing his bleak, strained expression, however, I realized that he must know, and I felt a rush of sympathy.

"Please let me explain," he said as a flock of chattering patrons streamed into the gallery. "I'm the vicar of a parish outside Canter-bury." His voice was quiet but resonant, with the same North Country accent as Isabel; he held a black hat in hands that were well shaped and clean. "Isabel and I had arranged to meet in London for a holiday together, but when I went to our rendezvous place yesterday, she never came. I didn't know what else to do except go to the police. They told me Isabel had been killed."

Gilbert White drew deep breaths; looking away from me, he blinked rapidly.

"I am so sorry for your loss," I said, moved by his grief and wishing I had more to offer than condolences. As a parson's daughter, I regularly have occasion to comfort the bereaved, but I always feel my helplessness.

"It is God's will, and I must accept it," he murmured. "Yet I shall have no peace until I know what happened to Isabel. Somehow I cannot believe she was killed by a common thief." He turned on me a gaze filled with anguish and frustration. "The police told me you knew her and that you witnessed the murder. I decided that I must speak with you and learn as much as possible about my sis-ter's death, so I went to the Chapter Coffee House—the police said you had lodgings there. The proprietor told me where to find you."

I did not recall telling the proprietor I was going to the National Gallery, but I supposed he had overheard Anne and me discussing our plans at breakfast. Neither did I think to wonder how Mr. White had recognized me, a stranger, in the crowd.

"Might I beg a few more moments of conversation with you, Miss Brontë?" His keen face alight with entreaty, Gilbert White said, "Would you let me buy you a cup of tea?"

Ordinarily I would have declined an invitation from a stranger, yet I could hardly refuse aid to a bereaved brother. He was a respectable man of the cloth, and drinking tea with him in public would harm neither my person nor my reputation. And perhaps he represented an opportunity to discharge the duty I felt towards Isabel White.

"Yes; I would be glad to tell you whatever I can," I said.

Anne came looking for me then, and I introduced her to Gilbert

White. We went to a coffee shop whose clientele consisted of modestly dressed ladies and a few clergymen. A maid in a frilled cap and apron served us tea. When I told Gilbert White about Isabel's behavior on the train, he reacted with bewilderment.

"I had no idea that Isabel was in such a bad state," he said. "Her recent letters to me indicated naught of the sort. Did you ever see the person she feared?"

"No," I said. "I couldn't be sure whether anyone was actually following her, or whether she just thought so."

"Did she say who it was?"

Regretting to disappoint him, I again replied in the negative, then described what had happened to me at the opera and the Chapter Coffee House. "I suspect those incidents might be connected to Isabel's murder, but unfortunately, I don't know who was responsible."

"That someone would attack innocent women!" Gilbert White exclaimed, clearly shaken. "The world has become a dangerous place."

"I wondered if Isabel was in trouble of some kind." I related Isabel's strange remark about hoping to escape punishment. "I also wondered if her trouble stemmed from her employment with Mr. Lock of Birmingham."

Gilbert White stirred sugar into his tea, his expression dazed as if he could make no sense of all he'd heard. Studying him covertly, I decided that most people would think him too dark, sharp-featured, and disheveled for fashion, but I found his looks oddly alluring. I couldn't help comparing him to George Smith. He wasn't as handsome, but I discerned in him a depth of character and feeling that George Smith lacked.

"I know my sister's character, and I cannot believe she would deliberately do wrong," Gilbert White said. "She must have somehow become associated with people who involved her in bad business." Anger glinted in his grey eyes, and his hands clenched into fists on the tablecloth. "Surely they are responsible for her death."

I sensed that he was capable of passions never experienced by my publisher. Intrigued by Gilbert White, I stole a glance at his left hand: He wore no wedding ring.

"I must learn who killed Isabel," he declared. Leaning towards me, his slender, strong figure tense with purpose, he said, "I beg you to tell me everything she said during the journey, in the hope that her words to you contained some clue to the mystery of her death."

Having failed to induce the police to search out the murderer, I desired to help Gilbert White achieve the same objective. I related what I remembered about my conversation with Isabel. As I spoke, Mr. White watched me closely.

"I regret that your sister and I talked more about me than about her," I said, flustered by his attention. "My experiences as a governess will contribute little towards identifying the killer."

"One never knows what information may prove useful in the future," Gilbert White said, "and I sincerely thank you for your assistance, Miss Brontë."

For the first time he smiled—a brief flash of white teeth that lent his face a radiance more striking than conventional good looks. The effect momentarily dazzled me. I reckoned that Gilbert White smiled neither often nor at just anyone; a smile from him seemed a gift. But a man like him could have no sympathy with anything in me, and I must shun him as one would fire, lightning, and all else that is bright but antipathetic. Gilbert White wanted facts from me, just as George Smith wanted me to write novels for him, and I wouldn't be a fool twice.

"Tell me, Miss Brontë," Gilbert White said, pouring more tea for Anne, who had been sitting timidly throughout the whole interview. "How did you come to be a governess?"

His interest seemed genuine, not merely polite, and it was balm to my injured pride. "I was born the third of six children," I said. "Our mother died when I was five, and my father was left alone to raise us all."

Sympathy softened Gilbert White's sharp features. "I know what it is to lose a parent. My mother was widowed when Isabel and I were quite young."

I felt drawn to him against my will, in spite of the lesson I'd learned from George Smith. "My father is a clergyman of limited means," I said, "and he determined on educating his children to support themselves. He sent my two eldest sisters and me to the Clergy Daughters' School in Cowan Bridge. Unbeknownst to him, the conditions there were unwholesome. My sisters contracted consumption and died."

Heartache and rage halted me as I recalled the bitter episode. I saw Anne puzzling at why I would talk so much to a stranger; yet Gilbert White's attention encouraged me. "Later, Anne and I attended a better school at Roe Head, where we received training to qualify us as governesses. We eventually obtained positions in private homes."

"Are you governesses still?" Gilbert White asked Anne.

She looked down at the table and remained silent, while I hesitated between opposing impulses. I had promised to protect the secret of our identity, but I found myself overcome by a desire to show Mr. White that I was more than the ordinary person I appeared to be.

"No," I said, "I am an author now."

"Indeed?" Surprise and growing interest animated Gilbert White's expression. "What have you written?"

"My book is called *Jane Eyre*," I said, lowering my voice so that the shop's other customers wouldn't hear. Anne kicked my foot under the table, but reckless daring spurred me on. "It was published under my pen name—Currer Bell." When Mr. White asked what the story was about, I said, "It relates the experiences of a governess."

"Based on your own experiences?" he said.

"It is more fiction than autobiography," I said, though I have since come to realize that Jane and I have much in common.

"Perhaps you described the life you wanted to live," Mr. White suggested.

I felt myself blushing. "Well, not quite." Although I wouldn't have enjoyed suffering Jane Eyre's woes, a passionate love affair with a man of kindred spirit was a different matter; indeed, fiction can fulfill dreams that life does not.

Another kick from Anne brought me to my senses. "I must ask you not to tell anyone I wrote the book," I said to Gilbert White.

"It's a secret known only to my sisters and my publisher."

"I shall be honored to keep your confidence," he said, as though he meant it. "I don't read much except religious works, but I shall certainly buy and read your book." His eyes sparked with sudden thought. "If I send you my copy, would you inscribe it for me?"

Pride and gratification warmed me as I nodded.

"How should I address the parcel?"

"It will reach me at the parsonage, Haworth, Yorkshire."

"I do thank you. I've never met an authoress before," Gilbert White marveled. Then he spoke in a voice tinged with caution: "Miss Brontë—"

Anticipation rose in me, and though I resisted defining what I hoped him to say, my breath caught.

"Did Isabel give you anything?"

"Why, no," I said, startled, disappointed, and vaguely disturbed. "What would she have given me?"

Gilbert White shrugged, his expression rueful. "I don't know. I don't even know quite why I asked. I suppose I was just hoping that Isabel passed on to you something—anything—that might explain what led to her death."

This sounded reasonable; yet uneasiness stirred in me, for I recalled Isabel White clutching her carpetbag as though she feared it would be stolen. What had she owned that someone else might want, perhaps badly enough to kill for it? I thought of the wreck of my room at the Chapter Coffee House. Did someone think I now possessed some unknown treasure?

Did Gilbert White seek the same object? If so, could he be involved in what had happened to me—and to Isabel?

I could not have guessed then that my suspicions might be justified. When I saw tears of grief and despair in his eyes, I inwardly rebuked myself for my distrust. Whatever crimes I witnessed or misfortunes I experienced, I ought not to suspect everyone I met of evil motives.

"I wish your sister had given me something of use," I said. "If she had, I would gladly give it to you; but alas, she did not. I wish I could be of more help."

"You've been very helpful," Gilbert White said with sincerity. "Now I fear I've imposed upon your kindness too long." Rising, he extended his hand to me. "Thank you and goodbye, Miss Brontë."

As I grasped his hand, our gazes met. I felt the warm, firm grip of his fingers, and the same electrifying sensation as when I'd first beheld him. It struck within me an unfathomable premonition that we would someday be important to each other. I saw my discomposure reflected in Gilbert White's eyes, and I knew that the same premonition had visited his mind, as well.

❖

"You think I spoke too frankly to Mr. White, don't you?" I asked Anne as we rode in a hansom cab towards Paternoster Row.

"Emily wouldn't like our secret told to a stranger," Anne said with quiet reproof. "However, he seems trustworthy."

"Do you think so?" I said.

"Yes. In spite of such a brief opportunity to appraise his character, I have the feeling that he is a person who keeps his commitments."

Still, my unease persisted. If Isabel had planned to meet her brother, why had she not said so? Was it he that she feared?

"Mr. White looks nothing like his sister," Anne remarked.

That I, too, had noticed the lack of resemblance caused me further disquiet. Yet I preferred to trust Gilbert White rather than admit that someone of bad character could inspire in me the peculiar feelings that arose in his presence. "Families vary in looks. After all, you and I are nothing like Branwell."

Our cab paused at an intersection. Looking out the window, I saw other black hired carriages. I recalled the one I had seen on the way to the opera, and I shivered at the thought that someone might be still following me.

If so, was it Gilbert White?

Despite my misgivings, I could not suppress the hope that we would meet again.

8

$$\star\!\!\!\leftarrow$$

THE INEXORABLE FORCE OF TIME CONVEYS US PAST GOOD AND BAD alike; all things must eventually end. My great adventure was over, and I could scarcely credit the reality of it. My body had become weak from eating and sleeping too little; yet even while I looked forward to going home, I wished I could live my entire London trip anew.

Rain beat against the windows in the second-class coach of the train carrying us northward. I gazed at the passing landscape, a dull scene of grey sky and sodden fields. Anne sat beside me, writing. The only other travelers present were two gentlemen—one sitting across the narrow aisle at the front of the coach, and the other at the rear. I observed them with only mild curiosity. Both wore city coats, trousers, and hats; both were reading newspapers. One had ginger hair and sideburns, while the other was dark.

With a despondent sigh, I opened my notebook and recorded our expenses for the trip. Anne and I had spent fourteen pounds— a vast sum. We had accomplished our initial purpose, but beyond that, what? I felt I had lived more in these few days than heretofore; yet now I was returning to the same quiet existence. Would I ever see London again? I nurtured faint hope of hearing from Gilbert White. The monotonous chugging of the train, its mournful whistle, the hard wooden seat, and the damp, chill air in the coach underscored how dreary and void everything appeared. There seemed little likelihood of learning the truth about Isabel White's murder. As the miles rolled by, I brooded about what awaited me at home. Would Emily forgive me? Would I find Branwell in a worse state?

That evening, as we entered Leeds, a storm engulfed the train. Thunder boomed above the metallic racket of the wheels. Outside the windows, lightning illuminated the city in flashes; rain slanting through the smoky air dissolved the lights into yellow streaks. Anne and I were collecting our books and satchels in preparation for our arrival at Leeds Station, when suddenly the dark-haired man seated in front of us rose. He strode towards us, seized Anne, and jerked her out of her seat. Anne gave a startled exclamation. I gasped in alarm.

"Sir, what are you doing?" Anne cried.

The man pinned her hands behind her and dragged her up the aisle. Anne shrieked in fear, struggling against him.

"Let her go!" I jumped out of my seat. The train's motion rocked me as I lurched after my sister. Horror flooded me as I realized that by leaving London, we had hardly escaped danger. I grabbed Anne's arm and tried to pull her free, but the man held tight. Why should this stranger attack her? Anne's screams pierced the thunder. A dreadful thought dawned. Was this man the murderer of Isabel White? Had he followed Anne and me here to kill us too?

"Please help us!" I called, turning to the ginger-haired man at the rear of the carriage.

He advanced up the aisle, gripping the seats to steady himself. Lightning blazed, and I glimpsed his face. His raw features wore an expression of sly malice: He was clearly no savior. Even as I recoiled from him, he snatched at me. I uttered a cry, dodged, and fell sideways into a seat. He grasped my collar. I realized that he and the dark man must be partners. He yanked me upright, and as my collar dug into my throat, I gagged. Anne's screams continued. With a strength born of panic and the desire to save myself and my sister, I lunged towards the window. My collar tore. I beat my hands against the glass and fumbled open the window. Rain blasted into the coach.

"Help!" I shouted. "Someone, please help us!"

The noise of the locomotive and storm drowned my voice. The train sped on. My attacker scrambled into the seat after me. I sobbed in terror as he hauled me backwards into the aisle; I kicked and thrashed. I saw the dark man wrestling with Anne, whose cries and attempts to free herself weakened as he forced her to the floor.

"Anne!" I screamed. "No!"

My attacker clamped a rough cloth that reeked of chemicals over my nose and mouth. The cloth smothered me, and I felt a cold, burning sensation across my skin. Sickly sweet fumes invaded my lungs as I gasped and choked. My vision blurred, and a dizzying faintness quelled my struggles. Thunder boomed, then, darkness claimed me.

>←<

Distant voices and hurried footsteps merged in the darkness with a great rattling, rushing din. The smell of smoke accompanied the sound of water spattering as I gradually returned to consciousness. I lay on a firm surface; my head throbbed painfully, and my mouth was dry. Alarm, inspired by terrifying memory, jarred my groggy mental faculties alert.

My eyelids flew open. Light glared across my vision. I tried to sit up, but vertigo assailed me. Coarse, heavy fabric covered me up to my chin, and I thrashed under it, crying, "Anne!"

Her hazy image bent over me. "Dear Charlotte!" Her face was pale and drawn. "Thank God you're all right!"

"Those men. Where are they?" Breathless with anxiety, I clutched my sister's hands.

Anne said with a reassuring smile, "Don't worry, Charlotte; we are safe now."

I relaxed, though I remained bewildered. "Where are we?"

"At Leeds Station, in the stationmaster's room."

"My spectacles—"

Anne positioned the spectacles over my eyes, and my surroundings came into focus. On the walls were colorful railway maps of Britain. I was in a room furnished with a desk, bookcases, a sofa upon which I lay beneath a blanket, and several chairs.

"How did we get here?" Now I recognized the sounds of trains entering the station and people hurrying about. Rain was falling outside the window. "What happened to us?"

The door opened. Anne called over her shoulder, "Come in—my sister is awake at last."

Gilbert White entered the room. What indescribable astonishment was mine!

"Hello again, Miss Brontë," he said, gazing down at me with concern. His dark hair was wet; his black suit clung damply to him. "How do you feel?"

"Extremely unwell, but alive." I pushed myself upright, fighting dizziness. "What are you doing here?"

"Mr. White saved us," Anne said, giving him a thankful look.

"I don't understand." Overwhelmed by the events of the past moments, I shook my aching head. "What happened?"

Gilbert White perched on a nearby chair. Bruises discolored his cheeks, and his white collar was torn, but he appeared vigorously alive, his masculine looks enhanced by his injuries. "I was riding on the same train as you. When I got off at this station, I saw two men climb out of the carriage ahead of mine, supporting a woman who seemed unable to walk."

"It was you, Charlotte," Anne said. "The men who attacked us put you to sleep somehow."

"It must have been the chemical on the cloth over my face." My dry throat rasped, and Anne handed me a glass of water, which I gladly drank. "What could it have been?"

"Probably ether—the new drug used by surgeons to render patients unconscious during operations," Gilbert White explained. "At first I didn't know the woman was you, because I couldn't see your face. Then I heard cries coming from the carriage that the two men had just left. I hurried over, looked inside, and found your sister lying on the floor, bound and gagged."

"Oh, Anne," I said, horrified. "Were you hurt?"

"Not at all; just frightened," Anne assured me. "When Mr. White removed my gag, we recognized each other. I begged him to rescue you. He called the railway guards to assist me, then ran after the men."

"I spotted them outside the station," said Mr. White. "They were putting you into a hired carriage. One man got in after you. I grabbed the other as he was climbing up and knocked him to the ground. As the carriage sped away, I jumped in. The man inside fought me, but I threw him out onto the street. I then ordered the driver to return to the station."

"He carried you inside," Anne said, "and obtained the station-master's permission for you to recover here."

"Sir, I sincerely thank you," I said, overwhelmed by gratitude. "Indeed, I believe I owe you my life. Where could those men have been taking me?"

"Unfortunately, I had no chance to ask them, for they fled with great haste."

Anne said, "Mr. White's first concern was your safety." She smiled at him, and I noted that his actions had won her esteem. "He couldn't abandon you to chase our attackers."

That a man should behave so towards me! This was the stuff of fantasies that had preoccupied me during my youth, when I day-dreamed tales of being rescued by the Duke of Zamorna, my imaginary hero. I felt a profound thrill.

Gilbert White scrutinized me. "Your color improves." A hint of mirth lightened his somber aspect.

Did he guess my thoughts? Ashamed that he should notice my blushing, I reminded myself that I was no longer a silly young girl, and tonight's adventure was not a fantasy. Any one of us could have been seriously hurt. "What could those men have wanted with me?" I said to Anne. "Did they steal anything from us?"

"Before they left the carriage, they looked through our books and emptied our satchels, but everything is here." Anne gestured towards our trunk, atop which lay our other possessions.

"They wanted only me," I said, even more disturbed and puz-zled. "But why?"

"I have heard that sometimes men abduct women for immoral reasons," Anne murmured, lowering her eyes in aversion to the crimes at which she hinted.

"But I am inclined to think that my experience was another in a series of events stemming from the murder," I said. "One of those men might have been the person who chased me at the opera, while the other ransacked our room at the Chapter Coffee House. Although I don't possess whatever it is that they seek, perhaps they think I can lead them to it."

"If so, then one of them must have killed my sister." Gilbert White rose, his expression animated yet troubled; he paced the office restlessly. "Unless we discover the truth about these crimes and catch the criminals, these attacks on you will surely continue. The only way to obtain justice for Isabel and to protect you is to catch those men. I've reported the incident to the local police, but I didn't get a good look at the men." He faced me, his brilliant eyes eager. "Perhaps you could describe them?"

"I'm sorry to say that I paid them little attention until it was too late," I said ruefully.

"As did I," Anne said.

"But we must try to remember as much as possible about them," I said.

Just then, the stationmaster entered the office. He was a florid-faced man dressed in a railway uniform. "Pardon me," he said. "Just checking to see how the ladies are."

Anne and I assured him that we both were well.

"It's a pity that such a thing happened to you on this railway," he said. "I'm afraid you've missed the last train to Keighley, but there's another tomorrow morning. In the meantime, if you want lodging, I suggest the White Horse Inn."

As I thanked him, my gaze alit on a framed picture on his desk. It was a miniature portrait of a woman and children who must be his family. Inspiration struck.

"Sir," I said, "may I please have a pencil and paper?" To Mr. White I said, "I shall sketch the faces of the men who attacked us."

Drawing is a favorite hobby of mine, although my talents are

modest. As I sat at the desk and began to sketch, my hand was subject to a fearful trembling which had little to do with the events just
past. My drawings—like my stories—are mirrors of my soul.
When I draw for someone, or read aloud my writing, I hunger for
praise and fear criticism. When my audience is a man, I feel most
vulnerable. And when he is a man towards whom I have particular
feelings, an intoxicating, shameful warmth spreads through my
body, almost as if I were disrobing before him. I felt the warmth
now as I drew the ginger-haired man. Anne offered suggestions,
while Gilbert White stood beside me, watching.

"Such impressive talent you have," he said.

"You are too generous, sir," I said with an awkward laugh.

Yet his praise delighted me. Unexpected memories arose to
increase my agitation. I saw myself in the parsonage nine years
ago, sketching William Weightman. When he stepped over to view
the portrait, he touched his lips to my cheek in a brief, daring kiss.
How I burned for days afterward! I recalled a schoolroom in
Belgium, where I read aloud a French essay I'd written. My professor—a man I once loved to distraction—hurled scathing criticisms
at me until I wept. Then he was all sympathetic kindness. Such passions he roused in me! Never could I let him know how much I
craved the touch of his hand.

Gilbert White's hands now rested on the desk near me—those
strong, clean hands which had wrested my life from the grip of
peril. The thought of his carrying me to safety stirred me powerfully. I hazarded a glance up at him—and straight into the impenetrable depths of his eyes. Mightily embarrassed, I averted my gaze.
I applied myself to drawing until the portraits were done.

"Very true and lifelike they are," said Anne.

"I'm sure they will help locate the men," Gilbert White said.
"But for now, please let me take you and your sister to safe lodgings, Miss Brontë."

I gladly agreed, for I welcomed his protection and company.
He installed us in a carriage and rode with us to the White Horse
Inn. As we disembarked, a sulfurous fog engulfed us. The chill
penetrated my damp garments, yet I was warm as from a fire

burning inside me.

"I apologize for disrupting your plans," I said, in fear of the possibility that Mr. White was merely discharging what he saw as a duty.

"I'm glad to help you." Mr. White paid the driver and lifted my trunk.

Heartened I was by his apparent sincerity; yet I thought to wonder how Gilbert White had happened to be on the same train as I. "May I ask what brought you to Leeds?" I asked.

"I'm on my way to Bradford, to inform my mother of Isabel's death," Gilbert White said as he opened the inn's door.

I pitied him this sad task, and my distrust shamed me.

"I, too, have missed my train and must stop the night here," he added.

Inside the inn, Anne and I engaged a room upstairs and Mr. White took one on the ground floor. He accompanied us to our room, to ensure that all was right. I heard him test the lock on the door—but avoided watching him; I pretended to study the white curtains and flowered wallpaper. His presence in the room where I would sleep caused me shameful thoughts.

"You should be safe tonight," Mr. White said. "I'm a light sleeper, and if anyone approaches you, I'll hear."

His words, meant to reassure, divided my emotions. Glad though I was to have him near, might our inhabiting the same house violate propriety? I recalled my unease when he had asked me if Isabel had given me anything. What did I know about him other than what he himself had told me?

Hesitantly I followed him into the corridor, while Anne remained in the room. "Sir," I began, seeking a way to dispel uncertainty without offending him.

I had only his word for what had happened between him and my attackers after he caught up with them. Could he be their accomplice? The ghastly notion stifled my voice as we stood facing each other. Mr. White waited for me to speak, his expression turning suddenly cautious. The narrow corridor confined us; a single lamp cast a fitful, smoky light. The inn's staff and other guests had retired, and in the silence I heard my rapid breathing—and his. My back was pressed against the wall; my heart thumped with an uncomfortable fusion of fear and an awareness of the improper feelings that had arisen in me towards this man I couldn't quite trust.

At last he spoke. "May I escort you to Keighley tomorrow?" His voice was soft, his gaze compelling. "After what happened tonight, you shouldn't travel alone."

That moment reminded me how fear can enhance attraction. I felt an almost irresistible urge to touch his bruised cheek. "But it would inconvenience you," I stammered.

"It would be my pleasure," he said with somber emphasis.

I was quaking inside, every particle of my being alert to the implication that Gilbert White felt the same attraction as I. Alive with hope that rivaled fear, I nodded wordlessly.

His rare smile flashed. "Then good night until tomorrow, Miss Brontë," he said, and descended the stairs.

Breathless and weak, I stood in the corridor, endeavoring to collect my thoughts. Likely, my recent mishaps had rendered me too leery of my fellow humans. If Gilbert White did have evil intentions regarding me, then he would not have saved me. We shared a mission as well as the potent alchemy that draws together a man and woman.

Thus I justified my good opinion of Mr. White; but later, while I lay in bed, I wondered more about him. Was I truly safe in the protection of my rescuer and possible suitor? Or was he a villain biding his time while scheming against me? Just before I finally slept, I recalled the premonition evoked during my first encounter with Gilbert White. What could it mean?

9

A S I PREPARE TO DESCRIBE THE
EVENTS THAT OCCURRED AFTER
my return to Haworth, I realize that my version of them comprises
but one portion of the story. Another belongs to my sister Emily. I
then had no idea of her state of mind, for we were on such poor
terms that we hardly spoke; and later, misfortune silenced Emily
forever. I now face a difficult choice: Shall I allow her to remain as
unknown to the world as she wished, or shall I reveal her nature
in all its tragic, human beauty? The truth requires that I defy her
wishes. It is my only hope of uncovering the complete facts of my
story.

The table before me is covered with journals that Emily left.
What she endured in the weeks following Isabel White's murder lie
in the words I have culled from these journals. May God forgive me
if I have defiled her memory for the sake of veracity. With great
foreboding I open the volume for that year and copy her account
herewith.

The Journal of Emily Brontë

Wednesday, 12 July 1848.

A sullen, unsettling day after a night of rain. More storms
threaten—I sense their approach rumbling in my bones. The
earth, the sighing wind, and the stone walls of the parsonage

breathe a fetid moisture. Oh, how this weather darkens my spirits, which are already in grievous state! Shall the very heavens weep for the troubled souls inside our house?

This morning, when I went upstairs to clean Branwell's room, I found him still abed, a ghastly, emaciated wraith.

"Emily, please give me some money," he moaned.

As I pulled the soiled coverlet off him, he clutched my hands. I twisted out from his clammy, revolting grasp, crying, "I won't. Let me go!"

"Just a sixpence," Branwell pleaded. "If I cannot buy laudanum, I shall die!"

Once I would have tried to coax him into resisting self-destruction, but I have no more patience nor compassion for the wretch. What are his afflictions compared to mine?

Branwell began sobbing. "Oh, heartless sister! Oh, cruel world! I'm dying, and nobody cares! Oh, my dear, lost Lydia!"

"Be quiet!" I shouted, incensed, because I have suffered a far greater loss.

Our commotion brought Papa hurrying to us. Branwell launched himself from the bed and fell on his knees in front of Papa. "Father, I need money. Please, you must help me!"

Papa shook his head in sorrow. "I've already spent a fortune paying your debts. I'll not indulge you anymore."

Desperate cunning shone in Branwell's eyes. "If you won't help me, I'll kill myself!"

He snatched a razor from the dresser; I grabbed his wrist. We struggled together in a mad dance, Branwell trying to slash his throat, I trying to prevent him. "Let me end my miserable life!" he screamed.

Perhaps I should, thought I. Perhaps I should afterward turn the weapon on myself—then neither of us need suffer more. But Papa wrested the razor away from Branwell. We locked him inside the room. He pounded on the door, ranting in maniacal fury. I went to the kitchen and began kneading bread dough, trying to distract myself from Branwell's uproar and my own worries.

Where are Anne and Charlotte? *Come back, come back!* my heart silently calls to them. But still I burn with my fury at their betrayal. Perhaps I should not mind so much if only I could write! But I cannot. Many are the stories begun since I wrote *Wuthering Heights*—all abandoned incomplete. Whenever I now try to write, I hear the damning words of the critics. They trumpet that my novel "shows the brutalizing influence of unchecked passion." They revile my characters as "most revolting to our feelings." What misery is mine! I can only pretend to work, covering pages with ramblings like these, while inspiration hides behind a locked door inside me. Fortunate Charlotte, who enjoys travel and is writing a new book! Fortunate Anne, who has published a second novel! Oh, my heart shall break!

Such bewilderment and consternation did Emily's words cause me! How could she consider the mortal sin of taking her own life? Had I but known of her pain, I would have been more sensitive towards her. But she never gave me a clue. She always appeared supremely confident of her talent, as well she should have been: Her poems and stories were things of splendor that never failed to move me. In literary expertise she was the leader, my idol, even though I was her elder. And I never suspected that she cared what the critics said; she seemed so indifferent to public opinion, even during her youth. When Emily was seventeen, she came with me to Roe Head School where I taught. As eccentric in appearance as ever, she was the target of bullies, from whom I could not always protect her. But she never flinched at their tormenting. She held her head high, a soldier in an enemy prison camp. How I admired her! My weakness is that I always want people to like me—and my work—even when I care not for them. How I wished I could follow Emily's example!

But now I understand that her attitude sheltered a tender soul. Emily pretended to scorn the critics while she bled inside from their harsh comments about *Wuthering Heights*. She hid her wounds from me.

When Anne and I at last returned to Haworth, we hurried into the kitchen, where Emily was kneading bread dough.

"Emily!" Anne cried. "How I've missed you!"

Emily glared. She showed no sign that she'd missed us or worried about us. Anne's smile faded.

"Has all been well here while we were gone?" I asked anxiously. Emily behaved as though she had not heard me.

Anne offered our sister the book she had purchased in London. "We've brought you a present—it's Tennyson's poems."

When Emily made no move to take the gift, Anne sighed and laid it on the table. Anne and I could only exchange worried glances and silently agree that we had best leave her alone until her mood passed. We crept out of the kitchen.

➤✦◄

Two days after that unhappy homecoming, a spell of wet, chill weather descended upon Haworth. I donned my bonnet and cloak, armed myself with an umbrella, and headed down Church Road to post a letter to Ellen Nussey, my dearest friend. Ellen was something of a busybody, so avid was she to know everything I did or thought. I had lately neglected my correspondence with her, and I'd written a letter of vague explanation.

Moreover, I could no longer tolerate confinement in the parsonage, where acrimony reigned. Emily continued sulking. Branwell had gone into the village and returned home uproariously drunk. Anne had received a review from the *Spectator* that read, "*The Tenant of Wildfell Hall*, like its predecessor, suggests the idea of considerable abilities ill applied . . ."

Although the wind now blew rain against me and tugged at my umbrella, I welcomed solitude. But solitude was not to be mine. As I neared the bottom of the lane, I was accosted by the Reverend Arthur Bell Nicholls.

"Good day, Miss Brontë," he said in his thick Irish brogue. "May I walk with you?"

Mr. Nicholls had come from Dublin to be Papa's curate. A man of twenty-nine years, he had heavy dark brown hair and eyebrows, heavy features, heavy legs, and a stolid, serious nature. I found him annoying, for he often sought me out although I could not imagine why. I reluctantly let him share my umbrella and accepted his company.

We walked down Main Street, through the village. The rows of stone cottages were grimy with peat smoke and dripping with rain. Mr. Nicholls and I skirted gutters overflowing with malodorous drainage from cesspits. Haworth is a poor, unhealthful place riddled with poverty born of slumps in the textile industry. Damp, tiny cellar dwellings house large families, fevers rage, and funerals comprise a large part of Papa's duties. That day the village seemed even smaller and poorer than usual, after my recent adventures in London.

I refrained from speech in the hope that my companion would grow bored and leave me, for I wanted to think about Gilbert White. Mr. White and I had talked together on the train all the way from Keighley to Haworth. We at first discussed Isabel, but soon our conversation turned personal. I told Mr. White how I had happened upon some poems written by Emily and thought to publish a book of poetry by my sisters and myself. I admitted that only two copies had sold, but the venture had spurred me to attempt novels. Mr. White told me about growing up in the town of Bradford, his father's fatal accident in a factory, and how charity had paid for his education at boarding school, then divinity college at Oxford. We had much in common—our Northern origins, our lives as charity children, our faith. He became the most intimate male acquaintance I'd ever had.

Before we parted at Keighley Station, he jotted on a paper the address of his vicarage, presented it to me, and said, "Shall we write to each other?"

"Do you mean—if I remember anything else about the men on the train—or if you learn anything from your mother?" I asked, astounded because no man I admired had ever before asked me to correspond with him. "Why, yes, of course."

"Whatever you choose to write, I'll be delighted to read," Mr. White said earnestly.

I thought it prudent to wait until he wrote before writing him a letter, and while I waited, I relived every moment spent with him. I dressed my hair with undue care, as if he could see me; we carried on imaginary conversations in my mind. For a woman to nurture affection without proof of requital is sheer folly, as I well knew, but I could not help myself.

Now Arthur Nicholls said, "Yesterday, at the stationer's shop, I met a stranger." Close beside me under the umbrella, he smelled of cooked cabbage. How I wished I had Gilbert White as my companion instead! "He asked about you, Miss Brontë."

"Oh?" I said, bored by anything the curate had to say.

"He wanted to know who your family and friends are, what you do, and what kind of character is yours," said Mr. Nicholls.

Uneasiness stirred in me; the rain and gusting wind seemed colder than a moment ago. "What was this man's name?"

"He didn't say."

My uneasiness quickened into alarm. "Well, what did he look like?"

"I didn't really notice."

"What did you tell him?"

"Nothing, of course. I don't gossip to strangers." Mr. Nicholls looked affronted.

There are people who have no notion of sketching a character or perceiving salient points of persons or things, and Mr. Nicholls belongs to this class. Would that he were as good at observation as he was discreet! Could the stranger be one of the men who had assaulted Anne and me on the train? I looked down Main Street towards the village green and the toll gate. Suddenly Haworth didn't seem so isolated as before.

"Miss Brontë, I hope you've not been doing anything to attract improper attention from strange men," Mr. Nicholls said in a tone of sententious concern. "As the daughter of a clergyman, you should be careful about your behavior, lest it reflect badly upon your father or the Church."

How dare he assume I was at fault and tell me how to act? "You do seize upon any chance to sermonize."

"Yes; it is my duty," Mr. Nicholls said seriously, interpreting my tart rejoinder as praise.

It was a pity that Mr. Nicholls couldn't be like Gilbert White, who'd cared more for my safety than about public opinion. Still, I knew Mr. Nicholls to be a good man, held in high regard by Papa and the parishioners. Perhaps Anne and Emily and I shouldn't have stolen his middle name as our nom de plume, although we'd enjoyed our secret joke.

Afraid that I would say something regrettable if Mr. Nicholls and I continued together, I halted. "Here's the post office. I must step inside." I said firmly, "Goodbye, Mr. Nicholls," entered the building, and left him standing alone in the rain.

Inside the post office, drawers and compartments lined the walls. Behind the counter sat the postmistress, Nancy Wills, a stubby woman with frizzy grey hair beneath her muslin cap.

"Oh, Miss Brontë," she said, "I heard tha was back from London. It were a nice trip, I hope? I saw your pa the other day when he come from visitin' the Oaks farm. They've got th' fever there."

More village gossip followed. When she paused for breath, I handed her my letter and said, "Is there any post for me?" As Nancy began searching through letters and parcels, a thought struck. "Has there been a stranger asking about me?"

"Matter of fact, there was," Nancy said. "It were two days ago. A man were botherin' me with all sorts of questions, like who do tha send letters to or get them from."

I felt a ripple of foreboding. "You didn't answer him, did you?"

Nancy's cheeks flushed. "Nor me. I told him to mind his own business." She turned away and mumbled, "I think I did see something for thee, Miss Brontë. Now where can it be?"

I shuddered to think that a murderer may have tapped her extensive store of knowledge about my family. "Can you describe the man?"

"Oh, he were a gentleman with black hair and city ways." Nancy tittered. "Fair handsome, too."

At least she had better powers of observation than did Mr.

Nicholls, even if she lacked his discretion. The stranger could have been the dark man from the train. If he now knew where I lived, why had he not approached me?

While I stood stricken by fear, the postmistress exclaimed, "Oh! Here it is!"

She gave me a flat rectangular package that was approximately seven inches long, wrapped in brown paper and tied with string. It had a London postmark, but no sender's address. "Whoever could have sent thee a present?" she said with expectant curiosity.

My thoughts flew to Gilbert White. Had he gone back to London and from there sent *Jane Eyre* for me to inscribe? Would there be a letter? Happy anticipation replaced my earlier fear. I hurried home and shut myself into the room above the front hall. With trembling fingers I unwrapped the package.

A letter is a wondrous treasure. Letters from my friends and family had comforted me while I was away from home. The absence of letters caused terrible unhappiness; I once had waited three years for a letter that never arrived. This time, however, fortune had blessed me.

Inside the package was a book wrapped in the same brown paper as the entire parcel—I could feel the curved spine and the edges of the binding. A sheet of white paper bearing a few lines of script accompanied the book. As I eagerly read the letter, anticipation turned to shock.

> Dear Miss Brontë,
>
> Forgive me for initiating a correspondence which you did not authorize and may not welcome. But I am in desperate straits, and I must presume upon you. Enclosed is a package. I beg you to deliver it, unopened, to my mother, Mrs. Mary White, 20 Eastbrook Terrace, Bradford, Yorkshire. Thank you for your kindness. I hope I will be able to repay it someday.
>
> Isabel White

10

> ⟩ ⟨

EVENING AT THE PARSONAGE GENERALLY FOLLOWS A LONG-standing routine, and so it did on the day I received Isabel White's package. My family ate a simple dinner, and by half past nine, we had finished our evening prayers. Papa had locked the parsonage doors and gone upstairs to his bedchamber, where he sleeps near his loaded pistol in case thieves or marauders should come. Branwell was out, presumably carousing at the Black Bull Inn. My sisters and I sat around the table to read aloud and discuss our literary works in progress. The wind from the moors wailed around the house; drafts rattled the windows. The flickering candlelight painted our shadows on the walls as I read aloud from the manuscript of my new novel.

On the surface this resembled any other of our gatherings, but I was uncomfortably aware of the difference. Emily had remained unrelentingly taciturn all day. Anne's hurt was palpable; there was none of our usual camaraderie. And I kept thinking of the package. What was the book? Was it the object sought by the thief at the Chapter Coffee House, and the reason I'd been chased at the opera then nearly abducted in Leeds?

While I read, the image of Gilbert White materialized upon the pages. He had asked me to write, and now I had something to tell him. Distracted by my pondering, I lost my place in the manuscript and ceased reading. I looked at Emily and Anne, but neither spoke. Anne unhappily watched Emily, who gazed downward, seething with ire.

"What do you think of my story, Anne?" said I.

Anne murmured, "It seems quite good to me," then fell silent, although she was usually an astute, voluble critic.

"Emily?" I said. "What do you think?"

Her head came slowly up. Her eyes were the turbulent dark green of stormy oceans; she rose and spoke in a hushed, ominous voice: "Do you really want to know what I think?" Pacing around the table, as was her habit, she said, "Well, I don't like it at all."

"Why not?" My chest constricted with alarm.

"Caroline Helstone is a weak, insipid, pitiful excuse for a heroine. Robert Moore is a cad." Emily's eyes shot vindictive sparks; her shadow followed her like a malevolent ghost. "And the curates are silly. In fact, all the characters are trivial and lifeless."

Her cruel criticism provoked a surge of anger in me. "Suppose you show me what good writing is," I said. "It's been months since you've read us a new story."

She recoiled as if I'd struck her, then muttered, "I've nothing ready yet. But that doesn't change my opinion of your book."

That I knew Emily was venting her rage at me upon my book did not relieve my fear that there might be some validity to her criticism. Perhaps *Shirley* was indeed a bad book. Yet its defects were of secondary concern to me at present.

"Emily, you are torturing me!" I cried. "I'm sorry I broke my promise. I've apologized over and over, and so has Anne. How can we gain your forgiveness?"

Hands clenched, Emily stood rigidly by the fireplace, her face ashen and her angry eyes reflecting the candle flames.

"No harm has come of telling Charlotte's publisher the identities of Currer and Acton Bell," Anne said in a pleading voice. "Smith, Elder & Company know nothing of you." She rose and moved towards Emily, her hand outstretched. "Everything is quite the same as before."

"Everything has changed!" Emily flinched violently away from

Anne's touch. "Mr. Smith will tell more people the secret, and soon curiosity seekers will be knocking on our door." Her voice ragged with hysteria, she began pacing the room, as if already under siege. "I can't bear that. I'll die!" It would do no good to tell Emily that she was magnifying the threat, for her fear of strangers was real and extreme.

"We must talk about what happened to Anne and me," I said.

"Anne has already told me everything. It makes me ill. I won't hear anymore." Emily pressed her palms over her ears. But as I told Anne how a strange dark man had questioned Arthur Nicholls and the postmistress about me, Emily's hands dropped. She crouched on the floor. "It's started," she whimpered. "The public has found Acton, Currer, and Ellis Bell. The hordes will invade Haworth, and we'll never have another moment of privacy!"

This explanation for the stranger in the village had not occurred to me. Had a reader of our books tracked the authors Bell to their lair?

Anne put her arms around Emily. "It seems more likely that the stranger is one of the men from the train, come to harm us again. Oh, Charlotte, we must keep the doors and windows locked. We must tell Papa, and we must never go out alone. Should we take turns staying up at night to watch over the house and keep Branwell inside?"

"Those measures might postpone trouble," I said, "but the only way to protect ourselves is to identify our enemies so that they may be apprehended."

"But how can we identify them?" Anne stroked Emily's hair.

"This may provide the answer," I said, and drew from beneath my notebook the package from Isabel White. "I retrieved it from the post office this afternoon. Miss White sent it the day we arrived in London. She must have conceived the idea while we were on the train—surely, that's why she took such pains to learn my address and the correct spelling of my name."

"How strange," Anne said, though Emily seemed not to listen. "Do you think Miss White's package contains clues as to who killed her and why?"

"I hope so; but alas, I can't look inside." I read aloud Isabel's letter. "My conscience won't allow me to open the package."

"Your conscience allowed you to break your promise to me," Emily said bitterly.

How well she knew how to worsen my guilt! "That was necessary. This matter is altogether different. Isabel White's letter represents her dying wish, and I cannot defy it."

"Will you tell Gilbert White about the package?" Anne said.

I had promised to tell him if I had further information regarding the murder. I also wanted to tell him that my attackers appeared to have located me in Haworth; yet my doubts concerning Mr. White had resurfaced. Was this package what he sought when he asked if Isabel had given me anything? Had he befriended me that I might lead him to the book? Would I receive aid by communicating with Mr. White, or further endanger myself and my family?

Before I could frame an answer to Anne's question, Emily exclaimed with caustic triumph, "Ah, I understand! This man Gilbert White is the reason for your interest in the murder. You've fallen in love with him, just as you did with Monsieur Heger in Belgium!"

I was shocked by her accusation and by the mention of a name I still cringed to hear. I stammered, "That's ridiculous. I am not in love with Mr. White, and I was never in love with—"

"Oh, yes, you were." A spiteful smile lit Emily's face. "I saw how you looked at him during our French lessons. I saw you writing letters to him and watching the post for his reply. Do you think I'm blind, that I wouldn't notice?"

Horror filled me. If my self-absorbed sister had noticed, how many other people had guessed my secret love for my professor, the married man over whom I had humiliated myself? I hated Emily for suggesting that I had fallen in love with Gilbert White as unwisely as with Monsieur Heger. She wanted revenge, and if I wanted peace between us, I should let her wound me; but I couldn't bear to discuss Monsieur Heger—or Gilbert White—in this manner.

"My feelings towards Mr. White are beside the point," I said coldly. Loath to mention my suspicions of him, I went on: "I may or may not write to him, but the fact is that Isabel has assigned me the duty of conveying the package to her mother. I must go to Bradford at once. Since I shouldn't travel alone, I need someone to go with me."

"Not I," Emily declared with a passion. She huddled closer to the floor, as if sinking roots in it. "When we returned from Belgium, I said I would never leave home again, and I—unlike you—always keep my word."

Anne's expression was pensive, worried. Still embracing Emily, she said, "Perhaps you should send the package by post."

"There must be a reason why Isabel didn't want to post the package directly to her mother," I said. "I must deliver it in person. Anne, since Emily won't go with me, will you?"

Emily turned a fierce gaze upon Anne, who looked torn asunder. I said, "The package is a possible clue to discovering who killed Isabel and attacked us. The only way to learn what's inside it is to obtain her mother's permission to look. Papa is too frail to travel, and Branwell too unreliable. Anne, you must go to Bradford with me."

Neither of my sisters spoke. They looked as they had in childhood, when they would whisper together, and if I came into the room, they would fall silent and wait for me to leave. "Dear Charlotte, I'm sorry," Anne said with quiet regret.

❧❦❧

As I recall the scene above, the wind wails round the parsonage; candles glow. But mine is the only shadow on the wall, for I sit alone at the table. The chairs once occupied by Anne and Emily are vacant. Emily's bulldog, Keeper, lies near the hearth beside Anne's little spaniel, Flossy. They prick up their ears and look towards the door, expecting the return of their departed loved ones. How my heart aches with loneliness! In the hope of distraction, I will relate a part of my story which occurred on the same night Emily and I quarreled, although at the time I knew nothing of these events.

John Slade's travels had again brought him to London. At midnight, the River Thames, black and oily under a clouded, moonless sky, flowed past the city, beneath the arches of London Bridge, and wended onward to the sea. By day, the Thames is a busy highway crowded with ships, barges, and ferries, but the traffic was now ceased, the shipyards deserted, the vessels moored at the wharves. The river slept—until a lone ship glided into view. Her tattered sails had borne her from the Orient. Painted in faded letters on her hull was the name *Pearl*. She approached the London Docks and navigated the canals along the quays. Warehouses loomed, dark and abandoned except for one: Here, lamplight shone through windows, and a man waited outside.

He was Isaiah Fearon, a prosperous merchant, once a trader in the East Indies. As he spied the *Pearl* drawing near, he shouted an order. The warehouse discharged a horde of dock laborers. They hurried along the quay to guide the ship into a berth and secure her; they transferred cargo from the *Pearl*'s hold to the warehouse. The captain disembarked, carrying a small wooden chest, and joined Isaiah Fearon. The chest exchanged hands. Fearon's men brought out scores of heavy crates, which they stowed aboard the *Pearl*. Soon the ship sailed away down the canal. Isaiah Fearon dismissed the men; alone, he locked himself inside the warehouse, a vast, dim cavern filled with goods and reeking of exotic spices. He went to his office, placed the chest on his desk, and opened it. Inside were hundreds of gold coins.

A sudden noise interrupted his contemplation of the profits earned from his secret venture: It was the sound of wood splintering under a hard blow. A distant door opened. There was an intruder in the warehouse. Fearon took a pistol from the desk drawer, snuffed the lamp, and tiptoed out of his office.

A wavering light moved behind the high rows of piled goods. Stealthy footsteps walked the stone floor and echoed in the gloom. Pistol in hand, Fearon stole through the shadows, circling his unseen adversary, determined to protect his property. Suddenly a cord whipped over his head and pressed tight around his neck, choking him. Fearon squealed; as his muscles tensed in shock and panic, he squeezed the trigger. The pistol discharged with a great boom. Fearon dropped the gun and clawed at the cord, which squeezed his throat harder. His attacker gripped him in an iron embrace. His body sagged to the floor. The terror in his expression faded as his features went slack. All was silent.

Over the corpse stood John Slade.

He held a lantern above Fearon's livid, swollen face. He breathed hard and fast, spent by exertion; his unruly dark locks were wet with sweat, his eyes afire. He hastened to the office and noted the chest of gold, then turned to the ledgers piled on the desk. He skimmed pages listing quantities of opium sold in China, and of silks and tea imported to England. Impatient, he yanked open the desk drawers, searching through the letters there. One document read as follows: "I am terminating our business agreement, and you should expect no more merchandise from my firm. Yours sincerely, Joseph Lock."

Slade folded the letter into his pocket, read the remaining correspondence, and cursed in frustration, for the name he sought appeared nowhere. Then he heard men's excited voices outside, and running footsteps: Fearon's gunshot must have alerted the dock guards. Slade fled soundlessly from the warehouse and vanished into the dark labyrinth of the docks.

11

>-<

I SPENT THE FOLLOWING DAYS WONDERING AND FRETTING OVER whether I should write to Gilbert White about the package. Each arrival of the post caused me a flurry of expectation that I might receive a letter from him; but time passed, no letter came, and my caution won out.

Emily observed my discomfort with grim pleasure. The burden of my duty to Isabel pressed upon me, and my previous adventures had left me hungering for more. Then on Thursday, July 20—six days after I had received the package—I heard a carriage rattling up Church Road. I dared to think that Gilbert White had come to call instead of writing me, and I hurried to open the door. Disappointment struck me.

My dear friend Ellen Nussey glided into the house, smiling. Ellen is plump and fair; her blue summer frock matched her round, light eyes. A straw bonnet covered her fluffy yellow curls. "My dear, the look on your face!" she exclaimed, enfolding me in an embrace as gentle as her voice. She always smells pleasantly of lavender pot-pourri. "Aren't you glad to see me?"

"Yes, of course," I hastened to say. "I'm just surprised." Ellen lives in Birstall—some twenty miles from Haworth—and never visits without prior arrangement. "You must be weary from your journey. Let me fetch you some nourishment."

I laid a light repast upon the parlor table. Pouring tea, I said, "What brings you here?"

As I passed the bread and butter, I contemplated the differences between us. Ellen is placid, while I am nervous. I am a daughter of a humble clergyman, but Ellen's father had been a wealthy owner of textile mills which still provided ample livelihood for the Nusseys. While I have worked to earn my keep, Ellen spends her days visiting, waiting on her mother, and fancy sewing. We first met seventeen years ago, at Roe Head School. I thought Ellen a prim, dull-witted busybody, and I did not like her; but over time, a mutual attachment had grown and flourished, and I learned to appreciate her good qualities.

"I came because of your letter," Ellen said. "Such dark hints about strange experiences! I felt certain that you were in a bad way and needed my help. I'm glad to find you in a good condition, but has something happened to your family?"

"They are all fine," I said, "except for Branwell, who's no worse than usual."

"Then my fears were unfounded." Clasping a hand to her bosom, Ellen sighed in relief. "But I was astonished to hear you had gone to London. Whatever for?"

Anxiety gripped me: Ellen didn't know the secret of Currer, Acton, and Ellis Bell, and I could not explain the trip without giving it away. "Anne and I had business in London."

"Oh. I see." I saw that Ellen was hurt by my evasion. Guilt pricked me, but before I could frame an explanation that would placate her without revealing too much, Ellen said, "There's something I've been meaning to ask you. It concerns that book everybody has been talking about, *Jane Eyre*."

A feeling of dread coursed through me.

"I heard a rumor that you are the author," Ellen continued. "At first I thought it could not possibly be true, because you wouldn't have published a book without telling me. But when I read *Jane Eyre*, I recognized Thornfield Manor as Rydings, where my family used to live. The grey house with its battlements, the rookery, and the thorn trees were all in the book, just as you saw them when you visited us.

And I could almost hear your voice speaking as I read. Now I must know for certain: Did you write *Jane Eyre?*"

Wincing inwardly, I clutched my teacup. Ellen had never been much interested in literature, and I never thought she would read *Jane Eyre*, let alone recognize anything in it. I had sworn to keep the secret, yet I didn't want to lie to my faithful friend.

"Ellen," I began.

As eager anticipation brightened her face, I spied Emily standing in the parlor doorway. Emily glowered at me, her meaning clear: She did not wish that Ellen be told, even though Ellen was one of the few people outside the family whom she liked. Then Emily turned and walked away, leaving me to choose between my friend and my sister.

"I did not write *Jane Eyre*," I declared. "If anyone tells you otherwise, you must set them straight."

"Oh. Yes, of course I will." Ellen looked unconvinced, even wounded, by my denial.

Anxious to atone for my deception, I clasped Ellen's hand and said, "I'm glad you're here, and I haven't even thanked you for coming. Please forgive me, and let me explain about the experiences I mentioned in my letter." I described Isabel White's murder and the incidents that followed, sharing with Ellen my belief that the events were somehow related.

"How awful!" Ellen exclaimed, clutching her throat as if she might faint. "My dear, how did you manage to find so much trouble?"

"I'm afraid that trouble found me, and it still lurks at my door," I said.

As I told her about the package from Isabel White and the inquisitive man in the village, I watched her expression turn aghast. She cried, "Oh, Charlotte, I can't bear for you to be in danger. You must come home with me this instant."

"That won't help me discover who's behind the attacks," I said. "Conveying the package to Isabel's mother and learning what I can from her represents my only hope of protecting myself and my family. But I cannot travel to Bradford alone under these circumstances, and Emily and Anne refuse to go with me. And Papa's health is too weak."

"How fortunate that I can be of use to you after all!" Ellen said, clapping her hands together. "My dear, I shall accompany you to Bradford."

Too late I realized that I should have anticipated this reaction. When Ellen is determined to help, nothing can stop her. "But those men might come after me again. I mustn't put you in danger."

Ellen waved away my protests. "I know you, Charlotte. You'll have no peace until you've done your duty to that poor woman, and if you don't have someone to accompany you, you'll make up your mind to go alone, no matter the risks."

There was truth in her words, but I could not put Ellen's safety at risk. "It's a journey of ten miles. We would have to stay overnight in Bradford. Surely you're not prepared for the trip, and your mother would worry if you were gone so long."

"Oh, but I am prepared." Ellen laughed merrily. "My trunk is outside. I came here expecting to stay with you at least a week, and I have Mama's blessing." Then dismay cast a shadow upon her countenance. "Unless—Charlotte, are you trying to say that you don't want my company?"

"No, of course I do," I hastened to assure her. As I tried to impress upon Ellen the serious nature of the threat, I could see that she remained hurt by what she saw as rejection, and unconvinced that any harm could befall her. Tears filled her eyes, and she dabbed them with a lacy handkerchief.

"I understand," she murmured. "I see that I'm not needed here, and I shall go home at once. Forgive me for bothering you."

It became clear that either I had to allow Ellen to accompany me to Bradford, or her feelings would be hurt beyond consolation. Moreover, I recognized that Ellen's proposal offered a solution to my problems. Should any persons wish to attack me, perhaps they would not if I was accompanied by someone outside my family, whom they wouldn't want to involve in their business. That Ellen had arrived today seemed almost a divine coincidence that enabled me to honor a murdered woman's last wish.

"We'll leave for Bradford early tomorrow," I said.

><

The town of Bradford is situated in the lower foothills of the Pennines. Its textile mills cluster along the valley like black, cancerous growths; coal mines mar the surrounding landscape. Mean tenements house men, women, and children who toil in the mines and mills from sunrise to sundown. The air resounds with the whine and roar of machinery.

The train conveyed Ellen and me to this hell on the morning of 21 July 1848. We left our bags at the station; then a hansom cab carried us through narrow streets amidst heavy traffic, past shops whose windows were so begrimed by soot that I couldn't see inside. Dense smoke laden with cinders stung my eyes and immersed the town in a perpetual dusk.

Ellen held a perfumed handkerchief over her nose and mouth. "This must be the most unwholesome place in the kingdom," she said. "I hope we do not take ill."

Illness was of secondary concern to me: I had spent the journey in dread of meeting again the two men who had attacked Anne and me. Although today's train trip had passed without incident, I nonetheless anxiously scanned the hordes of shopkeepers, laborers, businessmen, and servants on the streets.

The cab left Ellen and me at the entrance to Eastbrook Terrace. Carrying my satchel, which contained Isabel's package, I beheld a gloomy alley enclosed by two-story attached tenements constructed of dark, dingy brick. The pavement was covered by foul muck that was inches deep. I wondered how Gilbert White could allow his mother to live in such squalor. Surely he could afford better accommodations for his family. Did he shirk his duties as a son? Though disturbed by the thought, I held out hope that I might find him here. Perhaps he was staying with his mother, and had thus been too busy to write to me.

Boards had been set atop bricks to form bridges spanning the filth. Ellen and I gingerly walked along these, then up a staircase to Number 20. I knocked on the door.

"Come in," called a woman's faint voice from inside.

The room we entered was dim, its window partially covered with a muslin curtain. On a chair in the corner sat the woman, dressed in a white cap, white apron, and dark frock, her face in shadow.

"Mrs. White?" I said.

"Yes, who's there?" the woman replied in a timid tone, craning her neck.

"My name is Charlotte Brontë," I said, "and this is my friend Ellen Nussey."

As my eyes adjusted to the dimness, I saw that Mrs. White was perhaps sixty years old, frail of figure. Her face was gaunt, her pale skin lined; yet I discerned in her features the same delicately sculpted bones that Isabel had possessed. She held on her lap a cloth that looked to be a bedsheet. Her fingers plied a needle and thread, hemming the sheet in quick stitches. That she could sew in such poor light puzzled me, until a closer look at her showed filmy blue eyes gazing blankly up at me. Mrs. White was blind.

"I'm afraid your names are unfamiliar to me." She spoke in Isabel's voice, coarsened by age. "Have we met before?"

"I knew your daughter," I said, uncomfortably aware that the woman was still in mourning for her child and that I was intruding at a difficult time. "We met on a train to London. She asked me to call on you."

"Ah, you're a friend of Isabel. I'm fair glad to meet you." Half rising, Mrs. White extended her bony, delicate hand. I shook it, as did Ellen.

"Please, do sit down," Mrs. White entreated.

The room contained a divan, a table, a dresser, a chest, and a cupboard, all set against the walls; a hooked rug covered the floor. Everything was spotlessly clean, despite the foul odors from the street. Ellen and I settled on the divan; I placed my satchel beside me.

"Are you come to bring word of Isabel?" said Mrs. White. "Have you seen her lately? How is she?"

Ellen and I exchanged glances of alarm and puzzlement, for it appeared that the woman did not know her daughter was dead.

Mrs. White's expectant smile faded; she cocked her head, straining to divine the cause of our silence. "What's wrong?" she said, suddenly fearful. "Has something happened to Isabel?"

Alas, I had no choice but to deliver the news which Gilbert White had apparently not, although he had told me he was going to Bradford to see his mother. "I am so sorry," I faltered, "but your daughter is—Isabel has died."

Mrs. White sat frozen for a moment, her countenance blank; then she slowly released her grip on her sewing, which slid off her lap. She whispered, "No!"

"I'm sorry," I said again, wretched at the sight of the shock I'd caused.

Tears pooled in Mrs. White's eyes, though she shook her head in repeated denial. "But Isabel came to visit me not three weeks ago. She were in perfect health. How can she be dead?"

With great reluctance I informed Mrs. White of the murder, omitting the horrific details. A frenzy of weeping besieged the woman. "No! It can't be!" Her hands groped, as if in a desperate search for her daughter. "Isabel! Isabel!"

Ellen enfolded Mrs. White in her arms. I was glad Ellen had come, for she provided much better comfort than I could have. At last Mrs. White's sobs abated. Ellen went to the kitchen to make her a cup of tea, while I stayed by her. She looked shrunken and forlorn, and suddenly older than her sixty years; her eyes were red, and her complexion mottled from her tears.

"When I was in London, I met your son," I said. "He knows of Isabel's death. Has he not been here?"

"My son? I'm afraid I don't know what you're talking about. I've no son."

Her evident confusion was nothing to that which I experienced. "But he introduced himself as Isabel's brother. His name is Gilbert. He was coming here to see you."

"There must be some mistake," Mrs. White said. "Isabel is—or was—my only child."

What horror and surprise were mine! Gilbert White—I knew not what else to call him—had lied to me about his name, his past, and why he wished to know the truth about Isabel's death. He must have arranged a false address at which to receive my correspondence. Had his attentions to me been part of the lie? A dark emptiness opened inside me, then filled with panic. An idea surfaced from the chaos in my mind.

"Has any man been to visit you since you last saw Isabel?" I asked Mrs. White.

"Only a clergyman from the benevolent society. I forget his name. A bit odd, it were. While we was talkin', he tiptoed round the house, openin' cupboards and movin' things."

My heart began to pound. Perhaps Gilbert White was the stranger who had questioned people about me in Haworth. If he had also entered Mrs. White's house under false pretenses to search for Isabel's package, was he now on his way to Haworth to obtain it by whatever means necessary? The thought was horrifying.

Ellen came into the room, bringing a cup of tea for Mrs. White. I decided to say nothing of more of Gilbert White, for I did not wish to trouble Mrs. White nor Ellen. I did my best to hide my emotions, while Mrs. White sipped her tea. Presently, she began to speak in a small, sad voice.

"Isabel was my only comfort after her father died. He worked in the mill until a boiler exploded and killed him. Did Isabel tell you about that?"

"No," I said, for it had been Mr. White who'd told me. Whatever his real connection with Isabel, he must have known her well, and she had died violently. He now knew much about me. To what sinister purpose would he put his knowledge?

"When her father was killed, Isabel was ten." Mrs. White cradled her teacup in her hands as though craving its warmth. "I got a job running a spinning machine in the factory. Isabel was in school, but I couldn't earn enough to keep us, so she went to work at the factory, too."

My mind pictured a pretty blonde woman and girl laboring in the dirty, noisy mill, then trudging home through the dark, dreary streets of Bradford.

"I wanted better for Isabel, but there seemed no hope," Mrs. White continued. "Then one Sunday, some strangers came to our church. A Reverend and Mrs. Grimshaw. They said they ran a charity school in Skipton, and they was looking for poor girls who needed schoolin'. They came here and talked to Isabel alone for a long time. Afterward, they said she was just the kind of girl they wanted, and they took her away in their carriage. I hated to let Isabel go—we both cried—but I knew it was for the best."

I imagined a frightened young Isabel, riding off into the unknown, as I had done on my own first journey to the Clergy Daughters' School.

"While she was away," continued Mrs. White, "she wrote to me about all the things she was learnin' and all the nice people she'd met, and she sounded happy. But when she came home for the summer holiday, she was changed. They had fixed her hair, given her smart new clothes. She talked and acted like a lady. She was a stranger to me."

The shadow of past worries fell over Mrs. White's aspect. "Isabel had been such a happy, friendly, talkative child. But all the time we were together again, she never smiled nor said much. When I asked her if somethin' was wrong, she said no. She wouldn't talk about school at all. But at night I heard her cryin' in bed. I was afraid I'd done wrong to send her away, so I asked her if she'd like to stay home, even though there was naught for her here but the mill. She said no, and when her holiday was over, she returned to school."

A fragment of Isabel's conversation came back to me: *We are indeed products of our early training.* If something had happened to Isabel at school, was that at the root of her later troubles?

"The next holiday, she seemed more like herself," said Mrs. White, "so I stopped worrying. She were just growin' up, I thought. And later I was glad I had let her stay at the school, because when she was eighteen, the Reverend Grimshaw found her a good post as a governess for some rich folk up in London. By that time, my sight was going, and I couldn't work at the mill anymore. Isabel sent me money to live on."

I should be thankful that I was given an education that won me pleasant, lucrative employment, Isabel's voice echoed in my mind.

"She wrote to me, but she never said much about what she was doin' or the people she was with. She was always changin' posts and hardly ever came home. I asked to visit her, but she always had some excuse." Mrs. White said mournfully, "She didn't want my company. She was risen in the world and ashamed of her mum."

But a different explanation occurred to me: Perhaps Isabel had been ashamed of herself, for doing something she hadn't wanted her mother to know about.

"You mentioned that you saw Isabel recently," I said to Mrs. White. Three weeks ago would have been just before the murder. I understood why Isabel had been in Yorkshire when we met: She must have gone directly from here to the London train. "How did she behave?"

Mrs. White sighed, and her expression grew all the sadder. "She talked ever so cheerful, but I could tell she was nervous. I felt her fidgetin' and leanin' over to look out the window as if she was watchin' for someone. She started at every little noise. And at night, when she thought I was asleep, I heard her cry, just like when she were a child."

I asked Mrs. White if she knew what had ailed Isabel.

"She didn't say. And I didn't like to ask, because she was ever so secretive."

Alas, it seemed that I would not learn the reason for Isabel's death nor the identity of her killer from her mother. But my suspicions inclined ever more strongly towards Mr. White.

"Now I wish I'd made Isabel tell me what was wrong," said her mother. "Maybe I could have helped her." Sobs shuddered the frail old woman; her teacup sloshed, and Ellen gently removed it from her hands. "Now she's taken her troubles to the grave. She's gone forever, and I wish the Lord had taken me instead, for I can't bear to live without her!"

The time had come to discharge my duty. "Before Isabel died, she wrote to me and asked me to bring you this package," I said, and gave it to Mrs. White.

She eagerly accepted the last communication from her child. "Oh, thank you, miss," she cried. "I'm ever so grateful." She fumbled to open the package, then begged my assistance.

With great anticipation did I break the seal and remove the contents. There was a book bound in green cloth, and two papers—one a sheet of white stationery, the other a certificate from the Bank of England. Taking up the certificate, I said to Mrs. White, "Isabel sent you a banknote for a thousand pounds."

Such a vast sum I had never before handled, and my companions' faces reflected my amazement. Now I knew why Isabel wanted me to deliver the envelope: She'd deemed me less likely to steal than whoever else might have otherwise opened it for her mother.

Mrs. White exclaimed, "A thousand pounds! How generous Isabel always was! She didn't forget her mum." The old woman wept for joy. "But my heavens, where did she get so much money?"

I could not help thinking Isabel had come by the money dishonestly, for a governess's savings could hardly amount to such a fortune. Perhaps she'd been carrying her ill-gotten cash in the carpetbag that she guarded so closely, and exchanged it for the note at a London bank the day she died. She must have sought me out at the Chapter Coffee House because her killer was pursuing her and she had no one else to turn to for help.

"There's also a letter," I said. "Would you like me to read it to you?"

"A letter from Isabel! Oh, please do, miss!"

I read aloud:

Dearest Mother,

I'm sorry to say that I must go away. It is best that I not tell you where or why, or communicate with you while I'm gone. I promise to return if I can. In the meantime, I hope Miss Brontë has delivered this package to you and the money will supply your needs until we are reunited. Please take care of yourself and do not worry about me.

Isabel

Mrs. White and Ellen listened in obvious mystification. This message from beyond the grave sent chills through me, yet offered no enlightenment. I asked Mrs. White where Isabel might have meant to go, but she could offer no suggestion. I then turned to the book.

"Isabel also sent you a copy of *The Sermons of the Reverend Charles Duckworth*," I said, reading the title.

"But why would she send me a book?" Mrs. White shook her head in bewilderment. "She knows—she knew—I would be unable to read it."

Leafing through the soiled, musty volume, I scanned the dull ramblings of an ordinary clergyman who had immortalized himself in this tract. Surely, no one would kill to steal it. Then I noticed words filling the inner margins of the book's pages, penciled in Isabel's handwriting.

"Mrs. White," I said, "may I please borrow this book? I promise to return it."

"Aye, you can keep it if you like," Mrs. White said. "It's no use to me."

12

After Ellen and I left Mrs. White, we fetched our bags from the station, then engaged lodgings at a modest inn; we had tea and retired to our room for the evening. I explained to Ellen why I had taken the book from Mrs. White, and we sat on the bed to decipher Isabel's words. The writing was so tiny that my eyes had a difficult time of it; hence, Ellen read aloud while I copied the passages into my notebook.

With great trepidation do I embark upon recording the significant events of my life, for there is grave danger in hinting at what I have experienced. Furthermore, I am afraid that my narrative will show me to be a despicable sinner. Will I offend readers with a tale so sordid? Will they disbelieve me? These risks I must take, in the hope that writing my history will close a disgraceful chapter of my life. Perhaps they who would condemn me for the things I did will instead understand and pity me. And perhaps my words will reach the attention of someone able to combat an evil that is gaining destructive power even as I write.

My story begins when I met the man who became the master of my soul. I was at the time familiar with the nature of men, yet did not know that men such as He existed. The others had been coarse and ugly, but He was a creature from a different world. Dark was He, yet radiant, and possessed of great strength. From the very first moment, His strange beauty captivated me. His eyes—so fierce, so luminous—penetrated deep inside me. His voice was like velvet and steel, probing the recesses of my mind. Many questions did He ask me, and many secrets did He elicit.

I confessed to Him, as I had never been able to confess to any other soul, how, when I was a child, my father would creep into my bed at night. If I did not keep still Papa would beat me with his fist. He whispered that I was his darling and clamped one hand over my mouth to silence my cries. Oh, the tearing pain! He said that unless I promised not to tell anyone, he would send me to a prison for bad girls because I had tempted him. Even had I not feared his threat, how could I tell anyone of my shame?

When Papa died, my mother grieved, for she had loved him and I had kept my promise. His death impoverished us, and we were forced to go to work. I pretended to mourn him, but I was secretly relieved that he could never hurt me again. At night I dreamt that I was running through the mill, past rows of whirling, screeching spinning machines. They sucked me into their engines, and the mill exploded in a thunderous burst of bricks, metal shards, and boiling water. I would awake in terror. Every day as I worked in the mills I feared that my dream would come true and death would be my punishment for rejoicing that Papa was gone.

I never told anyone of this, other than the man to whom I made reference earlier. From Him I could hide nothing; nor did I want to, for He seemed the one person in the world who knew me and accepted me with all my faults. It was as if, when He coaxed from me the secrets of the horror and suffering I'd kept hidden from the world, I stood naked before Him with every scar on my soul visible. Every piece of myself that I gave Him purchased His favor in some inexplicable way, and I desired His favor above all else. I lived for His visitations, and I began to want Him in a way that I had never before wanted any man. His very presence reduced me to a state of hot, quivering need; His command was my law.

When she read this passage, poor Ellen began to cough and blush; however, she recovered herself and persevered with Isabel's account.

When He asked me to steal money from my employer, I did. At my next post, I was governess in a household that included a puppy, much beloved by the children. To test my loyalty, He ordered me to kill the dog. I was aghast, for I'd grown fond of it and its young owners. He didn't say that if I refused, He would abandon me—I could read it in His eyes. My need proved stronger than my conscience. One night I strangled the puppy. The poor creature squirmed and squealed in my hands until it expired. How sick I felt over betraying its trust; how guilty to watch the children grieve after the small corpse was found in the churchyard, where He had instructed me to lay it!

Yet all this faded to insignificance the moment I was reunited with Him. He caressed my cheek, and I thrilled to the touch that I'd longed for. Never had He given any sign that He wanted me, but now I saw desire in His eyes. He slowly undressed me, and the brush of His fingers kindled a fire in me. I wanted to cry out with impatience; I wanted to flee in terror, but His gaze held me still and silent: I could only submit.

How grateful I was that it fell upon Ellen to read aloud, and that I had but to copy! I blushed to think of pretty, demure Isabel White so forthrightly giving voice to these most intimate revelations, but I guiltily admit that I also burned with secret curiosity to hear more. Although she had turned a violent shade of crimson, Ellen steadfastly read on.

I swooned at the warmth of Him. Everywhere His hands touched me, flames leapt under my skin; I shuddered and moaned. He knew secrets of my body which I did not know myself. Willingly did I pleasure Him; eagerly did I open myself to Him. And when He entered me, there was no pain as in times past—only ecstasy.

But how could I commit such a sin as enjoying a man outside the bonds of holy matrimony? Should feminine virtue have not restrained me? Alas, I cared nothing for God, nor propriety, nor anything except Him. When He said, "What would you do for me?" I answered with all my heart: "Whatever you wish." He was my master, the source of all the meaning in my life. I was His devoted slave.

He introduced me to prominent men who hailed from all over the kingdom and the Continent. I entertained them at balls, taverns, gambling dens, and in bedchambers. The purpose of this was never explained to me, yet I deduced that my actions allowed my master to gain advantage over these men. Every one of them was damaged in some way by his association with me, while my master reaped the fruits of my labor. To what miserable depths did He sink me!

But I could not afford to care. The first time He ordered me to bed a man, I said I could not, for I wanted only Him. His countenance darkened, but His voice was quiet as He said, "You shall obey me." And my resolve crumbled because I saw that if I opposed His will, He would destroy me as He had destroyed other persons who defied Him. I obeyed, for the privilege of being with Him and keeping alive.

I trained myself to feel nothing towards the men I helped Him ruin. When I was presented to Lord John Russell, it mattered not that he was England's Prime Minister; I viewed him as but more prey for my master. But even a slave may reach the limit of her obedience; even a fallen woman retains a shred of morality. The time finally came when my love for my master was tested.

He sent me to work as governess in the house of Joseph

Lock, a Birmingham gun merchant. Mr. Lock was honest, kind, and a devout Christian. His wife was a fair, generous mistress to me, and their boys were affectionate and well behaved. They showed me the joy of an ordinary life. My heart began to ache for what I could never have, even as I sought to engage the affections of Mr. Lock. At first he resisted, ignoring my flirtatious gazes, avoiding me. Hating myself for the harm I would do him and his family, I went into his office, where he was working alone. He took me there on the floor, so great was the need I had aroused in him. Afterward, he wept, begging God to forgive his adultery.

Months passed, and our secret liaisons continued. His spirits declined, and his unsuspecting wife fretted over him, and how I pitied them both! He was clay in my hands, as was I in my master's. Then one night he told me what our affair had cost him, and what my master had gained by it. Mr. Lock knew only part of the story, but I deduced the rest from talk I'd overheard at my master's house. Shocked I was, for I had never suspected the breadth of His ambition; yet here was proof that He aspired to the power of kings. My discovery was the beginning of my disenchantment. I began to understand that I must free myself of Him, or consign my soul to eternal damnation. Still, I loved Him, and could not find the strength to break away —until He gave me His next command.

[Here some lines were scratched out.]

I was stunned by the audacity of His scheme. However, I did not doubt that He could succeed, for if He could compromise the Prime Minister, there seemed nothing He could not manage. The evil of it horrified me. How could I deliver helpless innocents into His grasp? How could I allow myself to be used as an instrument to shake the foundations of the world and bring disaster upon the kingdom?

I cannot, in spite of my fear of Him. To leave Him will cause me great agony, but leave I must, though my defiance will unleash the deadly force of His fury upon me. I write this on the eve before deserting my post at Mr. Lock's house. As soon as I pay a last visit to my mother, I will journey to London, then out of the country. I must tell no one where I am going. In truth, I myself do not know my ultimate destination. I only know that I must travel far and fast. I can already feel His mind sensing my traitorous thoughts. He is always watching me, and as soon as I am gone from Birmingham, He will send His minions after me, for He cannot allow me to live, knowing what I know.

May God protect me and forgive my sins.

"I've never heard such an extraordinary, disturbing tale in my life!" Ellen exclaimed when she'd finished reading.

"Nor have I." Indeed, I felt shaken and ill, as though I had absorbed the malignancy in Isabel's words as I transcribed them. What miserable degradation had she undergone; with what obscene depravity had she behaved! I was disgusted by Isabel, even as I pitied her. Setting aside my pen and notebook, I said, "How glad I am that I didn't tell Mrs. White about the hidden passages in the book."

"Who can be this man that forced Isabel to do those things?" Ellen asked.

I now confronted my suspicion that had turned to mortal certainty as Isabel's tale unfolded: Her unnamed master could be none other than the man I knew as Gilbert White. How well the description fit him! He must have discovered that Isabel had escaped his domination; he must have feared she would ruin his plans by refusing to obey him. He must also have guessed that Isabel had written their history, and he wished to destroy it to prevent exposure of his misdeeds. Had he not impersonated her brother to procure assistance from me, the last person to speak with her? Had he not also searched her mother's house? This seemed ample, damning proof that Gilbert White had killed his slave and pursued me solely to obtain her last testament.

I had other evidence which was less tangible yet more compelling: I had personally experienced the force of Mr. White's allure. Hence, I understood how he could have gained such power over Isabel that she would do his bidding, however evil. That I had let this man into my life, and desired him as Isabel had! What awful sins might he have seduced me into committing?

"My dear, what's wrong?" Ellen asked anxiously. "Your face has gone so pale!"

I was overcome by disgust at my own gullibility and my terror of Mr. White. I grew lightheaded and collapsed on the bed, my heart palpitating; yet I could not tell Ellen why. I had said nothing to her of Gilbert White, for fear that she would tease me as she did whenever a potential suitor entered my life, and I did not want her to know how I'd been duped. Nor did I think it wise to share with her my suspicions about this dangerous man.

"Isabel's story gave me a bad spell," I said. "Whatever shall I do with the book?"

"Give it to the police," Ellen suggested. "If the mysterious master killed Isabel—and if he really is going to bring disaster upon the kingdom—then the police need to know."

"But the London police think Isabel was the victim of a random attack," I said. "I doubt that a fantastic account scribbled in an old book could convince anyone to believe otherwise. Besides, nowhere does Isabel name her master."

All I could add was his assumed name and his description. I knew not where Mr. White was to be found. Of one thing was I certain: He would eventually find me.

"Then what will you do?" Ellen asked.

I knew I must do something, for the book had shown my situation to be much more serious than I had fathomed. That Isabel's master had subjugated the prime minister signified that her murder and my own troubles were but superficial manifestations of a far-reaching conspiracy, and that the impending disaster must be of vast proportions.

"I must identify and locate Isabel's master," I said.

Ellen stared in astonishment. "You? Why, the very idea!" She giggled merrily. "Oh, this must be one of your jokes, for how could you attempt such a hazardous task on your own?"

I could not explain that my only protection against harm was to deliver Gilbert White to the authorities before he found me. Nor could I admit that I wished for revenge upon the man who'd tricked me. I felt a new strength, fueled by anger, and a great determination to bring about his downfall.

"I am not joking. Someone must prevent the disaster," I said, "and who else is there but I?"

Exasperation colored Ellen's features. "This is another of your ambitious schemes, then. You should nip it in the bud, or you're sure to be disappointed." Her admonition eroded my determination, for who was I to pit myself against a murderer who apparently had the prime minister under his power? "Remember how you wanted to be an author, and it never happened."

After insisting that she believe this, I could hardly contradict her now. Still, she had reminded me that I had the talent to write a famous novel and thus achieve what no one had expected of me. I sat up as renewed self-confidence flowed through me like an invigorating tonic.

"I must at least try to find Isabel's master," I said, "for I am certain that everyone connected with Isabel is in danger from him, and I the most of all because I was her last companion. And I have her journal, which I believe he seeks because he thinks it reveals his secrets."

"But how can you hope to succeed, when the journal gives no particulars about this mysterious individual?" Ellen asked.

After some thought, I said, "I shall work with the facts about Isabel that we've gleaned today. The Charity School she attended is a place to start."

"It's been many years since Isabel left the school," Ellen said. "How can it have any bearing on her recent life?"

"Perhaps she kept in communication with the Reverend and Mrs. Grimshaw," I said. "Perhaps she told them things that she didn't tell her mother. Perhaps the school is part of the master's evil business. Instead of returning home tomorrow, I will travel to Skipton."

"Such a bold, drastic move!" With a gasp of horror, Ellen flung out her arms as if to restrain me. "My dear, you mustn't! If the

school is indeed associated with Isabel's master, you could be walking straight into the lion's den!"

"If it is, then it's the last place he would expect me to go," I
pointed out. "I shall be safer in Skipton than at home."

"But what would you do at the school?" Ellen demanded. "You
can't just walk in and start asking questions."

Indeed, I knew not how to go about obtaining facts from someone who might wish to hide them. Ellen and I argued: She chastised my impulsiveness and unladylike bravado, while I stubbornly
upheld my opinions. At last Ellen sighed in weary frustration.

"I see that you won't be dissuaded," she said. "I have no choice
but to go with you to Skipton."

There ensued another argument, in which I tried to impress
upon her the danger of the trip, while she swore to protect me. I
grew strident in my refusal, and Ellen began to weep.

"If you don't want me, and you insist on going alone, I'll return
home this very evening." She began packing her trunk while sobbing into her handkerchief.

I was torn between shame at hurting Ellen and irritation at her
for turning every dispute into a test of our friendship. But I didn't
relish the idea of confronting strangers at the Charity School alone.
I capitulated, agreeing that we would journey together to Skipton
on the morrow.

13

$\rightarrowtail\leftarrowtail$

TIME OFFERS NO INVINCIBLE BAR-
RIER AGAINST THE DARK FORCES
of the past. New places sometimes possess aspects of places I
thought to have left behind me forever; they evoke memories
preferably forgotten. This misfortune befell me during my visit to
the Charity School.

Ellen and I arrived in Skipton early in the afternoon of 22 July.
Skipton is a market town located on the Leeds and Liverpool
Canal. Its ruined Norman castle overlooks the village through
which we rode in a hired carriage. We journeyed some two miles
into meadowland. The Charity School occupied a shallow valley,
hidden from nearby farms by a birch forest. The path through this
was too narrow for our carriage, so Ellen and I asked the driver to
wait, then proceeded on foot.

"This seems a pleasant place for a school," Ellen remarked.

Indeed, the trees shaded us from the hot sun; birds twittered
around us; the air smelled cleanly fragrant. "But it's sufficiently remote
that evil things could happen here, with no one outside the wiser."

We emerged from the woods. Ahead of us appeared the
school—a two-story, stone structure with peaked slate roofs,
ruined turrets, and an arched doorway flanked by mullioned windows. A crumbling stone wall enclosed a garden filled with dark,
dense holly trees. Beyond the school's chimneys I saw the round

stone tower of an old windmill, its blades missing. A plaque on the wall bore the school's name.

At the door, Ellen grasped the knocker and rapped. We had agreed that she should take the lead during this expedition, for I wished to avoid, as much as possible, the notice of the people who had known Isabel White and might have had a part in her troubles and mine. If I effaced myself, perhaps I could induce them to think me insignificant and forgettable.

Presently, the door was opened by a severe woman dressed in a plain black frock, white apron, and white cap. "Yes?" she said. "Have you come to apply for the teaching position?"

"Oh, dear no. I am Miss Wheelwright of Birstall, and I wish to determine whether this school might be suitable for my young cousin." Ellen's voice exuded wealth, privilege, and refined breeding. "This is my companion Miss Brown."

These were the names, and this the story we'd invented in hope of gaining an inspection of the school. The housekeeper—as I assumed her to be—looked us over. We must have passed scrutiny, for she bid us to enter. As soon as I did, the smell hit me: an amalgam of soap, chalk, and damp plaster; of unappetizing foods; of the sweet, rank, urine odor of impoverished children. I was suddenly eight years old again, arriving at the Clergy Daughters' School at Cowan Bridge. Beyond the vestibule, where Ellen and I stood, a corridor extended between rows of doors. From these issued girlish voices reciting lessons in unison; in them I heard echoes from a bitter chapter of my life.

The housekeeper ushered Ellen and me into a parlor with dark paintings on the walls and old-fashioned furniture. She said, "I'll fetch the Reverend Grimshaw."

She departed, and we sat on a horsehair sofa. Ellen squeezed my hand. "That wasn't so difficult, was it?" she whispered, her eyes sparkling in enjoyment of our adventure.

I managed a shaky smile and endeavored to forget the school where I and my elder sisters, Maria and Elizabeth, suffered the inhumane deprivation that caused my stunted figure and contributed to their deaths.

"My dear, what's wrong?" Ellen gazed anxiously at me. "You look as white and queer as though you've seen a ghost."

There came a step at the door. Silhouetted in the light from the vestibule stood a man. I discerned his tall, upright figure in a frock coat and trousers, his head like a carved capital atop a black column, and the white clerical cravat at his throat. My heart lurched, for here, thought I, was the Reverend William Carus Wilson, evil proprietor of the Clergy Daughters' School. But of course, as I quickly realized when he walked towards us, this man was not my old enemy. His face, with its loose jowls, lacked the fierce austerity of Carus Wilson's. Greetings ensued; he introduced himself as the Reverend Grimshaw, and I endured the unpleasant clamminess of his hand shaking my own. I let Ellen do the talking, and when the Reverend Grimshaw sat opposite us, he addressed himself to her.

"You do realize that this institution is for girls who lack the financial means to obtain an education?" He had, I noticed, limp iron-grey hair and a moist, unhealthy complexion; he smelled of sweat. He gave Ellen a fawning, apologetic smile, his mouth puffy and sensual. "I fear that it is not an appropriate establishment for a child from a family such as yours. The accommodations are very plain."

"Oh, I quite understand," Ellen replied. "My cousin is a distant relative whose parents are in unfortunate circumstances." Her tone conjured up visions of an illegitimate child needing charity from affluent connections. "I am prepared to contribute towards her education."

God bless Ellen for saying what I'd told her to say in the event that the Reverend Grimshaw should question our motives, and for occupying him while I sat sick and tongue-tied.

"Ah," he said. "Well, then, perhaps you would like a tour of the school?"

"Yes, if it's not too much trouble." Ellen flashed me a covert, triumphant glance.

"No trouble at all." The Reverend Grimshaw rubbed his hands together, as eager to get them on Ellen's money as I suppose Carus

Wilson had been to get the fees that my poor father had paid for his daughters' schooling.

When he led us into the first classroom, a teacher was giving an arithmetic lesson to some twenty little girls. Our arrival halted the lesson; the girls stood. The sight of their wan faces and plain frocks reinforced my impression that I had returned to Cowan Bridge. Hollow coughs arose from their ranks, and a shudder passed through me: How well I remembered that sound of tubercular consumption wracking children's lungs!

The Reverend Grimshaw bade the lesson resume. As he explained the school's curriculum to Ellen, I noticed a girl who sat upon a high stool in a corner. She was slender, and her hair dark brown. A sign pinned to her frock bore the word SLATTERN. My chest constricted painfully, for the girl was the very image of my eldest sister. Maria had been a brilliant student, but untidy in her habits, and our teachers had punished her for them in the same manner as this girl. I was glad that Mr. Grimshaw led us out of the classroom before my emotions overcame me.

"We enforce strict discipline here," he said. "It teaches the girls respect for authority."

I choked back a bitter retort and endured the inspection of another class, where older pupils, some very pretty, labored on fine sewing. But the dormitory nearly shattered my self-control. Here stood rows of narrow beds covered by thin mattresses and ragged counterpanes. The bleak room, with its high ceiling, bare rafters, and but a single fireplace, would be terribly cold in winter, like the dormitory at Cowan Bridge. Every bed seemed occupied by the ghosts of Maria and Elizabeth, growing sicker until they were sent home to die.

"As you can see, we treat our pupils according to their social station," the Reverend Grimshaw said to Ellen.

He radiated the complacency of one who has never known privation and cares not about other people's suffering. Such a man had been Carus Wilson. Old grief and fresh outrage swelled in me, but I maintained my silence while the Reverend Grimshaw led us outside to a large garden behind the school. It was bordered on two sides by low stone buildings; on the far end, birches obscured the old windmill.

"Those buildings are quarters for myself and my family and the teachers," said Mr. Grimshaw. Pointing to an open expanse of ground, he said, "That is the pupils' recreation area. And beyond is the vegetable garden." There, girls weeded rows of plants. "Work builds character."

I recalled similar pronouncements made by Carus Wilson. I also recalled listening to him sermonize upon the deaths of children who had taken ill at his school: *I bless God that he has taken from us the children of whose salvation we have the best hope.* He was now beyond my reach, and I could scarcely restrain myself from berating the Reverend Grimshaw in his stead.

We went to the parlor and drank tea. As Ellen and the Reverend Grimshaw made polite chat, I stared down at my cup in morose silence. How clever and brave I had thought myself when I devised the plan to investigate the school and solve the mystery of Isabel White's murder! And what had I learned? Nothing— except that I was neither clever nor brave. Unable to discern whether the school was a den of sin or a noble institution, I was indeed the fool that Gilbert White thought me. Yet I couldn't bear the prospect of defeat.

Turning to Mr. Grimshaw, I blurted, "Recently I happened to meet a former pupil of this school. Her name was Isabel White. Do you remember her?"

He stared at me as if the teapot had spoken. Ellen's face proclaimed her alarm that I would introduce the matter of Isabel in such unsubtle fashion.

"Isabel White?" Mr. Grimshaw frowned; the perspiration beaded on his forehead. "I don't believe the name is familiar. You must be mistaken. There's been no Isabel White in our school." He pulled from his pocket a gold watch and said, "My heavens, but time passes quickly. If you'll excuse me, Miss Wheelwright and Miss, er—?" Amidst a flurry of courtesies, he ushered Ellen and me out the door.

We walked through the woods towards our waiting carriage, and Ellen burst into excited giggles. "Did you see how eager he was to get rid of us after you mentioned Isabel? He remembers her, I have no doubt of it."

"His behavior isn't proof that he was involved in her murder or knows anything about it," I said. "And fool that I am, I provoked him to expel us before we could learn more.".

"My dear Charlotte, your plan worked brilliantly!" Ellen took my arm and gave it a comforting pat. "It gained us an inspection of the school."

"For all the good it did us. I saw nothing about the place or the people that would seem out of the ordinary in a thousand schools in the kingdom."

"I think the Reverend Grimshaw is most sinister and unattractive," Ellen said with a little shiver. "I wouldn't put any relation of mine in his charge."

"I agree, but alas, our impressions aren't evidence to connect him with the crime. Besides, I cannot imagine Mr. Grimshaw as the master who seduced and enslaved Isabel." I favored Gilbert White for that role. "Perhaps Isabel experienced nothing more than the usual privations of boarding school, and it has nothing to do with what happened to her after she left." I sighed. "I don't know what else to do to expose her killer."

"Oh, you'll think of something," Ellen said.

As we rounded a curve in the path, our carriage came into view. A gig, pulled by a pair of horses, drew up on the road. Two men rode in the open seat. They climbed out and strode towards us. The sight of them—one dark, the other ginger-haired—froze my blood and halted me in my steps. Quickly I dragged Ellen off the path and into the shelter of the woods.

"My dear, whatever are you doing?" she said.

I hushed her. The men passed nearly close enough for me to touch them, but they didn't notice us. They continued up to the school and disappeared from sight.

"Who were they?" Ellen said. "Why did we hide?"

"They are the very same men who attacked Anne and me on the train."

14

>≺

I WISH I COULD SAY I CONFRONTED MY ATTACKERS AND DELIVERED THEM into the hands of the law. I wish I could say I forced them to reveal their connection with the events surrounding the murder of Isabel White and tell me who killed her. I wish I could say that I left Skipton possessed of the knowledge necessary to thwart the schemes of Isabel's master.

But alas! My actions were far less commendable. As we hid in the woods that day, Ellen urged that we leave at once, for those men were too dangerous to confront. I let her rush me into our carriage even as I deplored my cowardice. When I proposed going to the police, she reminded me that I could not just walk into a town where we are strangers, accuse people of wrongdoing, and expect to be believed. I had to credit her objections, and my nerves were in such a grievous state that she had no difficulty persuading me to board a train that very day. We parted at Keighley, where she caught a train to Birstall, and I proceeded, with utmost caution, to Haworth.

When I arrived shortly after nine o'clock that evening, a misty rain veiled the moors. I was exhausted from traveling, tense from looking over my shoulder to see if anyone pursued me, and downhearted because I felt little the wiser than when I'd left. I found Papa, Emily, and Anne kneeling in the study, their heads bowed as they said their evening prayers.

"Ah, Charlotte," said Papa. "How happy I am that you've come home."

Anne looked at Emily. Emily met my gaze with cold indifference: My absence had not softened her ill feelings towards me. I knelt, and we all prayed. Afterward, Papa went to lock the doors. I followed Emily and Anne to the parlor.

"Don't you want to hear about my journey?" I asked.

Emily gave a disdainful sniff. Anne murmured, "Perhaps later."

Less angry than hurt by their response, I said, "How is Branwell?"

"See for yourself," Emily said. "He's upstairs."

I mounted the stairs, pained by the memory of happier homecomings. I opened the door of Branwell's room, and the sour stench of illness nauseated me. My brother lay in bed, the covers twisted around his emaciated body, his bloodshot eyes half closed and his lips parted. His chest slowly rose and fell with each faint breath. He had procured laudanum and dosed himself into stupefaction. I left the room, shut the door, sat on the stairs, and wept.

>−<

I wish I could write that Branwell improved in the days that followed, but this wish, too, is in vain. The soporific effects of the laudanum wore off the next morning, and what tremors, violent sickness, and agony assailed him! He pleaded for money to buy more, and when we refused him, he cursed us. Emily remained hostile towards me, and Anne silently grieved at our estrangement. While we were at church the following Sunday, Branwell sneaked out of the house. Two days later, he still was gone. Our fears for him drove all thought of the murder, my adventures, and even Gilbert White from my mind.

On the second day, I walked the moors, thinking perhaps he might have wandered there and lost his way. The afternoon was cool and blustery. As I trudged up the hills, Emily's brown bulldog, Keeper, bounded alongside me, and the landscape began to restore my spirits. Those who do not know the moors think them dreary, but I find in them great beauty and comfort. The sky, animated by changeable weather, seems a living companion in my solitude. I watched billowy clouds race across a heavenly blue firmament, their shadows drifting on the sunlit land. The heather had begun blooming, and its purple blossoms misted the grey-brown hills. Swallows flitted between gnarled thorn trees; sheep grazed. Ivy and ferns grew on drystone walls; violets and primroses clustered in hedge bottoms. The wind breathed sweet flower scents, and Keeper chased butterflies.

We were heading for the waterfall that was a favorite place of my brother and sisters and myself, a place where Branwell might have sought refuge, when I heard a voice call my name. I saw a tall man striding towards me. He was dressed in black, with a white clerical collar; the wind whipped his tousled black hair. Terror struck ice into my bones. It was Gilbert White, the man who had deceived me, the man responsible for the attacks on myself, the murder of Isabel White, and a scheme that would bring disaster upon the kingdom. And I was alone on the moors with him.

"Miss Brontë," he called, raising a hand in greeting.

I whirled and began running for my life. "Keeper! Come!" I shouted.

We raced up and down slopes. From behind me I heard the rustling of grass crushed under rapid footsteps. I looked over my shoulder and saw Gilbert White cresting the hill; his long legs carried him faster than I could run. As I scrambled over a wall, crows wheeled overhead, their caws mocking me. My heart hammered; breathless fatigue rendered my limbs awkward. I reached the birches and alders that bordered Sladen Beck. I plunged between the trees, stumbled down the bank, and crouched to hide. Below me, the stream's clear, rushing water gurgled round the rocks where my brother and sisters and I had once played. The waterfall splashed down a staircase of boulders. But here I found no sanctuary, for Gilbert White burst through the trees and alighted on the bank above me.

"Miss Brontë, why did you run from me?" Hardly even winded, he spoke in surprise and bafflement.

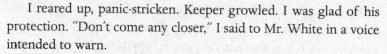

I reared up, panic-stricken. Keeper growled. I was glad of his protection. "Don't come any closer," I said to Mr. White in a voice intended to warn.

He hesitated, glanced at Keeper, and said, "I must have startled you by coming suddenly upon you like that. Please forgive me."

The very presence of him defiled this private place, and anger gave me courage. "What are you doing here?" I demanded.

"I wondered if anything had happened to you," Mr. White said. "Having heard not a word from you, I came to visit, and I saw you walking up the hill, and I followed." Now he seemed to realize that I felt something other than mere surprise at his unexpected visit. "I thought you would be glad to see me. Why do you look at me with such animosity?"

His eyes were as clear and brilliant as I remembered; his sharp features as compelling; the vigor of his body as masculine. I was ashamed that I had ever admired him or desired his regard. I was mortified to realize that I still did.

"You lied to me." My voice quavered with hatred as well as fear. I recalled my dreams about him, and I experienced afresh the painful disillusionment I had suffered at his deceit. With great satisfaction did I see his dismay.

"What are you talking about?" he asked.

"Your name is not Gilbert White," I said. "You're not Isabel White's brother. I was taken in by you at first, but I know better now. I also know you've been spying on me."

"Spying on you? Why, Miss Brontë, I've done no such thing." He took a step towards me, but when Keeper snarled, he moved back up the bank. "How can you think I would deceive you?" He feigned incredulity. "Where did you get these ideas?"

"I received a package that Isabel sent me before she died, and I went to Bradford to give it to her mother," I said. "She told me that Isabel was an only child."

He frowned, suddenly disturbed. "A package from Isabel? Did you see what was in it?"

That he should care foremost about the package! "You killed Isabel," I said. "It was you I saw struggling with her in that alley.

Your accomplices tried to kidnap me. You rescued me only to cultivate my gratitude, such that I might then do whatever you asked." I saw him stiffen and draw back, his face registering chagrin that he could no longer play me for a fool. "Who are you?" I demanded. "What do you want with me?"

Clouds gathered in the sky, and cold shadow doused the water's sparkling light. My adversary clenched his fists, and terror gripped my heart, for I expected him to strike me dead. But instead, he half turned away from me, gazing at the water. I might then have fled, yet I did not. I felt myself part of a story whose ending I must know, even at the price of my life.

The rushing water sounded loud in the silence between us. The wind quickened across the moors; I smelled rain. Starlings twittered, agitated by the impending storm. Keeper whined. At last my companion turned to me, and I beheld a stranger. Gone was the polite, humble cleric Gilbert White. This man's face was stern and formidable, his dark depths no longer masked by artifice. For the first time, I was seeing him as he really was.

"You have accused me of many evils, Miss Brontë, but I'm guilty of only one." His voice had altered to match his true self; the false Northern accent dropped away. "I did not murder Isabel White. The only harm I've done you is to win your friendship by false pretenses. I hope that when I explain why, you'll excuse my deception."

I knew not what he could say to earn my forgiveness; but I waited, for his gaze compelled me to hear him.

"My real name is John Slade," he said. "I'm a secret agent of Her Majesty's Foreign Office."

I stared, my mouth agape. I had heard of the Foreign Office, which managed the nation's affairs abroad; I had heard tales of the men who spied behind enemy lines, consorted with savages, and lived by their wits. A thrill of excitement coursed through me, but my distrust of him prevailed.

"Why should I believe you," I said, "after you've lied to me already? Why should I believe you're not still lying?"

John Slade answered my scorn with cool composure: "You are

a woman of rational mind. Listen to what I have to say, then decide whether to believe me."

I shook my head in defiance; but a hint of a smile touched his mouth. "You can go if you wish," he said. "But you are also a woman of insatiable curiosity. Shall I begin, then?"

Silence was my grudging assent. Too well did he know me!

"Since 1842 I've worked in France and Italy," Mr. Slade said. "Those countries are rife with secret societies made up of radicals whose purpose is to dethrone kings, foment wars, and spread revolution across Europe. My job was to infiltrate the societies. This I did by pretending to be a radical myself. I gained the trust of the leaders and reported their plans to my superiors. It was in Paris last year that I met Isabel White. She was a governess for an English diplomat's family. She was also a courier who conveyed money and messages between the French societies and their counterparts in Britain."

Amazement filled me. Though I'd known that Isabel had secrets, never had I imagined such a life for her. But I cautioned myself against taking Mr. Slade at his word.

"I befriended Miss White because I wanted to know who was employing her and financing the radicals," Slade went on. "She confided to me that she felt like a traitor for helping their cause, and she wanted to stop. I decided I could trust her to help me instead. That was in the beginning of this year, when it looked as though revolution would come to England. I told Miss White my true identity and hired her to work as my informant. When she had messages to deliver, she would copy them into the margins of old books. We met in crowded public places, where she would slip the books to me."

I thought of the book of sermons, which lay in the upstairs study at the parsonage. How would Mr. Slade know that Isabel wrote messages in books unless he was indeed an agent of the Crown and had done what he said? But Isabel's writing made no mention of secret societies, and if she had intended that book for Slade, why had she sent it to me? Still, his mention of messages in books weakened my suspicions.

He paused, scrutinizing me in an apparent effort to know my thoughts; then he proceeded: "Miss White gave me names of French radicals and Chartist agitators, as well as their plans for acts of violence, but she refused to tell me who was employing her to work for them. From hints she dropped, I deduced that she feared him too much to expose him."

A chill ran through me. This unidentified employer could be the man Isabel had called Master in her confession.

"In February of this year," said Mr. Slade, "Miss White said she had an especially important message for me. We agreed to meet at Notre Dame Cathedral, where she would give me a book containing the message. I arrived at the appointed time, but she never came. She had vanished from Paris. I feared that her employer had discovered she was giving away his secrets."

Mr. Slade regarded me closely as he continued. "I traced her to England, and I learned that she was a governess in the house of Joseph Lock, a Birmingham gunmaker. I kept secret watch upon Lock. At first I thought him to be directing subversive activities in England and abroad. My suspicions grew when I discovered that he was smuggling guns out of England through an intermediary, a China trader named Isaiah Fearon. But Lock shot himself dead the day before Isabel's murder. I later found Isaiah Fearon strangled in his warehouse. I now believe that all three were players in a conspiracy devised by a leader whose identity remains unknown. I believe Lock killed himself because he wanted to get out, and he saw suicide as the only way. This leader had Isabel White and Isaiah Fearon killed because he suspected them of disloyalty. It's my wish to capture him, because I'm certain he'll commit other, far worse, crimes unless I do. And it's in your interest to help me, Miss Brontë."

I could only gaze at him in alarm at learning of the string of violent deaths.

"Isabel White knew this leader, and she could have exposed him." Mr. Slade moved closer to me, until Keeper's growl halted his steps. "So, perhaps, could Fearon. They were weaknesses in the barrier he created to protect himself. He has eliminated those weaknesses—but one remains."

Distant thunder rumbled; the wind keened as the sky turned greenish grey. I was stricken by Mr. Slade's suggestion that I could be the next to die. My sense of adventure had blinded me to the danger I had stumbled into.

"I must find the leader of the conspiracy," he said, his voice edged with determination. "You can draw him into the open. What say you, Miss Brontë? Will you help me trap him?"

He had observed that the villain was after me, and he wanted to use me as bait to catch his quarry. He clearly expected me to agree; but I said, "When you rescued me in Leeds, you were not on your way to visit your mother. Why were you on that train?"

"I was going to Bradford. I wanted to learn what Mrs. White knew about her daughter's associates. But I was also following you, because I suspected that Isabel's enemy would make some move against you, and I wanted to protect you."

This was a reasonable explanation; yet Mr. Slade's glibness perturbed me. I did not like that he thought me so gullible as to trust him again. "Did you also stay by me in Leeds and on the train home because you wanted to protect me?" I said, sounding more hopeful and less challenging than I intended.

"Yes," Mr. Slade said, "but I also enjoyed your company. I beg you to forgive me, and I hope we can be friends again."

When Mr. Slade extended his hand to me, when he flashed his rare, dazzling smile, fury consumed my heart. He might have won me by logic, but not by calculated charm. Wounded pride swayed my judgment.

"Should I believe you came by all this information as innocently as you say you did?" I flared, backing away from Mr. Slade.

Withdrawing his hand, Mr. Slade frowned at my belligerence. "It's the truth."

"So you say!" I laughed in derision as the wind dashed raindrops at us. "But *I* think you know those things about Isabel because *you* were her master. You discovered she was betraying you, and you killed her. Now you pose as a spy so I will reveal the content of Isabel's package. Well, I'll have nothing to do with you!"

I turned and clambered up the bank; Keeper followed me. Mr. Slade hurried after us, saying, "Wait, Miss Brontë."

"Leave me alone!" I screamed in panic.

I thrashed through the trees, tripping on my skirts. If I didn't escape, he would kill me, hide my body on the moors, and no one would ever know what had become of me.

"Please forgive me if it seems I've trifled with you, but my feelings of friendship towards you are genuine," he called after me urgently. "I am an agent of the Crown. If you want proof of that— or of my good character—we've a mutual connection who can provide it. Do you know Dr. Nicholas Dury? He's a friend of your father's. He'll vouch for me. Just ask him."

I had heard Papa speak of Dury; but Mr. Slade's mention of him inspired terror rather than trust in me. If Mr. Slade had discovered Dury, his spying upon my family was extensive indeed. That he thought I would accept his reference without bothering to verify it enraged me all the more.

"I'll hear no more lies!" I shouted.

Now we were racing across open land, beneath turbulent dark clouds. The howling wind swept the grasses into waves like the sea, and rain lashed me in torrents. Mr. Slade caught my cloak, and I cried out. A brilliant vein of lightning split the heavens; thunder quaked the earth.

"Keeper!" I called. "Save me!"

I heard the bulldog barking. Mr. Slade turned me towards him and grasped my shoulders. "I'm not the one you should fear." His face, streaming with rain and afire with intent, was close to mine. "I can help you if you'll help me."

I screamed, but the storm drowned my voice. I writhed and flailed. His hands restrained mine and I clawed his wrists. Drenched from the rain, scourged by the wind, we struggled together. Mr. Slade shouted words that I ignored. I tore my hand loose and struck his face. Blood spurted from his lip, and horrifying impulses leapt in me. I wanted to press my mouth to Mr. Slade's, to taste his blood. I wanted to surrender to him so that I might feel pleasure beyond my experience. Though fury blazed in his eyes and his grip on my arms was cruel, at that moment I feared myself more than I did Mr. Slade. With all my strength I twisted free of him. I stumbled backward, so shaken I could barely stand. Mr. Slade advanced on me as lightning seared the sky and thunder boomed. He was breathing hard, his white collar stained with blood, his expression ominous.

"Keeper!" I screamed. "Attack!"

Barking and growling, the dog launched himself at Mr. Slade's throat. Mr. Slade flung up his arms to ward off the assault. Keeper's paws struck against Mr. Slade's chest, and he fell backward. Savage delight filled me. I turned and ran for home.

15

$\rightarrow\!\!\leftarrow$

KEEPER AND I ARRIVED HOME DRENCHED AND SHIVERING. MY family was sitting at tea, and my appearance provoked alarmed questions about what had happened. I described meeting John Slade, his bizarre tale of espionage, and how Keeper had defended me— though I did not confess those feelings I preferred to keep secret.

Emily hurried to embrace her dog. "Did that man hurt you?" she cried, clearly more concerned about him than me.

"Where is John Slade now?" Anne asked.

I said I didn't know.

"Well, let us hope he is gone, and there will be no more trouble," Papa said.

That seemed a rather insufficient response to what had just occurred, but there was nothing else to be done at the moment. All through the evening, I waited in dread. For what, I did not know.

That night, while we were asleep, Branwell came home. I never learned where he had been. But my brother unwittingly influenced the course of events.

$\rightarrow\!\!\leftarrow$

A thunderous commotion awakened me. I heard, from downstairs, someone screaming, "Help! Help!"

"Branwell?" I cried, glad that he had returned home at last.

I hurried from my room. Emily, Anne, and Papa joined me on the landing. My sisters looked frightened. Papa clutched his pistol. Peering down the stairs, we all exclaimed in horror. Branwell thrashed on the hall floor, wrapped in flames.

"I'm burning in the fires of hell!" he shrieked.

We rushed down the stairs. Emily ran to the kitchen, fetched a bucket of water, and hurled it at Branwell. The splash doused the flames. He sat up, sputtering and dripping, clad in the charred remains of his clothes, his thin body shivering.

Papa crouched beside him, asking querulously, "Where have you been? What have you done to yourself?"

"He's been drinking. I can smell it on him." Emily gazed at Branwell in disgust. "He obviously sneaked into the house, went to sleep, and left a candle lit and set himself on fire again. Then he panicked and tumbled downstairs."

Some two years ago, Branwell had nearly burned to death in his bed. I said, "Let's take him upstairs. He doesn't seem to have broken anything. The burns on his arms and legs don't look serious, but still, the doctor ought to examine him."

When Papa and I moved to raise Branwell to his feet, he batted our hands away. "No!" he cried, his eyes wild. "This was no accident. There was an intruder in the study. He attacked me!"

"What did this intruder look like?" I asked, skeptical.

"He was tall and dressed in dark clothing," Branwell said. "That's all I could see."

"Drunken delusions," was Emily's scornful pronouncement.

"There really was an intruder," Branwell insisted. "He almost killed me!"

Just then there came a loud crash from the rear of the house. Clattering noises and rapid footsteps were followed by the sound of the back door opening. Papa, my sisters, and I hurried through the kitchen and down the passage to the door, which stood open. We saw, running up the hill behind the parsonage, the dark figure of a man.

"Stop!" Papa shouted.

Aiming his pistol out the door, he fired. The shot boomed. The intruder raced onward and vanished over the hill. We exchanged glances of wordless bewilderment, while in the hall, Branwell burst into hysterical laughter.

"Either you believe me now," he called, "or Father is shooting at phantoms of my imagination!"

We helped Branwell upstairs. Papa dressed him in a nightshirt and put him to bed, then fetched the doctor and the constable. The doctor salved and bandaged Branwell's burns. The constable deduced that the intruder had come in through the front door, which Branwell must have forgotten to lock, and left no trace of his presence other than a broken plate in the kitchen. When at last the men had departed, Papa, Emily, Anne, and I gathered in the parlor.

"Do you think this was related to the series of attacks on you, Charlotte?" asked Papa.

Emily spoke in a barely audible voice: "We've never had a burglar before." Huddled in the corner of the sofa, she was so pale that her lips had gone white.

"This can't have been an ordinary burglar," Anne said. "Nothing was taken."

A thought struck me. I ran upstairs to the study and looked on the desk. I searched through the books and papers atop it, then went back to the parlor. "Isabel White's book is gone. The intruder must have stolen it."

My family absorbed the news with the air of people already numbed by too many shocks. The intrusion was clearly another episode arising from Isabel's murder, exactly the sort of event I had been anticipating since John Slade accosted me on the moor.

"They were in this house," Emily said. "They handled our things." Panic tinged her voice. "Maybe they even came into our rooms while we were sleeping."

That evildoers had invaded our home horrified me no less than Emily. Papa stood at the table, reloading his pistol; his hands shook. Anne sat on the sofa and put her arm around Emily.

"Branwell could have been killed," Anne said, "perhaps the rest of us, too." She asked me, "Do you think it was John Slade? He knew Isabel sent you the package, because you told him. He want-ed it badly enough to come to Haworth. When he didn't get it, he could have decided to steal it tonight."

I nodded, as that explanation had occurred to me. "Mr. Slade does fit Branwell's vague description of the intruder. But he thinks I gave the package to Mrs. White. Therefore, he wouldn't have come here to get it." In spite of my rage at his deception, I found that I wanted to believe Mr. Slade innocent. How my feelings for him managed to persist against my will! "He doesn't know I have a transcript of Isabel's story." It was locked safe in my drawer. For once in my life I was thankful for my poor sight, which had required Ellen to read aloud the words Isabel had written and me to copy them out in case I should want to study them at a later date.

"What's going to happen next?" Emily demanded of me.

"I fear that whoever stole the book won't stop at that. They must know I've read what Isabel wrote. They could very well sup-pose she also entrusted other information to me." Distraught, I twisted my hands and paced the floor. "And if they think it's infor-mation that endangers them or their plans, they will come back for me."

Emily looked terror-stricken, and Anne was anxious. Papa said, "What is to be done, Charlotte?"

"Shall we ask the police for help?" said Anne.

"They can't capture our attackers or thwart the schemes of Isabel's master based on the little information we have," I said. "Nor can they stand guard over us day and night."

"Then what do you propose we do?" Emily cried.

I liked that she and Anne appeared ready to forget our quarrel and unite with me against our enemies. But I liked less the plan which I had in mind, although it seemed our only hope.

"We must turn to John Slade," I said.

Anne regarded me with disbelief. "After he misrepresented him-self and terrified you—and may have murdered Isabel, among oth-ers? My dear Charlotte!"

"If he is an agent of the Crown as he claims, then he would have the wherewithal to help us, as well as to protect us." And despite my antagonism toward Mr. Slade, my heartbeat quickened at the thought of seeing him again.

"Can he truly be an agent?" Papa said doubtfully. "How can we know he's not an imposter?"

"He might have lied to you again," Anne said.

Though I shared these same reservations, the night's events forced me to appeal to this man I reviled for dashing my hopes as well as using me. "We needn't take his word for what he is," I said, and I told them how Mr. Slade had claimed that Dr. Dury could vouch for him.

Papa pondered the surprise of his and Mr. Slade's mutual connection with Dr. Dury, his old schoolmate, a don at St. John's College in Cambridge, where they had studied together. "I've not seen Nicholas in many years, although we've corresponded. He has an unimpeachable reputation. Charlotte, we must consult him about Mr. Slade at once."

16

$>\!\!-\!\!<$

PAPA AND I JOURNEYED THE NEXT DAY TO CAMBRIDGE, SITE OF THE famed university. Across this ancient town spread the various colleges, reminiscent of medieval castles, with towers, spires, and fortified gates. Venerable walls, adorned by sculpture and ivy, sheltered gardens and cloisters. Water flowed from elegant fountains; stained glass gleamed like gems; and stone bridges arched over the swans and punts drifting upon the River Cam. The afternoon of our arrival was rainy, the town devoid of the black-gowned fellows and students who flock the streets during the academic terms. Papa led me to St. John's College, which occupies four magnificent red brick quadrangles with profuse battlements, dormers, and chimneys. We were fortunate to find Papa's friend Dr. Dury in, for we had arrived without invitation or notice. He received us in his rooms at the top of a narrow staircase.

"My dear Patrick," he exclaimed in warm greeting. "After all this time! And this must be your daughter Charlotte."

He was Papa's age, rotund of figure and hardly taller than I. Thin grey hair fringed his scalp. His eyes were bright blue and keen-sighted in a cheerful, rosy face.

"Can it be forty years since we last met?" Papa said.

"Indeed," Dr. Dury said, "but a mutual connection, John

Slade, has alerted me to expect you and Miss Brontë. Please join me for tea. We have important business to discuss."

His parlor was paneled in mellow wood. Books filled the shelves, covered the desk, and lay piled on the mantel and floor. We sat in armchairs before a crackling fire. A servant brought the tea, and Dr. Dury toasted crumpets.

"Being here brings back so many memories," Papa said, "that I can almost imagine myself a raw youth again."

Dr. Dury chuckled. "I'll never forget my first sight of you, arriving from Ireland with your great height, flaming red hair, and strong brogue. You certainly stood out among the pupils."

"Ah, to be sizars together again," Papa said.

He and Dr. Dury had both belonged to this group of impoverished young intellectuals who worked as tutors in exchange for their education and board. "At least we need no longer sleep on the floor of a crowded attic," Dr. Dury said.

"Nor study with our feet wrapped in straw to keep them warm," Papa agreed, sipping tea.

"Despite the privations, you graduated in the first class," Dr. Dury said. "But it's the present, not the past, that concerns us now." He turned to me. "What has happened that you need the services of my friend John Slade?"

I briefly described my recent experiences and watched his kind face grow grave. "We must know whether Mr. Slade is what he claims to be. Are you well enough acquainted with him to assure us?"

"Indeed," said Dr. Dury. "I first met Slade when he came to study here in 1831. He was the most outstanding pupil I've ever had. His father was an army colonel, and his family traveled widely. Slade had a gift for language and was proficient in French, Italian, German, and Russian. He possessed great intellect and a passion for learning that went beyond the theology he studied. He aspired towards a career in the Church, but he took extra classes on history, natural science, economics, and politics. We had furious debates about those subjects during his tutorials. Slade also excelled in fencing and shooting. He had such a zest for life."

These were good things to hear of Mr. Slade; yet doubt remained. How had this paragon turned from the Church to a life of underhanded pursuits?

"But he had a wild side." Dr. Drury shook his head regretfully. "He liked women, drink, and gaming. When he wounded a townsman in a duel, he was almost sent down. His father's influence saved his college career. He was ordained in 1835 and obtained a curacy in Wiltshire, but lasted only two years. Life as a country cleric was too quiet for him."

I was interested to learn that Mr. Slade had once been a clergyman, yet not surprised, for he had convincingly played his rôle as the Reverend Gilbert White. I had sensed the wildness in Mr. Slade, but saw no remnant of the boisterous young reveler. What had changed him?

"Slade then joined the army of the East India Company," Dr. Dury said. "That, as you may know, is the great mercantile concern that trades in the Eastern Hemisphere. It earns a fortune from cotton, spices, indigo, silks, and tea. It governs India in the name of the Crown, and its army protects the colonial territories and citizens of the British Empire. Slade served the company in Kabul."

Dr. Dury explained that this savage kingdom of mountains, plains, deserts, steppes, and tribal chiefs had become during those years a battleground in the rivalry between Britain and Russia, who fought for control of Turkestan. When Russia had earlier supported Persia's siege of the Kingdom of Kabul, the Crown feared that the region would fall completely under Russian influence, threatening Britain's Indian empire. A British invasion of Kabul was therefore mounted.

"The East fascinated Slade. His letters were filled with his discoveries about the culture, and his flair for language was put to good use. He dressed as a native holy man and wandered enemy territory, gathering news and surveying the land. He brought back valuable information on enemy activities. But the trouble there undid his military career."

The East India Company's army had entered Kabul in 1839 and installed upon the throne a king sympathetic to the British, Dr. Dury related. Insurrections broke out among the natives, and the

British occupation failed. "John Slade was discharged and returned to England. His talents and his exploits in the East recommended him to men in high places. He became an agent of Her Majesty's Secret Service."

That mysterious organization is the subject of much rumor and speculation; few facts about it are known. Frowned upon by polite society, it reeks of the treacherous spy methods practiced by Continental police, so repugnant to the honest British. Yet it has always borne a whiff of glamour that appeals to me.

"Slade infiltrated radical societies in Europe, reporting their activities to his superiors in the Foreign Office," Dr. Dury said, then paused and pondered. "Something happened to him in France. His letters stopped for a year, and we lost contact. When we renewed our friendship in 1845, I found him drastically altered. He had become serious, solitary, and focused on his work to the exclusion of all else. He never told me what troubled him, and his manner discouraged my asking. But I can assure you that Slade remains in the employ of the Secret Service to this day. Reliable sources tell me that he is one of its best agents and defenders of the Crown. I believe his character to be strong, steady, and virtuous."

"That is high praise indeed, and proof enough for me that Mr. Slade is what he has represented himself to be," said Papa. "What say you, Charlotte?"

Our host's commendation had removed much, but not all, the doubt in my mind. "Can we really trust Mr. Slade?" I asked Dr. Dury. "Should we ask for his help?"

Dr. Dury contemplated the fire; its intermittent glow played upon his pensive countenance. "I know persons who have placed their trust in Slade and lived to thank him." Dr. Dury lifted his keen blue gaze to me. "But keep in mind that a spy lives by treachery."

This advice did not quench my misgivings, yet swayed me in favor of Mr. Slade. Furthermore, I knew not what else to do to protect my family and prevent worse disaster. "Then we shall accept Mr. Slade's help," I decided.

Even as I spoke, the earth seemed to fragment under me. What business had I to involve myself with a man who belonged to such a different world? I recalled that day on the moor with him, and I felt again the fierce, savage excitement. What forces would my decision unleash?

Papa nodded. "It is for the best, Charlotte."

"Very well," Dr. Dury said, though not without reluctance. "I shall contact Slade, and you will hear from him soon."

17

> ✷⟨

John Slade returned to Haworth on 30 July.

My family rose early that Sunday for church. As Emily, Anne, and I took our seats in our pew, villagers filed into the galleries, and the sonorous music of the organ echoed. Papa preached while the sexton walked the aisles and awakened slumberers with a tap of his long staff. A sudden stir arose in the congregation; I turned and saw the man who had entered the church.

Although a letter from him had prepared me for his arrival, it did not lessen my shock at seeing Mr. Slade again. My heart began to pound. Mr. Slade, wearing black clerical garb, paused and looked around while curious villagers scrutinized him. His gaze lit on me, and I felt that all the world had acquired a new life. The sunlit arched windows and the flowers on the altar seemed brighter; Papa's voice reading the Gospels sounded more melodious. I breathed intoxication from the very air. Mr. Slade bowed slightly, then seated himself in an empty pew. I averted my face, overwhelmed by shame that I would experience profane sensations in church. In the wake of my shame galloped fear. What had I done by agreeing that Mr. Slade should come?

When the service ended, my sisters and I rose. Mr. Slade walked up the aisle to meet Papa. "Greetings, Uncle Patrick," said Mr. Slade. "'Tis I, John Brunty, your nephew from Ireland."

I recognized the story that his letter had said would disguise his true identity and explain his presence among us. He spoke in an Irish brogue so perfect that I would easily have believed his ruse, had I not known better.

"Welcome," Papa said, shaking Mr. Slade's hand. He studied his "nephew" and seemed to approve of what he saw. As Emily, Anne, and I approached, he called, "Girls, meet your cousin."

Papa introduced me first, and so flustered was I that I looked up at Mr. Slade barely long enough to see the conspiratorial gleam in his eyes. He said, "Hello, Cousin Charlotte." I felt my hand gripped by his, and a fresh onslaught of emotion. Now that my rage at his deceit had passed, my other feelings towards him had become unbridled. The strange intimacy fostered by our encounter on the moors, and my newfound knowledge of him, had increased my desire for his regard. And without my anger to shield me from him, I was defenseless.

Next Papa presented Emily, who stared at the floor and bobbed a silent curtsy at Mr. Slade. Anne met him as calmly and pleasantly as if he were really our cousin. "Please come with us to the house," she invited.

Exiting the church, we greeted villagers and walked up the hill. The church bells sang across the village, the sun turned the moors golden, and all was peaceful except my heart.

The Reverend Arthur Nicholls hovered near us, eyeing Mr. Slade with alarm and me with concern. "Is there adequate room at the parsonage for your nephew?" he asked Papa. "Maybe he would be more comfortable at the Black Bull Inn."

I supposed Mr. Nicholls felt possessive towards my family and jealous of the newcomer. "We'll manage," I said tartly, though I quaked at the idea of having Mr. Slade under my roof.

It was strange to see him drinking tea in the parsonage. He sat in a chair beside Papa's, opposite the sofa occupied by Anne and me. Emily and Keeper sat on the floor. Keeper eyed Mr. Slade with distrust.

Mr. Slade got right to business: "We must lose no time. The sooner we apprehend the villain, the sooner you will all be safe. Please tell me what you've learned about Isabel White."

I described my visits to Isabel's mother and the Charity School. I nearly quailed under his intent gaze. Discovering the truth about Mr. Slade had rendered him even more handsome, and although he was now friend instead of foe, I knew that my feelings must remain unrequited, for what could a man of his accomplishments want with a dreary spinster? As I told Mr. Slade about Isabel's diary, I realized that after he knew everything I did, I would be of no more value to him.

"May I see your transcript of the diary?" Mr. Slade asked, upon learning that the diary itself had been stolen.

"First tell me what you know of this business that we do not," I said, deliberately withholding information.

He obliged, and his account furnished the facts that I have previously related about his actions while we were apart. After he finished I said, "Now what is your plan?"

Slade raised an eyebrow at my reluctance to cooperate, but he said, "Agents from the Foreign Office will spy on the Charity School and attempt to identify the men from the train. They'll also keep watch on the household of Joseph Lock, the gun maker, and look for clues regarding the evil scheme that Isabel mentioned in her diary and the identity of her master." He turned to Papa. "In the meantime, I shall stay here and guard your family. I believe the villain will eventually try to attack your daughter again. When he comes, I shall capture him."

Papa nodded, but I did not like Mr. Slade's idea; nor did Anne, as I could tell by her perturbed expression. He said, "Is something wrong? Do you object to my plan?"

"It gives me nothing to do except wait, like cheese in a mousetrap," I said. "I can't bear to sit idle until the trap springs." Nor did I like to think I was useless to him except as bait.

"There must be something we can do," Anne added.

Mr. Slade frowned. "These matters are best left to professionals."

I observed that he disliked opposition; yet pride forbade me to let him govern my behavior as well as torment my heart. "If you are going to live in our home, you must respect our right to help ourselves."

"I respect every right of yours." Mr. Slade spoke cautiously, aware that we were on new, untested footing. "But I don't see what you could do for this investigation, except what I've proposed."

I have always hated to be underestimated, especially by those for whom I care more than I should. "How will your agents get inside the school or Mr. Lock's house to gather clues? Someone with good reason to be there would be more likely to discover something worthwhile."

"Surely you don't mean yourself?"

Mr. Slade's incredulity encouraged my contrariness. "I do. Mightn't the Lock family need a new governess now that Isabel White is gone? And the Charity School needs a teacher." The housekeeper had indicated as much when she'd answered the door. "I am qualified to fill either post."

"That is out of the question," Mr. Slade said, adamant. "Even if you were to be hired, I could not protect you. And if the villain should discover you snooping, you would be in great trouble. You cannot go."

"I could," said Anne.

"You mustn't," I exclaimed. "There's no telling what would happen if you were found to be a spy." I was afraid for her safety, if not my own. "It's too dangerous."

"It's too dangerous for either of you," Mr. Slade said.

Ignoring him, Anne turned to me. "Are you saying you wouldn't get caught, but I would? I, too, am an experienced governess; do you not trust me to play the part?"

"I don't doubt your competence," I said, although I did. "I just prefer to risk myself rather than you."

Anne could see that I thought her weak and ineffectual. "Dear Charlotte, this is my chance to show you that I'm capable of more than you believe."

A critical choice lay before me: I must either recognize her as my equal by letting her prevail over me, or override her and permanently damage our sisterhood. "Then you'd better go to Mr. Lock's house," I said reluctantly, "because if the men who attacked us on the train return to the school, they might see you and recognize you."

"They wouldn't recognize me," said Emily.

Anne and I beheld her with surprise. Keeping her face averted, she went on: "Those men have never seen me. Neither they nor anyone else associated with Isabel White would know of my connection to Charlotte." Emily paused, gathering breath and courage. "I've been a teacher. I look the part of a destitute gentlewoman. I daresay the Charity School would hire me."

Imagine my shock! "Do you mean you would go away and live among strangers?" I stared at Emily in disbelief, as did Anne and Papa. Mr. Slade, unaware of Emily's disinclination to leave Haworth, merely looked puzzled.

Emily swung her gaze to me. "I can't hide at home while your life is in peril," she said bravely, though she hugged Keeper the way a person lost at sea clings to a raft.

My earlier narrative portrays Emily as self-centered and unlikable; yet she had a generous spirit that surfaced in times of dire need. She also possessed great courage under circumstances that would challenge the bravest of us. I recalled the time, several years ago, when she'd been chased and bitten by a mad dog. She had simply cauterized the wound with a hot poker, then gone about her business, despite the fact that she might have been fatally infected. Now she would extend herself for my sake, with the same noble stoicism. Love and admiration for her swelled my heart.

"Thank you, Emily," I said with tenderness.

A sound of protest issued from Mr. Slade; he stood. "This discussion is pointless." Anger and dismay darkened his face. "None of you shall set foot out of Haworth."

We heeded him not, for the joy of renewed harmony, and the thrill of collaboration, carried us beyond his control. Alone, I might have been subjugated by him; partnered with my sisters, I felt my power over my own fate multiplied threefold.

Anne said, "If I obtain a post in the Lock house while Emily goes to the Charity School, what will you do, Charlotte?"

"There is an important clue in Isabel's diary that remains to be investigated." Turning to Mr. Slade, I said, "Wouldn't you rather investigate it yourself, than rely on your associates?"

"What clue?" he demanded.

"If you won't allow us to participate in the investigation, I won't give you my transcript of the diary or tell you what is in it besides that which I've already told you," I retorted.

Outrage filled his expression. "This is akin to blackmail!"

Yet I sensed that he admired my cleverness, albeit grudgingly. This gave me much satisfaction. "So be it."

Mr. Slade looked confused, then vexed. "Even if I were to let your sisters have their way, I couldn't go off and leave you unprotected."

"Then take me with you," I said. Carried away by excitement, I didn't think about the impropriety of our traveling together. I knew only that I must prove my worth to him, and take a hand in protecting my family and myself, no matter the risks.

"You've gone mad," Mr. Slade said with a derisive laugh. "The idea of your accompanying me while I make inquiries—" He ran a hand over his tousled hair in a gesture of exasperation. "It's impossible."

He looked to Papa, who only shrugged and said, "I fear I am powerless to influence the girls when they've made up their minds."

I almost laughed with giddy delight at Mr. Slade's chagrin. He said, "You are all amateurs, and you wouldn't know what to look for, or how to avoid detection. You could ruin our chances of capturing the villain and thwarting his scheme, in addition to endangering yourselves." Mr. Slade folded his arms and his expression turned obstinate. "If you want my help, you'll follow my plan."

I saw in him the authority of a man accustomed to leading; I also perceived the fiery aura of ambition that surrounded him. "If you want our cooperation, you will honor our wishes."

My pulse raced as Anne, Emily, and I rose simultaneously and stood together, united against Mr. Slade. Often my sisters and I had been downtrodden, imposed upon, and disregarded. Singly we were weak, but our alliance now generated a mystical, strengthening force. Mr. Slade retreated a step backward from us, and his face took on the wonder of a man viewing a phenomenon he doesn't understand. I beheld the hands that had once restrained me, the face I had struck, the body whose strength I'd opposed, and the mouth I had wanted to kiss. My heartbeat thundered like the storm on the moors; my blood rushed like the wind.

The wonder in Slade's gaze changed to something akin to enlightenment. Unspoken words parted his lips, and I waited, breathless—for what revelation? Then the lucid depths of his eyes went opaque, as though he had closed some internal barrier against me. His features darkened with grim resignation.

"God help us all," he said.

18

>−<

A WEEK PASSED, DURING WHICH MR. SLADE REMAINED IN THE parsonage, taking meals with us and sharing our nightly prayers. He also spent much time writing letters, and reading letters he received, in the upstairs study where he lived. Whenever I went out, he accompanied me as my protector. His Irish charm won him general acclaim in the village and caused quite a stir among the young ladies. Papa respected him; Anne treated him fondly. Emily even stopped hiding from him, and Keeper now wagged his tail at Mr. Slade.

One might think that all the hours we spent together would have fostered a new acquaintance between Mr. Slade and myself. Yet I was afraid of saying anything that would reveal my feelings for him; consequently, my manner towards him was taciturn. His towards me exemplified cautious restraint.

At night Mr. Slade stayed downstairs, guarding the house, though he never seemed the worse for his wakeful nights. Perhaps his vigilance kept danger at bay, but still, I did not feel safe. Matters could not continue thus. Mr. Slade, through some arcane means, obtained for Anne the post of governess to Joseph Lock's children. She left for Birmingham on Monday, 7 August, the same day Emily journeyed to the Charity School. Mr. Slade and I set out for London that very morning.

I had kept my bargain, showing him my transcript of Isabel's diary and pointing out the mention of the prime minister. Now we sat in the train, on our way to investigate the very same man. With every revolution of the wheels, my own rashness appalled me more. What could I hope to accomplish? Did anyone deduce that I was traveling with a man who was only posing as my kin? I feared disgrace as much as I did the possibility that Isabel White's killer pursued me.

After we had gone many miles, Mr. Slade produced a book and said, "Do ye recognize this?" In public, he maintained his Irish brogue for my safety.

The sight of *Jane Eyre* in his hand gave me a turn. "I believe I do," I murmured.

"The author has a remarkable talent for storytellin'. I stayed up all night readin' until I finished."

I blushed with pride, as I always do when someone praises my work. I dreaded to continue the discussion, for they who praise a book often disparage it in the next breath.

"The tale did strike me as rather improbable," Mr. Slade said.

My guard enclosed me like a suit of armor. "In what way?"

"Jane and Rochester were an odd pairing," Mr. Slade said. "In real life, they'd never have formed an attachment."

Stung by his criticism, I said tartly, "May I ask why not?"

"Rochester is a man of property and position, and Jane a penniless orphan. They're from different worlds."

"Similar status is not the only basis for a union between a man and woman," I said, growing flustered as I defended my book. "Compatibility of minds is also important."

"In fiction, perhaps," Mr. Slade said. "But if Jane and Rochester were to exist, he would never discover their compatibility. A man like him, who has always required beauty and vivacity in a woman, doesn't so easily forgo those attributes. And Jane quite lacks them."

His words flayed me. "Jane's character and judgment compensate for her lack," I protested.

"True. But Rochester would never have noticed those good qualities behind her plainness, if not for the author's guiding hand."

Mr. Slade added gently, "Forgive me if I've upset ye. *Jane Eyre* is a fine tale, and I don't mean to diminish it."

Alas, he had done more than diminish my book. He had ground my heart under his heel. I sought a change of subject. "Dr. Dury told me you'd been a soldier in Turkestan," I said, then indicated a wish to hear of his experiences there.

Nostalgia veiled Mr. Slade's eyes. "Middle Asia is a land of wild, savage beauty," he said, and described its deserts, high mountains, exotic bazaars and mosques, and tribal warriors. "It's also a troubled land that has been invaded throughout history by the Greeks, Persians, Mongols, Arabs, and Turks."

He described the invasion of Kabul by the British East India Army and how it had gone wrong. "Forty-five hundred British troops and twelve thousand women, children, and Indian sepoys retreated from the kingdom in January 1842. The weather was bitterly cold, and the country deep in snow. Native partisans fired on us as we struggled through the Khurd Kabul Pass. Almost all of us were massacred."

"You were on the march?" I said in surprise. "I read that there was but one survivor: an army doctor."

"I was wounded and left for dead." Mr. Slade's grim manner hinted at horrors seen and suffered. For the first time since he'd come to Haworth, I glimpsed his true self through his genial Irish guise. "Later, I was discovered by natives I'd befriended. They hid me and cared for me. Eventually I made my way back to England."

In awe of him, I said, "Working in France afterwards must have been more pleasant."

His face went rigid and a shadow darkened it. "Not in the end," he said coldly, and turned away.

I felt mortified because I had intruded on private ground and he had spurned me. I wished to know what had happened to Mr. Slade in France, but dared not ask. Little more conversation passed between us.

When we reached London, Mr. Slade hired a carriage. We drove around the streets, and after he ascertained that no one was following us, we proceeded to the home of his elder sister, with whom he had arranged for us to stay. Katherine Slade Abbot was a respectable, well-to-do widow; she lived in an elegant house in Mayfair. Mrs. Abbot, or Kate, as Mr. Slade fondly called her, had his coloring and eyes; she was pretty, vivacious, and kind. After we dined, Mr. Slade hurried me into another carriage. We rode by an indirect route to the Foreign Office to confer with his superiors.

The Foreign Office was situated on Downing Street, in bleak, grimy brick buildings. We went to a room paneled in dark wood and lit by gas lamps. Seven men sat at a long table. The man at its head was some fifty years old, with a rigid bearing and sleek hair the color of his sallow, pallid complexion; he wore a gold satin waistcoat. Reader, you will recognize him as Lord Unwin, the man whom Slade met in the Five Coins Tavern after the murder of Isabel White. His companions were nondescript and dressed in drab hues. The smoke from their pipes hung in the air. Everyone rose when Mr. Slade and I entered the room. Being the only woman present discomposed me. That I'd had the temerity to demand participation in a matter within their purview now seemed ludicrous.

They greeted Mr. Slade, who turned to me, indicated the man at the head of the table, and said, "May I introduce Lord Alistair Unwin, deputy chief of the Foreign Office." He had dropped the Irish brogue and spoke in his own voice. To Lord Unwin, he said, "This is Miss Charlotte Brontë."

Quaking inside, wishing myself at home, I curtsied. Lord Unwin bowed politely, but his arched eyebrows and sharp, haughty features conveyed disdain towards me, and I took an immediate dislike to him. "Please be seated," he said.

I was not introduced to the other men. Mr. Slade and I took chairs at the end of the table. Lord Unwin addressed Mr. Slade: "You've chosen an inconvenient hour to meet. I'm late for a ball."

"My apologies, Lord Unwin," Mr. Slade said, "but Miss Brontë and I have only just arrived in town, and there are matters that must be discussed without delay."

Lord Unwin glowered at Mr. Slade, and I observed the animosity between them. "I presume these urgent matters concern the murders of Isabel White, Joseph Lock, and Isaiah Fearon, as well as your investigation of a conspiracy against the Crown?"

"They do, my lord," said Mr. Slade. The other men watched in somber silence.

"Well, tell us what you have to report, and be quick about it."

"Miss Brontë has visited Isabel White's mother and the school Isabel attended," Mr. Slade said. "She has come to relate her discoveries to you."

Self-conscious and faltering under the men's scrutiny, I told what I'd learned. When I finished, Lord Unwin said, "How admirable, Miss Brontë. Our sincerest thanks." He gave Mr. Slade a contemptuous smile. "So Miss Brontë has obtained Isabel White's missing book and the important clues therein. She has also linked the Charity School to the men who attacked her on the train and who have an apparent connection with the mysterious criminal we seek. That's more than you've accomplished lately. How fortunate for us that she happened along."

Anger smoldered in Mr. Slade's eyes. I could hardly enjoy praise given at his expense, and I wondered at the reason for Lord Unwin's ill treatment of him. Mr. Slade said evenly, "It is fortunate indeed that Miss Brontë is helping with our inquiries."

"What have you done to further them?" Lord Unwin frowned at his gold watch.

"I've sent Miss Brontë's sister Anne to be a governess in Joseph Lock's house," Mr. Slade replied. "She'll try to learn why Lock killed himself and what connections the gun factory may still have with our criminal. Her other sister, Emily, has gone to teach at the Charity School, in the hope of discovering how it fits into the criminal's scheme, and what that scheme is."

Lord Unwin received this news with amazement. "You allowed Miss Brontë's sisters to undertake the work of professional agents?" he said, his voice rising to a shrill pitch. "My dear fellow, have you gone mad?" His subordinates' faces reflected his disapproval. "Should these women bungle the attempt, our mission could be compromised." He was more concerned for his mission than for my sisters' safety, and I liked him even less.

"Anne and Emily Brontë are experienced teachers, and they'll perform their roles more convincingly than could agents posing as teachers," Mr. Slade said. "They understand the need for caution, and I have confidence in them."

Though he spoke with patient calm, I sensed how much Lord Unwin's reproof disturbed him. By insisting on our involvement, my sisters and I had undermined Mr. Slade's standing in the Foreign Office. That he took the blame for our actions instead of laying it on us did his manners credit.

"If your amateur spies do cause trouble, you shall be held personally responsible," Lord Unwin said in a threatening tone. "What other plans have you?"

"Isabel White wrote that her master had drawn the prime minister into his scheme." Mr. Slade rose, gave Lord Unwin my copy of the message from the book, then took his seat again.

Lord Unwin peered down his sharp nose at the lines Mr. Slade had marked. "How fantastic! It is beyond belief that Lord John Russell should be involved in these affairs."

"The matter merits consideration," Mr. Slade said.

A leery, indecisive look crossed Lord Unwin's features. "Isabel White was a woman of base morals. She could have lied about the prime minister."

"Granted," Mr. Slade said, "but if her message tells the truth, then the prime minister represents another connection to the criminal. We cannot afford to overlook that possibility."

Lord Unwin propped his chin on his hand and regarded Mr. Slade through hooded eyes. "What do you propose doing?"

"I propose an audience with the prime minister for Miss Brontë and myself, in order that we can tell him what we've learned and find out what he knows."

Incredulity was Lord Unwin's response. "You would confront the prime minister and accuse him of consorting with a trollop? You would claim to his face that he has fallen under the sway of a man who plans an attack on the kingdom?"

"We wouldn't accuse him," Mr. Slade said. "We would discreetly question him, then ask his help in apprehending the criminal."

"Discretion would not make Isabel White's story less insulting to Lord John Russell." Lord Unwin smacked his palms down on the table. "Permission is denied."

Although Mr. Slade maintained his composure, I sensed his anxiety. "But the prime minister may possess information that could advance our investigation," he said. "He may even know the criminal by name, or have learned what his scheme is."

"Maybe; maybe not," Lord Unwin said with a reedy chuckle. "We've only Isabel White's dubious claim to support your conjecture."

"It is imperative that Lord John Russell be questioned." The set of Mr. Slade's jaw betrayed his anger at Lord Unwin's opposition.

"Provoking his wrath could bring worse disaster than whatever the criminal intends," Lord Unwin said waspishly. "If you offend the prime minister, the repercussions will be farreaching."

I realized that Lord Unwin cared more to safeguard himself than to protect England from further violence, and he was more concerned that the prime minister would punish him for Mr. Slade's actions than about the success of the investigation.

"We must take the risk." Leaning towards his superior, Mr. Slade entreated, "Please reconsider."

Lord Unwin folded his arms resentfully. "My decision is final. Stay away from the prime minister."

"You can't close off an entire avenue of inquiry!" Mr. Slade protested, leaping from his seat.

"Indeed I can," Lord Unwin sneered. "You'd best hope that your amateur spies can elicit the facts we need. I now adjourn this meeting." Chairs scraped as Lord Unwin and his men rose; he bowed to me. "Good evening, Miss Brontë."

❖❖❖

"Lord Unwin fears to risk his own neck," Mr. Slade said with bitter ire as we rode away in our carriage. "That a man like him should have charge over the nation's affairs! God save us all from cowards!"

I confess that I savored the feeling of comradeship that stemmed from our siding together against Lord Unwin. "Why does Lord Unwin dislike you so much?"

"For common reasons as old as history." Mr. Slade gave a humorless laugh. "Lord Unwin belongs to a proud, noble family that lost its land and wealth. He was forced to go to work instead of enjoying the life of an idle aristocrat. Family connections got him a post in the Foreign Office, and he's been promoted to a high rank merely because of his name. I, on the other hand, am an upstart son of a nobody. My achievements rankle Lord Unwin because they, not birthright, have won me a place in the world. He would like to see me fail, disgrace myself, and prove his superiority." Mr. Slade mused, "Lord Unwin's kind are fast losing their domination over England, and he has chosen to punish me for that."

How well I understood. While a governess, I had been abused by rich employers who resented my education, as if I had insulted them by possessing what they lacked. My sense of camaraderie with Mr. Slade increased. "What shall we do?"

Mr. Slade's teeth flashed white in a brief, cunning smile. He said, "I have ways to circumvent Lord Unwin's orders."

My hopes buoyed me yet again, with their sudden resurgence.

19

DURING THE NEXT FEW DAYS, MR. SLADE LEFT HIS SISTER'S HOUSE early every morning, before I awakened, to pursue inquiries whose nature he did not elucidate to me. In his absence he stationed two Foreign Office agents in the foyer to guard me. I kept to my room, where I endeavored to finish writing *Shirley*, waited for news from Mr. Slade, and grew ever more anxious. At night I lay awake and heard him come home very late. Our previous sense of partnership had vanished, to my vexation and disappointment.

My solitary wait was enlivened by letters from Anne and Emily. Here I reproduce Anne's:

My dear Charlotte,

I am glad to report that I arrived safely in Birmingham and am now ensconced as governess at the Lock house. My role as secret observer is one for which I am much less qualified, and I hope I shall perform creditably.

The family consists of Mrs. Caroline Lock, who is the widow of Joseph Lock, her two sons—Harry and Matthew, aged seven and six—and Mr. Henry Lock, her brother-in-law. Mrs. Lock is a pale, haggard wraith. Her blue eyes are sunken and the effort of conversation seems to pain her. When we met, I caught the odor of spirits on her person. She spends all her time in her chamber, tended by her maid, who carries in trays of food and glasses of wine. The trays come out barely touched, the glasses empty.

My two pupils are both fair, sturdy, handsome lads; but oh, how obstreperous Master Harry is! During our first lesson he chattered constantly. When I told him to be quiet, he hurled his books out the window. Young Matthew never speaks at all, and his eyes are solemn. He wets his bed, as if he were a much younger child. But I suspect that he is more sad then feebleminded, and Harry more confused than evil. Their father's death seems to haunt the entire household, and not the least of all Mr. Henry Lock.

Mr. Lock is a fair, slender man with a perpetually worried face. He manages the family gunworks and spends long days there. While the nursemaid gives the boys their supper, Henry Lock and I dine alone together (Mrs. Lock never joins us). We sit at opposite ends of the table in the elegant candlelit dining room. He always greets me politely, then retreats into his private thoughts. We nibble at the food, for which neither of us has much appetite; then he excuses himself and withdraws to the study on the top floor. I know he works very late, because the study is directly above my room, and I can hear him moving about.

A more troubled family I have seldom seen. The Locks' melancholy might have depleted my own spirits, had I not a purpose to accomplish. With that purpose in mind, I ventured to the kitchen on the afternoon of my second day, on the pretext of begging some water to drink. The cook and the scullery maid were quite willing to gossip about Mrs. Lock's grief and about her husband's suicide. But before I could hear more than I already knew, the housekeeper came into the kitchen and scolded us for idle talk.

My subsequent attempts to obtain information from the servants met with evasion. I began to fear I would never learn why Mr. Lock took his own life, nor what was his connection to the murder of Isabel White. I doubted that I would ever glimpse her "master" or anyone associated with him—until tonight.

The hall clock chiming midnight roused me from a fitful doze. Then came a knock at the front door. As I wondered who called so late, I heard the door open, and Henry Lock say, his voice shrill with alarm, "What are you doing here?"

A man replied in menacing words that I could not discern. I crept from my room onto the landing and peered over the banister. Henry Lock stood at the open door. Beyond the threshold stood a man with a beaked nose, jutting chin, and ominous expression.

"I won't," Henry Lock said. "We've done enough for you. Go away and leave me alone!"

The man seized him by the collar. Henry Lock lurched and cried out, his hands splayed. The visitor murmured threats that were indistinguishable to me, yet struck fear into my heart.

"No!" I heard Henry Lock say; then: "Yes! Whatever you wish. Just please don't—"

The visitor released him. He staggered backward. There was a last mutter from the visitor, whose shadowy figure withdrew. Henry Lock slammed the door, secured the bolt, and sagged against the wall, gasping. What had transpired between him and his caller? Does my wishful imagination convince me that the caller is an emissary of Isabel White's evil master? I feel certain that dire peril threatens this house. I shall wait and watch for the opportunity to solve the mystery.

I hope you and Emily are well, and that your own inquiries are progressing.

With love,
Anne

Her letter engendered in me both fear and, at the same time, the hope that Anne had found a path that would lead to the truth. I know how much she craved independence and wanted to prove her worth, but how I regretted allowing her to go to Birmingham! Yet my anxiety concerning Anne was far less than that I felt for Emily.

Emily was never a fulsome correspondent; her letter was brief. She merely said that she had arrived at the Charity School and been taken in as a teacher. I didn't discover what happened during her time there until after her death, when I read the following passages in her journal:

The Journal of Emily Brontë

Skipton, 10 August 1848.

The train carried me northwest, like a coffin speeding towards doom. The passengers in the carriage numbered more strangers than I had seen in years. With every passing mile, my heart yearned more desperately for home.

A thunderstorm coincided with my arrival at the Charity School, which was as forbidding as a ruined castle. I stood, wet and shivering, for some time at the door, my heart pounding while I fought an urge to flee. At worst there were evil criminals inside; at best, strangers to face. I summoned all my courage and knocked. When a maid answered, I forced myself to say, "I am in need of work. Might you need a teacher?"

My appearance must have convinced her that I was the correct sort of destitute gentlewoman, for she admitted me into the building. "Wait here. I'll fetch the mistress."

The blood coursing wildly through me blurred my vision of the place in which I found myself. I heard the voices of teachers lecturing and students reciting lessons. The frightening cacophony shrank my soul into a kernel of terror as a small, buxom, brassy-haired woman approached me.

The woman, Mrs. Grimshaw, introduced herself and scrutinized me with her sharp hazel eyes. Her figure was tightly corseted into a green paisley frock. The unnatural shade of her hair suggested henna dye. By her accent, she was clearly of common birth, pretending to a higher social station. "And you are?"

"Miss Emily Smith," I whispered, remembering to give my false surname.

"What brings you 'ere?"

I stammered out my preconceived tale of having been a teacher at a distant school that had closed, leaving me with nowhere to go, as I had neither family nor friends. I thought Mrs. Grimshaw would surely notice that I lied, so unconvincing did I sound to myself. But she nodded and said, "What subjects did you teach?"

"Music," I said.

She led me into a room with a piano. "Let me 'ear you play," she ordered.

As I sat at the instrument, I felt all my terror of making a show of myself. For one panic-stricken moment, my mind could not recall a single bar of music. But somehow my hands played a hymn.

Either Mrs. Grimshaw didn't notice my mistakes, or she cared not about them, for when I finished, she said, "You can begin giving lessons tomorrow."

That I had gained a position at the school seemed more a grief than a triumph. A teacher named Miss Rathburn took me into the teachers' residence, a low stone building divided into cells. Miss Rathburn is about forty years of age, willowy and tall; she has a queer habit of fondling her large bosom.

"You'll share this room with me," she said.

She then told me the hours for lessons, meals, prayer, and rest, but I scarcely listened. The tiny room appalled me; I could not bear to live in such close proximity with a stranger.

"Teachers have free run of the school," Miss Rathburn said. "The only places off limits to everyone are the Grimshaws' quarters and the old windmill."

Then we went to supper. Some seventy girls occupied tables in the refectory, but they could have been hundreds, so loud were their shrill voices. I sat with the Reverend and Mrs. Grimshaw and the four other teachers. After the Reverend Grimshaw led a prayer, his wife introduced me to the school.

"Girls, this is Miss Smith, your new music teacher," she said.

As I rose and all eyes fixed upon me, I almost fainted from embarrassment. When the meal commenced, every bite nauseated me. The teachers attempted to engage me in conversation, and I made brief, awkward replies. The girls glanced in my direction, whispering and giggling: Already I was an object of mockery, as I had been at other schools. At bedtime I lay awake while my chamber mate slept. Her breath filled the room; I heard the other teachers stirring in adjacent chambers. How I wept for the parsonage and the moors! In my sad state, how could I accomplish here what I had sworn to do?

At last I fell into exhausted slumber. I dreamed I was suffocating. I awoke to find myself screaming and thrashing and the other teachers gathered around me, staring in fright. They now treat me with the wary reserve accorded to people of questionable sanity, but my pupils display no such caution.

The leaders of the school are Abigail Weston and Jane Fell, both handsome, insolent girls of sixteen. They expend no effort at learning the piano, and when I correct their mistakes, they laugh at me. The other girls follow their example, but for one Frances Cullen. She is a plain, shy little thing, thirteen years old, the object of much teasing. With her I feel a sad kinship.

On my second evening at the school I craved solitude so much that I thought I would die of the need. I waited until everyone else was asleep, then slipped outside. It was a hot, windless night. A swollen moon spread a hazy glow over the school. Deep shadows cloaked the garden. Crickets chirped, and the perfume from flowers hung heavy in the air. I inhaled invigorating breaths of freedom as my beleaguered soul drew comfort from nature . . .

. . . until the Reverend Grimshaw emerged from his quarters. I hid behind an oak tree. He hurried past me and disappeared between the birches at the end of the garden. Jane Fell came out of the house and followed Grimshaw. The round stone tower of the windmill rose beyond the birches. Jane and the Reverend Grimshaw must have gone there, but what were they doing in that forbidden place? I wondered how Jane could roam about when all the other girls were locked in their rooms, and what business she had with the Reverend Grimshaw.

Perhaps their business concerned the matter I had come to investigate. I decided I must see what went on in the windmill, but then I heard the clatter of horses' hooves and carriage wheels, nearing the school. Suddenly Mrs. Grimshaw appeared in the courtyard. Her sharp eyes glinted in the moonlight, surveying the school, as though in search of trespassers. Fearing she would discover me, I crept back to my bed, certain there is something amiss here.

The next day Jane Fell was vanished from the school. When I asked where she had gone, Miss Rathburn said she'd taken ill in the night and her parents had fetched her home. Yet I had seen her looking in perfect health, and I could not help but wonder if whatever happened to Jane has any connection to the life or death of Isabel White. And perhaps I shall soon find out.

That afternoon, Mrs. Grimshaw called me into her office. She asked me, "Does your work suit you?"

I replied that it did, and I thanked her for her charity.

Mrs. Grimshaw preened. "Many women 'ave reason to thank us," she said. "An' some expresses their gratitude with donations." She showed me an envelope that contained ten pounds. "We've just got this from a former pupil."

She carelessly dropped the envelope on her desk, then bustled from the room, leaving me behind. I had the peculiar feeling that she wanted to see if I would take advantage of the opportunity to steal the money. At first I had no wish to steal, and no doubt that I must prove my good character or be expelled. But my thinking suddenly altered. Under ordinary circumstances I should leave the money where it was and show my virtue; yet this was not an ordinary school, and I was no ordinary teacher. Divining that Mrs. Grimshaw wanted something other than virtue from me, I slipped the envelope into my pocket.

Fearful anticipation gnawed at me all day. Had I passed her test? What was to come? Then, after evening prayers, Mrs. Grimshaw appeared at my side. "May I 'ave a word with you, Miss Smith?"

We went again to her office, she severe, I cowed and cringing. "This afternoon I showed you some money," Mrs. Grimshaw said. "It was there when I left the room." She pointed at the desk. "Do you see it?"

"No, ma'am," I whispered, quaking as would any thief who feared punishment. My fear was real; I didn't need to pretend.

"Nor do I," Mrs. Grimshaw said. Her eyes gleamed, and a cruel smile curved her moist, full lips. "Whatever could 'ave become of the ten pounds?"

"I don't know," I said, though guilt at the lie undermined my show of innocence.

"Oh, but I think you do know." Mrs. Grimshaw prowled around me, her footsteps trapping me in a circle. "I left you alone in this room with the money. Now it's missing. An' you're the only person besides me that's been 'ere all day." She halted like a cat ready to pounce. "Empty your pockets," she ordered.

Quailing from the menace in her eyes, I obeyed. Out came the envelope of money.

"Aha!" Mrs. Grimshaw exclaimed, snatching it from my hand. "Wretched thief! After we've fed an' sheltered you and given you employment, you betray our trust!" Righteous indignation swelled her countenance; yet I perceived that my guilt gratified her. "I should throw you out!"

"No, please, don't!" I said in sudden panic, as I began to think I'd misjudged the situation and would lose my position at the school. How could I then discover facts that might save my family? "I've nowhere to go!"

"I ought to turn you over to the law," Mrs. Grimshaw said.

A vision of myself locked in prison horrified me. Gasping, I fell on my knees before Mrs. Grimshaw. "Have mercy. I beg you to forgive me."

"But you must be punished." That Mrs. Grimshaw relished my terror and humiliation was evident.

"Do to me what you will," I said, "but please let me stay. I promise I'll never steal again."

"There is a way you can avoid punishment and prove you deserve to be kept 'ere," Mrs. Grimshaw said with a show of reluctance.

"I'll do anything," I cried. "Anything you ask!"

Folding her arms, Mrs. Grimshaw beheld me, her shrewd gaze taking my measure. She nodded, and her smile turned conspiratorial. "We'll just forget about your mistake. Quit your sniveling, and go to bed. Tomorrow you'll do a special little task for me."

I felt overwhelming relief that she had given me a second chance, and shame that I had been branded a criminal. "Thank you," I whispered. As I fled the room, apprehension clutched my heart. I had put myself in the power of a woman whom I believed was up to no good, and what did she expect of me?

20

>‒<

ON THE MORNING OF MY FOURTH DAY IN LONDON, I BREAKFASTED with Kate in her spacious dining room. It was decorated in shades of yellow. Sun shone through the windows, and fresh flowers adorned the table. I wished I could absorb some of the brightness around me and enjoy the generous meal of eggs, breads, ham, and jellies, but I worried about Emily and Anne, and I had begun to fear that my presence in London was unnecessary.

At that moment Mr. Slade strode into the room. "Good morning," he said casually, and sat at the table as though his sudden appearance were not remarkable.

I looked down at my plate, for fear he would see the joy that rose in me. Kate exclaimed happily, "My prodigal brother! To what do we owe the honor of your company?"

"There have been some new developments," Mr. Slade said. "Please forgive me for leaving you uninformed so long, Miss Brontë. I've been investigating the prime minister through indirect channels, in vain. Lord John Russell has no apparent connection to Isabel White, Joseph Lock, or Isaiah Fearon. To discover his part in this business, we must ask him directly."

"Lord Unwin has ordered us to stay away from the prime minister," I reminded Mr. Slade. "Dare we disobey?"

He frowned as if he wished his superior to the devil. "We

must, or lose a chance to acquire whatever facts Lord Russell may have about Isabel's master."

"How shall you approach him, when he's occupied with government affairs day and night and surrounded by men who protect him from interruptions?" Kate asked.

Mischief glinted in Mr. Slade's eye. "Lord John Russell plans to attend a certain event. And I have secured an invitation."

He handed me a square of heavy, cream-colored paper. Printed in elegant script, it read, "The Duke and Duchess of Kent request your presence at a ball."

"The ball offers an opportunity for a chance encounter with the prime minister," Slade said. "Miss Brontë, shall we go together?"

My first reaction was my usual, dire dread of social occasions. My second was anxiety concerning practical matters. As I sat tongue-tied, Slade said, "Have you some objection?"

Kate took the invitation from me, examined it, and cried, "The ball is tonight! My dear brother, Miss Brontë fears there's not enough time for her to prepare."

"The ball doesn't start till nine o'clock," Mr. Slade said to me. "Can you not be ready by then?"

I could not be ready ever, for I possessed nothing to wear. Kate flashed me a look of comprehension and said, "Miss Brontë will be ready."

She whisked me upstairs to her chamber, where she laid out beautiful, shimmering silk frocks. "It's fortunate that we're nearly the same size. I shall happily lend you a ball gown."

I was grateful to her, yet still apprehensive; what business had I in such fine raiment? Since bright colors and low necklines don't become me, we selected a modest grey satin. That night, when I stood ready before the mirror, I thought I wouldn't disgrace myself. The gown's narrow bodice and flounced skirt lent me stature, and the emerald sheen of the fabric lit auburn lights in my hair, which Kate had dressed in fashionable style.

"Your eyes are as bright as diamonds," Kate said fondly. "They're all the adornment you need." Then she leaned close and whispered: "Though he may seem unresponsive, don't despair.

Even the most broken heart can mend. Fate can work magic even on a man who has for years shunned romantic attachment."

I saw my face blush redder, thinking that Kate had noticed my feelings towards her brother; yet I wondered at her remark. Did she mean that he had suffered a broken heart? And if so, who had been the object of his love?

Shaky with anticipation, I descended the stairs. In the foyer Mr. Slade paced. His black evening clothes and unruly hair gave him a look of raffish elegance. When he spied me halfway down the stairs, I saw the surprised admiration that I had hoped to see in his eyes, but as I nervously smiled, his countenance turned aloof.

"Shall we go?" he said indifferently.

He neither looked at me nor spoke during our carriage ride through London. We alighted in Belgrave Square, outside a magnificent mansion. We joined the splendidly attired gentlemen and ladies parading up to the doors, from which emanated violin music. My hand trembled on Slade's arm, yet I wasn't quite so nervous as on the night at the opera with George Smith. The finery I wore clothed me like armor; having a mission to accomplish fortified my courage. Inside the vast ballroom, we were engulfed by a horde of guests. A crystal chandelier blazed. Mirrored walls magnified the room and the crowd; a roar of voices and laughter echoed over the music from the orchestra.

"We must find the prime minister," Mr. Slade said. "Let's dance. That will allow us a view of everyone."

The orchestra commenced a waltz. Before I could protest that I did not know how to dance, Mr. Slade had led me out on the floor. At first I stumbled, but then I found myself caught up in the music, waltzing effortlessly. The lights, the dancers, and their reflections spun around me. Mr. Slade's face was the single clear image in the blur of color and motion. His gaze scanned the room; but as we whirled together, his eyes met mine, briefly at first, then for longer intervals. His frown signaled reluctance to behold me; yet he did, as if unable to prevent himself. My heart was beating fast. Did Mr. Slade draw me closer? Did his hand tighten on mine?

Just when I thought I would faint from intoxication, Mr. Slade said, "There is the prime minister."

He hurried me from the dance floor to a cluster of people. At their center was a man in his fifties whose massive head and broad shoulders seemed too heavy for his short, frail body. His face was unwholesomely pale, its skin masking prominent bones. Mr. Slade maneuvered us through his entourage to his side.

"My lord," Mr. Slade said. The prime minister turned to us, his eyes shrewdly inquisitive. "I am John Slade, and this is Miss Charlotte Brontë. May we have a word with you?"

Lord John Russell had been born to wealth and privilege, but he embraced modern ideas and belonged to the Whig Party, which represented the interests of businessmen and opposed the Tory royalists. He had distinguished himself by introducing the famous Reform Bill that extended voting rights and shifted power from the landed aristocracy to the men of commerce. Its passage had won him enormous popular acclaim. He had ascended to the supreme post of prime minister, but his two-year tenure had been plagued by Chartist insurrection, worsening poverty and violence in Ireland, and the threat that revolution on the Continent would spread to England. Now he cast an uninterested glance at me, then looked Mr. Slade up and down. He seemed ready to brush us off without a reply.

"This concerns Isabel White," Mr. Slade said.

The prime minister's face blanched paler; his throat contracted. "I do not know anyone by that name." His voice was incongruously affected, mincing, and uncertain for a man of his status. "Excuse me." He turned and fled, ignoring the stir that his abrupt departure created.

"Come," Mr. Slade said, grabbing my hand. "If he gets away, we may never have another chance at him."

We hastened in pursuit across the dance floor. We followed Lord John Russell down a winding staircase and outside to a garden. Trees arched between the star-jeweled sky and the garden's brick paths and flowerbeds. The lighted ballroom windows cast their radiance over all. The air was redolent with the smells of flowers and cesspools. I gasped, breathless from running. We caught up with the prime minister near a pond centered by a marble statue of Aphrodite. The prime minister faced Mr. Slade with jaw thrust out and fists clenched.

"Isabel sent you?" he demanded. "Well, you can tell her that I'll have nothing more to do with her. And unless you leave these premises at once, I'll have you imprisoned for trespassing!"

He must have thought we were in league with Isabel and her master, and he had run to avoid public exposure. The same realization flashed across Mr. Slade's face. "Isabel didn't send us," he said. "I'm an agent of the Crown, employed by the Foreign Office."

The prime minister shook his massive head, glowering at us. "I'll believe none of your filthy lies. Go to the devil!"

In desperation I cried, "Please, my lord, we mean you no harm. We've come to help you."

He turned to me in surprise, as though wondering how such an obviously insignificant person would dare to entreat him.

"Isabel White has been murdered," I hurried on. "We believe that the same man who forced you to serve him is responsible. His henchmen tried to abduct me and nearly killed my brother. Isabel claimed that he has launched a plot that threatens the kingdom. Our only chance to stop him is to band together."

Lord Russell's hands slowly unclenched; he regarded me with shock. "Isabel was murdered? How did it happen?"

I was filled with relief that he appeared ready to listen, and amazement at my own boldness. I recounted the details of Isabel's death; then Mr. Slade described the murder of the merchant Isaiah Fearon. As he told about discovering that Isabel was a courier between radical societies and her master who abetted them, the prime minister took on the aspect of a man beholding the ruin after a siege of a city.

"How did you connect me to all this?" he said.

I explained what we had read in the book Isabel had sent me. Now Lord John Russell staggered over to a marble bench and sat down heavily.

"Then it's true that an intimacy with Isabel put you in thrall to her master?" Mr. Slade asked.

Lord Russell nodded, in evident relief at confessing what he must have kept a dark secret. "It all began in the year 1844," he said. "I was battling the Tory opposition to grant civil rights to the Irish and regulate the factories. My wife was gravely ill. I had invested money in ventures that proved unsound, and I lost a fortune. I was forced to borrow heavily to cover my expenses. I became so distraught I could not rest. I took to roaming the town at night, in search of a diversion. One evening I found myself in a gaming club. It was there that I met Isabel."

Shadows like bruises obscured the prime minister's face; the gay music from the house mocked his unhappiness. "She was a hostess at the club. Ordinarily, I would never consort with a woman of her kind. But Isabel was beautiful. I was lonely and vulnerable and smitten."

Here was verification of the tale in Isabel's diary, I thought, glancing at Mr. Slade. But his attention remained focused on Lord John Russell.

"I continued to meet Isabel, at disreputable taverns and lodgings," the prime minister went on. "Eventually I began to tell her my troubles, as I suppose many men do with their mistresses." He grimaced in self disgust. "She said she knew someone who could give me financial assistance. At first I refused, for I knew the money would come with strings attached. But as I neared the verge of financial ruin and a mental breakdown, Isabel's repeated offers grew more tempting. One night she brought me five hundred pounds from the man she called her master. I accepted it, as I did further payments."

His posture withered with shame; I pitied him.

"What was asked of you in exchange?" Mr. Slade said quietly.

"Nothing at first," Lord John Russell said. "I severed my relations with Isabel in 1845, when I took my wife to seek medical advice in Edinburgh. My financial position improved, and I thought myself rid of problems. But then . . ." His expression turned doleful. "Early in 1847—some six months after I became prime minister—Isabel waylaid me outside the Houses of Parliament. She told me that her master ordered me to pay him ten thousand pounds. I was horrified. I said I could not and would not pay. But she said that unless I did, my wife would be told of my adultery. My wife was still in poor health, and the shock might have killed her. Therefore, I did an unpardonable thing.

"At the time I was responsible for the Treasury and funds earmarked for relief efforts in Ireland. From those I stole ten thousand pounds to pay Isabel's master. Yet his demands did not end there. Soon Isabel told me that he wanted me to ensure that certain ships left England without inspection or interference."

"Which ships?" Mr. Slade said in a tone of controlled eagerness.

"I don't recall, but they belonged to various trading firms," Lord John Russell said. "They all were bound for the Far East."

"What was their cargo?" Slade asked.

"I preferred not to know. I deduced that they conveyed Englishwomen to be sold to wealthy Oriental men. I told Isabel to inform her master that I refused to aid an illegal, immoral trade. But she said that he had spies at the Treasury, and he knew how I had obtained the money I had paid him. And unless I let the ships pass unimpeded, her master would expose me as an embezzler. The scandal would ruin my political career."

These, then, were the threats by which her master had subjugated the prime minister. Greed, poor judgment, and fear can weaken the most powerful of humanity.

"I had no choice but to obey. But since you've told me that Isabel's master finances radical societies, I fear that the ships had a purpose even more harmful than I believed." Lord John Russell's pallid face looked ghastly ill. "He must intend to disrupt order in Asia and undermine British dominance there, as he has in Europe. His ships must have carried information, troops, and weapons to confederates overseas."

Mr. Slade nodded. I wondered if guns manufactured by Joseph Lock had comprised part of the ships' secret cargo. Perhaps he, too, had been forced to serve Isabel's master and had provided the guns against his will. Had he later discovered the treasonous purpose for which the guns were meant, then killed himself rather than face exposure? Perhaps Isaiah Fearon had transported the guns, and died because he was a link in the chain that joined Isabel White and Joseph Lock to the man who had ruled them all. I recalled Isabel's claim that the villain aspired to the power of kings.

"Who is this man that coerced you?" Mr. Slade urgently asked.

The prime minister shook his head. "I never met him. I don't know his name. Isabel refused to tell me. She was my only link with him."

And the deaths of Isabel, Lock, and Fearon had broken the chain. Slade said, "Can you direct me to the gaming club where you met Isabel?"

Lord John Russell said he couldn't recall, for he had tried to forget those troubled times. Animosity sharpened his expression. He rose stiffly and said, "I could be hanged for what I've done. If you tell your superiors what I've said, I shall deny everything. My word should easily prevail against yours, and you'll find yourself in graver trouble than I." Yet he couldn't hide his terror that his deeds would come to light.

It was clear that Mr. Slade perceived the advantage he held over the prime minister, for he said, "Miss Brontë and I will protect your secrets, under one condition."

A dour, raspy chuckle emanated from Lord John Russell. "You would bargain with me? Your audacity is remarkable." He made as if to leave, but ventured only a few steps before reluctantly pausing.

"Should Isabel's master contact you and demand more favors, inform me at once," Mr. Slade said. "Determine who owns any ships you're asked to give safe passage from England and what cargo they carry. Help me identify and apprehend the villain, and I will shield you from exposure and punishment."

Lord Russell considered. "If you receive an anonymous letter addressed to you at the Foreign Office, you should heed it," he finally said, then left us.

"There seems little more to be learned here," Mr. Slade said. "We may as well go."

Yet he did not move. He regarded me with a strange look that stirred a fluttering sensation in my breast. The trees and darkness isolated us from the crowd at the ball; our only companion was the marble Aphrodite, immobile and silent.

"Your speech to the prime minister carried the day," said Mr. Slade, and I heard new respect and warmth in his voice. "I congratulate you." He added gruffly, "I must also tell you how lovely you look tonight."

Such a stir of pride and happiness arose in me that I could not answer. The night seemed to swell with a freshening breeze, the slow turning of the heavens, and the tide of hope that lapped at my heart.

I am no fanciful young maiden who believes that a summer eve harbors magic, or that a beautiful gown, a waltz, and a successful collaboration can influence destiny. But my relations with Mr. Slade altered that night, and in the days which followed, they continued altering, to my joy and hazard.

21

> ✦

WHAT TRANSPIRED AT THE BALL CAUSED ME SUCH TUMUL-TUOUS emotion that I tossed in my bed that night, my mind awhirl; I then fell into dreams of waltzing with Mr. Slade. I awoke breathless with anticipation of what the day would bring.

When I went into the dining room and joined Mr. Slade and Kate at the breakfast table, he handed me two letters. "These came in the morning post."

One letter was from Anne, the other from Emily. I opened Emily's first, and as I read, consternation filled me. "Emily writes from Haworth. She's left the Charity School. She gives no explanation. What can have happened?"

Mr. Slade's grave expression said he feared that Emily had somehow compromised our inquiries. "What does Anne say?"

Her letter was even more disturbing, as her own words can attest.

My dear Charlotte,

I write in haste to convey important news.

The day after the mysterious visitor came, Mr. Lock and I again dined together. He looked so much more haggard and preoccupied than usual that I was emboldened to ask him what was amiss. With unconvincing haste he attempted to assure me that all was well.

When I confessed I had seen him arguing with a man last night, and asked him if it was this man who troubled him, his countenance went deathly pale. He swayed in his chair. Perspiration on his face glistened in the candlelight. I hurried to him and poured him a glass of wine, which he gulped. I blotted his forehead with a napkin, and he drew shuddering breaths as his color returned.

As soon as he was able, he thanked me for my assistance and apologized for disturbing me. His courtesy while in distress increased my sympathy for Henry Lock. He seemed little more than a boy, and I had an urge to cradle him in my arms. Hesitantly, I suggested he tell me his worries, that perhaps I could help.

There must be something about me that engages other people's trust. Friends, employers, and total strangers have told me their woes. Now Henry Lock confided how he had tried to dissuade his elder brother Joseph from placing him in charge of the family gunworks, for he sensed that his brother had been compelled to retire against his will. Regardless, Mr. Joseph Lock announced his decision to his workers the very next day.

A shudder passed through Henry Lock as he reached this point in his sad tale. "Joseph's wife sent me a message to come home at once. When I arrived, she said he had locked himself in his office and she'd heard a shot." He looked haunted, as though he were reliving his discovery. "I broke down the door and found Joseph slumped over his desk. His head lay in a pool of blood. The room smelled of gunpowder. The pistol had fallen from Joseph's hand, onto the floor."

After murmuring my condolences, I ventured to ask why his brother had taken his life. Mr. Lock told me his brother had left no explanation, but a week after Joseph Lock's death, he began to understand.

"I was working late at the gunworks, reviewing the account books," he told me. "It was after ten at night, and I was alone at my desk. Suddenly the man who came here yesterday stalked into the room. I asked him who he was and what he wanted. The man never gave his name, and to this day, I do not know it. He said, 'I'm here to fetch the guns I ordered from Joseph Lock.'"

A stir of excitement passed through me, for I sensed that I was about to hear something important.

Henry Lock continued, "The man told me to unlock the warehouse. Then he walked out of my office as if he expected me to follow and obey him. I ran after him, calling, 'My brother is dead. I know nothing of your transaction with him. I must see some proof of it before I can give you any guns.'

"There were four other men standing by the warehouse. They grabbed me and threatened to beat me unless I cooperated. I watched helplessly as they carried out crates of guns and loaded them on a wagon. The men all climbed on the wagon and prepared to drive off. The leader told me that my brother had already been paid an agreed-upon price, and that I was bound to keep his bargain now that Joseph was dead. He told me he wanted hundreds of rifles, pistols, and cannons and he would come for them in two weeks.

"I argued that those guns were more than the factory could produce in that time, and I called him a thief. I said I would report him to the law. But he said there were things that my brother wanted kept secret. He mentioned that one concerned a Miss Isabel White, and that this and other secrets would ruin not only Lock Gunworks but Joseph's memory and my good name if they were made public."

Henry Lock exhaled in desolation. "I surmised that Joseph had committed improprieties with the childrens' governess. But it was obvious that he'd done something else, something even more terrible, that had put him under this man's power, and he'd bartered the guns to protect himself, our family, and the firm. I thought that if I honored the bargain, I could avert whatever disaster Joseph had feared. But when the two weeks were up and the men came for the guns,

I had completed only half of them. That man came here yesterday to demand that I deliver the rest."

The candles burned low. Henry Lock, crumbling with despair, admitted that he feared that even should he be able to deliver the guns, the demands would never stop. His firm would go bankrupt, and his family would be destroyed.

"Surely there's some other recourse," I said. "Perhaps your brother's secret isn't as dangerous as you've been led to believe. Have you any idea what it is?"

He had none, he told me. He supposed he would never know the whole truth until the blackmailer made good on his threat and a scandal broke.

Thinking of Mr. Slade, I mentioned I had a friend connected to the Crown who might be able to help him. But Henry Lock begged me not to involve my friend or anyone else. He knew his brother had broken the law, he said, and he could not allow his family to be punished for his sins. The wine in the glass he held trembled as his body shook with fear, but he proclaimed that he would endeavor to produce the guns and pray that the business would be resolved.

I could not share his blind faith, for I believed Isabel White's evil master was behind his troubles and would have no mercy on him. I determined on learning more, and the next day brought an opportunity.

The children went on a holiday with friends. I was left with no duties and a great wish to escape the gloomy house, so I asked the coachman to drive me into Birmingham. There I noticed a man outside a tobacconist's shop. I recognized his distinctive beaked nose and jutting chin. He was the man who had threatened Henry Lock. As he walked away, rash impulse seized me.

I told the coachman to wait, and I hurried out of the carriage. Crowds around the shops blocked my view of the man, and I almost lost him. But I spied him passing the church and ran to catch up. We traversed districts that grew shabbier until the man turned down a dark, forbidding road.

There, moldering tenements bordered a narrow cobblestone pavement. The man entered a dingy brick public house called Barrel and Shot. I peered cautiously through its window into a dim room. The man I'd followed sat drinking amidst others who looked to be crude, unemployed laborers.

So occupied was I that I didn't notice two men enter the street until they neared me. They were rough young scoundrels, their smiles malicious. They advanced on me, and fear caught my breath.

"What in there was you so interested in?" the first man said, pointing towards the Barrel and Shot. I shook my head in mute terror.

"Might be she was lookin' for a man," the other taunted. Nudging elbows, they exchanged sly glances and snickers replete with insinuation, then grabbed my arms. Panic assailed me. I struggled to free myself and pleaded for them to let me go. The men laughed, jeered, and propelled me along the road.

I screamed for help and a constable strode towards us. Some blows from his stick sent my attackers fleeing. He inquired after my well-being, and I replied that I was unharmed and thanked him. The constable escorted me to my carriage, chastising me that this was no place for a lady. I took the opportunity to describe the man in the public house, Henry Lock's tormentor, and asked, "Could you tell me who he is?" The constable said, "No, but he's someone you'd best not associate with, I'm sure."

Yet I felt sure that the man in the public house is a link to the person responsible for Isabel White's murder and Joseph Lock's suicide, as well as the attacks on you, dear Charlotte. I regret that I was unable to discover his identity, and I hope for a chance to rectify my failure.

Anne

After Mr. Slade and I had read this letter, I exclaimed, "If the constable hadn't been near, Anne might have been hurt by those scoundrels! I should have anticipated that she would get herself in trouble. She must leave Birmingham at once!"

That Mr. Slade didn't remind me how he'd warned us of the danger was a credit to his tact. "Indeed, Anne should leave. She has learned more than she realizes. We have her description of Henry Lock's mysterious tormentor, as well as the name of the public house." Mr. Slade narrowed his eyes in contemplation. "The Barrel and Shot is a notorious meeting place of Chartist agitators. I begin to see how the man fits into the scheme of Isabel's master."

"I shall write immediately to Anne and tell her to return home," I said, rising from my chair.

Mr. Slade rose too. "Better yet, we'll fetch her. A trip to Birmingham to find the man Anne saw promises us more good than staying in London in case the prime minister should contact us."

Kate ordered the carriage, while I hurried to pack. Mr. Slade and I boarded the train to Birmingham that very morning.

22

＞✦＜

WE ALL EXPERIENCE EMOTIONS THAT WE WOULD RATHER DIE than confess, and sensations we experience with shame and guilt. To relish what is deplorable seems a sin; that evil can inspire such pleasure shows how wayward is the human flesh. The spectacle of human violence should repel me; yet under some circumstances, I instead feel the same exhilarating passion as when I watch storms rage or the ocean's waves crash. This I learned, to my disgrace, on my trip with Mr. Slade to Birmingham.

When we arrived there, he deposited Anne and me in a lodging house owned by a respectable married couple he knew—the man was a retired East India Company sergeant with whom Mr. Slade had served. Anne and I were given a comfortable room upstairs, where we rejoiced to be together again and talked over our experiences. Our hosts had two sons who worked as police constables. That night, they and Mr. Slade went out to seek the man who had extorted guns from Henry Lock. Anne retired to bed, but I sat up, too restless for sleep. I mused upon how my relations with Mr. Slade had evolved. Although my feelings towards him had gained power, I felt easier with him than any other man I'd ever met. It seemed we had reached some unspoken accord, the paths of our lives had converged, and we traveled side by side towards some unknown destiny. But who was John Slade? I could now count many hours we had spent together; yet all I knew beyond doubt was that he was a man inclined to disappear and leave me waiting.

At dawn, Mr. Slade returned. I hastened to meet him. "What has happened?" I said.

"We arrested three men at the Barrel and Shot," said Mr. Slade. His hair and clothes were disheveled. "One of them may be familiar to you. Another fits Miss Anne's description of the man she followed there. I must ask you both to come to the prison and identify the men."

Mr. Slade escorted us in a hackney cab to the Birmingham prison, a forbidding, brick-built dungeon in Moor Street. Through its barred windows, inmates shouted rude remarks at passersby. Sharp spikes topped the surrounding wall. Outside, constables unloaded shackled men from a horse-drawn van. A warden unlocked the massive, ironclad gate for us. In the lodge, he sent Anne and me into a cubbyhole where a hatchet-faced woman groped over our bodies and under our clothes, seeking hidden weapons or other contraband. While Mr. Slade and the warden escorted us through a maze of gloomy passages lit by guttering gas lamps, I experienced increasing trepidation.

Through rusty window gratings I spied male prisoners marching around the yard. A stench of urine, excrement, and misery grew worse as we proceeded deeper into the prison. The walls and floor of the passage were slick with fetid moisture. Yells, groans, and raucous babble echoed from the prison galleries. Guards dressed in blue uniforms patrolled the corridors, the keys on their belts jangling. Chained prisoners leered at Anne and me as they were marched by. Mr. Slade halted us outside a door that had a small glass pane set at eye level.

"Look inside," Mr. Slade told Anne. "Do you recognize the man you described in your letter?"

Anne peered through the glass; I looked over her shoulder into a room with a scarred plank floor, whitewashed walls, and exposed gas pipes. The two constables stood guard over three men seated on benches at a table. One man had a craggy, beak-nosed face. His right eye was blackened, his clothing stained with blood. Mr. Slade must have fought a strenuous battle to capture the prisoners.

"That is the man who threatened Henry Lock," said Anne.

My attention was caught by another prisoner, seated opposite the one Anne had identified. He wore a black suit, and his head was wrapped in a bandage; he had ginger hair and a cruel, coarse face I would never forget.

"The bandaged man is one of the pair that attacked us on the train and came to the Charity School," I exclaimed.

Mr. Slade flashed a brief, triumphant smile. "I thought I recognized him from your drawing. It seems our hunt was doubly successful. What about the third prisoner?"

This was a fellow whose thin figure, sleek hair, and pointed features gave him the appearance of a greyhound. His narrow eyes shifted and his foot tapped nervously. His suit boasted scuff marks and torn sleeves. Neither Anne nor I had ever seen him before.

Mr. Slade thanked us for our help, then said, "The cab will take you to your lodgings while I interrogate the captives."

Though Anne readily acquiesced, I said, "I want to watch and hear what those men reveal."

Mr. Slade moved between the door and myself, his expression disapproving. "This is not what a lady should witness."

"It can't be worse than the murder I saw," I retorted.

He frowned, clearly impatient to begin the business at hand and loath to argue. "If you insist."

The warden ushered Anne away. Mr. Slade led me into an adjacent room. A window, covered by an iron grate, gave a view into the room which held the prisoners. Mr. Slade drew a chair up to the window for me. "Look all you wish, but be quiet," he said, then departed.

Eagerly I sat. A moment later I saw Mr. Slade enter the other room. The constables stood alert; the prisoners tensed, eyeing Mr. Slade with hostile wariness. I must confess that I felt much sympathy towards the Chartist cause—in spite of the riots perpetrated in its name—for I believed that its demands for a voice in the government were reasonable and its proponents well intentioned. But these men seemed the despicable sort that takes advantage of social unrest as an opportunity to cause trouble

"I've done nothing wrong," my ginger-haired attacker said haughtily, in the voice of a man educated above low-class origins. "Why am I under arrest?"

"I'll ask the questions," Mr. Slade said.

"You might as well let me go," came the reply, "because I've nothing to tell you." The other captives nodded defiantly.

"Oh, but you do," Mr. Slade said. His manner was calm, though edged with determination. "First, you'll tell me your names."

"Joe Blow," my attacker said sardonically.

"Peter Piper," the gun thief and blackmailer said in a rough Northern accent.

"John Jones," said the greyhound. His voice was London Cockney.

Mr. Slade and the constables seized the prisoners, twisted their arms behind them, and slammed them against the wall. The men struggled and shouted curses.

"Your real names, please," Mr. Slade said.

A lady should turn away from the sight of violence and close her ears to foul language. I should have experienced disgust at watching Mr. Slade coerce the prisoners, but his action roused some primitive instinct in me. My breaths came faster; I thrilled to a stir of dark pleasure and leaned closer to the window.

The prisoners capitulated. My attacker revealed himself to be Charles Ogden; the blackmailer was named Sid Jakes; and the third man, Artie Crowe.

"Thank you," Mr. Slade said, as polite as if this were a social occasion. He and the constables shoved the prisoners towards the benches. "You may sit down now."

The men obliged, glaring at Mr. Slade, their hatred like blood in the air. Though dismayed that Mr. Slade would use force to obtain facts, this hitherto unseen dimension of his personality fascinated me. And I had no sympathy towards these criminals.

"Mr. Ogden, why did you and your friend attack the Misses Brontë on the train near Leeds on the eleventh of July? And on whose orders?"

"I don't know what you're talking about," said Ogden. "You have the wrong man." His manner was so plausible that even I, his erstwhile victim, almost believed him.

Mr. Slade turned to Jakes. "Who receives the guns you stole from the Lock Gunworks?"

"I never stole nothing," the blackmailer huffed, but I spied guilty fear in his eyes.

Crowe, the third man, watched this exchange with such caution that I surmised he had something to hide. Mr. Slade flicked a glance at him, then addressed the whole group: "Why were you in the Barrel and Shot?"

"I wanted a drink," said Ogden. I perceived that he was the ringleader. He said belligerently to Mr. Slade, "This is an outrage. You've no right to keep me here. I'm going."

He rose, as did the other men. Mr. Slade blocked the door. "Try if you like." As the men hesitated, a disdainful smile twisted Mr. Slade's mouth. "Ah. You beat helpless women, but you'd prefer to avoid a fight with me. What a coward you are."

Ogden clenched his fists. I saw how much he disliked being mocked in front of his friends. I sat on the edge of the chair, my face close to the grating.

"And you're a fool to obey a master who leaves you to take the consequences of the crimes he orders," Mr. Slade added provocatively.

Angered beyond prudence and forced to assert his masculine courage, Ogden charged at Mr. Slade, who dodged his blows and struck Ogden in the stomach. Ogden bellowed in pain, doubled over, then rammed his head into Mr. Slade's chest. They crashed against the door and grappled with each other. I feared that Mr. Slade would be harmed; yet I trembled with exultation to see his face and muscles strain. I thought of his days as a soldier in the East and as a spy on the Continent. The same hands that had touched me must have done harm, even killed. I did not care.

As Mr. Slade and Ogden fought, Jakes rushed towards the door. A constable grabbed him, and a storm of flying fists engulfed the pair. Mr. Slade flung Ogden at the other constable.

The constable caught Ogden, and they struggled together. My heart beat wildly; gasps parted my lips. Now I understood why men in Haworth flocked to the boxing matches at the Black Bull Inn. Mr. Slade advanced on Crowe, who backed fearfully away.

"Please don't 'urt me!" Mr. Crowe said.

The constables wrestled Ogden and Jakes facedown on the floor and straddled their backs. "I'll spare you if you'll talk," Mr. Slade said to Crowe.

I realized that Mr. Slade had marked Crowe as the weakest member of the group. By overpowering the others, he'd aimed to win a turncoat. Crowe exclaimed, "All right! It's true! Charlie attacked them women. Sid took the guns."

"Shut up!" yelled Ogden, pinned under the constable. His nose bled; his ginger hair dripped with sweat.

Jakes, lying limp and defeated, said to Crowe, "Bloody traitor, you'll pay for ratting on me." In retaliation he addressed Mr. Slade: "He killed that yellow-haired bitch who was governess at Mr. Lock's house."

I stared dumbstruck at Crowe. He was the man I'd seen stabbing Isabel White! Mr. Slade momentarily froze in astonishment that his hunt had netted the murderer. I could scarcely believe that Anne, my little sister, had led us to this revelation. Mr. Slade glanced at me, and we shared satisfaction that one mystery had been solved.

"It was 'im said to do it," Crowe babbled, desperate to excuse himself. "It was 'im told Charlie to kidnap the Brontë woman, and Sid to get the guns."

"Who?" Mr. Slade asked, looming over the cowering man.

"He'll kill us if you tell, you fool!" Ogden shouted.

"Don't say nothin' else!" said Jakes.

They obviously feared their master more than they did the law. Mr. Slade's eyes glinted, registering this fact. "Mr. Crowe, you've confessed to murder. You'll hang for it." Crowe sat on a bench, huddled in dejection. Mr. Slade turned to Ogden and Jakes. "I have witnesses to the blackmail of Henry Lock and the attack on the Misses Brontë. Ordinarily, you would go to prison. But your employer leads a conspiracy to destroy civil order in Europe and undermine the British government. The crimes you have all committed for him make you accomplices to treason, and the penalty for treason is death."

Ogden and Jakes scowled; I could feel panicked thoughts racing through their heads.

"But if you cooperate with me, I'll reduce your sentences," Mr. Slade said. "Give me the name and whereabouts of the man who ordered your crimes, and I'll protect you from him."

I was horrified that these criminals might not be punished to the fullest extent of the law, but I understood Crowe, Ogden, and Jakes were but small game, and Mr. Slade wanted larger prey. Leniency towards them was the price he must pay to capture their master.

Jakes uttered a scornful laugh. "There's nowhere safe from him, and none what can protect us. Betray him, and we're dead."

"Betraying him is your only chance to survive," Mr. Slade said. "When he learns of your arrest, he'll assume you talked whether you did or not. Here are your choices: Help me catch him so that he can't harm you, and you'll go free. Refuse my offer, and either you'll hang or he'll kill you."

A short eternity passed. Jakes and Crowe looked to Ogden, who heaved a breath of resignation and nodded. I admired Mr. Slade because although his strength had gained him an advantage over the men, his cleverness had won him victory. The constables returned Ogden and Jakes to their seats. There the men slumped, diminished by defeat.

Mr. Slade walked to the head of the table. "Who is your employer?"

"He's a Frenchman named LeDuc," Ogden said reluctantly.

At last we could put a name to Isabel White's mysterious master.

"Where can I find him?" Mr. Slade's manner was quiet; only his intense gaze bespoke his eagerness for the information.

"He lives in Brussels," said Ogden.

At Mr. Slade's prompting, Ogden gave an address I did not

catch because such emotion besieged me. The mention of Brussels inevitably recalls the torment I experienced there.

"Who is LeDuc?" Mr. Slade said.

"He belongs to the Society of the Seasons." This, I later learned, was a radical French secret society. Ogden revealed that LeDuc was wanted for fomenting insurrections in Paris and had gone into exile in Belgium.

"How did you meet him?" Mr. Slade asked the prisoners.

"We never did," said Ogden, and the other men echoed him. "He hired us through the Birmingham Political Union." I recognized the name of a local Chartist organization. "He and those union men wanted to spread the revolution to England. He gave them money to pay people to stir up the townsfolk and start riots."

Evidently, a faction within the union had chosen violence as a means to social reform, with the support of the radical Frenchman who must have employed Isabel White as a courier between himself and secret societies around the world. The riots were easy money for Jakes, Ogden, and Crowe, and when the Chartist movement died down, LeDuc found other work for them. Mr. Slade pressed the men for details about the nature of their work.

"'E paid me to snoop around Yorkshire and find out about the Brontë woman," Crowe mumbled, fidgeting. "I broke into the parsonage to steal a book 'e wanted, but someone almost caught me. I 'ad to run." He had been the stranger who'd questioned the Haworth folk and nearly killed Branwell!

And with more pressure, it came forth that Ogden had been the man who chased me at the opera and searched our room at the Chapter Coffee House.

"What did you plan to do with Miss Brontë after you kidnapped her?" Anger tinged Mr. Slade's calm voice, and I liked to think it signified more than ordinary concern on my behalf.

"I was supposed to drive her to Kirkstall Abbey," said Ogden. "Someone was to meet us and take her someplace. I don't know who nor where."

A shiver passed through me. Had Mr. Slade not rescued me,

would I have been transported across the ocean into the hands of the evil LeDuc? Did he want me yet?

Mr. Slade interrogated the prisoners for quite some time, but they appeared to have no further information about LeDuc. "What's going to happen to us?" Jakes demanded.

"For now, you'll stay in prison, under constant guard," Mr. Slade said.

The men sullenly accepted their fate. Mr. Slade exited the room; I met him in the corridor. We walked from the prison, both of us rendered uncomfortable by what I'd seen him do. It was not until we were riding in the carriage that Mr. Slade spoke.

"I'm sorry," he said, looking out the window. "Know that the requisites of my work are as disturbing to me as they must be to you." His profile was strained. "Will you forgive me?"

I said, "I forgive *you*." But I couldn't forgive myself for the thrill I had felt watching him.

Mr. Slade turned to me. Our gazes met, and I saw that he discerned what I'd felt while he'd coerced the criminals. I burned with shame—what a perverse, unnatural woman he must think me! But his face relaxed, and from him eased a breath that was part mirth, part relief. A strange sweetness warmed me. He would not condemn me for the guilty pleasure I had felt because he'd felt it, too. The episode at the prison had been a kind of intimacy we had shared. As the carriage sped through the streets of Birmingham, I waited to hear what Mr. Slade would say.

"It seems that M. LeDuc is the criminal we're looking for," Mr. Slade said. Although he spoke of our investigation and not ourselves, his voice was unsteady. "Perhaps the solution to the mystery lies in Belgium."

23

>+<

H ERE I MUST PAUSE IN MY OWN
NARRATIVE TO RELATE IMPOR-
tant events that concerned my sister Emily. On the evening of the
day we encountered the Birmingham criminals, Anne and Mr.
Slade and I returned to Haworth. I treated Anne with a newfound
respect that she seemed to appreciate. Emily was oddly preoccupied. When I asked her what had happened at the Charity School,
she was reluctant to tell me. I never knew the whole story until
after I read in her journal the following account:

The Journal of Emily Brontë

11 July 1848.

At dawn, I emerged gradually from sleep to find Mrs.
Grimshaw at my bedside. She whispered, "Get dressed, then
meet me in the school hall."

Her stealthy mien lent a sinister air to her command, but
I obeyed. Inside the silent, deserted school, Mrs. Grimshaw lit
candles for us both, unlocked the cellar door, and led me
down the stairway to a dungeon of passages with dirt floors
and damp, rank stone walls. I shuddered, for I sensed the
place to be evil. We entered a cell carved out of the earth. A
little girl stood tied to a wooden pillar by ropes that bound
her wrists and ankles. It was Frances Cullen, my shy pupil.

She wore a thin white shift, and her feet were bare. Her hair was disheveled, her face tearstained. She cringed from us and whimpered. I stared in shock.

"Frances has been naughty," Mrs. Grimshaw said, "and naughty girls must be punished." She handed me a leather strap. "Whip her twenty lashes. Do it hard enough to hurt, but not to leave permanent scars."

This was how I must pay her for excusing my theft! Dumbstruck with horror, I stood frozen. Mrs. Grimshaw walked out of the room and shut the door; her footsteps mounted the stairs. I turned to Frances. She was watching me, her eyes huge with terror. I flung away the strap, set down my candle, knelt beside Frances, and put my arms around her.

"Don't be afraid," I said. "I won't hurt you." Frances's rigid, quaking body went limp against me, and she sobbed. Her misery tore my heart. "Why does Mrs. Grimshaw want you punished so harshly?"

"I made the Reverend Grimshaw angry," Frances whispered.

"How?" I asked, wondering what wrongs this meek, gentle child could have done. She gulped, as if choking on the recollection. "What happened, Frances?" I said urgently.

"I'm not supposed to tell!" she cried.

"I won't tell anyone you did," I promised.

This seemed to reassure Frances. "He bade me accompany him to the windmill," she said in a quavering voice that was so low I could barely hear. "He . . . he ordered me to take off my clothes and lie on the floor and—oh, I'm ashamed to say any more!"

She underwent a spate of trembling, and I felt sick with dismay. It now seemed certain that the Reverend Grimshaw used the windmill for immoral relations with pupils, including Jane Fell and now Frances. I then noticed the blood that trickled down her bare legs, and fresh horror assailed me. Such blasphemy!

"I started to cry," Frances continued in a whisper. "He told me to stop. He said he'd sheltered me and fed me, and I should be glad to repay him." She began to weep. "He hit me and held me down. He said I must learn how to please men and not complain. He hurt me so much." Frances's sobs rose to a hysterical pitch. "He . . . he told Mrs. Grimshaw I'd been bad. She brought me here and tied me up. I've been alone in the dark for hours."

Rage at the Grimshaws burned in me as I unknotted the ropes. "Fear no more," I said. "I won't whip you."

"But you must!" Frances protested, to my surprise. "If you don't, Mrs. Grimshaw will, and she'll do it harder."

We heard footsteps on the stairs: Mrs. Grimshaw was coming to see how the punishment progressed. "Please!" Frances cried.

I took up the strap, raised my skirt, and said, "Scream and cry as loudly as you can."

Twenty times I lashed the strap hard against my own leg and endured the pain, while Frances screamed as though I struck her. After it was done, I felt sore but virtuous for having spared Frances. She later appeared at breakfast looking chastened, and Mrs. Grimshaw gave me a nod of approval. My hatred for the school burgeoned. I could not bear to stay in this place where children were tortured; yet I didn't want to abandon Frances. Though I yearned for home, I couldn't forsake my mission. It seemed likely that Isabel White had suffered the same evils as Frances, but perhaps the school harbored more secrets that I must learn for the sake of Charlotte and our family. Hence, I resolved to stay and persevere.

But after the pupils retired to the dormitory, Mrs. Grimshaw waylaid me. "I saw Frances undressing, and there's not a mark on her," she said, bristling with anger. "You didn't whip her. Next time, do as you're told, or I'll 'ave the police on you."

She left me shaking with dread. I realized I must leave the school, no matter my regrets. That midnight, I quietly dressed, then packed my satchel. I crept outside, intending to walk to town and board the earliest train home. A cool, rest-less wind blew clouds across the stars and the full moon. The trees in the garden tossed their boughs; shadows stirred. As I sped down the path, I noticed a light. It came from the forbid-den windmill.

Curiosity delayed my flight. I crept up to the windmill. Its door was closed, but the lighted window was open. Through it I heard men's voices inside the mill. I peered through the window and saw the Reverend Grimshaw standing in the light from a lantern he held. I had a clear view of his face, but the two men opposite him stood with their backs to me.

"Gentlemen, I no longer wish to do business with you," the Reverend Grimshaw said, his manner at once pompous and fearful.

"It's too late for you to terminate our association," one of the other men said in a high, cultured voice.

"But this has become too dangerous. Rumors about the school are circulating in town. The Church has sent officials to inspect the premises. And the more girls who pass through the school, the greater the chance that one will talk." The Reverend Grimshaw seemed on the verge of weeping. "Please, good sirs—if you don't release me, I shall be ruined!"

"If you renege on your promise, you'll have worse to fear than that the Church will discover the fate of the girls in your charge," said the other man. His voice was deeper, and men-acing. "Would you like everyone to know that you satisfy your carnal desires with your pupils?"

Even in the meager light I could see the Reverend Grimshaw's complexion turn pale.

"You can either fulfill your obligations to us," his adver-sary said, "or be exposed as a foul sinner."

The Reverend Grimshaw cast his gaze upward, as though he expected the heavens to rain fire. Defeat settled upon him. His pomposity deflated, he seemed aged and shrunken. I pitied him not. "I'll fetch her," he said.

He and his companions left the windmill; I followed,

undetected. The Reverend Grimshaw entered the house. The two men walked to the front of the school. I hastened after them, my heart beating fast, my blood racing. In the road stood a carriage and horses. The two men waited beside the carriage, while I hid in the moonlit woods. Presently, down the lane from the school came the Reverend Grimshaw with his lantern. Beside him walked Abigail Weston, once friend to the now-absent Jane Fell. They halted at the carriage. The driver opened its door.

"Where are you taking me?" Abigail asked the men.

Giddy excitement, tinged with fear, inflected her voice. One of the men said, "You're going to London, to live in Paradise."

Was she following in the footsteps of Isabel White? I felt certain that both young women had been mistreated in the same manner as had Frances, and both schooled for some evil purpose. Isabel White's path had led to the criminal she called her master, and a life of sordid intrigue. Alas, I believed that Abigail, Jane, Frances, and other girls at the school were destined for the same.

Abigail and the men rode away in the carriage. The Reverend Grimshaw returned to the school. I trudged along the road until I reached the village.

I write this account as the train carries me homeward. Morning sun now gilds the countryside, but my thoughts dwell in the dark realms of uncertainty. Will my discoveries be of any use to Charlotte and Mr. Slade?

I regret that Emily underwent such distress for my sake. All she told us when Mr. Slade, Anne, and I arrived home was how the girls in the school were beaten and that one had been taken to London by men who promised she would live in Paradise. Mr. Slade received this meager news with profound appreciation.

"Paradise is the name of a London gaming club and house of ill repute," he told Emily. "Its clients are English and foreign politicians, businessmen, diplomats, and nobility. Your observations suggest that Monsieur LeDuc employs girls from the school to draw prominent men into his schemes. He must have discovered Isabel at the school, used her as a courier between himself and the radical societies, and put her to work in the Paradise, where she met the prime minister. You have done well by giving us a place to investigate his doings. I'll put the club under surveillance at once."

Emily seemed indifferent to Slade's praise. We could not have suspected at the time how important her discovery would turn out to be.

"That a school which purports to be a charity would ruin help-less, innocent girls is an outrage!" I exclaimed.

Papa said, "I shall report the Reverend Grimshaw to the Church so that he may be censured and the school closed."

"As they should be," said Slade. "But your taking action against the school will drive Monsieur LeDuc deeper into hiding. I am afraid we must leave it alone until our work is done."

"He's right, Papa," said Anne.

"But the girls will suffer in the meantime," Emily objected in alarm.

"Therefore, it's more important than ever that we find Monsieur LeDuc and put a stop to his evildoing as soon as possi-ble," I said.

"We can catch a train to London tonight and book passage on a ship for Belgium tomorrow," Mr. Slade said to me.

I was thrilled that he would include me in his journey. He prob-ably wished to avoid another argument, yet I dared to wonder if he might have another, more personal motive.

The thought of traveling again, while I was on the verge of col-lapse from exhaustion and nervous strain, was appalling; still I jumped at the chance for another venture with Mr. Slade, and I heard the siren song that the thought of Belgium always stirs in my heart.

"I will be ready," I said.

24

THE STEAM PACKET LABORED ACROSS THE ENGLISH CHANNEL, the paddle wheels churning noisily, funnels belching smoke, and sails billowing. I stood on the deck, my eyes dazzled by the vast ocean that sparkled with cobalt, emerald, and aquamarine lights. Ships dotted the rolling waves. Seabirds wheeled high against the sky's blue brilliance and majestic white clouds. I relished the salty wind. Mr. Slade and I had sailed from London on that day of 14 August, then boarded the Channel packet in Dover. Now the Continent came into view. The coast was a line of golden sunshine, touched with viridian green. As the ship bore me toward that coast I marveled that my quest had once again led me into the past.

Twice before had I made this journey. The first time, in 1842, Papa had escorted Emily and me to school in Brussels. There I found the new sights, acquaintances, and knowledge I had longed for. I also gained other experiences that I could never have anticipated.

It began innocently enough. At age twenty-five I was older than my classmates at the Pensionnat Heger, a Protestant among Catholics, a shy Englishwoman surrounded by gregarious, French-speaking Belgians. The only person who paid me any particular attention was Monsieur Heger, husband of the school's mistress, a professor who instructed his wife's pupils. His ruthless criticism of my essays made me cry; his praise thrilled me. He was a small, black-haired, black-bearded man of ugly face and irritable temper, but his keen intellect stimulated my mind. Soon my heart beat fast at the sight of him. In the evenings I chanced to meet him in the garden, where he smoked his cigars and we debated the merits of various authors. I thought of us as master and pupil, nothing more. Not until Emily and I returned home did I realize that I had deeper feelings for M. Heger.

My second voyage across the Channel occurred in 1843. I returned alone to Brussels, eager to take up a position as an English teacher at the school. But Madame Heger began watching me and behaving coldly towards me. I never saw M. Heger except from a distance. Our lessons and talks ceased. Madame had discovered I was in love with her husband, and she had separated us. I stayed in Belgium until my health and spirits failed, and I at last recognized the sin and futility of loving a married man. I returned home, broken and grieving. My punishment was years of writing to M. Heger, begging him for letters that never came. That I loved him, and he cared naught for me, still hurts me. I am still plagued by a sense of unfinished business.

Yet now, by a strange fortune, I found myself again bound for Brussels. I felt a familiar jumble of excitement, fear, and hope. I traveled as if upon a dark, turbulent sea of memory.

Mr. Slade joined me at the railing. His folded arms rested close beside mine; the wind ruffled his black hair. My heartbeat quickened for him as it once had for M. Heger.

"The sea refreshes even the most aggrieved mind," Mr. Slade said in a quiet, musing tone.

I had discovered this to be true, and I wondered what experience had inspired Mr. Slade's remark. "Whenever I am near the sea, I feel such awe, exhilaration, and freedom." Those emotions surged through me now. "Its magnificence elevates me above my petty concerns."

Mr. Slade gave me a sidelong look. "Such magnificence dwarfs mankind and shows us how weak we are compared to the forces of nature."

"Indeed," I said, "but for me, the ocean inspires a glorious sense that anything is possible. I feel myself to be in the presence of God."

Mr. Slade's expression turned remote. "I wish I could share your delight in His presence," he said. "There was a time when I renounced God for His cruelty."

His harsh words shocked and appalled me.

"There was a time when I wished never to cross this sea again because I couldn't bear to face the past," he said.

I saw that Mr. Slade was reflecting upon memories which were no less bitter than mine. The sea had worked some enchantment on us, bringing our deepest secrets close to the surface. Launched free from land and ordinary restraints, we could talk frankly.

"Did something go wrong in your work as a spy?" I asked.

A humorless laugh gusted from Mr. Slade. "Had I concentrated solely on spying, misfortune would have spared me." Silence ensued while he contemplated the distant shore. Then he began to speak in a voice drained of emotion: "One of the men I spied upon was a French professor at the Sorbonne in Paris. He led a secret society that aimed to overthrow King Louis Philippe. I posed as an aspiring radical French journalist and was admitted to the society. The professor had a daughter named Mireille. She kept house for him and wrote political tracts about corruption in the court. She was the most beautiful, enchanting woman I had ever met."

A note of yearning nostalgia crept into Mr. Slade's voice. Much as I wanted to hear his story, I did not like to listen to him praise another woman for traits I clearly lacked.

"Mireille was a Catholic and a fiery, passionate Frenchwoman," Mr. Slade continued, "while I was a serious Briton and ordained clergyman of the Church of England. She was a rebel, and I the agent bound to destroy her and her comrades. In spite of our differences, we fell in love."

Though my spirit recoiled from hearing of his love for another woman, I felt a poignant kinship with Mr. Slade: We both had loved unwisely. I recalled his sister Kate's allusion to a broken heart and presumed that this affair had not ended well.

"Mireille and I married," said Mr. Slade. "We were very poor and lived in a garret, but we were happy together. Soon she was expecting our child. She didn't know that I wasn't what I seemed— until one night shortly before the child was due to be born. A man in the society had learned my true identity. He told her I was a British spy. That night she confronted me with her knowledge. She was enraged, hysterical. She accused me of betraying her and her cause. I tried to calm her and apologize for lying to her. I said that since we'd met I had grown sympathetic to the rebels, which I truly had. I swore that I'd never reported on her or her comrades to my superiors, as indeed I had not. I had betrayed my own cause for love of her. But Mireille refused to believe me. She called me a filthy scoundrel, then ran out of the house."

Mr. Slade stood motionless, his hands steady on the railing, his manner stoic. "I let Mireille go because I was too proud to follow. I thought she would soon return and we would make peace. But the next night, the police raided the professor's house during a meeting of the secret society. They arrested all the members. Mireille was among them. The police took everyone to prison. The professor was executed for treason. And Mireille—"

The muscles of Mr. Slade's throat contracted. "She gave birth to our son in prison that night. He was stillborn. She died some hours afterward, hating me." Mr. Slade paused and, with a visible struggle, regained his composure. "Never have I spoken of this to anyone."

What shock, horror, and compassion I felt! "I am so sorry," I murmured, inadequate to comfort him, yet glad he'd confided in me.

His gaze was fixed on some inner horizon. "Seven years have passed since Mireille's death. Seven years during which I threw myself into my work because I had nothing else, though I'd come to doubt the morality of what I did. Mireille taught me to see the rebels as people oppressed by their rulers, the allies of my superiors. I closed my mind to those thoughts, and closed myself to anybody who might gain my affection and cause me more pain. But now I see the sun rising after a night I expected to last forever. I begin to think that God is benevolent as well as cruel; He compensates for what he takes away."

Bemusement inflected Mr. Slade's quiet voice. He glanced at me, but I instinctively averted my eyes so that I missed the look in his. He spoke in words almost inaudible: "I begin to find happiness and meaning in life again."

My hands tightened on the rail. I wanted to believe that our companionship was the cause of his renaissance; yet I knew that his beautiful, beloved wife was my rival, even though she was dead. Now I faced a dismal fact: I was as much in love with Mr. Slade as I had been with M. Heger, in spite of there being as little prospect for requital. Perhaps the search for Isabel White's master was what had diverted Mr. Slade from his grief; perhaps he endured my company only because he wanted me to draw the criminal out of hiding.

As with my previous journeys, what happened in Brussels was something I could never have anticipated.

> ←

We disembarked at Ostend, where we caught a train for Brussels. As we traveled across the flat, bare Belgian countryside, I gazed out the window. The sky was a leaden, uniform grey; the air was warm, stagnant, and humid. Pollarded willow trees edged fields tilled in a patchwork of green hues; torpid canals lined the roadsides. Painted cottages added specks of color to the serene landscape which gave no hint of the many wars fought here. First conquered by Julius Caesar, Belgium was later ruled by the Franks, by the Dukes of Burgundy, and then the Hapsburgs; these were followed by the Holy Roman Emperors of Austria and Spain, by France under Napoleon, and by Holland under the Prince of Orange. Belgium finally won independence in 1831, and it kept peace during the revolutions this year. Here I, too, had won a battle—to tear myself away from M. Heger before my love for him destroyed me.

Upon reaching Brussels, I rode with Mr. Slade in a carriage

through the avenues. Medieval houses still sheltered in cobbled lanes near boulevards lined with stately mansions. Colorful open-air cafes and markets still bustled; the air still smelled of the foul River Senne. Burghers clad in dark coats and hats abounded, as did peasants in rustic garb. Voices babbled in French and Flemish. I couldn't help searching the crowds for M. Heger. We entered the Grand Place, the main square in the lower city. The bell in the tower of the Gothic town hall tolled seven o'clock. Gas lamps illuminated the scrolled gables, fanciful statuary, and elaborate gold ornamentation that graced the merchant guild houses. In the east, the towers of the Church of St. Michel and Ste. Gudule rose majestically on the hillside. I gazed beyond it, towards the aristocratic upper city, where the Pensionnat Heger stood.

Mr. Slade secured us lodgings in the Rue du Marché aux Herbes, at the Hotel Central. Such palatial elegance! Such glittering mirrors and chandeliers! Such a smart clientele! My spacious room was furnished with brocade chairs, fluted lamps, and luxurious Flemish carpets and tapestries. I spent my first evening there, and much of the following day, while Mr. Slade went out to recruit his friends among the Brussels police on a hunt for the exiled French radical LeDuc.

He returned the next day at dusk. We sat together in the hotel's candlelit dining room, where ornate silver and fine crystal sparkled on tables laid with white linen. Suave waiters served us wine, mussels in garlic and cream, and rabbit stew. The rich food overwhelmed my palate. I felt drab among the fashionable diners. Mr. Slade looked handsome in his evening dress, but weary and discouraged.

"We found LeDuc," he said. " An odd, repulsive fellow he is—not above four feet high, with a bald head, pale, blazing eyes, and an arrogant manner. He lives in a dirty attic room, and he was conveniently at home."

"What happened?" I asked, wondering why he didn't act happier to have located our quarry.

"At first he denied any connection with the Birmingham Chartists, but after the police roughed him up a bit, he changed his mind. He claims to take orders from a man who is immensely wealthy and extremely secretive. This man told LeDuc to instruct the Birmingham Chartists to take guns from Joseph Lock and murder Isabel White. He paid well for these services, and his money also went towards financing the recent insurrection in France. However, LeDuc doesn't know the man's name. They are in frequent contact, and they meet in person, yet LeDuc has never set eyes on him."

"How can that be?" I said in puzzlement.

"Whenever the man wants LeDuc, he sends a carriage. The driver blindfolds LeDuc and drives him to a house. When he arrives, he and his master talk together. His blindfold stays on the entire time, so he doesn't know where the house is or what it looks like. Nor can he describe his host. Afterward, the carriage takes him home. LeDuc stuck to his story even when the police threatened him with prison." Mr. Slade drank his wine, as if to swallow his exasperation. "I'm forced to believe Leduc is telling the truth, and the criminal we seek isn't him, but his nameless master."

We had come all the way to Brussels to discover that we had misidentified our quarry and the chase was at a dead end. "LeDuc must have noticed something about the man that might identify him, or something about the house that will help us locate it," I said.

"He furnished two observations," said Slade. "The house has a peculiar, sweet smell. And the man speaks French with an odd foreign accent that LeDuc didn't recognize."

These seemed meager clues to me. As Slade and I sat in mutual discouragement, a waiter approached me. "*Excusez-moi, Mademoiselle, mais vous avez un visiteur.*"

"A visitor? For me?" I said, so startled that I forgot my French and spoke in English.

The waiter said, "*C'est un gentilhomme, qui vous attende au jardin,*" then departed.

Mr. Slade regarded me with alarm. "What gentleman knows you're in Brussels?"

"I cannot imagine," I said.

"He must have traced you here." Excitement animated Mr.

Slade, and I knew he referred to the criminal we sought. "He has come to you, or sent one of his henchmen, as we hoped he would."

We hurried to the glass doors and peered out at the garden, but trees concealed my visitor. "I cannot go out there," I said, shrinking back in terror.

"You must. This may be our only hope of capturing the criminal." Mr. Slade took hold of my shoulders, gazed intently into my eyes, and spoke with adamant insistence: "You've nothing to fear. You won't be alone. I'll be watching every moment."

His determination overcame my resistance; I nodded. "Wait a few minutes while I steal into the garden from the back," he said, then rushed from the room.

I stood quaking with fright, unwilling to leave the safety of the hotel. But I could not throw away what might be our mission's only hope of success. Nor could I waste the work for which my sisters had risked their safety. I opened the door and stepped outside.

The setting sun gilded the garden. The day's lingering heat engulfed me as I crept down the flagstone path. I heard crickets chirping, birds singing, carriages in the streets, and the pounding of my own heart. Rosebushes bordered the path, and each ragged breath I drew filled my lungs with the sweetness of the blossoms. Ahead stood a gazebo. I perceived a man standing inside at the same instant I smelled pungent smoke from the cigar he held. Memories too potent to articulate halted my progress. I stared in astonishment as the man stepped out of the gazebo and walked towards me.

"So, Miss Charlotte," he said in the brusque, heavily accented English that I'd not heard for almost five years, other than in my dreams. "We meet again."

He doffed his hat to me. His black hair and beard were streaked with grey, and time had etched new wrinkles around the eyes behind his spectacles; but otherwise his stern visage was the same as that which lived in my memory.

It was M. Heger.

25

⇥⇤

I STOOD TRANSFIXED WHILE MY LIPS FORMED SOUNDLESS WORDS. I FELT faint and dizzy; a violent trembling seized me.

"Is this how you greet your old teacher?" M. Heger snapped. His face took on the same fierce scowl as when he'd discovered mistakes in my essays long ago. "Shameful! Deplorable!"

Composure failed me: I burst into hysterical weeping. M. Heger's expression softened, the way it always had after his savage criticism wounded me. He tenderly dried my tears with his handkerchief.

"Ah, *petite cherie*, do not cry," he said. "The shock, it was too much for you. I should not have arrived without warning. My sincerest apologies."

While M. Heger patted my shoulder and murmured endearments, I cried for anguish remembered; I cried for joy. And when it ended, I was calm as the sea after a storm.

"How did you know to find me here?" I asked. "Why have you come?"

"It is a strange story," he said with a characteristic shrug. "This morning I received a letter from someone who did not sign his name. This letter said that my old pupil Charlotte Brontë was at the Hotel Central, and would I kindly deliver to her the enclosed message."

M. Heger gave me a small white envelope. So dazed I was that

I didn't think to wonder at the meaning of this happenstance. I simply put the envelope in my pocket.

"I must admit that this errand for a mysterious stranger was just a—how do you say it?—a pretext for coming," M. Heger said. "I wished to see Miss Charlotte, to know how the years have treated her."

His penetrating gaze examined my face. I worried that I must seem aged and ugly to him. Concern, sympathy, and sadness played across his Gallic features. "Life has brought you suffering, *oui?*" he said. Then he smiled. "But the impassioned spirit still burns bright within you."

His perception had always rendered me transparent. Now I felt a tinge of anger that he should treat me with such familiarity. "If you wanted to know of me, then why did you break off all communication between us? Why did you not answer my letters?"

Sorrow and guilt clouded M. Heger's face. "How I treated you has long disturbed my conscience. I will explain, if you will grant me the honor of listening. Shall we walk together?"

M. Heger drew my arm through his, and we strolled the paths. It was as if some magic spell had transported us back in time to the garden behind the Pensionnat. The smoke from his cigar and the scent of the roses completed the illusion.

"Let us imagine that there was once a man who lived in this very city," said M. Heger. "He was respectably married to a woman of impeccable character. He was a teacher, she the *directrice* of a school for young ladies. A fitting match, *non?*"

I nodded as I understood that M. Heger was telling his own story.

"Perhaps their marriage had been arranged for convenience," M. Heger went on, in the same dispassionate voice. "Perhaps their souls spoke different languages. But they had four beautiful children, the esteem of their acquaintances, a modest fortune, and a comfortable place in the world. The man had his profession. He thought himself happy. Then one day the man met a new pupil at his wife's school," M. Heger said as we circled the gazebo. "This pupil was *une demoiselle anglaise*. She was little, poor, and plain, but such a rare, wonderful intellect she had!"

Awe inflected M. Heger's tone, and I grew hot with embarrassment at my entry into the story.

"Such a thrill it was for the man to instruct *la demoiselle anglaise*," said M. Heger. "She responded to his teaching as no other pupil ever had. She read, she wrote, she studied with a passion that matched his own. At first he thought his interest in her to be purely professional. When he noticed her growing attachment to him, he told himself it would benefit her education." Self-mockery tinged M. Heger's smile. "But alas, things are never so simple between male and female, are they?"

My heart began to pound in anticipation.

"The man believed he was only flattered by his pupil's affection. He believed that the new meaning he had found in life was due to his success in teaching her. When they walked and talked together in the evenings, he convinced himself that he regarded her only as his star pupil. He did not notice that all his attention was for her, until his wife confronted him. 'You have fallen in love with *la demoiselle anglaise*,' she said." Exhaling deeply, M. Heger shook his head. "And the man realized it to be true."

M. Heger was confessing that he had loved me! This was shock upon shock, and my legs buckled. M. Heger hastened me into the gazebo and seated us on a bench.

"Why didn't you tell me then?" I cried. "Why did you let me think you cared nothing about me and withdraw your friendship from me?"

"Ah, *petite cherie*, what else could I have done?" M. Heger's voice was rueful. "To have revealed my feelings for you would have encouraged yours for me, *non*? Together we must surely have succumbed to temptation. I had no choice but to cast you off. And although I treasured every letter from Miss Charlotte, I could not reply, lest our correspondence provoke me to rush across the sea towards her."

His revelation was balm to my hurt pride. A peaceful quiet enveloped us as the sunlight faded to a coppery glow and cool shadows gathered in the garden. "Time quenches desire and transforms love into affection," M. Heger said, voicing my own thoughts. "Can we put the ills of the past behind us and remember its good? Can you forgive me?"

"Gladly," I said with all my heart.

A look of worry persisted on M. Heger's face. He said, "Yet I wish I had given you more than pain."

I felt like a fairy tale princess awakened by the shattering of a spell. I thought of the stories I'd penned before we met—those pointless, rambling, overwrought tales that are fit only for scrap paper. I recalled the days of writing *Jane Eyre* and hearing M. Heger's voice inside my head: *Clumsy expression! Unnecessary verbiage! You must sacrifice, without pity, everything that does not contribute to clarity, verisimilitude, and effect!* The suffering I endured as a result of my love for him now seemed worth the book which was as much a product of his teaching as of my own creation.

"You gave me something more valuable than you ever thought," I said.

I told M. Heger about my literary success, and he was deeply gratified. When I told him of my business in Belgium, he expressed surprise, wished me good fortune, and clasped my hands. He espied that I wore no wedding ring.

"You are not married," he said regretfully. Then a mischievous twinkle lit his eyes. "But perhaps your state may change." He cocked his head towards the hotel. "Who is that gentleman over there who has been watching us?"

To my surprise, I saw Mr. Slade standing not far away. I had all but forgotten our plan for him to protect me and trap the criminal. He had apparently deduced that I was in no danger. I was mortified that Mr. Slade had witnessed my display of emotion, yet amused by his obvious perplexity.

"He regards you with a possessive interest." M. Heger asked slyly, "Is he your suitor?"

"No," I said, abashed.

M. Heger smiled in a manner that said he, with his worldly Gallic wisdom, knew better than I. "I wish happiness to you both," he said.

We bade each other an affectionate farewell. M. Heger kissed my hand; then I stood in the gazebo and watched him walk briskly away. He paused to give Mr. Slade a formal bow. Then M. Heger was gone.

Mr. Slade hurried to me. "Who the devil was that?"

I felt as though I had journeyed into another sphere and abruptly returned, with an enormous weight lifted off my shoulders. "An old friend. His name is Constantin Heger."

"How did he find you here?"

I explained. Now that my shock at seeing M. Heger had abated, the circumstances that brought about our reunion seemed more and more implausible.

"For your friend to be mysteriously sent to you can be no harmless coincidence," Mr. Slade said. "Where is the letter he brought?"

"Here," I said, producing it from my pocket. Mr. Slade sat on the bench beside me as I opened the envelope and removed two sheets of white paper exuding an unfamiliar sweet, exotic fragrance. They were covered with elegant handwriting in black ink. I read aloud:

> My dear Miss Brontë,
>
> Please forgive me for addressing you before we have established a formal acquaintance. Although we have yet to be introduced, you certainly know of me. Indeed, you ventured to Bradford, and to the Reverend Grimshaw's Charity School, in search of information regarding myself. Perhaps our mutual friend Isabel White mentioned me when you traveled to London together, or in the book she gave you. Therefore, you cannot regard me as a stranger. And I, who have closely studied you in recent weeks, have learned much about you.
>
> I know that your father is vicar of St. Michael's Church in Haworth and that he was widowed upon the death of your mother in 1821. Your brother is the village wastrel. You were educated at the Clergy Daughters' School in Cowan Bridge, Miss Wooler's School in Roe Head, and the Pensionnat Heger in Brussels. You and your sisters have eked out a meager living as governesses.
>
> I am intrigued that you, with your humble history and impoverished circumstances, should involve yourself in world affairs far beyond the realm of your existence. That you have followed my trail, and come so close to me, indicates that you

are a woman of rare character. My interest in you, and yours in me, have induced me to take the liberty of sending you this message by way of M. Heger, the Belgian gentleman to whom you once sent many letters.

It is with regret that I confess to a previous attempt at contacting you. That was, as you might surmise, the incident at Leeds Station. My two colleagues disobeyed my orders to treat you with proper courtesy. Please accept my apologies for their rudeness. Now let us make our acquaintance under more civilized conditions.

Will you do me the honor of dining with me tomorrow evening? I wish to discuss with you a proposal to serve our common interests. I will send a carriage to your hotel at six o'clock. Should you decide to accept my invitation, all you need do is enter the carriage, and you shall be brought to me.

Much as I would like to include your cousin who is traveling with you, I must ask that you come alone.

I hope that tomorrow will mark the onset of a mutually rewarding association.

"There's no signature," I told Mr. Slade. "But can there be any question about who wrote this letter?" Horror filled me. "It was Isabel White's master!"

"How extraordinary that he should communicate with you, just when we thought we would never find him," Mr. Slade said.

I hurled away the letter as though it carried the plague. "He knows so much about me. Your true identity seems one of the few things he hasn't learned from spies he sent to loiter in Haworth and question the villagers."

He must have heard from the gossipy postmistress about my letters to M. Heger. My revulsion immediately turned to terror. "He's been following me all along, waiting for his moment to approach me," I cried. "He knows where I am. He's here in Brussels." I jumped up, and my frantic gaze roamed the garden, the roofs of the buildings surrounding the hotel, and the darkening sky.

"If he wanted to attack you, he would have done so already,"

Mr. Slade said. "He means to lure you with this." Mr. Slade retrieved the letter, which had fallen to the ground.

"I can't go," I said, aghast at the thought of delivering myself to the man whose minions had murdered Isabel White and Isaiah Fearon and who had almost killed my brother.

"And you won't," declared Mr. Slade. He examined the letter and envelope. "These give no clue to who or where the criminal is, but when the carriage comes for you tomorrow, the police and I shall follow it."

"Will the carriage go to him even if I'm not inside?" I said doubtfully.

"If it doesn't, we'll arrest the driver and force him to reveal who his master is."

I hated to find fault with Mr. Slade's plan, but I said, "The criminal keeps his identity a secret even from his henchmen. What if the driver knows as little about him as M. LeDuc did?"

"He should at least know where he was ordered to take you," Mr. Slade said.

"By the time you find out, the criminal might have already vanished," I said. "We'll have lost what may be our only chance to catch him. He'll realize that I have tried to trap him, and he'll go to ground." Another possibility frightened me: "He may retaliate against me by attacking my family again."

Mr. Slade regarded me with exasperation. "Then tell me what you think we should do."

Despite my terror, I didn't wanted to go home empty-handed, to face my family's disappointment and admit that I was neither as brave nor capable as I had purported to be. I confess that I hoped to impress Mr. Slade, for what else did I have to offer him beyond my willingness to risk my life in his service?

"I must accept the invitation," I said. Mr. Slade exclaimed in protest, but I told him, "When the carriage arrives, I will go where it takes me. You and the police can follow. I will lead you to the criminal."

26

>‹‹

DUSK DESCENDED UPON BRUSSELS AS I STOOD WAITING OUTSIDE the Hotel Central. Lights shone from streetlamps and crowded cafes along the boulevard. People strolled; carriages escorted by liveried footmen sped past me. The sky glowed lavender; the mild air sparkled. Lively orchestral music drifted from the park, while I shivered in my plain cloak and bonnet. The evening ahead of me spread like a black abyss from which I might never emerge. How I regretted persuading Mr. Slade that I should accept this invitation! Too soon would I venture within reach of the hands that had instigated murder. I longed to dash into the hotel and hide, but the church bells rang the hour of six o'clock. A black carriage drawn by black horses stopped at the hotel. The driver stepped down and approached me.

"Mademoiselle Brontë?" he said.

He wore a black cape, and a black hat obscured his face. I nodded. The presence of Mr. Slade and the police, waiting in carriages parked along the street, did not ease my trepidation. The driver opened the carriage door. Compelled by the momentum of the events that had led up to this instant, I stepped into the carriage and sat. The driver shut the door, enclosing me in darkness. His whip cracked. The carriage began to move amidst such racketing wheels and clattering hooves that I couldn't determine whether Mr. Slade and the police were following. I tried to open the windows to look, but I found them fastened shut. I rattled the door; it was locked. I was trapped in the vehicle, which gathered speed and bore me towards an unknown fate.

The carriage veered sharply around corners. The driver seemed determined to evade pursuit. Our route comprised many twists and turns through the city. Motion and fear engendered nausea as I braced myself for a collision. I heard water flowing and felt the carriage rise, then descend, crossing a bridge over the river. I smelled rotting fish in the quayside market. But I soon lost all sense of direction. I prayed that Mr. Slade and the police would be able to keep up with me.

On and on we sped. The city noises faded; clattering cobblestones gave way to rutted earth; I smelled damp soil and fetid marsh. Perhaps two hours passed before the carriage abruptly stopped. Silence rang in my ears. My fear congealed into a cold sickness. I heard the driver climb down from his perch, and his footsteps approaching. The door opened, and lantern light diffused around his figure, which blocked my view of what was outside. He handed me a soft, dark cloth.

"*Bandezvous les yeux,*" he said.

I recalled that M. LeDuc had gone blindfolded to meet his master. Now I must do the same. With unsteady fingers I tied the cloth over my eyes. The driver pulled me from the carriage into the night. Through the utter darkness that shrouded me I heard wind whispering through trees and insects shrilling. Hands grasped me and propelled me forward. Two pairs of footsteps accompanied mine as I stumbled on broken flagstones. My unseen escorts never spoke. I gasped with terror, on the brink of fainting.

Was Mr. Slade near? I almost called out his name. Would the criminal guess we meant to trap him? If so, would Mr. Slade rescue me, or would this journey end in catastrophe? Death had become a clear, immediate danger rather than a vague threat in the distant future.

My escorts led me up a flight of stairs. A door creaked open, and the hush of an interior space surrounded me. I breathed stale, musty air. Our footsteps rang on a stone floor. The door closed behind us with a heavy, echoing thud, and my heart sank, for I feared I was locked in a place where Mr. Slade could not reach me. Finally my escorts and I halted. I smelled savory food odors and the same exotic scent that had perfumed the invitation. My escorts seated me in a chair, and their footsteps receded.

"Good evening, Miss Brontë," said a man's voice that was quiet, low-pitched, suave, and foreign. "You may remove your blindfold now." He blurred his consonants in an odd, musical accent that I could not place.

I pulled off the blindfold. I was sitting at the end of a long table lit by candles. Before me lay a meal of soup, roast fowl, potatoes, vegetables, bread, cheese, and a tart, served on flowered china and accompanied by ornate silver, wine in a crystal goblet, and a linen napkin. The room was large, the windows covered in tattered red velvet, the walls hung with faded tapestries that depicted mounted hunters pursuing stag in a forest. The coffered ceiling was festooned with spiderwebs. But where was the man who had just spoken?

"Your presence does me an honor," he said. "A thousand thanks for accepting my invitation."

His voice emanated from behind a lattice screen at the far end of the table. He could see me through the lattice, but I could not see him.

"Who are you?" I said in a quavering voice. "Why did you bring me here?"

He laughed—a hushed, silvery sound that prickled my skin. "All in good time, my dear Miss Brontë. First you must please eat."

Fear clenched my stomach into a knot that spurned food. None was set before him: He intended to remain hidden while watching me. I fought an urge to run. If Mr. Slade and the police were near, I must wait for them to capture my host and rescue me. If they had lost track of me during that wild ride, then I was on my own, I knew not where, at the mercy of a criminal. I lifted my spoon, dipped it into the soup, and pretended to sip the steaming liquid.

"The philosophers of my kingdom believe that one's fortune can be read in the face," said my invisible host. "Will you allow me to tell you what I see in yours, Miss Brontë?"

His voice possessed a strange quality that calmed me as though I'd drunk a soporific, and it inclined me to let him lead the talk where he wished. I nodded.

"I see intelligence, courage, and honesty," he said. "I see kindness, loyalty, faith, and a struggle between fear and will, desire and caution, in your beautiful eyes. The ravages of suffering accompany the strength of spirit. The future promises you danger, adventure, sorrow, and happiness."

Perhaps I shouldn't have been susceptible to flattery at such a time, but the power of the fortuneteller strengthened his hold over me. However, I was not yet so beguiled that I forgot my own purposes. "Now that you have appraised me, might I see you and read your character and fortune?" Now that I was almost face to face with evil, I wanted to look it in the eye.

Again he laughed, as though pleased by my wits even while he mocked me. "Ah, Miss Brontë, you must earn the privilege."

"How?" I set down my spoon, abandoning any pretense of eating.

"You must describe for me the events in your life that shaped you into the woman who has traveled across land and ocean in search of me," he said. "Where shall we begin?" There was a suspenseful, anticipatory pause. "Tell me about the death of your mother."

My mother's death was a wound that still caused pain. My defenses bristled that this arrogant stranger would dare to probe that wound. "I would rather not," I said coldly.

His shadow stirred behind his screen; I heard the silken rustle of his garments. "Come now, Miss Brontë. Your honorable mother deserves a better tribute than your silence." His tone was reproachful. "And I wish to hear the story."

I realized that if Mr. Slade were able to save me, he would have by now. I was alone, and I must obey my host or risk provoking his wrath. And strangely, I felt a need to talk: It was as if he had unlocked some door inside me. I recalled a passage from Isabel White's book: *His voice was like velvet and steel, probing the recesses of my mind. Many questions did He ask me, and many secrets did He elicit.*

"She took ill when I was five," I said, halting and nervous. "She went to her bed and was unable to get up. Papa insisted that my sisters and brother and I play outside because she couldn't bear our noise."

Memory showed me Papa's careworn face, the closed door behind which Mama lay wasting, and Maria, Elizabeth, Emily, Anne, Branwell, and myself walking the moors together. My childhood feelings of woe and confusion now returned "When we went home in the evening, we could hear her moaning. Papa sat and prayed by her all night." I remembered his prayers rising above the terrible sounds of Mama's anguish, and experienced anew the fear I had felt. "She grew weaker, until one day Papa called us into her room."

The image of my mother, so thin, pale, and still, rose up before me. Papa sat beside her while we children stood at the foot of the bed. "We stayed with her until she died."

As Mama drew her last breath, Branwell slipped his hand into mine. I had forgotten that, and telling the story had restored this lost detail of Mama's passing. Tears streamed down my cheeks.

"How sad that the untimely death of your mother was not your only childhood misfortune," said my host. "Did you not also lose your two elder sisters?"

Though his voice exuded sympathy, his words compounded my pain. I could not bear to think of Maria and Elizabeth now, let alone submit to interrogation about them.

"Did you stand by their deathbeds?" my host pressed. "Did you pray for their spirits as they departed this world?"

"I did for Elizabeth," I said, compelled to answer in spite of myself. *From Him I could hide nothing,* Isabel had written. "But I didn't know Maria was dying until it was too late. She and Elizabeth took ill at our boarding school. They were sent home, while I stayed at school. Papa brought me home in time to see Elizabeth again." The candle flames quivered and reflected in my tears. "But I never got to say goodbye to Maria."

"Your story causes me sorrow beyond words," my host said. Indeed, he sounded sincerely grieved. As I wept, his compassion soothed me, and I quite forgot that it was he who had dredged up my worst memories. After my tears subsided, he said, "We shall dwell no longer upon tragedy. Let us next discuss your experiences in the noble profession of teaching. How admirable that you once attempted to found your own school."

Alas, the school was another painful episode of my life that his spies had uncovered. "I obtained a Continental education so that I could offer lessons in French," I said. "I sent prospectuses to everyone I knew, but not a single pupil could I get. Haworth is too remote and dreary a location."

"The school was doomed despite all your effort," said my host. "It is not your fault that you were unable to assure independent means for your sisters and yourself."

This I believed; but there persisted a nagging suspicion that my dislike of teaching, and a secret wish to fail, had undone my best efforts. And though my host's voice conveyed no criticism, I thought I deserved the blame. I felt like a pathetic wretch, despite my literary success, which he seemed unaware of; at the time, even I could almost believe it had never happened.

"A woman in your position can secure her future by marrying," my host said. "Why did you not?"

He seemed to know my every sensitive spot, and now he had touched the sorest. "I didn't want to marry either of the two men who wanted to marry me," I answered, driven to justify myself. "They were as ill suited to me as I to them."

"Perhaps your unique character has destined you for solitude."

He spoke this as a compliment, yet with a ring of prophecy that discouraged my lingering hope that I would find love. That Mr. Slade did not come to my rescue seemed incontrovertible proof that he was not meant for me.

"But do not despair, Miss Brontë," my host said. His voice breathed comfort through his screen towards me. "I appreciate you as other men cannot. You have in me a friend who values the rare qualities that everyone else overlooks. I shall reward you for your many hardships and failures."

I felt so lost, hopeless, and alone that I could almost believe him to be the only person in the world who cared for me. I dimly realized that he had worked this same spell on Isabel White. *He seemed the one person in the world who knew me and accepted me with all my faults. Every piece of myself that I gave Him purchased His favor in some inexplicable way, and I desired His favor above all else.* He must have shown her the futility of her life, then drawn her to into his treacherous web.

"Now has come the time to discuss the proposal that I mentioned in my letter," he said. "I offer you a position in my employ."

How he worked his spell had been amply demonstrated to me; his motives concerning myself remained obscure. I said, "Why would you wish to employ me? Why go to such lengths to bring me here?"

With sly amusement he replied, "Perhaps you have heard the saying, 'An intelligent enemy is preferable to a stupid friend.' However, I believe that an intelligent friend is most desirable."

He thought he could turn me into a confederate and use my cleverness to his advantage. Then he needn't fear that I would report him to the authorities. He was clearly trying to master me by demolishing my self-pride.

"What is the position you are offering?" I asked.

"I can only tell you that should you accept it, you will be a rich woman," he said. "Your every desire will be satisfied. You will live in luxury, assure yourself a better future than you could imagine, and fulfill your destiny."

He had judged my character based on what his spies had learned about me and what he'd elicited from me tonight. He thought me a woman who was clever yet luckless, who was daring yet had failed at every venture she'd attempted heretofore, and who could thus be bought with a vague promise of financial security and a renewed sense of purpose in life. But he had misjudged me. He was unaware that I was the author of a famous novel, and that I was in league with a spy for the Crown. Mr. Slade had kept his identity as secret as I had mine; the villain had yet to detect that Mr. Slade was after him. He, like so many others, had underestimated me. Now, if I wanted to remain safe, I must play along with him.

"Your kindness is much appreciated," I stammered, "but—"

Even in my addled condition, I perceived that here was the devil incarnate, offering to purchase my soul. If I accepted, he would

force me into immoral acts as he had done Isabel. If ever I disobeyed him, I would meet a similar violent end. The price I would
pay for wealth and gratification was my soul's eternal damnation.
Yet an impulse to leap at his offer vied with my distrust and natural caution, so alluring was he. He had shaken my self-confidence,
and what better could I expect from life? And although I wanted
never again to endure his company or his ruthless examination of
me, I feared what he would do if I refused.

"But you need time to consider my proposal," he said smoothly. "I do not expect you to decide in such haste. After you return to
England, you will place an advertisement in the *Times* stating that
Miss Brontë does or does not accept the position offered her in
Belgium. Now the carriage will return you to your hotel. I bid you
farewell, and thank you for a most delightful evening. Please put on
your blindfold, Miss Brontë."

➔←

When the carriage left me at the hotel, I fled inside—and collid-
ed so violently with Mr. Slade that he put his arms around me to
steady us. I clung to him as shudders convulsed me.

"Thank God you're all right," he exclaimed in relief.

"I was so afraid," I cried. "Why did you not come?"

"Your driver managed to elude us."

This was exactly as I had feared. Now I quaked harder at the
realization that I had been utterly alone and defenseless.

"I came back to wait for you," Mr. Slade said. "The police are
still out searching."

Belatedly I realized that we held each other in too intimate an
embrace. I stepped away from Mr. Slade. He seated me on a divan
and summoned a maid to bring me tea. The cup and saucer were
placed in my hands, which trembled so much that the china rattled,
but the strong, bitter brew invigorated me.

Mr. Slade sat by my side. "Where did you go?"

"I don't know," I said, then explained why. "But it seemed to be
a large house in the country."

"What did the house look like?"

Alas, I had to tell him that the blindfold had prevented me from seeing anything except the dining room, which I described in detail.

"Tell me about the man you met," Mr. Slade said.

"He would not tell me his name. And I never saw his face. He sat behind a screen. But I know he is a foreigner." I tried to imitate his accent, but I am hopeless at mimicry. Mr. Slade could no more identify the villain's land of origin than I could. When Mr. Slade asked what we had talked about, I related the proposal the man had made me.

"Is that all?" Mr. Slade said. "You were gone for quite some time. What else happened?"

"Nothing." I averted my eyes, too ashamed to confess the man's strange effect upon me.

"Perhaps the police can find the house," Mr. Slade said.

➤✦

The next afternoon, while riding along the country roads where my driver had shaken them off his tail, the police stumbled upon the house in the Forêt de Soignes, a tract of woods southeast of Brussels. They took Mr. Slade and me to the ancient, ruined brick chateau. Its walls were crumbling and mossy, the window-panes shattered, the gardens overgrown by weeds; the turrets and gables had collapsed in places. Mr. Slade and I walked through corridors hung with peeling wallpaper, and vacant chambers stripped of furniture, into the dining room.

"This is the place," I said.

The candles had burned out. My meal lay cold on the table, and a rat nibbled the food. No one sat behind the screen, but the exotic perfume lingered on the air. As I shivered at disturbing memories, the police inspector joined us.

"This house is the ancestral estate of an impoverished noble family," he said. "Last year they rented the house to a Mr. Smith from England. They communicate with him only by letter and have never met him. Neither have the local people, for he keeps to himself. We've searched the property, but found no trace of the tenants."

"'Mr. Smith' is apparently gone and not to return," Mr. Slade said, his expression grim.

"We cannot catch him if we don't know who he is," said the police inspector.

Mr. Slade met my gaze, and we shared a thought that caused me tremors of dread. "It seems that the only possible means of locating the criminal is for me to accept his offer," I said.

27

ALAS, MR. SLADE AND I WERE NOT
THE ONLY ONES DISAPPOINTED
by our misadventure in Brussels. We traveled posthaste to
London and there presented ourselves to Mr. Slade's superiors in
the Foreign Office. Again we sat with Lord Unwin and his officials
at the long table in the smoky chamber on Downing Street. After
Mr. Slade described my rendezvous with the villain and his own
thwarted pursuit, Lord Unwin regarded him with contempt.

"You had this man within your reach and allowed him to elude
you." Indignation elevated Lord Unwin's reedy, affected voice.
"Your ineptitude appalls me."

Yet the sparkle in his pale eyes attested to how much he relished
Mr. Slade's failure. Mr. Slade endured the reprimand with clenched
jaws. I knew he excoriated himself no less than did Lord Unwin. I
sat silent and mournful to hear Mr. Slade abused.

"The trip was not a complete loss," Mr. Slade said. "Communication was established between the villain and Miss Brontë. Should
she place the advertisement in the *Times* and accept his offer of
employment, he'll contact her again. That will give me another
chance at him."

"Another chance, perhaps, but not for you," Lord Unwin said.
"We cannot afford the risk that you might blunder again. As of this
moment, I am removing you from this inquiry."

"You can't!" Mr. Slade was outraged. "Not after I've handled the investigation this far, and it has produced what information we have about the villain. Not after one unfortunate mishap!"

"Indeed I can." Lord Unwin's cruel, haughty smile deepened. "And it's not just one mistake you've made." He lifted a paper that lay in front of him and passed it to Mr. Slade. "This letter came for you while you were in Belgium. I took the liberty of reading it."

As Mr. Slade scanned the letter, a frown darkened his brow. He silently handed the paper to me. On it I read the words written in a hasty black scrawl: "No luck yet identifying the owner of the ship used by Isaiah Fearon to smuggle weapons out of Britain. No further contact with the person responsible." There was no signature, but I deduced that the author must be the prime minister. My heart sank; our hopes of learning anything from him had been dashed.

"It seems that your other inquiries have also proved fruitless," Lord Unwin said, clearly gratified at the second blow he'd delivered Mr. Slade. "You will go back to France and resume spying on the secret societies. Other agents will be dispatched to Belgium to trace the villain's movements from there, and to Haworth to guard Miss Brontë. After she places the advertisement, they will report to me any communication she receives from the villain."

Mr. Slade and I looked at each other in extreme dismay. I knew he didn't want to return to the place where he had lost his wife. I also knew how loath he was to quit our mission after we had come this far.

"You'll not disrupt the pursuit of a killer and traitor because of your personal grievances with me!" Mr. Slade rose so abruptly that his chair crashed to the floor.

Lord Unwin sneered. "You'll obey my orders, or face punishment for insubordination."

Belatedly, my mind absorbed what he proposed regarding me. Not only must my family tolerate strangers in our home; I would lose Mr. Slade and our friendship. Such heartache filled me that I blurted, "I won't have anyone but Mr. Slade!"

The men all turned to stare at me, surprised by my outburst. "My dear Miss Brontë, I'm afraid you have no say in the matter,"

Lord Unwin said in a tone of polite disdain.

"If your agents come near my house, I won't let them in." I knew I sounded rude, and even childish; but I cared for nothing except to bind Mr. Slade to me. "If I receive a communication from the villain, I'll not tell them."

Before Lord Unwin could reply, one of his associates said to him, "A lack of cooperation from Miss Brontë could jeopardize our mission. Under these circumstances, I advise against replacing Mr. Slade."

Lord Unwin pondered, frowning as he looked from me to Mr. Slade. Then he nodded grudgingly. "Very well."

My heart rejoiced. Mr. Slade gave me a look that was as quizzical as grateful. Did he guess why I had so vehemently taken his side? I averted my gaze from him.

"Lest you think I've conceded because of your protests or Miss Brontë's threats, I must disabuse you of the notion," Lord Unwin said to Mr. Slade. "The search for this criminal has gained a level of urgency such that we cannot afford the slightest disadvantage. Last night there was a fire at the Paradise Club."

I recognized the name of the den of iniquity where girls from the Charity School were sent to work and where Isabel White had brought the prime minister under the villain's influence.

"The blaze was extinguished before it did much damage. You've had agents watching the club since you discovered its connection with our criminal, and they summoned help," Lord Unwin continued, sounding reluctant to give Mr. Slade credit for anything. "Most of the patrons escaped without injury, but three women, and the men with them, were found strangled upstairs in private rooms."

Horror chilled me. Mr. Slade's gaze darkened with consternation. "The criminal has eliminated more people who had connections to him," Mr. Slade deduced. "Could the fire have been set to cover up the murders?"

"It seems likely. There was a strong smell of kerosene near the rooms where the victims died." Lord Unwin added, "Two of them were Jane Fell and Abigail Weston, former pupils at the Reverend Grimshaw's Charity School."

They had died because we had not yet caught the killer. Guilt lowered upon me.

"The men came from noble families, who have besieged the government with demands that the killer be brought to justice," Lord Unwin said. "We now need Miss Brontë's cooperation more than ever." He shot me an ireful glance. "Miss Brontë shall place her advertisement tomorrow morning. Immediately thereafter, you and she shall return to Haworth to wait for a response." Lord Unwin pushed back his chair; his subordinates followed suit. The gaze he bent on Mr. Slade turned colder. "This is your one chance to make amends for your Belgian escapade. Disappoint me again, and you'll be out of Her Majesty's service despite your illustrious career."

It suddenly occurred to me that Emily had saved the day for Mr. Slade and me. Had she not gone to the Charity School and linked the villain to the Club Paradise, Lord Unwin would never have connected the murders to the villain, and nothing would have swayed him in our favor. We owed Emily a great debt indeed. How strange that she who had been least interested in our business should have the responsibility for its continuation.

As we all rose, Lord Unwin bowed with mocking courtesy to me. "I hope for your sake that henceforth Mr. Slade will do better at protecting you than he did in Brussels."

>‹

Mr. Slade and I passed four days in Haworth—days that were uneventful yet strained with the tense pitch of waiting. On the last morn, Mr. Slade accompanied me on my visits throughout the parish, which I had shamefully neglected of late. He again sported the clerical garb and the guise of my cousin John from Ireland. He walked by my side, carrying the basket of food for the needy, across moors in their full summer glory. Flowers colored the cottage gardens and the hedgerows; thrushes swooped over meadows where fat sheep grazed. The sky was such a serene blue that I could almost forget the dangers that menaced my world.

"This is the existence that would have been mine had I not chosen a different path after I took my orders," Mr. Slade said.

Once more he appeared such a convincing clergyman that I could well imagine him as the vicar of some country parish. "Have you ever regretted your choice?"

"I didn't when I was younger. To tread an unvarying routine, to be confined within narrow environs, seemed repellent to me then." Mr. Slade gazed across the hills that receded in hazy green swells. "Yet now, after all I've seen and done, I can understand the value of a life spent ministering to souls rather than adventuring in foreign lands. I find pleasure, instead of boredom, in England's peaceful countryside."

As we descended a slope towards town, I reflected that while Slade had come to appreciate the pleasures of a village parish, I had developed a taste for intrigue. The divide between us had narrowed. But I again recalled what Mr. Slade had said about *Jane Eyre*, and his implication that a man like him could never love a woman like me. The happiness he'd expressed on the ship must have resulted not from our comradeship but from the natural end to his mourning for his dead wife. I couldn't know whether my regard for him was any less unrequited than before our trip to Belgium. I did know that this time we had together was but a transient interlude.

"What will happen when the villain contacts me?" I asked.

"He'll instruct you as to where to meet him. My superiors will use the information to find and capture him."

After the villain was caught, the Foreign Office would have no further need of me, and Mr. Slade would have no reason to dally in my vicinity. I couldn't wish to prolong our mission, or for England to remain in danger, in order that the dreaded separation would be postponed; yet the thought of ending our association opened a chasm of emptiness and anguish before me.

Stepping back from the edge of the chasm, I said, "What if the information is insufficient to find the villain? Must I do his bidding and go to him?"

"Indeed not," Mr. Slade said with firm resolve. "One way or another, we'll get him without endangering you."

Yet his reassurance didn't negate the possibility I feared. "Suppose I did go. What would happen?"

Mr. Slade gave me a look that scorned what he thought was unnecessary speculation, but he humored me: "You wouldn't go alone. I, and other agents, would follow you."

"And after I arrive at my destination?"

"We would remain within your reach and protect you from the villain until his capture."

"What should I do until then?" I said. "How should I behave that he would fail to see me as a decoy to draw him out of hiding?"

"Just be Miss Charlotte Brontë, the humble governess," Mr. Slade said. "That's what he thinks you are. He'll never know otherwise."

I hated to think that was how Mr. Slade viewed me too. "What might he want me to do for him?"

"Whatever it is, you won't have to do it, because we'll have him in chains first," Mr. Slade said as we traversed the village along Main Street. Sunshine brightened the grey stone houses. "But this is idle talk. Don't worry yourself. You won't be going near that criminal. Besides, he hasn't even summoned you yet."

Walking the road uphill towards the parsonage, we met the postman. He handed me a letter that struck ice down my spine. It was enclosed in a plain envelope addressed to me in the same elegant script as the letter that the villain had sent me via M. Heger in Brussels. I opened it with trembling hands. Inside I found banknotes, a railway timetable, and a letter that read:

> My dear Miss Brontë,
>
> How pleased I am that you have accepted my offer. Please take the train to Cornwall that I have marked in the timetable. You will receive further instructions at the station in Penzance. I wish you a safe journey.

28

>+<

WHEN WRITING A FICTITIOUS STORY, ONE SHOULD ALWAYS choose the most exciting possible course for the story to follow. Characters in a book should experience action rather than inertia, and thrills rather than contentment. How fitting, therefore, that what I would write in fiction is what transpired in actuality. But life, unlike fiction, guarantees no happy ending. The dangers I faced were not mere words that could be expunged by the scribble of a pen. The villain who had summoned me was not harmless ink on paper but flesh and blood.

These notions haunted me as I journeyed by rail towards Penzance. That town is located in Cornwall, the county at England's southwest extremity. Dread of an evil, ruthless man sank deeper into my bones while I traveled past fishing villages that clung to cliffs above the glittering blue sea. In meadows green and gold beneath the southern sun rose dark stone pillars, monuments built by ancient folk for mysterious rituals. The ruins of Roman fortifications dotted the countryside. This was the land where King Arthur was born at Tintagel. Would that I were an ordinary traveler, come to explore the scenes of legend!

A casual observer might suppose I journeyed by myself; but Mr. Slade had kept his promise that I should not go unaccompanied. He rode, disguised, somewhere on the train. At all times seated near me was a Foreign Office agent, duty bound to protect me. Other agents had been dispatched to Penzance to arrange for the surveillance and capture of our quarry. Yet I felt as alone as if I had entered another world. How I wish I had heeded the objections raised by Papa, Emily, Anne, and Slade when they learned I'd been summoned!

"Dear Charlotte, you mustn't go," Anne had said.

"How else will we locate the villain?" I countered.

"We now know he is in Cornwall," said Papa. "Let Mr. Slade and his colleagues seek him out."

"He could be anywhere in an area thousands of acres in breadth," I said. "Or perhaps he's not there at all. Perhaps the instructions I receive in Penzance will send me on to some other, unknown place where he awaits me."

"Mr. Slade can intercept the instructions," Emily said.

"But what if the villain sends a henchman to deliver the instructions only to me?" I said.

"We can watch the station for anyone who looks to be waiting for you," Mr. Slade said. "When he leaves, we can follow him to his master."

"That would do very well, if you pick the right person," I said. "Bear in mind that he may not know where his master is, and may only have orders to deliver me to some place to be fetched later by someone else."

"He can direct us to the next link in the chain leading to the villain," Mr. Slade said.

"If I don't appear," I said, "the villain will know that something has gone awry with his plans. He'll go deeper into hiding."

"Even worse, he may deduce that Charlotte betrayed him and seek revenge," Emily said, reluctantly taking my side.

"We shall all be in more danger than before." Worry shadowed Anne's face.

"And no one can recognize him except me," I said. "I have at least heard his voice."

Papa nodded, unhappy but persuaded by our logic. Together my family and I convinced Mr. Slade that I should obey the summons. I must confess that I did so for other reasons than those I'd spoken, and not only out of a desire to protect Britain. Although Isabel White had been reduced to a small portion of a larger concern, I still felt a duty to gain justice for her. My sense of obligation extended to Mr. Slade. If the villain remained free, Mr. Slade would bear the blame. Furthermore, going to Cornwall would prolong my association with him the only way I knew how.

Hence, we traveled to London to report our plan to his superiors and procure their aid. We expected opposition from Lord Unwin, but received none. The murders at the Paradise Club had outraged the government's highest echelons. Pressure to apprehend the culprit had been brought to bear upon Lord Unwin. His own welfare was more important to him than my safety, and his need to win favor among his superiors outweighed the risk that Mr. Slade might fail him again. Therefore, he quickly supplied all the helpers and funds that Mr. Slade requested.

Now, on 29 August, the train approached Penzance. The village climbed the hills in tiers of whitewashed stone houses around Mount's Bay. A causeway extended to St. Michael's Mount, a rocky islet crowned by a castle. Seabirds screeched from rooftops and harbor; brick chimneys arose from tin mines. Grey clouds blanketed the sky; the fishing fleet drifted on the lead-colored ocean. Through the open window blew the smells of sea, fish, and tar; the misty drizzle tasted of salt. My dread expanded so large in me that I almost suffocated. In the station, I faltered onto the platform amidst citizens who spoke the strange Cornish dialect. Suddenly a man jostled me. He pressed into my hand a small, folded square of paper.

"Excuse me," he said.

No sooner did I recognize Mr. Slade's voice, than he was gone so quickly that I barely glimpsed him. As I secreted the paper in my pocket, I heard my name called. I turned and found myself facing a tall man, some forty-five years of age, with a languid, slouching stance. His hair was blond, his features handsome, his country tweeds impeccably tailored.

"Yes?" I stammered in reply.

The man smiled and bowed. "An honor to make your acquaintance. Kindly allow me to introduce myself. My name is Tony Hitchman. I've been appointed to meet you."

I realized at once that Mr. Hitchman was not the man who had invited me: His speech was the proper diction of the British upper classes, free from any foreign accent.

"Had a pleasant journey, I hope?" Mr. Hitchman said.

As I answered that I had, I gleaned a closer inspection of him. Behind his languid posture I sensed the alertness of a predatory beast ready to spring. His smile had a roguish cast, emphasized by a scar that snaked down his left cheek. His pale green eyes were cold, their appraisal of me too direct. All told, I doubted that Hitchman was the respectable gentleman he seemed on the surface. My distrust of him exceeded what I would have felt towards anyone associated with the villain who'd brought me here. And I perceived that the distrust was mutual.

"This is Nick," he said, indicating a man hovering near us.

Nick was swarthy, his strong build clothed in rough garments, his dark eyes shadowed by heavy lids. He nodded me a silent greeting and lifted my bags.

"If you'll please come this way?" Hitchman said.

Everything in me rebelled against going with them—but I had promised to lead Mr. Slade to the villain. Quaking from fear, I allowed Hitchman to guide me to a carriage. Nick stowed my bags and took the reins; Hitchman sat beside me. The carriage wended through narrow, rising crooked lanes, past fishermen's cottages and the brick buildings of shops. Below us I saw boats clustered in the harbor, and a handsome promenade along the shore.

"Ever been in Penzance before?" Mr. Hitchman asked.

"No," I said, fighting the urge to look backward and see if Mr. Slade was following us.

As we drove through the town, curiosity momentarily abated my terror. Here had my maternal grandfather been a tea merchant and my grandmother the daughter of a silversmith. After their deaths my mother had left Penzance; I had never ventured to these parts. I wondered if any of the people I saw on the streets were my relations, whose acquaintance I would have liked to make.

"What have you been told about the terms of your employment?" Hitchman said.

"Nothing," said I. "Perhaps you could tell me what my duties are?"

"You're to be a teacher."

Never had I imagined that I'd been hired to practice my former profession. "Who is to be my pupil?"

"My partner's son," Hitchman said.

A ray of illumination shone through the veil of mystery that shrouded the villain. I now knew that he had a child. And I knew that Hitchman was no mere minion, but the villain's coconspirator. My distrust and fear of Hitchman increased.

"What subjects am I to teach?" I inquired.

"English," came the answer.

I began to suspect that the villain intended other uses for me. I hoped he would be caught—and I would be rescued—before I found out what they were.

We drove out of town, along the shore, past hills covered with cedar and pines that looked black in the wet, dark day. I heard a carriage behind us and took courage from the notion that surely Mr. Slade followed me. We turned onto a lane that wound down into a narrow cove; the other carriage continued along the road. Twisted cypress trees clung to the rocky cliffs that sheltered the cove. On a rocky outcrop of land, a lone house perched above the sea. The low tide lapped over the rocks. The house had a slate roof and thick granite walls built to withstand storms. It was square and stark, with three floors. Nick halted the carriage outside the attached stable.

"I'll show you to your room," Hitchman said. "After you've had a bit of a rest, you can meet your pupil."

Nick carried my bags up the steps to the house. I saw no alternative but to follow. Inside the house, I hesitated in the foyer, which had a bare stone floor and cracked plaster walls. A cold, damp draft wound through doors to various rooms. From beyond the stairway came a woman and two men. Hitchman introduced the stern, black-clad woman to me as Ruth the housekeeper, but he did not name the men, who were of the same silent, tough sort as Nick. I felt desperate to escape, but I must first draw the villain out of hiding.

"May I meet my employer now?" I said.

"Sorry; he's away on business," Hitchman said. "He'll return in a day or so."

My heart plummeted.

"After you, Miss Brontë?" Hitchman gestured with mocking courtesy towards the stairs.

I doubted that Mr. Slade would want me trapped here to wait for the villain; yet I knew that his career—and the lives of innocent people—hinged on me. Thus, I preceded Hitchman upstairs, into a chamber. The furniture was carved in elaborate, unmatched designs, its surfaces marred; the porcelain jug and basin on the washstand were chipped, and the mirror's gilt frame tarnished; the Turkey rug was discolored. I had a sudden memory of tales my mother had told me of Cornwall. Wrecking and piracy had once been common occupations here. Cornish folk would watch for ships to founder on the rocks offshore, then pillage the cargoes; they also attacked the ships at sea. I wondered if my quarters had been furnished with salvage and loot.

Nick set my bags by the bed and departed. Hitchman said, "Is there anything you need? A bite to eat, perhaps?"

I answered in the negative: I could not have swallowed food. I peered through the window, whose glass was scarred by wind and salt. Behind the house, a dock rose on pilings from the sea. The cove was hidden from the view of everyone except fishermen on the distant ships. I remembered that Cornwall's other famed pastime was smuggling. The smugglers had once conveyed tin from local mines to the Continent, and spirits, tobacco, and silks to England. Secluded coves such as this had provided hiding places for boats laden with contraband. Perhaps this house had once belonged to a smuggling baron.

"By the way, I should mention a few rules for you to observe." Hitchman spoke in a casual tone, but when I turned to face him, his gaze promised harsh retribution for disobedience. "You'll con-

fine yourself to this floor and the one below. The upper story and
the cellars are off limits. After dark, you'll stay in your room. And
you'll not leave the premises without an escort. Nor will you speak
about the household's business to outsiders. Do you understand?"

"Quite," I said coolly, though I despaired to realize how little
freedom I would have.

Hitchman smiled, as if he sensed my unhappiness and relished
it. A current of antipathy flowed between us. "I'll leave you, then.
Come downstairs when you're ready. Dinner will be served at six."

He walked to the door, turned, and added, "Your predecessor
broke the rules. She didn't last long afterward."

Then Hitchman was gone. As his footsteps receded down the
stairs, I absorbed the impact of his parting words. I had been
brought here to fill the vacancy left by Isabel White, whom his
associates had murdered; a similar fate awaited me should I defy
him and his partner. I sank into trembling fear, when suddenly I
remembered the paper given me at the station. I closed the door,
brought out the paper, and read the following message:

> If you need me, come to Oyster Cottage, Bay Street. We'll be
> watching you. Good luck. Destroy this note.
>
> J. S.

Even as the reassurance from Mr. Slade lifted my heart, I despaired
anew. How could I reach him without disobeying Hitchman's rules
and imperiling my life? I saw that I must not count on Mr. Slade for
help; my own resources must suffice. Overcome by fatigue, I lay on
the bed and rested for an hour. I then rose, washed my face, and tidied
myself. Then I crept downstairs and entered the front parlor. It was
furnished with the same battered opulence as my room. As I peered
into a curio cabinet, someone lunged out from behind it.

"YAH!" he shouted, arms raised in menacing fashion.

All my stifled terror and anxiety exploded like a thunderbolt in
my chest. I screamed. Recoiling, I flung up my hands and stumbled
backward.

"Ha, ha!" my attacker chortled. "I scare you!"

It was a boy, short and slender. He wore a dark blue cap that fit tight around his head. His black hair was in a long plait. I formed an impression of a high-collared blue jacket that was fastened with frogs, and loose black trousers above feet clad in black slippers, before his round, laughing face captured my attention. His eyes were narrow and tilted. These, along with high cheekbones, marked him as a Chinese—the first I'd seen outside pictures in books.

"You look so surprise. Funny!" Pointing a finger at me, he doubled over in a fit of giggles.

"Who—who are you?" I gasped.

The boy's mirth vanished; he stood up straight and fixed an imperious gaze on me. "I am Kuan T'ing-nan." Instead of asking me who I was, he said, "You my teacher."

I realized that this boy must be the son of the villain. Logic decreed that the villain would also be Chinese. The son spoke English with an accent similar to the father, although far less capably. How had a Chinaman come to this kingdom? Why would he wish to scheme and murder here, far from his native land? The answers must wait. Survival must be my concern, and the boy before me represented the first challenge.

Drawing myself up to my full height, I spoke in the severe tone I had often used while a governess: "I am Charlotte Brontë. Your father has engaged me to teach English to you. It appears that you will benefit from a few lessons. You will also never startle me like that again."

But my manner failed to produce the desired respect from T'ing-nan. Disdain twisted his mouth. "I no need teacher," he said. "I not a child."

A closer look showed me the dark stippling of whiskers on his face. He was not a child, but a young man, perhaps eighteen years of age. His small size had misled me to think him much younger.

"You no tell me what to do," he said. "You servant. I the master." His expression of smug superiority reminded me of many privileged, spoiled children I had taught. He reached out and shoved my shoulder. "You go away."

Affronted, I stood my ground. "Your father engaged me. Whether I go or stay is his decision, not yours. And I doubt he'll be pleased to hear of your misbehavior."

Even while a scowl darkened T'ing-nan's aspect, his boldness visibly deflated. I sensed in him a fear and dislike of his father. But the mischief in his eyes kindled anew. He prowled in a circle around me, forcing me to turn so I could watch him.

"Where you come from?" he said.

"Yorkshire," I said. "That's in the north of England—"

"England!" He spat the word in disgust. "It is small country. I see map. England look like bird shit on ocean." Whoever had taught him what little English language he spoke, he had learned a coarse vocabulary. "England ugly. People ugly." T'ing-nan's look said this judgment included me. "I from China." Now he swelled with pride. "China big. China beautiful." He had also learned manners that would disgrace a ditchdigger. "Ladies in China wear pretty clothes. Why you wear plain, cheap dress? Your family have no money?"

"They have less than some people but more than others," I said tartly. "As long as you're in England, you should learn that proper behavior is expected here. A gentleman does not make insulting personal remarks to people, nor shove them, nor criticize their country."

T'ing-nan waved away my instructions. "I no want learn. I hate England. My father hate, too. Someday we go home to China. Then I no need speak or act English."

I spied a chance to learn more about my mysterious employer. "Why does your father hate England?"

"England bad for China," T'ing-nan said.

"What do you mean?" I asked, eager to know what grudge his father had that justified murder.

But T'ing-nan only smirked, like a child enjoying a secret.

"If he hates England, then what is he doing here?" I said.

"Business," T'ing-nan said bitterly.

"What kind of business?"

The youth stopped circling me, and his expression turned wary.

"My father go here, go there," he said, gesturing ambiguously. "Sometime make me go with him. Other time, leave me someplace. While he gone, men watch me. They keep me in house. Lock me up. Never let me outside except at night. Never by myself." Angry resentment gleamed in his eyes. "At home, in China, I go wherever I want. I have friends. I have fun. But here, nobody. No fun. In England, I am prisoner."

"Why?" I said.

"My father want no one see us."

Chinamen are rare in England, and I surmised that the villain wished to avoid the notice that his and his son's appearance would attract. Pity leavened my dislike of T'ing-nan. His loneliness and confinement must exceed that which I'd ever known.

"But surely you could be allowed to walk in the cove?" I said. "There you would be hidden from the public."

T'ing-nan's narrow gaze rebuffed my suggestion. "You watch."

He stalked from the room, along a passage towards the back of the house. I followed. Nick suddenly appeared, interposing himself between us and the door.

"You let me out," T'ing-nan said.

Nick shook his head, held his position.

"I go," T'ing-nan insisted, grabbing for the door handle.

Hitchman and one of the men I'd seen earlier joined us. "You aren't going anywhere, young fellow," Hitchman told T'ing-nan. "Your father's orders."

As the youth yelled protests in Chinese, Hitchman and the other man seized his arms. They bore the kicking, screaming T'ing-nan up the stairs.

"Sorry for the trouble, Miss Brontë," Hitchman called. "We'll just let him calm down awhile, and you can start his lessons tomorrow."

They passed from my view. I heard a door slam upstairs, and T'ing-nan pounding on it and shouting. Nick still guarded the door. His glowering silence spoke a clear warning to me: I, too, was a prisoner.

29

$$\rightarrow\!\!\!\leftarrow$$

T HAT EVENING I ATE A DINNER OF ROASTED PILCHARDS, SERVED BY Ruth the housekeeper, alone in the dining room. Hitchman ushered me upstairs to my room, where I lay awake, listening to the sea, until sleep claimed me. The next morning, I began teaching T'ing-nan. He was sullenly uncooperative. At noon he announced that he'd had enough learning, flung the schoolbooks onto the floor, and stomped off to his room. I coaxed and scolded him through the door, but he refused to come out.

"Lost your pupil, have you?" Hitchman said.

"It seems that way," I said, irked by his mocking manner. But T'ing-nan's behavior afforded me a pretext for leaving the house. "Since I have nothing to do here, I should like to go into town."

"Very well," Hitchman said.

He summoned Ruth to accompany me, and Nick drove us to Penzance. The weather continued cool and drizzly. As Ruth and I walked up the main street, Nick trailed close behind us. We passed stalls at which fisherwomen in scarlet cloaks and broad hats hawked their wares to town ladies wearing fancy lace caps. Ruth paused, her attention caught by the pungent displays of fish. A peddler's cart separated me from her and Nick. Swiftly, I edged away from them; I looked frantically around. Where would I find Oyster Cottage? I saw Nick roving the street, scanning the crowd for me. I hurriedly bent over a basket of cockles at a stall. He walked on without noticing me.

A man's voice hissed in my ear: "What in the deuce is going on?"

Startled, I turned and saw Mr. Slade standing beside me. He wore shabby clothes like a fisherman's, and a cap pulled low over his face. A sob of relief welled in my throat.

"Don't look at me," Mr. Slade ordered in a harsh whisper. "Act as though we don't know each other."

I tore my gaze from him and pretended to examine the cockles as I whispered, "The man we seek is not at the house. He's expected to arrive later."

Mr. Slade stifled a curse. I saw Ruth and Nick approaching. "Here they come," I said in a panic.

"Look upward to your right," Slade said urgently. "Do you see that house with the blue trim and two gables?"

I saw it, on a hillside street beyond market, and nodded.

"That's Oyster Cottage," Slade said. "Go there if you feel in danger."

There was no time to advise him of the rules that hindered my freedom. We moved apart, and the crowds separated us. Ruth and Nick joined me.

"Find what you wanted?" Ruth asked.

I picked up a cockle and paid the proprietor for it. "Yes," I said.

A storm blew in from the sea that night, lashing the waves against the cliffs and rain against the house. Foghorns moaned through my sleep. I was awakened by thumps and voices that echoed up from the cellars. Footsteps mounted the stairs. I listened, but nothing more happened. I slept until the parlor clock chimed seven. After washing and dressing, I ventured downstairs. Ruth served me a solitary breakfast. Outside the dining room window, a pale, drifting mist obscured the sea. The dampness, chill, and seclusion produced in me a languorous depression of my spirit. No sooner had I finished eating, than Hitchman appeared.

"My partner arrived last night," he said. "He wants to see you. Come with me."

The source of the sounds I'd heard now became apparent: The man must have arrived by boat and entered the house through a subterranean passage. This abrupt summons left me no time to inform Mr. Slade that our villain was at hand. Even if Mr. Slade had been watching the house, he would not have observed the arrival of its master. Fear choked the breath in my lungs, but it was easily outweighed by my strong curiosity.

Hitchman led me up the stairs, to the forbidden third story. It smelled of the perfume I remembered from the chateau. We followed a dim passage lined with doors. The last one stood open; Hitchman ushered me inside a small, dim chamber that resembled the cabin of a ship. A round window like a porthole overlooked the mist-shrouded sea. A telescope sat upon a table; maps hung on the walls above a rusted brass-bound trunk. Near the desk stood the man I had waited so long to set my eyes upon.

He was little taller than his son, but his proud carriage lent him a semblance of height. Unlike his son, he wore the dark coat and trousers of a British gentleman, and his gleaming black hair was cut short in corresponding fashion. Perhaps he had eschewed his native garb in order to blend in with the local citizens and move about freely. While the son was all restlessness, the father was all repose.

"So we meet again, Miss Brontë," he said.

His silky, suave voice again worked an eerie magic upon my mind, dissolving my ties to Mr. Slade, the outside world, and everything sensible and sane. His face had a waxen gold skin that stretched tight over the curved planes of his bones. His age was indeterminate. With his haughty, sculpted nose and lips, he was at once repulsive and alluring. Words from Isabel White's diary whispered in my mind: *His strange beauty captivated me.* His eyes, set beneath high, arched brows, were shaped like half moons. Their steady gaze drew me into their black depths. I feared that if I looked too long into them, I would lose myself. I struggled to think what Mr. Slade had told me to do, and I recalled my aim of learning as much as possible about this man.

"Now that I have entered your employ," I said with a calmness I did not feel, "may I know your name?"

His half-moon eyes narrowed in faint amusement. "I am Kuan Tzu-chan. You may address me as Kuan."

I later learned that this was his family name, which, in Chinese fashion, he spoke before his personal name. To Hitchman, who stood beside me, he said, "Leave us."

Surprise, and offense, disrupted Hitchman's genial expression. "I'll stay, if you don't mind."

"I do mind," Kuan said simply.

Hitchman stood irresolute for a moment, then departed. I saw that while he fancied himself as Kuan's partner, he was clearly the subordinate.

"Come, Miss Brontë," said Kuan, "let us converse." He pointed me toward a chair and took for himself the wooden captain's chair behind the desk. It was too big for his slight frame, but he sat regally. "Are your quarters satisfactory? Have you everything you need?"

I had engaged in similar conversations at every establishment where I'd worked; but Kuan's voice imbued the mundane exchange with portentous significance. His keen scrutiny of me implied an interest in more than my comfort. "My physical needs are met, but I expected a little more. You promised me that if I accepted this position, I would live in luxury. And I prefer that my freedom not be so restricted."

He heard my complaint with a look of condescension. "There are times in life when we must delay gratification and tolerate minor inconveniences in order to earn our rewards. Now then: I understand that you have met my son and begun his lessons. How does he progress?"

"Your son is intelligent, but he refuses to apply himself," I said. "His antipathy towards my country has set him against mastering the language."

A shadow of displeasure crossed Kuan's smooth face. "My son must learn to accept the circumstances that fortune has thrust upon him. And you, Miss Brontë, must overcome his resistance. Have you ever had difficult pupils in the past?"

"Far too many," I said.

"Were you ultimately able to tame and instruct them?"

"Not all," I admitted. Were this an interview with any other employer, I would have tried to conceal my failings so he would not think ill of me; but the force of Kuan's nature compelled me to honesty, as it had in Brussels. "It is impossible to teach someone who refuses to accept instruction."

"So you blame the pupils, and not yourself, for their failure to learn?" Kuan said with a glimmer of a smile.

I didn't want to anger him by implying that if T'ing-nan failed to learn English, it was his own fault; yet I wished to defend myself. "Medieval alchemists claimed to convert base metal to gold, but not even the best teacher can effect a similar transformation in a pupil."

"In my land, a good teacher is one who acknowledges her own mistakes and endeavors to correct them, rather than giving up," Kuan said.

He displayed the same arrogant superiority that I had observed in his son. I replied tartly, "With all due respect, sir, this is not your land."

A look of secretive gloating came over Kuan. "I detect in you a harsh attitude towards children, Miss Brontë. Do you dislike them so much?"

My candor faltered; his observation was astute, and a woman who admits disliking children risks seeming a monster. "I like them very well," I replied.

I could see that my falsehood did not deceive Kuan; yet satisfaction wreathed his features. "But still you would vigilantly protect any children in your charge?"

"Of course I would," I said.

"You would endanger your own life before letting them come to harm?"

Although I could not imagine sacrificing myself for any of the brats I'd taught—nor for Kuan's rude, petulant son—I nodded, rather than contradict my previous answer.

"You would place yourself between your charges and someone

who attacked them?" Kuan said. "In fact, you would do anything rather than hurt a child?"

My nods grew weaker, for I did not have much enthusiasm for children and could not commit to risking my life for an unknown hypothetical child; yet his satisfied expression deepened. I felt that I had passed some arcane test he had set for me. He steepled his hands under his chin as he continued to scrutinize my face. "Why did you choose a profession that is so ill suited to your nature?"

"There are few others open to women," I admitted.

"But many Englishwomen stay home rather than enter the service of strangers," Kuan said. "Why did you not?"

"I was determined not to be a burden on my father," I answered. "I considered it my duty to contribute to the household income."

"Duty to one's parents is the highest virtue," Kuan said. "But how onerous must be the burden of supporting a brother and sister who are unfit to earn their own living."

This description of Branwell and Emily enraged me, as did Kuan's familiarity with our business. "They are not a burden," I said in an icy tone. "Whatever I do for them and the rest of my family is done out of love, not obligation."

Kuan contemplated me. "For love of family, then, you would go to lengths that you would not for anyone else." He seemed pleased to have deduced this.

His questions had grown increasingly personal, and increasingly offensive. "May I ask the purpose of this discussion?"

He waved away my query. "Its purpose will become evident in good time."

"Then until that time, I'll not answer any more questions."

Kuan placed his hands on the arms of his chair, conjuring the image of an emperor on a throne. "I am your master, and you are my servant. You shall do whatever I decree."

Anger made me incautious. "I may be a servant, but you do not own me. Here in England, the law does not tolerate slavery." I rose, flustered as usual while asserting myself. "If you will please excuse me, I must go now."

Sudden malevolence glimmered through Kuan's calm visage. "Here in my domain, the laws of England do not apply. Sit down, Miss Brontë."

Now was the time to flee the house before he could pry more deeply into my mind; now was the time to fetch Mr. Slade to capture Kuan before he could fulfill his secret, evil purpose. I rushed to the door and flung it open—only to find Hitchman standing in the hall, barring my path.

"You will remain until I determine that our conversation is finished," Kuan said evenly.

I sank into my chair. Hitchman closed the door, imprisoning me with Kuan. Yet even a caged animal will snap at its jailer.

"I will answer more questions from you, under the condition that you answer questions from me," I said, despite knowing that I was in no position to bargain.

I expected Kuan to be angry, but he seemed gratified that I had stood up to him. "Your courage delights me, Miss Brontë." A smile of arresting charm transformed his face. "Valor while under threat is a rare and admirable trait."

My emotions underwent a sudden, unsettling shift. I felt no longer defiant towards him, but flattered by his praise. Once more, as in Brussels, he had invoked his power to make me desirous of his good opinion, even though I knew him to be my enemy.

"The bargain you propose is a fair one," Kuan said. "I shall postpone my interrogation of you, and you may interrogate me. Is it agreed?"

He extended his hand towards me. My small, unexpected victory startled me so much that my mouth fell open. We shook hands. His grasp was firm, his slender fingers like iron sheathed in silk. I had a disturbing sense that I had agreed to much more than an exchange of information. Even more disturbing was the way our new comradeship gladdened my spirits.

"Well, Miss Brontë?" said Kuan. "I await your questions."

All I could think to say was, "Who are you?"

Kuan nodded his approval; he settled himself more comfortably in his chair. "This is an instance when a short question requires a long answer. I trust you are intelligent enough that by the time I am finished, you will deduce why I wish you to know my story in such detail. Who I am extends beyond my mere identity and has deep roots in the past. In China, a man's history begins not with himself, but with his forebears. Mine were rice merchants in Shanghai, the great trading city on the eastern coast. The family business was prosperous, but my father aspired to join the ruling mandarin class, and I—his eldest son—was chosen to elevate our family's station. His wealth bought the best tutors for me. I studied for long years. At age twenty, I passed the examination for entry into the civil service of the emperor."

This sounded indescribably foreign to me. Kuan's words seemed to waft me upon a breeze laden with Oriental spices. I found myself mesmerized by his voice. Vague scenes of Chinese pagodas and palaces took shape in the mist outside the window; the gulls' cries became the babble of Chinese merchants.

"I was then appointed district magistrate of a village in Fukien Province," Kuan continued. "There I learned the skills of statesmanship and administration. For the next seventeen years, I worked in various posts throughout the land."

I found myself unable to look away from his steady, black, vertiginous eyes; an eerie stupor relaxed me. Kuan's beauty grew more alluring and less repellent by the moment. I didn't feel the same attraction towards him as I felt towards Mr. Slade; yet he exerted upon me a pull that I couldn't define. Did my character predestine me to be smitten by Kuan? Did some magnetic current flow from him to me, as between lodestone and iron? I began to fathom some part of his motive for telling me his life story: He sensed how drawn I am to the lure of things dramatic and fantastical, and he wanted to sink his hooks into my mind.

His suave, musical voice went on: "Those were tumultuous years. While I was a judicial commissioner in Sinkiang Province, it became embroiled in a war against the followers of a prophet called Mohammed. Two years later, when I was financial commissioner in Hunan, rebel attacks beset the province. By this time I had married; my wife had borne my son T'ing-nan. Our two daughters followed." Dark memories swirled in Kuan's eyes. "I eventually attained a post as secretary to the governor of the city that your people call Canton."

The part of my mind that remained rational comprehended that Kuan hadn't yet said anything to explain his actions.

"Canton is located in the tropic region of south China," he continued. "It is a busy port where merchants from Europe, Arabia, the Orient, and the New World come to trade. These foreign traders live separate from the townspeople, in factories on the bank of the Whampoa River. There are vast fortunes to be made in tea and silk, by Chinese and foreigners alike. It was a most advantageous post for me."

"Then why did you leave China?" I asked boldly. "What brought you to England?"

He regarded me in silence, his eyes narrowed to slits, as though measuring how much I deserved to hear—or how far he could trust me. At last he folded his hands on the desk and said with an enigmatic smile, "Those are questions that I shall answer on a future occasion. You are dismissed. Until I summon you again, you will continue teaching my son—if you can."

30

I SPENT THE REST OF THE DAY IN SOLI-
TUDE. T'ING-NAN NEVER REAPPEARED
for more lessons. I surreptitiously tried the doors and windows—
and found them all tightly secured: I was a prisoner. That night I
heard an argument between Kuan and T'ing-nan. The son screamed
in Chinese; the father never raised his voice. Later I heard stealthy
movements in the cellar. I had a frightening sense that there were
many more people in the house than I had encountered. The
atmosphere was so turbid with menace that I vowed to stay not a
moment longer. The next morning, I was dressed in cloak and bonnet when the key turned in the lock and opened my cell. I hurried
out and intercepted Hitchman in the foyer.

"Good morning, Miss Brontë," he said, surveying me in his
insolent fashion. "Are you going somewhere?"

"To town, if you please," I said.

I regretted that I could not take my bags, which would alert
him that I had no intention to return; but I would gladly escape
with only the clothes I was wearing. I tried to hide my nervousness,
but I must have failed, because Hitchman looked askance at me.

"Why must you go to town again so soon?" he said.

"I need to post a letter," I said, holding up the envelope that
contained a message written to Papa, Emily, and Anne. "My family will wish to know that I arrived here safely."

Hitchman said, "Give me the letter. I'll see that it's posted."

"Oh, but I'd rather do it myself and spare you the trouble." Dismay sank my spirits, for he had clearly been instructed not to allow me to leave.

"Hadn't you better attend to your duties?" Hitchman said.

"I doubt that Master T'ing-nan will mind waiting for his lesson," I said.

Hitchman regarded me with suspicion alerted by my urgent need to be gone. "Go to the schoolroom, Miss Brontë. I'll send your pupil to you."

Defeated, I turned to obey, but he grabbed my arm and swung me around to face him. "I have something to say to you first. You have somehow earned Kuan's good opinion, but until you've proven to me that you're trustworthy, I'll be watching you. Do you understand?"

"Yes, sir," I said, breathless with fright. He, unlike his master, had no gentleness nor magic to lull me. "May I go now?"

"Not just yet." Hitchman smiled, relishing my fear. "I'll have you know that I owe my life to Kuan. I've repaid him by doing more than I'll mention now. And I'll do more yet to further the plans we've laid and reap the rewards we expect."

Was it more than lucre and gratitude that inspired his loyalty? Perhaps he, too, had fallen under Kuan's mysterious spell.

"Isabel White stole money from Kuan before she ran away from him," Hitchman said, and finally I learned how she'd come by the thousand pounds she'd sent her mother. "She died for her mistake. If you do anything to betray Kuan, I'll kill you."

Hitchman's merciless gaze and emphatic manner assured me that his threat was sincere. I went faint with the terror that he would discover my deception—or that Kuan would. Hitchman released me, but I felt the lingering ache from his grasp as I stumbled into the schoolroom. Overwhelmed by helplessness, I collapsed in the chair at my desk and cradled my head in my hands. What if I was never to escape the house? Would Mr. Slade rescue me?

Presently, T'ing-nan arrived. He mumbled a greeting and seated himself at his table. He seemed unnaturally subdued, perhaps because of the altercation with his father the night before. I set him a lesson in writing. He clenched the pen in his fist and produced an illegible scrawl.

"Hold your pen this way," I said, demonstrating.

He tried, but seemed unable to follow my example. "You please show me?" he said humbly.

I should have known that he had mischief up his sleeve, but I was too addled by my encounter with Hitchman to be on my guard. I positioned myself beside T'ing-nan, took his hand in mine, and arranged his fingers around the pen.

He seized my wrists. "Hah!" he crowed. "I got you!"

"Let me go," I ordered, angered by his trick and my own gullibility.

His eyes danced with malicious glee as I struggled to pull away. He rose and jerked me to and fro, twisting my arms.

"Stop that!" I cried, fearful that he meant me serious harm, perhaps because he wanted to vent on me his anger at his father. "Help! Help!" I screamed.

A loud voice commanded, "Stop!"

We both froze, then turned to see Kuan standing in the doorway. He spoke disapprovingly in Chinese to his son. T'ing-nan released me and glared at Kuan.

"Come with me, Miss Brontë," said Kuan.

As he ushered me up the stairs, into his office, I felt as though I'd been plucked from a frying pan and cast into fire. He seated me in the chair I'd occupied yesterday, and himself at his helm behind the desk.

"I apologize for the crude behavior of my son," Kuan said; yet he did not appear sorry. Rather, he seemed gratified, as if at an opportunity that T'ing-nan had furnished him. "But then he is not the first unruly young man you have ever had the misfortune to know."

"What do you mean?" I said.

"I am referring to your brother."

My defenses reared inside me as they always did upon mention of Branwell. "Branwell is nothing like your son."

"I beg to disagree," Kuan said, calmly folding his hands. "Your brother is, according to the people of your village, a constant trial to his family, as my son is to me."

"Branwell would never attack a woman," I protested.

Kuan gave me a pitying smile. "Would you like to hear what my spies have learned from your village folk?"

I didn't want to learn more than I already knew about my brother's misdeeds, and particularly not from Kuan. Goaded and indignant, I said, "What I would like is that you should honor your promise to let me inquire about you." If I couldn't yet deliver him into Mr. Slade's hands, at least I might learn what he was and what were his intentions.

Again he seemed pleased, rather than annoyed, by my forwardness; perhaps he welcomed an audience. Contemplation narrowed his gaze. "Perhaps the time has come for me to answer the question you asked me last night: Why did I leave China?" His eyes took on that distant, musing look of recollection. "Why indeed, when Canton had everything to offer an ambitious civil servant such as I was."

Once more, his mellifluous voice and the mention of foreign locales began weaving a spell around me. On the sea outside the window, a ship seemed a Chinese junk floating on eastern waters. I fell into the same languorous yet attentive state as yesterday.

"Wealth flowed into Canton from distant lands," Kuan said. "Foreign merchants paid duties to the emperor and fees for lodging. Chinese merchants paid taxes and tributes. Much of this money found its way into the hands of officials like myself, the secretary to the governor. And the most profitable commerce was the trade in opium."

I flinched at his mention of the drug that had ruined my brother and caused my family such woe. Kuan's spies must have discovered Branwell's habit. It seemed no coincidence that Kuan would speak of Branwell and opium in the same conversation.

"Opium is the fruit of the poppy and a substance of miraculous powers," Kuan said. "When ingested—or smoked in a pipe, as is done in China—it eases pain and induces a feeling of tranquillity and euphoria. Worries fade; the senses grow keener. The world seems delightful."

Often had I wondered why Branwell took opium, to his own detriment. Now I began to comprehend.

"Hence, the use of opium is widespread in Canton," said Kuan. "The servants in my house indulged. So did clerks and officials in the governor's service. But opium is not a pure boon to mankind. It induces a disinclination to do anything but lie dreaming amidst clouds of smoke. A habitual user abandons his duties, ceases to eat, and grows weak. Even should he wish to reverse his decline, he finds the habit most difficult to break. Cessation causes stomach cramps, pains, nightmares, and extreme nervous agitation."

How well I knew, from observing Branwell.

"The poor wretch will do anything rather than give up his opium," Kuan continued. "When he has spent all his funds on the drug, he will steal. Money has vanished from the government treasury, stolen by officials. Thieves roam the city. And the problems extend far beyond Canton. Across the kingdom, merchants, peasants, soldiers, priests, and the finest young men and ladies of society have taken up the habit. So have the emperor's bodyguards and court eunuchs. It is estimated that China harbors some twelve million opium smokers."

I was amazed to hear that what I'd thought a private problem was such a vast calamity in the faraway Orient.

"And the scourge continues," Kuan said. "Every autumn, the ships arrive in Canton, laden with thousands of chests of opium from British poppy plantations in India. British merchants in the foreign settlements strike deals with Chinese opium brokers. Chinese silver pours into foreign hands, while the opium is carried inland along creeks and rivers, like poison flowing through the kingdom's blood."

Kuan suddenly addressed me: "What did you do when your brother fell under the evil spell of opium?"

Startled into frankness, I said, "I tried to stop him using it." Indeed, I'd searched the house for bottles of laudanum, thrown them away, and remonstrated with Branwell.

"That is exactly what we in China attempted with our many opium smokers," Kuan said. "Imperial edicts were issued, outlawing opium use and trade. Under orders to stem the scourge, I led raids on opium dens, arrested dealers. I seized Chinese opium boats and confiscated the cargo. Smokers were punished by beheading. Dealers and opium den operators were strangled. By discharging my duty, I made myself unpopular with the users whose opium I made scarce, the officials who profited by the trade, and the dealers whose property I destroyed." Kuan's expression turned dark with memory. "There was a price on my head."

His crusade to save his people had earned him threats. I had experienced the same from Branwell by trying to save him. I began to see another piece of his intention in telling me his story: Kuan meant to forge our common experience into a bond between us— and in spite of my awareness, he was succeeding.

"But the profits from the opium trade were so great," Kuan said, "that new dealers replaced those executed. The only solution was to attack the source of the opium: the British merchants. They who brought their foreign mud to poison our people must be banished from China."

The hatred I saw in his eyes when he spoke of the British merchants surprised me. I had never thought to hate the people who supplied opium to Branwell; I had blamed him alone for his condition. Now I felt my perspective revolving, like a globe turning in Kuan's hand to reveal new continents.

"The importation of opium was banned," Kuan went on. "British ships were searched, and their opium cargo seized. But corrupt officials pocketed bribes from British merchants and turned a blind eye to the trade. Although opium ships were barred from Chinese waters, they still came, for we lacked a navy strong enough to repel them. Chinese brigands formed secret societies to smuggle opium from the ships into China. Nonetheless, during the winter of 1838, we executed more than two thousand opium smugglers."

Kuan sat motionless while he spoke, yet radiated the fire of a zealot championing his cause. I watched him like a disciple mesmerized by a prophet.

"A new imperial commissioner arrived from Peking the next spring. Under his orders, I investigated civil servants and army officers suspected of collusion in the opium trade. By summer, I had caused the downfall of some sixteen hundred people. The commissioner ordered the British merchants to surrender all their opium and pledge to refrain from the trade forever. But they refused. The commissioner then halted all trade and imprisoned them inside their settlement. Finally, after many days under armed guard, the British surrendered their twenty thousand chests of opium, which we dumped into the ocean.

"But our triumph was brief. The British were outraged by our treatment of them, and their financial loss. They demanded reparations. They concentrated fifty battleships and several thousand troops at Hong Kong. There, the first shots of the war over opium were fired. The British forces began arriving in Canton the following year, in June 1840."

An image of battleships in full sail, heavy with guns and troops, advancing on a harbor, filled my mind. I saw the scene in more vivid detail than Kuan depicted in words. Was this my vision, or was his memory transmitted to me by some magical power?

"We were aghast at the size and strength of the fleet," Kuan said. "When it began to bombard our fortresses, we were horrified that our actions had provoked such retaliation."

My heartbeat sped with the fear that he must have experienced. I heard cannons booming across water, saw towers on shore in flames. Kuan's consciousness seemed to merge into mine, so that I lived his story—as he intended me to do.

"Our army fought valiantly, but it was no match against the British," Kuan said. "They blockaded the river and seized Chinese merchant junks. As they stormed nearby coastal cities, they revived the opium trade. They furnished arms to Chinese smugglers, who fought their way past our army. Sentiment in the kingdom turned against those of us who had most zealously pursued the crusade against opium. We were blamed for the war. The emperor decided that the British could be pacified, and the war halted, if he punished us. That August, I was among various officials relieved of their duties and assigned to faraway posts. My dedication had brought me the worst disgrace."

My perspective revolved further beyond my own moral foundation. I could not help but view Kuan as heroic and unjustly disgraced for trying to protect a kingdom from the ills that Branwell suffered.

"I did not leave Canton at once," Kuan continued. "The war required the military expertise I'd gained at my previous post. I stayed until the next spring. During that time, the British captured our forts and occupied Hong Kong. Their ships roved the Canton delta, sinking war junks and destroying defenses, then mounted an assault on the waterfront. Thousands of citizens fled Canton. Thieves looted abandoned houses. The troops I commanded built batteries along the shore, mounted guns, and fired on the British . . . in vain. British troops disembarked in May 1841 and amassed outside the city wall."

His mesmeric voice fostered in me visions of a city in chaotic peril. I saw the flames, smelled the smoke; I heard the screams of people fleeing the horde that besieged them.

"A general panic ensued," Kuan said. "Soldiers deserted their posts and plundered the city. Riots broke out. The governor of Canton called a meeting of his officials. I advised that we continue fighting. I reasoned that although the British were likely to take Canton, they could not conquer all of China; they would weaken before they reached the interior. But other officials advised negotiating a truce."

Kuan grimaced in contempt. "Their cowardice prevailed, and I, the lone dissenter, was ordered to leave for my new post. That evening, while the British clamored outside the city wall and the officials prepared to accept defeat, I hurried about town, settling my affairs. My son T'ing-nan and my personal retinue of ten men accompanied me. When we arrived home late at night . . ."

Kuan paused, and I perceived that powerful emotions were getting the best of his customary self-control. I sat alert, sensing that his story was approaching its climactic revelation. Rising, he said, "Come with me, Miss Brontë. I wish to show you something."

He led me to the room next door. It was unfurnished except for a table upon which stood a miniature framed portrait, painted in

Oriental style, of a pretty Chinese woman and two little girls, dressed in bright, exotic costume, their hair studded with ornaments. Candles flamed before the portrait. A brass vessel held sticks of smoking incense. At last I identified the source of the perfume in this house and in the Belgian chateau.

"These are my wife, Beautiful Jade, and my young daughters, Precious Jade and Pure Jade," said Kuan. "That night I arrived home to find them brutally murdered."

Reader, these were the murders I described earlier. I learned of them from Kuan, at this moment in my tale, and his spell and my imagination breathed life into his recital of the facts. Now I was to discover how the murders had set in motion the events I experienced.

"They lay slashed to death, awash in blood, in the wreckage of the bedchamber," Kuan said in a tone of deliberate detachment as we contemplated the funeral altar. "While I was gone, the servants had deserted my estate, leaving my wife and daughters alone. Someone had entered the mansion and slaughtered them."

The entirety of his motive for relating the events of his life to me became clear at last. Kuan wanted to engage my sympathy for his cause. A part of me understood that he was manipulating me; yet I couldn't but pity a man who'd lost his family by violence.

"On the wall, written in their blood, was the insignia of a secret society whose members traded in opium," Kuan said. "The insignia was their notice to me that they had murdered my family as revenge for my crusade against them."

Alas, his portrayal of himself as a hero and martyr was having the desired effect upon me, even as I knew him to be a murderous blackguard himself!

"Had I been home," said Kuan, "they would have killed me, too, and collected the price offered for my death. As I fell to my knees beside my wife and children—as I howled in grief—I felt rage leap like flames within me. My spirit demanded retribution. I wanted to punish the murderers for their crime, but how? I had no official standing in Canton; I couldn't mount a search for the killers, nor order their execution." The helplessness Kuan must have felt colored his tone. "And Canton had become a lawless place. What hope had I of justice?

"It was then that I broke the bonds of duty that I had honored all my life. I swore that I would pursue my family's killers and deliver them to justice myself." Kuan's eyes glittered. "I removed the gown and cap that had signified my official rank. I gave my son into the care of a trusted friend. Then I armed myself, and the ten loyal men from my retinue, with muskets and swords. I prayed one last moment over my wife and daughters, and I promised them that I would avenge their deaths. Then my men and I went hunting for the killers. We tracked them to their opium dens and we shot them dead. I did not care that I had become an outlaw and murderer myself. All I cared for was to kill every last one of them."

I pictured him and his henchmen bursting upon the surprised scoundrels, gunning them down amidst screams and blood. Though his remorseless violence horrified me, my spirit applauded him. I know what it is to hate someone with such venom, and I might have done similar harm to those who had wronged me, had I the power and not feared the consequences.

"During the next few days, we slew eighteen men," Kuan said. "In that time, the Canton officials and the British negotiated a truce. It was agreed that China would pay six million pounds—an enormous sum—to the British. In return, the British would spare the city and withdraw their ships from the waterfront. Despite the blood on my hands, my need for vengeance remained unsatisfied. The deaths of eighteen miserable opium smugglers could not restore my wife and daughters to life. And China had suffered a terrible defeat."

I thought that at last Kuan had explained why he'd left China. His womenfolk had been slain, his country humiliated; China harbored memories he must have longed to escape. I understood that Kuan, once a civilized, honorable man, had turned into a criminal because rage had twisted his mind. Yet still I didn't know why he had chosen to come to Britain—or what he wanted with me. Before I could ask, Hitchman appeared.

"What do you want?" Kuan frowned in annoyance at Hitchman.

"Sorry to interrupt," Hitchman said, "but I must speak to you. It cannot wait."

The two of them went out to the corridor, where they exchanged low, urgent words. Then Kuan hurried down the stairs without bidding me farewell. Hitchman came to me.

"Kuan asked that you excuse his abrupt departure," Hitchman said. "He'll resume your conversation later. In the meantime, he wants you to remain in your room."

As Hitchman escorted me there, not a word of explanation did he give; but clearly there was trouble. I would not learn until later what had happened—and later still, how its repercussions would ultimately put me in peril.

31

❖

I LANGUISHED IN MY ROOM, WONDER-
ING WHAT HAD HAPPENED. FOG
swept in from the sea, and a malaise enshrouded the house, which
was as silent as a tomb until that evening, when I heard footsteps. I
went to the door, and to my surprise it opened at my turn of the
knob; Hitchman had forgotten to lock it. I crept to the stairway and
spied Kuan and Nick in the hall below.

"Have you found any sign of my son?" Kuan asked.

Nick shook his head.

"Keep looking," said Kuan.

They parted company and disappeared from sight. I realized
that T'ing-nan must have gotten out of the house and run away.
Everyone was apparently occupied with bringing him back. I felt
pity for the boy, who had lost his mother and was now abroad in a
strange land, and for his father, too, because Branwell had taught
me the torment that ensues when a loved one goes missing. But
T'ing-nan's disappearance spelled opportunity for me.

The clock struck eleven o'clock, its chimes echoing through
the empty house. I dressed in my cloak and bonnet and stole
downstairs. The front door was unlocked; preoccupation with
finding T'ing-nan had rendered the household careless. Outside,
the dense, swirling mist obscured my vision of anything beyond
twenty paces distant. It muted the sea's roar and settled upon me,

damp and chill. As I hastened along the road towards Penzance, I had a disturbing sense of being watched. I paused to listen, but heard nothing.

At last I reached town and ascended the streets. Houses were densely packed in the twisted tangle of alleys. Their windows cast oblongs of faint light on the moist, slick cobblestones. Cats prowled past me; I heard them foraging and screeching in the darkness. The clattering of clogs heralded the approach of village folk who loomed suddenly out of the fog then disappeared. Smoke rose from chimneys atop the crooked slate roofs. I breathed the smells of fish frying, the salt sea, and the effluvium trickling from drains. Somehow I located Oyster Cottage, a tiny house built of rough-hewn stone, streaked brown by the weather. I rushed up the crumbling, uneven steps and pounded on the door.

"Mr. Slade!" I cried.

Mr. Slade immediately opened the door, pulled me inside, and held me while I sobbed from relief and lingering fright. "What are you doing here?" he said. "What's happened?"

I became aware of his body's heat warming me through the white shirt he wore, and my face pressed against the skin bared by his open collar. Embarrassed, I stepped away from him and tried to compose myself.

"I ran away," I said, and explained the circumstances that had allowed my escape. "I had to see you."

"I'm glad you're here," Mr. Slade said. "I'm even gladder to see you safe."

His voice was rough yet gentle, his gaze warm with something more than the happiness felt by comrades reunited. Could it be that my absence, and the danger to my life, had increased his affection for me? Flustered, I turned my attention to my surroundings. We stood in a small room with whitewashed walls and a low, slanted ceiling. The window was open to vent smoke from the fireplace. A table held books, papers, and a burning lamp. There was one plain chair where Slade had apparently been sitting at the table, and an armchair in the corner.

"You must be tired," he said. "Come, rest yourself."

He seated me in the armchair, then drew his chair opposite me and perched on its edge, leaning forward. I noticed how quiet the house was. There was no sign of Slade's fellow agents. The ease I'd learned to feel in his presence vanished. The room seemed too small, the dim lamplight too intimate, and Mr. Slade too close. I could see the dark stubble on his face, the reflections of the lamp in his eyes. But I should not allow myself to be distracted by personal thoughts. Quickly I told Mr. Slade about Kuan and what he'd said to me.

"So Mr. Kuan is a Chinaman," Mr. Slade said, amazed and enlightened. "That explains his strange accent and his connection with Isaiah Fearon, the China trader. It's a wonder that he's made such inroads into British society. But we knew he had a brilliant mind." Mr. Slade shook his head, deploring Kuan. "It's a pity that he has applied it to waging a personal war against us."

"Perhaps he has a good reason." My words, spoken without conscious thought, surprised me.

"What are you talking about?" Mr. Slade frowned in surprise even greater than mine.

"His family was murdered by opium dealers who were in collusion with British traders." Although I knew Kuan had done wrong, something in me wanted to explain his motives. "His homeland was invaded by ours."

I had been accustomed to think that Britain was good and noble and to respect its intentions, if not always its politicians. I didn't want to believe that my country would deliberately harm another for no just cause. I had always preferred to believe that people in the Far East were savage, ignorant heathens, and if they only knew better, they would understand that we wanted what was best for everyone. We, after all, were more advanced in science and philosophy; we were Christians, with God to justify our actions.

But now I realized that I had adopted Kuan's way of thinking. He had personified the Chinese for me, had made them seem human and their suffering real. He was akin to David fighting Goliath, and I could better identify with the small and weak than with the mighty. Though the Chinese were heathens, they were as much God's creatures as we, and as deserving of compassion. I was dismayed at how much influence Kuan had gained over my mind; yet I felt an irresistible urge to speak for him.

"Mr. Kuan is avenging the death of his wife and children and the humiliation of his country," I said.

Mr. Slade drew back from me, as much offended as he was puzzled by my vehemence. "Kuan has no right to punish innocent people in Britain for what happened to him in China," he said. "Isabel White, Joseph Lock, and Isaiah Fearon weren't responsible for the murder of his family or the attack on Canton. How can you defend that madman?"

All that was rational and moral in me rebelled against my own defense of Kuan; but alas, he had undermined that part of me. I couldn't admit to Mr. Slade how far Kuan had swayed me towards his side; nor could I stifle my compulsion to make Mr. Slade understand Kuan's point of view. "The actions of the British government have driven him mad. He's not to blame," I said, although I knew this was faulty reasoning. "In his mind, we, as a nation, have done far more wrong than he has. Were China to harm us, or England, in such a way, we should feel and react in kind. Can't you see that?"

"I can see that Kuan is a criminal," Mr. Slade said, adamant. "Whatever his justifications are, they don't excuse murder. And the situation in the East is more complex than he has represented to you. It's not for him to settle international disputes."

I flared with anger at Mr. Slade for arguing with me, and at Kuan for suborning me; given that Kuan wasn't there, my anger focused on Mr. Slade. At that moment I forgot I loved him; indeed, I almost hated him. He seemed a self-righteous brute. Some of my suspicion and disapproval of Kuan had transferred to Mr. Slade; some of my loyalty to Mr. Slade has transferred to Kuan.

"Are you so blindly certain of our goodness and his evil?" I demanded.

Mr. Slade's response was a look of grave concern for me that extinguished my irrational temper. Now I felt sick that I had allowed Kuan to come between us. I sank in my chair while contradictory impulses battled inside me and Mr. Slade regarded me with caution. The emotion that prevailed was a desire to regain our comradeship.

"Please forgive me," I said. "I didn't mean to speak as I did. So many upsetting things have happened to me that I hardly know what I'm saying."

"Yes, of course," Slade said, although he seemed not quite convinced by my disclaimer. "Have you learned what Kuan is planning?"

"Not yet," I said.

There ensued an awkward pause, during which Slade scrutinized me more closely than I liked. I could tell that he thought I was withholding information, and he was correct: Not one word about Kuan's strange influence on me had I breathed. I sensed that Mr. Slade was wondering whether I would share with him Kuan's plans if I knew them. Suddenly I wanted to flee him as much as I longed to stay with him.

"I must return to the house before Kuan misses me," I said, rising.

Mr. Slade stood between me and the door. "I have a better idea. You stay here. I'll fetch my comrades, and we'll storm that house and capture Kuan."

"No," I said. "He sneaked into the house by a secret passage; when he hears you coming, he could slip right through your fingers. I have to go back. Don't worry; I'll be safe."

"It's not just your safety that concerns me." Mr. Slade clearly sensed my divided loyalties.

"I'm all right," I said. "I have to go. Otherwise we may never learn what Kuan intends."

As much as I feared Kuan, I needed to show Mr. Slade that we were on the same side and that I would do my part. I edged around him towards the door, but he caught my hand and drew me to him. My heart began to pound with the fear that he would force me to tell him how I'd fallen under Kuan's sway, and an equal fear of what can happen when a man and woman find themselves alone together. Slade touched my cheek; it burned in response. Our faces were so close that I could feel our breath mingle. As he bent his head towards me, how I yearned for the touch of his lips on mine!

A sudden disturbing thought quenched my desire. Was Mr. Slade trying to seduce me because he truly wanted me, or did he have another, less flattering purpose? Perhaps he knew that his command over me had weakened and he sought to ensure my obedience. Kuan had poisoned my relationship with Mr. Slade. Once I would have eagerly welcomed his kiss; now I turned my face away. Mr. Slade hesitated, then dropped my hand. I couldn't look at him, so I know not whether his face showed hurt because I'd rejected him or vexation that his ploy had failed.

"Goodbye, then, Miss Brontë," he said, cool and formal. "Take care."

I fled the house in fear that I'd ruined the hopes I still cherished even while I distrusted Slade's motives. Outside, the wind had risen; the fog receded towards the sea. Midnight must have come and gone; the houses were dark. The moon and stars glowed through shreds of mist in the black sky as I rushed through the town and along the road. I had an even stronger sense of being followed than before. I imagined I heard footsteps echoing mine, and someone else's breaths. At last I reached the cove, where the sea's thunder drowned all other sounds. I crept down the path towards the house. Lights shone in the windows, and I despaired: The searchers had returned home during my absence. Even if Kuan, Hitchman, and Nick didn't know I wasn't in my room, I dared not attempt to sneak past them. How I wished I hadn't come back! Had I been thinking clearly, I would have encouraged Mr. Slade to raid the house. As I hesitated in the darkness some twenty paces from the house, a hand seized my wrist and pulled me into a stand of pines on a ledge overhanging the sea. I cried out in alarm.

"Miss Brontë, you be quiet, or I throw you in water," T'ing-nan said.

His menacing voice, and my knowledge of his character, told me that his threat was in earnest. I said, "Where have you been?" His face was dirty and streaked with tears, his clothes disheveled. "Everyone's been looking for you."

"I try run away," T'ing-nan said. Shivers and whimpers disrupted his breathing. "But no place to go." He clutched at me. "You help me go back to China!"

"I'm sorry, but I can't," I said, amazed that he would think me willing or capable of such. "I've no money; I don't even know how one goes about traveling to China." Although I'd known how much he longed for his homeland, I hadn't imagined him desperate enough for this. "Besides, your father would never approve."

"Please!" T'ing-nan, all but a grown man, burst into hysterical sobs. "You must help. I have nobody else!"

Lights shone down the path. T'ing-nan and I froze silent. His eyes gleamed with panic in the sudden illumination. I have no doubt that mine did the same. We heard Hitchman say, "I heard voices over there."

Rapid footsteps behind two moving lanterns approached us. T'ing-nan shrank into the trees and whispered urgently, "Please! No let them catch me!"

I had even more to fear than did T'ing-nan. As the light spilled over me, I was momentarily blinded; I then discerned Hitchman and Nick carrying the lanterns. They saw me; it was too late to evade them.

"Miss Brontë, what are you doing out here?" Hitchman demanded.

Two choices lay before me: I could help T'ing-nan hide and face questions I didn't want to answer, or I could give him away in the hope that it would protect me. "I came outside for a breath of air," I said. "I heard a noise, and I went to investigate. I've found T'ing-nan."

I pointed at him. As Hitchman and Nick shone their lanterns on him, he looked wildly around him for escape. But they blocked the path, while behind him was a vertical drop to the roaring, foaming sea. T'ing-nan wept in despair. He let Nick lead him up the path, but as he went by me, he muttered, "Someday you be sorry. Someday I make you pay."

Hitchman walked me to the house. "Well done, Miss Brontë. But in the future, obey orders."

I thanked Heaven that he had believed my story. After he locked me in my room, I knelt and prayed to God to help me survive. I tried to sort out my confused feelings. Certainly I had allowed myself to feel too much sympathy towards Kuan. Now that I was away from Mr. Slade, I thought better of him, and I chastised myself for throwing away an opportunity that might not come again. I hoped I hadn't alienated him forever. I hoped I would live long enough for us to reconcile.

There was a knock at the door. Hitchman appeared and said, "Kuan wants to see you."

He escorted me to the attic chamber, where Kuan sat at his desk. A single lamp burned. His face above his dark clothing seemed to float in the dim room, like an Oriental god above an altar in a temple. The smell of incense completed the illusion. He dismissed Hitchman and invited me to sit.

"A thousand thanks for restoring my son to me," he said.

"I'm glad to be of help," I said, relieved that he apparently intended to forgo punishing me for leaving the house. I was sorry I'd betrayed T'ing-nan, but he was safer here than wandering alone.

Kuan's luminous black gaze studied me. "Your hair is wet with mist. Your cheeks are red from the cold night air."

Fear trickled into my heart. Did he suspect I'd been outside longer than I'd implied when Hitchman found me? But he merely said, "You must have some wine to warm you."

He produced a bottle and poured a goblet for me. The wine gleamed ruby red. I am wary of imbibing liquor—perhaps from fear that it will enslave me as it has Branwell—and I would have declined, but I was wary of offending Kuan. I accepted the goblet and drank. The wine was sweetly potent, with a bitter aftertaste.

"You deserve a reward for finding T'ing-nan," Kuan said. "What shall it be?"

What I wanted was that he should go back to China and never harm anyone again. What I said was, "I should like to hear the rest of your story." Then God help me convey the information to Mr. Slade and effect Kuan's capture!

Kuan nodded. "Your choice pleases me." He resumed his tale as though we had never been interrupted: "After I took revenge on the men who killed my family and the Canton officials surrendered to the British, I could not remain in Canton. I had taken no care to conceal what I had done, and word that I had slain the opium gang spread through the city. My life as I had known it was over. I was a criminal, with the law after me. I fled into hiding in the delta. In the meantime, other events transpired."

His eyes looked inward and far outward at once, searching memory and space. "The war did not end with the truce. The British weren't satisfied with the money paid them for the opium that had been destroyed. They remained determined to conquer China, and they sailed their warships up the river. Brave folk in the country villages rose up to resist the barbarians. It was in one of these villages that my men and I had found shelter. The residents formed militias, arming themselves with cudgels, swords, match-locks, and spears. I became commander of my village's militia. My appetite for revenge extended beyond the Chinese gangsters who had slaughtered my family, to the British traders who were ulti-mately responsible."

Kuan paused, and his gaze concentrated on me. "Miss Brontë, you're not drinking your wine. Do you dislike it?"

"No, it's fine," I said, and sipped more, although the bitter taste put me off and my head was getting light.

"We fought a valiant, losing war against the British," Kuan went on. "By October they had occupied and looted two major cities, Tinghai and Ningpo. Chinese resisters everywhere were massacred, their houses burned, their families killed."

The wine blurred the room around me; visions of bodies drenched in blood and piled high in the streets flickered before my eyes, while gunfire and screams rang inside my head. These illu-sions were even more frighteningly real than those Kuan had inspired in the past. My glass was empty, and he refilled it. I drank in spite of a terror that he had doctored it with some potion that induced trances while it eroded the will.

"We, in our small efforts at fighting the barbarians, were like gnats buzzing around a giant. We were only delaying their inevitable victory," Kuan said, his hypnotic voice weaving through my confused thoughts. "I wasn't satisfied to fight to the death or to run away. I began to plot alternate strategies against the British. During my forays through the delta, I had the good luck to meet Tony Hitchman. He was captain of a merchant ship, the son of a duke with a proud heritage and no wealth. One night in Canton, Hitchman quarreled with the captain of another ship and stabbed the man to death. He was arrested, convicted of murder, and sentenced to hang."

I felt a chill of terror; my intimation that Hitchman was dangerous was now confirmed.

"While Hitchman was in prison, the war broke out," Kuan said. "During the confusion, he escaped. He fled to the marshes outside Canton, where a band of my soldiers caught him. They would have killed him, but I realized that he could be valuable. I ordered my men to desist. We gave him food and shelter. In return, he taught me English and captained the ship that brought us to Britain. Here, he introduced me to people who helped me establish a foothold in the West. We made perfect partners. I had allies in the form of my loyal retainers and the soldiers from the militia. Hitchman had maritime skills and advantageous connections."

At last I understood how a Chinaman had gained influence at high levels of society, through contacts obtained by his aristocratic underling. But dizziness and stupor rendered me silent, passive.

"One night we spied a British scout boat that had become lost in the delta. We killed the crew and stole the vessel. Thus began my career as a pirate. We made our way back to Canton to raise money to finance the plans I'd made. Our target was the opium trade. It seemed fitting." Irony colored Kuan's voice. "Opium money was stored in receiving ships moored offshore. We raided and plundered them until the British forces became too aggressive in their pursuit of us. We ventured farther out to sea to prey on opium clippers journeying home with their ill gotten bounty. Our biggest prize was a steamship carrying fifty thousand pounds in silver."

Kuan's face glowed with satisfaction. "Now I had my war treasury. I had a seaworthy ship. We set out for England and arrived in 1842. Here I used my stolen fortune, and Hitchman's contacts, to build an empire. I induced businessmen to give me war supplies and money, and traders to smuggle weapons to my allies in China. British politicians proved useful in shielding my secret efforts to mount an army that could drive their own nation out of China."

I knew how he'd exploited vulnerable men such as Joseph Lock and the prime minister, but I'd never dreamed he had so ambitious a goal as to wage a one-man war on Britain. His grandiosity amazed me; intoxication caused the peculiar sensation that my head was drifting free from my body. Kuan seemed far away, yet his voice infected me all the more deeply.

"The times favored me." Kuan seemed to appraise my condition; he smiled. "Many other men were as eager as I to overpower the leaders of Britain and other kingdoms. I forged alliances with revolutionaries both here and abroad. My intention was to foster instability in Britain while building my own power and wealth over the years, then to return to China, where I would drive the barbarians and the opium trade out of my homeland forever. But a certain event disrupted my plans."

Emotion darkened Kuan's face. I could feel his anger and hatred enfolding me like tentacles. The lamplight wavered. Strange echoes wailed in my ears as my head drifted higher.

"In June of 1842 came news from China," Kuan said. "The British forces had captured Shanghai. They then headed up the Yangtze River, wreaking terrible carnage. The Chinese army was powerless to stop them. The British reached Nanking in August, and China was forced to surrender."

Kuan's voice tightened with an effort to control the rage that suffused his features. "In Nanking Britain and China signed a treaty that ceded Hong Kong to Britain and ordered China to pay an indemnity of twenty-one million pounds. This loss of territory was a disgraceful humiliation for China. And the opium trade flourished bigger than ever. I realized that I could not afford to delay taking action. Britain might overrun China while I was slowly building my army. Hence, I plotted a more immediate, daring scheme to make Britain pay for the deaths of my wife and children, and at the same time force it to renounce the new treaty and leave China."

Fanatical determination smoldered in his eyes. "Innocents shall suffer as recompense for the suffering of innocents. I shall take them hostage to my cause and bring the British Empire to its knees. For six years I have been gaining the influence of the right people and planting my allies in strategic places. The time is almost at hand."

This was the closest I had come to learning Kuan's intentions, and excitement reverberated through me; but still he spoke in only vague terms. In my entranced condition, I couldn't fathom his meaning. A question surfaced from amidst the whirl of sensations that possessed my mind. "What innocents?" I whispered. "Who are your hostages?"

"Be patient, Miss Brontë. You will know soon enough," said Kuan. His secretive smile teased me. "In fact, you will play a role of the utmost importance in my scheme. It is the role I once intended for our mutual friend Isabel White. You will take her place."

Across my vision flashed the image of Isabel's murder in that London alley. I heard the words from her diary as if she spoke inside my head: *How could I allow myself to be used as an instrument to shake the foundations of the world?* Should I refuse to comply with Kuan, I would share her fate. Should I obey him, I would share her sins. *I must free myself of Him, or consign my soul to eternal damnation.* A heart-pounding fright stirred in me an urgent desire to run for my life. I tried to stand, but my limbs were as heavily inert as sacks of flour.

"Why have you chosen me?" I whispered.

Kuan rose, moved behind my chair, and leaned close to me. "You, Miss Brontë, are a woman of intelligence, honor, and righteousness." His warm breath hissed the words into my ear. "Together we will triumph over evil."

His strange magic combined with the effects of the wine, subduing my urge to resist. It blurred my ability to distinguish between justice for Isabel White and Kuan's other victims, and justice for Kuan's family and China. Now Kuan caressed my cheek. To my horror, I felt my skin tingle alive under his fingers, and the heat of desire spread through me.

I thrilled to the touch that I'd longed for, said Isabel's voice in my memory.

"Your face is as beautiful as your spirit," Kuan whispered. "You enchant me."

His words fed a lifetime's hunger for such praise, even if it was false. How much I had yearned to hear it from Mr. Slade, who had never expressed such admiration for me. Kuan raised me to my feet, easing me so slowly and smoothly away from the chair that it seemed to vanish. He held me with my back pressed to him. The room faded from my perception; we were afloat in some alien place where lights flickered and eerie noises sounded through black shadows. Kuan's lips grazed my neck; his hands moved over my breasts. No man had ever touched me thus. Intoxicated and dizzy, I moaned as pleasure overwhelmed me.

I wanted to flee in terror, but . . . I could only submit.

Mr. Slade had instilled in me this desire, but had not fulfilled it. Now I responded against my will to Kuan, craving from him what I couldn't have from Mr. Slade. The animal in me was a blind, lusty creature, unable to distinguish one man from another. I hardly knew what I felt for Mr. Slade and what for Kuan.

But how could I commit such a sin as enjoying a man outside the bonds of holy matrimony? Should feminine virtue have not restrained me? Alas, I cared nothing for God nor propriety, nor anything except Him.

My mind pictured Mr. Slade holding and caressing me, as real as life. I sighed with rapture. *His very presence reduced me to a state of hot, quivering need. . . .* The image of Mr. Slade and myself dissolved into a shocking, obscene picture of Kuan with Isabel White, naked and entwined. But at that moment I didn't care that Kuan had been Isabel's lover. I didn't care that he wasn't Mr. Slade. I forgot he was a murderer. All I was aware of was his power to satisfy my desire.

"Will you do my bidding, Miss Brontë?" Kuan murmured. I heard Mr. Slade's voice echo his. "Will you help me achieve justice?"

When He said, "What would you do for me?" I answered with all my heart: "Whatever you wish." He was my master, the source of all the meaning in my life. I was His devoted slave.

"Yes," I whispered, not knowing whether it was Mr. Slade or Kuan to whom I was pledging my loyalty.

32

I AWAKENED TO FIND MYSELF LYING ON MY BED, FULLY DRESSED, MY SPECTA-cles askew on my face. Pale daylight shone through the white curtains; gulls screeched outside. My head ached, my stomach was queasy, and there was a sour taste in my mouth. My wits stirred sluggishly to life. I sat up with a cry of dismay as I recalled how Kuan had begun to seduce me. Yet I couldn't recall anything else, for the wine must have rendered me unconscious. Panic clutched my heart. What, in my inebriated condition, had I allowed that madman to do?

I made a hasty inspection of my clothes and person, and found no evidence that Kuan had maltreated me. It seemed that he'd conveyed me to my bed and left me to sleep. I was vastly relieved, but also shamed and horrified that last night I had succumbed to Kuan. Was it only poisoned wine that had undermined my will? With its effects worn off, could I still resist him? Or was I his creature, over whom he would always exert control? I moaned at the thought that here was another day to face. How many more must I pass in Kuan's company before I could learn who were his intended hostages and what were his plans for them?

When fortune gives us no alternative but to go on, we somehow manage. I rose, washed, and tidied myself. This took a bit of time, as my stomach kept heaving, and dizziness spun the room around me; I frequently had to stop and lie down. Finally I tottered downstairs.

I was surprised to find Kuan, Hitchman, and T'ing-nan in the dining room: This was the first time I would have their company at a meal. Kuan and Hitchman bade me a polite good morning, to which I replied with as much composure as I could. T'ing-nan only glared at me: He was still angry that I had given him up to his father last night. I perceived the echo of a conversation that my arrival had interrupted.

"Please join us, Miss Brontë," said Kuan.

I sat at the end of the table, opposite him. Ruth served me tea, bread, and eggs. Hitchman was eating the same meal as I, but Kuan and T'ing-nan had bowls of what appeared to be gruel with fish and strange herbs. T'ing-nan held his bowl up to his mouth and shoveled in the food with chopsticks, never once taking his hostile gaze off me.

"Did you sleep well last night?" Kuan asked me in a tone that hinted at the drama we had enacted together.

"Yes, thank you," I said, although my face burned.

Hitchman regarded us with suspicious curiosity. I lowered my gaze to my plate, but the food turned my stomach. I sipped the strong, bitter coffee, which somewhat restored my health and courage.

"I beg permission to go into town," I said. I must tell Mr. Slade what Kuan revealed to me last night, and here I presented my excuse: "I wish to go to church. I've not been since I left home."

"You can wait awhile longer," Hitchman said.

"No," Kuan overruled him. "Miss Brontë must be allowed to observe her religious rites."

"Very well," Hitchman said, though clearly disgruntled.

I wondered whether Kuan thought the spell he'd worked upon me last night had secured me in his power and he'd come to trust me enough to let me go, or whether he wished to assert his superiority over Hitchman. Whatever the reason, I was glad to climb into the carriage. To escape Kuan's frightening pres-ence, if only temporarily, was a boon. As Nick drove me towards town, a storm commenced. Rain battered the carriage; lightning seared the deluged coastline and sea. Between cracks of thunder I heard hoofbeats following us. I looked out the window and saw what appeared to be·a farmer riding a horse. He tipped his hat at me, and I recognized Mr. Slade, who must have been secretly watching Kuan's house in case I should come out. Relief swam over me.

In Penzance, Nick drove up wet cobblestone streets where townspeople walked sheltered under umbrellas and brick town-houses abounded. He stopped the carriage outside St. Mary's Church. Its stone walls promised age-old sanctuary to souls in need. I climbed out of the carriage, trying not to look about for Mr. Slade. The rain drenched Nick and me as we hurried past a churchyard filled with tombs and lush with tropical vegetation. Inside the church, Nick stationed himself by the door while I walked up the aisle between the pews. Among these were scat-tered some dozen worshippers. Lightning illuminated them in flashes. Their soft spoken prayers and the rumbling thunder echoed in the chill, dank space. I anxiously scanned the church from beneath my bonnet. Would Mr. Slade come? How might we talk without Nick's noticing us?

I heard a soft hiss, glanced to my right, and saw Mr. Slade crouching on the floor inside a pew. He must have watched me stop at the church, where he hurried to enter by some other door and lie hidden in wait for me. My steps faltered, and he gestured for me to sit by him. Conscious of Nick's gaze on me, I did.

"Act as if I'm not here," Mr. Slade whispered. "Pretend you're praying."

I bowed my head over my clasped hands. My mind teemed with memories of the previous night, while my heart beat fast with emotions I had no time to sort out. "Kuan has told me some part of his plan for revenge," I whispered. "He means to take hostages and force the British out of China." I regretted that my news was so vague. "But I don't know who the hostages are or how Kuan means to take them."

There was a brief silence from Mr. Slade, during which I

sensed his shock. He said, "I do know. Yesterday I received a letter from the prime minister. He says he was accosted by one of Kuan's henchmen in London. The man ordered him to use his authority to persuade the Queen that her children need a new governess, and to recommend Charlotte Brontë for the post."

Amazement and horror overwhelmed me as Mr. Slade's news and mine combined like pieces of a puzzle fitting together to complete a terrifying picture. "The royal children are the hostages Kuan intends to take! I am to help him kidnap them!" I fought to lower my voice and maintain the pretext of prayer.

"So this is how he means to strike at the British Empire." Revelation inflected Mr. Slade's voice. "Not by military force, but by ransoming its most precious treasure—the royal bloodline. If he succeeds, he will usher in a new, horrific era of warfare. No longer will enemies need huge armies to cripple us—just the wherewithal to kidnap, extort, and terrify. It could begin the downfall of not just Britain, but the civilized world."

We sat speechless in awe and dread of such a future, until I voiced the question that Kuan had evaded answering: "Why has Kuan chosen me, of all people?"

"I can only speculate that you have the traits he needs in an accomplice. He surely knows other people who are capable of kidnapping the children but none responsible enough—as you are—to ensure their well-being until he's done with them." Slade added, "Yours must be the role for which he intended Isabel White. No wonder she balked and ran away from him. The kidnapping must have been the last straw for her."

"It's the last for me as well!" I exclaimed, distraught and frantic. "I cannot do it any more than Isabel could!"

Now I understood why Kuan had questioned me about my feelings towards children: He had wanted to ascertain that I was capable of harming them if need be—and he had misinterpreted my lack of enthusiam to mean that indeed I was. Though I bore them not much affection, I could never conspire to make the six royal children "the innocents who shall suffer as recompense for the suffering of innocents."

"I know you don't want to," Mr. Slade said, "but forestalling it won't be that simple."

My terror increased a hundredfold. "Kuan will kill me if I resist. What am I going to do?"

Mr. Slade pondered while our time together swiftly fled. I saw, with a sinking heart, that there was no safe way to end my ordeal. Now I heard Nick's footsteps coming towards me. Fearful and desperate, I beseeched Mr. Slade again, "What shall I do?"

"Prepare to resume your old occupation as a governess."

❧❦

Nick drove me back to the house. There I spent the day alone, for T'ing-nan refused to come out of his room for lessons, and I didn't see Kuan or Hitchman. The house seemed deserted, except for Ruth, who served my meals. That night after dinner I became so drowsy that I must have been drugged again. I slept so soundly that I was aware of nothing until morning, when I again awakened feeling groggy and ill. I rose and dressed, then heard a knock at my door. I opened it to find Hitchman outside. He was wearing his coat, carrying his hat.

"Pack your bags, Miss Brontë," he said. "We're leaving."

I was alarmed by the realization that Kuan's plans were being set so abruptly in motion. "Where are we going?"

"To London," Hitchman said.

"Why?" I said. But I already knew. Fear and anxiety rushed upon me.

"I'll explain on the way," Hitchman said.

"What about Mr. Kuan?" I said, trying to stall the inevitable. "Are he and T'ing-nan coming with us?"

"They've already gone." Hitchman's cruel smile mocked my dismay. "They left last night."

I comprehended that I had indeed been drugged last night, so that I wouldn't hear their departure. I felt an awful despair. Kuan had vanished again, probably through the house's cellars and the smugglers' caves, then by boat out to sea. While I was still under the power of his henchman, I faced the threat of death unless I cooperated with his scheme.

"Make haste, Miss Brontë," said Hitchman. "The train leaves in an hour."

33

> ✦ ✦

Hitchman accompanied me to London on the train. He told me nothing of our plans, other than that I would receive further instructions when we arrived. While riding in the carriage, he sat beside me; at stations along the way, he rarely let me out of his sight.

"If you have any thoughts of absconding, you had best forget them," he warned me. "Kuan has men besides myself watching over you."

I didn't see Mr. Slade during the trip, and I feared that we had become separated. The mundane business of eating box lunches and changing trains took on a nightmarish quality. The combination of terror and monotony was almost unbearable.

We arrived at Euston Station on 4 September. Hitchman helped me out of the train onto the platform. Exhausted and disoriented, I wondered what misadventure lay in store for me. Then I saw, loitering amidst the crowds, a familiar figure. It was Lord John Russell, the prime minister. His hat shielded his face, as though he wished to obscure his identity. Hitchman called his name; Lord Russell turned. His startled, wary look of recognition encompassed Hitchman as well as me.

"I've been ordered to meet you," he said to Hitchman in a low voice; he didn't want to be overheard. He pretended not to know me. "Here I am." His scowl expressed bitter resentment.

"And here is Miss Brontë," Hitchman replied. "Do as you've been told, and all will go well for you." The threat showed through his genial manner. "That applies to you, too, Miss Brontë. *Au revoir*," he said, then slipped away and was lost in the crowds.

Lord Russell led me to a carriage without looking at me. His face was grim; he didn't speak a word until we were riding slowly through the London traffic. "Forgive me if I don't seem happy to see you again. Do you know that I have been forced to obtain for you a position as governess to Her Majesty's children?"

"Yes," I said. "Mr. Slade told me about your letter."

Lord Russell clenched his fists and glared about as if looking for somebody to pummel. "The villain's audacity defies belief! Have you met him? Who is he? What does he intend?"

I described Kuan and his motives as best I could. I explained that Mr. Slade and I had deduced that Kuan meant me to help him kidnap the children, so that they could be used as hostages to force Britain out of China. Lord Russell's sickly countenance turned even sicker. Cursing under his breath, he pulled a handkerchief from his pocket and wiped sweat off his forehead.

"I cannot possibly abet such a scheme," he said. "What he plans is the blackest treachery against the crown! Yet he holds my life in his hands. God help me!"

As the carriage inched along, a man jumped inside. He wore the shabby clothes of a beggar and a cap pulled low over his eyes. He sat next to the prime minister.

"Sir, this a private carriage," Lord Russell said in a startled, offended tone.

The intruder removed his cap. It was Mr. Slade. "Thank Heaven!" I exclaimed. "I thought never to see you again!" Tears welled in my eyes as the emotions I'd suppressed during my journey with Hitchman found release.

"I followed you all the way from Cornwall," Mr. Slade said. "You weren't alone."

His manner was businesslike and impersonal, but I could discern that he was glad to see me, too. I felt happy and safe in his presence, even though still under mortal threat from Kuan. How could I have ever divided my loyalty between them?

Lord Russell greeted Mr. Slade without enthusiasm. He obviously had not forgotten the humiliating confession he had made at the ball.

"Kuan is gone," I told Mr. Slade.

"I know. My men searched his house as soon as you and Hitchman left." Mr. Slade turned to Lord Russell. "Have you arranged Miss Brontë's new post?"

"Yes, I have," Lord Russell replied in a hateful tone. "I'm taking her to Buckingham Palace now. We have an audience with the Queen at one o'clock."

I cowered at the very idea. How unworthy of the honor I felt! To think that I must meet Her Majesty under such ignoble circumstances! "What will we do?"

"We must tell the Queen everything," Mr. Slade said.

Lord Russell looked anxious. "Not everything, surely."

"We'll keep your connection with Mr. Kuan a secret," Mr. Slade assured him. "We'll persuade the Queen to let Miss Brontë stay in her employ long enough for us to find out who Kuan's agents are and apprehend them and him."

"How do you propose to persuade Her Majesty?" Lord Russell said, clearly deeming this a futile plan.

"That's what we must determine before you take Miss Brontë to the palace," said Slade. "She would probably like some luncheon first. Take her to the Warwick Club. I'll meet you there."

Lord Russell shook his head as though in disbelief that any good could come of whatever we did, but he said, "Very well."

The traffic cleared; the carriage began moving faster. Mr. Slade opened the door. "Where are you going?" I said, loath to lose him.

"To gather our forces," Mr. Slade said, then jumped from the carriage.

➤✦

Lord Russell and I dined in a private room, at a table laid with heavy silver, fine linen, and china. Velvet draperies covered the window; with candles burning, it felt like night. We had finished and were sitting in grim silence when Mr. Slade arrived with Lord Unwin and a man I didn't know. This man was in his sixties and handsome with an elegant figure, wavy grey hair, and a jaunty step. Lord Russell and I both rose.

"Lord Palmerston," the prime minister said, speaking and bowing stiffly. He barely acknowledged Lord Unwin, whose haughty countenance showed resentment at the snub.

Lord Palmerston returned the greeting with cool civility. Mr. Slade said, "Miss Brontë, may I present the foreign secretary?"

I had recognized his name. This was the man charged with managing England's relations with foreign kingdoms and protecting the interests of the crown. The newspapers extolled his skill at diplomacy as loudly as they criticized his policies. "It is an honor, sir," I said, awestruck.

He took my hand and gracefully raised it to his lips. "The honor is all mine." His smile was shaped like a Cupid's bow; his eyes sparkled with intelligence and zest. His voice was suave, and I felt the power of his charm. "I had the pleasure of knowing your father long ago. Pat Brontë and I were at Cambridge together."

"Yes, I know." I recalled Papa talking about how, in 1804, when Britain was bracing for an invasion by Napoleon's army, volunteer militias were formed. Papa and other university men had drilled under the command of Henry Temple, the officer in charge. Papa took pride in this connection between himself and the man who was now foreign secretary, but I never expected Lord Palmerston to remember Papa.

"When you see your father, please give him my best regards," Lord Palmerston said.

"I will, sir." I could see that his prodigious memory, coupled with his skill at pleasing people, had contributed to his political success.

"If you'll excuse my haste, time is short," Lord Palmerston said, and I glimpsed the man of purpose beneath the charm. We all sat at the table. "Mr. Slade has briefed me on the situation, and we are in agreement on what must be done." He ignored

Lord Unwin, who compressed his lips, disgruntled. "Now I shall tell you how I propose to handle Her Majesty."

His self-confidence was supreme. I envisioned Papa as a university student, marching at a young Lord Palmerston's orders. Now I was under the same command.

✦✦

The unpredictability of life astounds me. My adventure had already taken me beyond the limits of where I had ever envisioned going. I had traversed England and crossed the sea; I had found myself among the dregs of society and then among the rich and powerful; I had journeyed into my past. Caught between two men who represented the poles of good and evil, I had done things of which I had never thought myself capable, and enacted dramas more intense than any in my dreams. But even with all that, I would never have imagined meeting Victoria Regina, Queen of England.

We arrived at Buckingham Palace, whose vast grey bulk of Classical architecture dominates the Mall that encompasses Trafalgar Square and Westminster. Red-coated guards armed with rifles stood sentry outside. A flag bearing the royal standard fluttered over the roof, indicating that the Queen was in residence. Mr. Slade, Lord Palmerston, Lord Russell, and Lord Unwin escorted me so quickly through the palace that I had only a blurred impression of marble pillars, wide hallways, grand staircases, hordes of servants, abundant mirrors, ornate furniture, and gilding everywhere. I found it to be as vulgar as it was magnificent. All I remember clearly is the stench of bad drains and stagnant cesspools.

My presentation to the Queen took place in her sitting room. She and her Prince Consort were seated on a brocade-covered divan amidst many figurines, gold-framed portraits, and brass cages of pet birds. Dolls and other toys lay strewn about the floral carpet. Through open windows hung with gold draperies came the noise of children at play outside. The informality of the situation surprised me, although I remembered that I was here as a servant, unworthy of a lavish, ceremonial presentation at court. Trembling and awkward, I didn't dare look up from the floor until curiosity triumphed over timidity.

This was not the first time I had seen Queen Victoria. While I was at school in Belgium, she had visited Brussels. I'd stood amidst the crowds to watch her procession. When she flashed by in a carriage, I had thought her not beautiful, and I found my impression still valid now, five years later. She was prettily dressed in a summer gown, but even more stout than before, having borne six children, one of them that past spring. She wore her brown hair in a simple knot. She had a florid, heavy-featured face with a pointed nose and receding chin. The Prince Consort, Albert of Saxe-Coburg-Gotha, was tall, rather stiff, and clad in an elaborate coat, breeches, and boots. He wore a mustache and whiskers in foreign style, and looked far less handsome than his portraits.

Formal greetings were exchanged. The Queen extended her hand to Lord Palmerston, who politely kissed it. She said, "The Queen is delighted that her foreign secretary chooses to grace her with his presence." Her voice was well bred yet girlish; she was only twenty-nine, very young for a ruler of the Empire. I detected sarcasm in her courteous tone. "His behavior has led her to believe that he preferred to avoid communication with her."

Later Mr. Slade explained to me that the Queen and Palmerston were at odds because she wanted to approve all official correspondence from the Crown before it was disseminated, but that he had repeatedly taken action on her behalf and informed her only after the fact.

"Not at all, Your Majesty," said Lord Palmerston. "Were it not for the demands of my office, wild horses could not keep me from seeking your delightful company." He spoke with such gallantry that the Queen visibly softened.

Lords Russell and Unwin made their obeisance to the royal pair. The Prince Consort was uniformly cordial to everyone. He spoke with a heavy Germanic accent. Although the same age as the Queen, he appeared much older due to his ponderous manner. The Queen was cool towards Lord Russell. I later learned from Mr. Slade that she thought the cross, unhandsome, and brusque little man failed to measure up to his predecessors, of whom she'd been quite fond. She paid Lord Unwin scant attention. When Lord Palmerston introduced Mr. Slade, she studied him with interest as he kissed her hand. Her cheeks flushed brighter; she smiled. Then came my turn. Shaking in my shoes, miserably aware of my plain looks and travel-worn clothes, I tiptoed up to the Queen. I felt like a criminal, approaching my sovereign under false pretenses. Keeping my gaze downward, I watched the hem of my frock move nearer hers. I made an awkward curtsy, murmuring my respects in a scarcely audible voice.

"This is Miss Charlotte Brontë, Your Majesty's new governess," said Lord Russell.

"Welcome, Miss Brontë," said the Queen.

Her voice compelled me to raise my head that she might inspect me. My heart pounded as I stood face to face with the Queen, close enough to touch her. She had round, protuberant, luminous eyes whose intelligence rendered her better than plain. A regal aura surrounded her despite her youth. Her expression indicated that she didn't think much of me.

"That the prime minister has recommended you satisfies me that you are qualified to be governess to my children, Miss Brontë," she said. Mr. Slade later told me that her high officials had a say regarding who worked in her household, and she must often acquiesce, given that handing out political favors was essential to maintaining good relations with them. "But I should like to know something about you." I saw that she was a mother concerned about the character of the person charged with tending her children. "Who is your family? Where is your home?"

When I told her, she seemed satisfied, albeit unimpressed. I sensed Mr. Slade and Lords Palmerston, Russell, and Unwin marking time until they could attend to their real business.

"Where were you educated?" the Prince Consort asked me.

After I replied, he questioned me in detail regarding the subjects studied and the posts I'd previously held. He was more interested in the education of his children than were many fathers I had encountered while a teacher. I began to understand that he was at least half the brains at the helm of the nation. He conversed with me in French and studied me with earnest, somber attention. When he expressed his opinion that I would do very well, his wife concurred. He had a strong influence over the Queen.

"You should meet the children now, Miss Brontë," she said.

Lord Palmerston cleared his throat. "In a moment, please, Your Majesty." She raised her eyebrows, surprised that he should contradict her. "My apologies, but there's an important matter we must discuss."

"Very well," she said, her interest piqued in spite of herself. "What is it?"

"Miss Brontë has been approached by a man who has offered her a bribe in exchange for helping him kidnap Your Majesty's children," said Lord Palmerston. This was the story that he and Mr. Slade had invented in order to shield the prime minister.

"Kidnap my children!" Breathless with horror, the Queen clapped a hand to her bosom. Her gaze flew to the window, through which we heard the children laughing in the garden. She glared at me, as if I were at fault, then at Palmerston. "But this is outrageous!"

The Prince Consort's expression was troubled, but he remained calm. "Who is it that means to engage Miss Brontë in such an evil conspiracy?"

"Mr. Slade has identified the man as a criminal he's been hunting for some time," said Lord Palmerston. "His name is Kuan. He hails from Canton, China. He's a pirate and renegade whose purpose is to upend order in our hemisphere." He gave a brief, edited history of how Kuan had abetted revolutionaries in Britain and abroad. He spoke rapidly, with an authority that discouraged questions. The Queen and Prince Consort looked too shocked to ask any. Lord Palmerston omitted my role, thinking they might disapprove of my sleuthing. "He has murdered many people in his quest for power. He must be stopped."

"Well, then stop him!" the Queen cried with a grand, sweeping gesture, as if to send the entire British army in pursuit of Kuan. "Don't let him come near my children!"

"We shall ensure that he won't," said Lord Palmerston. "However, we need Your Majesty's cooperation."

"You shall have it," the Prince Consort said as he laid a soothing hand on his wife's arm. "But first, we must reconsider Miss Brontë's employment. In view of her connection with this criminal, we cannot allow her to join our household, even if she is innocent of any wrongdoing."

"My dear Albert is right," the Queen promptly agreed. She gave me an icy look. "I regret to inform you that you must seek another post elsewhere." She then addressed Lord Unwin: "Would you be so good as to escort Miss Brontë out?"

I felt like a leper banished from society, tainted by my unwilling association with Kuan. I would have meekly gone, but Lord Palmerston lifted his hand, stopping me.

"I must beg you to reconsider, Your Majesty," said Lord Palmerston. "We need Miss Brontë."

The Queen regarded Palmerston as if he had asked her to take a viper to her bosom. Her eyes blazed with her dislike of his overbearing manner. "Whatever for?"

Lord Palmerston glanced at Mr. Slade, who said, "Kuan has gone into hiding. We don't know where he is. But he has told Miss Brontë that he'll be in communication with her as regards kidnapping the children." The Queen listened, compelled by his personality and the urgency in his voice. "Miss Brontë is a loyal, law-abiding citizen with no intention of abetting Kuan, and she is our only link to him. Unless she is permitted to assume the post of governess, the link will be broken. We'll lose our chance to catch him."

"Oh, Albert, what shall we do?" the Queen wailed, on the verge of tears. I recalled that she had just had a baby; perhaps she was in a more excitable state than usual.

After careful deliberation, the Prince Consort said to Slade, "You must find some other way to catch this criminal than by planting Miss Brontë among our children and waiting for him to show himself. Even if she means them no harm, we would prefer some other governess."

Slade inclined his head. "With all due respect, Your Royal Highness, I must persuade you otherwise. We have good reason to believe that Kuan has accomplices already inside your household. Even should Miss Brontë refuse his bribe, he can enlist others to harm the children."

"My God!" the Queen exclaimed, looking around as if suddenly surrounded by enemies. "Can no one near me be trusted?"

"Not until Mr. Kuan's henchmen have been identified and removed," Slade said. "And the best way to accomplish that is to plant Miss Brontë here among them. I predict that they shall reveal themselves to her when the time comes to carry out the kidnapping."

The Queen shook her head, too distraught to reply.

"But when will that be?" her husband asked. "How long must we wait?" When no one could furnish an answer, he said, "Here is a better idea: We shall interrogate everybody in the household and determine who are Kuan's confederates."

"That's reasonable, Your Highness," Mr. Slade said with careful courtesy. "The problem is that Mr. Kuan's accomplices may be clever enough to escape our detection."

The Prince Consort conceded with a reluctant nod. "Then I propose dismissing all our servants and attendants. That way, there can be no question that we have rid ourselves of everyone who means us harm. We shall replace them with new persons of impeccable character."

"That's quite a good alternative," said Lord Palmerston.

"Indeed, Your Highness," said Mr. Slade.

Lord Unwin echoed them. Lord Palmerston and the Prince Consort began discussing people who might fill various posts. I watched the Queen, whose expression turned stormy as she listened. I saw that she didn't like the men, her subordinates, leaving her out of the conversation and making decisions for her.

"This is impossible!" she exclaimed. "I won't allow a purge of my entire household!"

"My dearest," the Prince Consort soothed her while he patted her hand.

"It's in your best interests, Your Majesty," Lord Palmerston said gravely.

"Nonsense!" The Queen flung off her husband's hand and swept away Palmerston's words with an imperious wave. "My ladies-in-waiting and servants are some of my most loyal, beloved friends in the world. I'll not throw them all out just because there might be a few bad apples in the barrel! Nor will I tolerate an entire house full of strangers!"

"But you must, for the sake of the children," her husband coaxed.

"Their safety must be our primary concern," Mr. Slade said.

The Queen huffed. "I am the mother of the children. I'll decide what's best for them!" I wondered how often she'd been pushed around; it was clear she hated it.

"Then what will you have us do, Your Majesty?" Condescension edged Lord Palmerston's deferential air.

Her eyes darted and rapid breaths fluttered her bosom; she rose from her divan and paced in search of an answer. Her feverish gaze lit on me. "Miss Brontë will take up her post as governess. She will help us to thwart and capture our enemies, as was originally suggested."

I could see that she liked the plan no better than before, yet was determined to oppose the men and unable to think of an alternative. The Prince Consort rose, put his arm around her, and led her back to her chair, saying, "Calm yourself, or you'll be ill. Think of the danger to the children."

The Queen sat with a heavy, graceless thump. "They're in danger as long as this villain Kuan is at large, whether or not I replace my attendants. He might suborn the new ones as well as the old. Trapping him, with Miss Brontë's assistance, is the only solution."

"But the plan is neither that simple nor so foolproof, Your Majesty." Lord Palmerston's tone derided her judgment. "Something could go wrong, despite our best endeavors."

She glowered at him, showing a hint of the formidable old

woman she might well become, many years hence. "Your best endeavors must suffice. I've made my decision. And you had better not fail me."

Her tacit threat encompassed Mr. Slade, Lord Russell, and myself. The Queen had spoken.

"Yes, Your Majesty," Lord Palmerston said meekly.

Slade nodded while the Prince Consort sat in glum, troubled defeat. Lord Palmerston hid a smug smile behind his hand, for the Queen had done exactly as he'd predicted when he'd described his strategy beforehand at the club. He had expected that pushing her in one direction would cause her to move the opposite way. By pretending to support the Prince Consort's idea of replacing her attendants, he had manipulated her into allowing the royal children to be used as bait for the purpose of entrapping Kuan. Such a wily, conniving character was Lord Palmerston! I thanked God that he was working *for* the British Empire and not against it.

The Queen smiled, placated. "Now that this matter is settled, I trust it shan't interfere with our journey to Scotland."

Her husband's expression grew all the more troubled. Mr. Slade frowned. Even Lord Palmerston looked disconcerted as he said, "I'd quite forgotten that Your Majesty and Your Highness were planning to visit your new estate in Balmoral."

"We are set to depart tomorrow," said the Prince Consort.

"I must respectfully advise that you postpone the trip," Lord Palmerston said.

"But we've so been looking forward to it," the Queen protested. "As have the children." Her gaze hardened. "Why should we disappoint them?"

"You'll be extremely vulnerable to attack while you're traveling," Lord Palmerston answered.

If the Queen and her children should go to Scotland, then so must their governess. Alarm filled me. Things had seemed difficult enough when I thought I would be fulfilling my duty here in London. Traveling with the Queen was far beyond the scope of my experience and capabilities. I desperately hoped that Lord Palmerston would dissuade her.

"Under such conditions, protecting Your Majesty and the children would be difficult," Slade said.

"Certainly no more than here," the Queen said. "Your security precautions on my behalf are so lax that intruders can come and go as they please. Need I remind you of that boy named Jones who wandered round inside the palace for days before he was caught and arrested?"

"Yes, well," Lord Palmerston said, abashed. "But Your Majesty had best stay in London until Kuan is apprehended and the danger is past."

Her eyes flashed with renewed anger. "Oh, is the Queen of England to be a prisoner in her own home?" She tossed her head. "I will not bow to some foreign criminal, and I refuse to cower inside the palace. I might just as well hand over my kingdom to anyone who threatens me! We shall go to Scotland as planned."

I saw resignation on the faces around me. The pride of Britain was at issue and the Queen's cooperation had reached its limit.

"Very well, Your Majesty," said Lord Palmerston.

Lord Unwin, tired of being ignored, thrust himself into the conversation: "May I at least arrange a special escort to guard the children?"

"Certainly." Ready to be agreeable again, the Queen turned to me. "Have you ever seen the Highlands, Miss Brontë?"

"No, Your Majesty," I said.

She gave me a look that said she would endure my presence as a necessary evil, and woe betide me if I did anything to cross her. "What a wonderful experience our holiday will be for you."

And thus I found myself bound for Scotland with the Queen.

34

✦

THE ROYAL YACHT, CHRISTENED
VICTORIA AND ALBERT, SAILED
from Woolwich on the morning of 5 September 1848. The sun
sparkled on the Thames, along whose docks huge, noisy crowds
had gathered to admire the magnificent paddle steamer decorated
in white and aquamarine blue with richly carved crowns.
Spectators cheered as the Queen and Prince Consort boarded the
yacht, accompanied by their entourage. Behind them up the gang-
plank, I shepherded the Princess Royal, aged eight years, the Prince
of Wales, aged seven, and their four-year-old brother. I was glad
that the other three children had been left at home, reducing the
number of my charges as well as targets for abduction. Looking
towards the three ships that would carry the equerries, royal physi-
cian, steward of the household, and more court attendants, I
glimpsed Lord Unwin strutting on deck, but Mr. Slade was
nowhere in sight. Along the river floated the Royal Squadron—four
armed warships ready to escort the Queen to Scotland. I felt reas-
sured that Kuan couldn't possibly breach such heavy defenses, yet I
knew that he was biding his time. The journey ahead seemed an
undertaking composed of equal parts grandiosity and terror.

When everyone had boarded, the gangplanks lifted; moorings
were cast off. The fleet moved up the Thames, while the crowd
roared and waved. A band played a rousing, cheerful tune.

Streamers, confetti, and flowers fell like colored rain. Pleasure boats filled with more spectators followed the royal fleet. The spectacle dazzled me as I stood watching on the deck. I could hardly believe I was part of it. Yesterday I'd written my family to tell them where I was going, and I doubted they would believe me.

Presently, the river and noise gave way to the sea, and we sailed along the coast. The Queen and Prince Consort retired to the cabin, while I began my duties, for they'd made clear to me that I would not merely pose as their children's governess; they expected me to earn my keep. Little Prince Alfred stayed constantly with his mother, but I supervised the Princess Royal and the Prince of Wales on deck. The Princess Royal, called Vicky, was a perfect little lady, and mature beyond her years. Her manners were courteous and charming, her clothes immaculate.

"Look, Miss Brontë," she cried. "Those sailors on that ship are saluting us!" She smiled, nodded, and waved at them like the royalty she was.

Her brother Albert—called "Bertie"—was the sort of child that every governess dreads. The heir to the throne had a fair-haired, fair-faced, angelic countenance behind which lurked the very Devil. He raced about, yelling as he bounced a ball along the deck.

"Stop making such a racket, Bertie," the Princess commanded. "You'll disturb Mama and Papa."

Bertie paid no attention to her—nor to me when I warned him that his ball might bounce overboard. "I don't have to obey you," he said in a childishly imperious manner. "Someday I'll be King of England, and everybody will obey me."

Someday I should like to boast that I'd once administered a thorough paddling to the King of England. But I hesitated to punish him, lest I displease his parents and sink myself further in their esteem. I begged Bertie to quiet himself, but he ignored me. His ball bounced over the railing. He let out a yelp as it bobbed on the waves and the ship moved away from it. He climbed upon the railing.

"No, Bertie!" exclaimed Vicky.

"I must get my ball back," he said.

"If you jump in the ocean, you'll drown," I said, attempting to tug him off the railing. "Come down at once!"

Impervious to common sense, he struggled. He seemed—dare I say?—a rather stupid boy, more intent on getting his way than mindful of danger. It boded ill for the future of the nation when he ascended the throne.

"Let me go!" he shouted.

He struck out at me and kicked me, all the while he kept shouting. Vicky ordered him to stop, but he refused. As I tried to restrain him, he swung his leg over the railing. This was a child I had sworn to protect! Our noise brought the crew and royal entourage running towards us. The Queen and Prince Consort rushed from the cabin.

"What is all this commotion?" the Queen demanded.

"Bertie is trying to jump off the ship," Vicky said. "Miss Brontë is trying to stop him."

The annoyance on Her Majesty's face turned to terror as she beheld her son, who was now dangling overboard while I desperately clung to his ankles. "Bertie!" she shrieked. Turning to her husband, she said, "Don't just stand there, save our darling boy!"

Before the Prince Consort could react, the captain of the royal guard hurried to my aid. Captain Innes was a soldierly man some fifty years of age, resplendent in uniform. He grabbed Bertie, hauled him up, and set him on his feet on the deck.

"There, Your Highness," he said. "Safe and sound."

His bright blue eyes twinkled at me from beneath his bushy grey eyebrows. His bushy grey mustache didn't quite hide a sympathetic smile as I murmured my thanks and the assembly breathed a collective sigh of relief. "No harm done," he assured the Queen.

Bertie, overwhelmed by all the attention he was getting, began to cry. The Queen hugged him. "Come along, my darling," she said, and held out her hand to her daughter. "We'll have some cake." She shot me a look so acid that it could have dissolved steel. "Take better care of them in the future, Miss Brontë."

She, the Prince Consort, and both children went into the cabin. The crew returned to their duties, and the entourage to whatever their business. I sensed everyone's unspoken disapproval. I had almost let England's future monarch drown. Standing at the rail, gazing at the sun-dappled waves and coastline, I felt a gloomy amusement that such twists of fate had landed me in a profession at which I had always been incompetent. I had disgraced myself in front of employers more exalted than any others I had served. To them I must seem an unlikely person to save the kingdom from evil, when I could not even control a seven-year-old boy.

The Queen's chief lady-in-waiting came beside me. She was the Duchess of Norfolk, a woman whose elegant dress and poise intimidated me. Now she smiled at me in a friendly, conspiratorial fashion.

"Don't feel that you're to blame, Miss Brontë," she said. "The fault is Her Majesty's. She is prone to spoiling Bertie. How can anyone expect him to learn good behavior when she constantly rewards him for bad?" The Duchess shook her head, which was crowned by an upswept mass of yellow hair and a wide-brimmed hat laden with flowers. "I fear he will grow up to be the worst tyrant that England has ever known."

"You are too kind, Your Grace," I murmured.

"Oh, there's no need for such formality between traveling companions," she said. "Please call me Mathilda. May I call you Charlotte?"

"Certainly," I said.

She chatted with me, attempting to put me at ease and make me feel welcome. I was grateful to her and to Captain Innes, who had saved Bertie and spared me the ruin that would have followed had any harm come to the boy. Yet I remembered that someone among the royal household was Kuan's accomplice. Until I knew who, I dared trust no one.

❖✦

While on this exhilarating journey, I had not forgotten those dear to me whom I'd left behind. I often wondered how Papa, Anne, Emily, and Branwell were faring in my absence. I judged that my pretense of cooperating with Kuan would protect them from him, and that I was the only one in danger. I remembered the parsonage as a haven of tranquillity.

How wrong was I!

I present my sister Emily's account of events at home during the night I spent aboard the royal yacht:

The Journal of Emily Brontë

I dreamed I was chasing a golden book which flew on golden wings and gave off a splendid, unearthly golden light. It was the book I longed to write, and unless I caught it, I never would write it. Down a dark, winding tunnel I ran, while the book flitted just out of my reach. It disappeared around a curve, and suddenly a loud, rapping noise startled me. I awakened standing in the front hall at home: I had sleep-walked from my bed. The noise was a knocking at the door.

Anne came down the stairs, saying, "It's after midnight. Who could be calling so late?" Fear resounded in her voice as she answered her own question: "No one who can mean us any good."

But I was so drowsy that I forgot the dangers that threatened the household. I could still see the golden book; I heard its wings fluttering outside. I started towards the door. I heard Anne call Papa, and both of them hastening after me. Before they could stop me, I unlocked the door and opened it. Three men burst across the threshold. Anne gave an alarmed cry.

"What do you think you're doing?" Papa demanded of the men. "Who are you?"

The tallest of the three held a pistol, which he aimed at Papa. "Raise your hands," he said. "Don't move, or I'll shoot you."

His speech told me he hailed from the upper social strata of England, but I was too confused to observe more about him. I could neither speak nor move.

Papa stood frozen for a moment; then his hands crept

skyward. The man pointed the gun at Anne, who also lifted her hands as she edged close beside Papa.

"If it's money you want, we haven't much," Papa said, "but I'll give it to you if you'll only go and leave us unharmed."

"Be quiet," ordered the man with the gun.

My dream dissipated like mist in the wind. Shocked alert, I realized that I had let evil into our house. "No!" I screamed. "Get out!"

One of the other men was near me, and I flew at him in outrage. He grabbed my arms. As I howled and kicked his shins and we struggled together, horrified exclamations came from Anne and Papa. Hysteria filled me: I fought harder. The third man leapt to his comrade's assistance. Together they pinned my arms behind my back. The man with the gun seized Anne and jammed its barrel against her throat.

"Be still, or she dies," he told me.

Anne's mouth gaped with silent terror. Papa said, "Emily, please. Do as he says."

My mind at last absorbed the idea that the man would kill Anne unless I obeyed him. Fear drained the resistance from my muscles.

The man with the gun ordered Anne: "Light a lamp."

She obeyed, her hands trembling. The lamp illuminated the men, who were all dressed in dark clothes, their hats shading vicious faces. One kept hold of me; the other bolted the door. He then snatched the lamp and roved around the house, while the man with the gun held us paralyzed. Soon he returned and said, "There's nobody else here."

Branwell must have sneaked out to the Black Bull Inn while we slept. Luck had favored him for once in his miserable life.

"These three will do." The gunman told Papa, "Show us to the cellar."

Papa reluctantly unbarred and opened the cellar door, beyond which a dark staircase led beneath the house.

"All of you go down," ordered the gunman.

We went in single file, Papa first, Anne next, then the man with the lamp. My captor propelled me after them. The gunman followed close behind. None of us called for help; the village was too far away for anyone there to hear us. As we descended, the narrow stairwell enclosed me. I breathed the dank odor of earth and experienced the suffocating sensation that the very idea of captivity provokes in me. I suppressed an urge to fight my way back above ground. We reached the cellar, a room whose walls are made of stone and earth, in which my family rarely sets foot. The intruders flung Papa, Anne, and me on the floor amidst the odds and ends that had accumulated there over the years. They backed up the stairs.

Papa said, "Please have mercy." His voice wavered. Anne and I huddled together; she moaned, and my terror choked me. "Please let us go."

"Keep still," said the gunman.

He and his comrades vanished through the door and banged it shut. The cellar was immersed in darkness. I heard the bar drop into place. Then there was silence, except for our breathing.

"This must be another in the same series of troubles that have plagued us," said Papa.

"There can be no doubt. I sense the hand of the same villain at work," Anne said mournfully. "I had hoped that the danger from him was past; but alas, it seems that it is not."

"But why would he have us imprisoned in our own home?" Papa said. "And for how long do these men intend to keep us here?"

Anne made no reply. The suffocating sensation constricted my chest. Trapped in the subterranean darkness, I gasped for air.

"They can't lock us up forever," Papa said, as if trying to reassure himself as well as Anne and me. "People in the village will notice our absence. They'll come to investigate. They'll rescue us."

The cold, damp gloom seethed with our horrified thoughts of what might happen to us in the meantime. I heard muffled voices from above: The intruders were still in the house.

Anne said, "Branwell is bound to come home eventually."

We knew better than to expect deliverance from that drunken, hapless, opium-besotted wreck. My heart thudded with my craving to be free. I hurtled blindly up the stairs, tripping on them and falling on my hands and knees, crawling until I reached the top. I beat my fists against the door.

"Let me out!" I screamed.

No one answered; the door remained shut. I fought until my hands were bloody, screamed until my throat was raw. Finally, in a state of despair and exhaustion, I slid down the stairs. Anne held me and murmured soothing words as I wept. I wept for my lost liberty, for the book I would never write.

"If this is happening to us," Papa said in a voice of dawning dread, "then what has become of Charlotte?"

35

HE REMAINDER OF THE VOYAGE TO SCOTLAND PASSED WITHOUT incident. The Queen and Prince Consort kept Bertie by them, relieving me of his irksome care; I had only the well behaved Princess to amuse. If there was danger on the royal yacht, I saw no sign of it. Indeed, I felt safer than I had since before Isabel White's murder. Thirty-seven peaceful hours after setting sail, we arrived at Aberdeen on 7 September. Carriages and horses that had been shipped to Scotland ahead of time conveyed us to the new royal estate at Balmoral.

The Queen was as popular in Scotland as at home. Along our way, the Scots turned out to greet her. The Queen, Prince Consort, and their two elder children rode in an open carriage at the head of our procession. Crowds cheered them uproariously. The entrance to each village was decorated in the Queen's honor with a triumphal arch made of barley or wheat sheaves, flowers, evergreens, or stags' heads. The day was a whirlwind of happy faces, voices shouting greetings in a strange dialect, music from bagpipes, speeches by local gentry, and guns firing salutes. Riding in a carriage with the Queen's other attendants, through a landscape of farms and distant, snow-capped peaks, I felt myself part of a grand, historic spectacle. In the joy of our reception, I was temporarily distracted from the horrific events that had brought me to this very place.

We reached Balmoral to find a Scottish Regiment's Guard of Honor waiting at attention. Balmoral, located on the River Dee, on the eastern side of the lofty Cairngorm Mountains, comprised ten thousand acres of fields, woods of towering birch and pine trees, and meadow. The Forest of Ballochbuie abutted its northern border; on the south rose the dark crags of Loch-na-gar. The pretty white castle had many turrets and gables, gingerbread trim, an ancient square tower surmounted by a battlemented parapet, and a glass conservatory. It was surrounded by expansive gardens that sloped towards the river in a series of natural terraces.

Inside the castle was a hall paved with Dutch tiles; a broad staircase led to the upper floors. The rooms were furnished like a grand country house, with chintz upholstery and curtains; they were fewer and smaller than I'd expected, insufficient for the royal family and entourage. The servants and attendants—Mr. Slade, Lord Unwin, and other Foreign Office agents among them—were quartered in neighboring cottages. I had a tiny chamber upstairs in the castle, near the children's nursery and the Queen's chambers. The gentlemen of the household had rooms above us; the ladies-in-waiting below. After lunch in the crowded dining room, I walked behind the royal family on an inspection of the estate. Not until that evening did I have a chance to speak with Slade.

Local citizens staged a celebration for the royal family. A huge bonfire was lit upon Craig Linne. Fireworks spangled the sky above Balmoral. We gathered on the terrace to watch. Bertie and Vicky jumped up and down, squealing with excitement at the glowing streamers, rosettes, and exploding bursts of colored stars. Rockets boomed, echoing off the mountains. Guards, courtiers, and ladies-in-waiting cheered. The Queen and Prince Consort smiled happily. I stood apart from the others, an interloper. My presence could only remind the Queen of the threat that haunted her and spoil her enjoyment. Presently, Mr. Slade appeared at my side.

"Is all well with you, Miss Brontë?" he said.

"For the time being," I said.

My senses quickened with the delight that his presence always

caused me. I lifted my eyes to the distant heights, where the bonfire's flames danced in the wind. Smoke and gunpowder scented
the air.

"I've been inspecting the estate," said Mr. Slade. "So have the
twelve constables sent from London. We found no signs of trespassers or anything else suspicious."

"I am relieved to hear that," I said.

All through the journey, despite its many diversions, I had been
tense with waiting to see him again. Yet so much time had passed
since we'd been alone together, so many things had happened, and
we seemed reverted to strangers.

"Would I be correct to assume that no one has yet approached
you on behalf of Kuan?" Mr. Slade's tone was cautious.

"You would," I said, uneasy because I thought Mr. Slade must
be remembering that night in Penzance, when I'd spoken in
defense of Kuan's motives. Did he still wonder if the Chinaman
had compromised my loyalty to him and my country? "Had anyone approached me, I would have sought you out and informed
you immediately."

"Of course," Mr. Slade said, although doubt tinged his voice.

I compelled myself to look directly at him, lest my avoidance
of his gaze provoke further suspicion. The fireworks illuminated
his face. On it I saw shadows cast by weariness; the burden of his
responsibilities, and his vigilant attention to duty, had taken their
toll on him. His expression combined concern for me with
uncertainty as to where we stood with each other. I thought I perceived in him a wish to regain the comradeship we'd shared.
Here, in the lofty altitude and fresh, clear air of Scotland, my time
in Cornwall seemed but a fading nightmare. Distance had weakened Kuan's spell over me; I could scarcely credit that I had ever
sympathized with him. Mr. Slade was once more the primary
object of my regard.

As our eyes met, the doubt in his eyes subsided; he smiled. His
hand clasped and held mine; I enjoyed a warm, glad certainty that
nothing could defeat us. The sky dazzled in a booming explosion of
red, orange, and gold cartwheels. The audience exclaimed, and the

children danced with delight. My happiness was such that I knew it could not possibly last.

Events were to prove me sadly correct.

→⤜←

The celebration soon ended. The bonfire burned out; the last sparkle of fireworks faded. The royal party retired to the castle. Slade went off to his cottage, and I tucked the children into their beds. The Queen and Prince Consort came to bid them goodnight. I walked the corridor, allowing the family their privacy, and there I met Captain Innes, the valiant soldier who had averted the crisis at sea.

"Just checking to see that everyone is safe," he said, lowering his cheerful, hearty voice to a loud whisper and walking beside me.

"Everyone is well, thank you," I said.

We reached the landing that overlooked the entrance hall. Dim light from a few lamps shone there; laughter drifted up to us from the chambers of the ladies-in-waiting. Captain Innes signaled me to halt, and his voice rumbled softly against my ear: "Mr. Kuan sends his greetings."

Shock assailed me. This was the moment I had been dreading. The kindly, jovial Captain Innes was Kuan's accomplice, bearing the summons to enact my part in his evil scheme. "Why . . . how . . . ?" was all I could say.

Captain Innes made a rueful face. "Got myself into debt at one of Mr. Kuan's gambling clubs. Couldn't pay. Had to agree to do him a favor instead. He'd have killed me otherwise. But enough of that. You and I will take the children the night after tomorrow."

I looked around with some notion of rushing to tell Mr. Slade that the accomplice had revealed himself to me, but Captain Innes seized my wrist, preventing my flight. "What's the matter?" he said. "Changed your mind about your arrangement with Mr. Kuan? Well, hear me out before you think of reneging on him. He has men holding your family prisoners as we speak. He'll set them free after you bring him the children. Unless you do as I say, they'll die."

Horror gained ascendancy over all other emotions as I grasped Kuan's motive. He had never trusted me as fully as I thought; he was too clever to assume that I was firmly under his sway. He knew I would do anything for my family's sake—he had elicited that fact during his interrogation of me. And now he had taken my loved ones hostage to guarantee my obedience.

"Do you understand, Miss Brontë?" An edge of steel cut through Captain Innes's cheerful voice.

"Please don't let him hurt them," I said, gasping with terror.

"Their lives are in your hands," Captain Innes said. I struggled to break free of him, but he held tighter to my wrist. "Here's the plan. Before you put the children to bed the night after tomorrow, give them each a few drops of this in their cocoa."

He lifted my hand, placed a vial in my palm, and closed my fingers around it. "It's laudanum. They'll sleep so soundly, nothing will waken them. You wait up for me. I'll come to the nursery after everyone else is asleep. We'll carry the children out of the castle. Understood?"

Captain Innes's usual pleasant smile had become a ghastly caricature. Desperation burned in his twinkling eyes. Fright and helplessness compelled me to nod in spite of myself, as I realized that I must either commit a terrible crime or doom those that I loved best.

"Should you be tempted to tell tales and upset Mr. Kuan's plan," Captain Innes said, "just think of your family."

Two maids approached us along the passage. Captain Innes let go my wrist, stepped back from me, and bowed with gallant, false courtesy. "Good night, Miss Brontë."

36

A WAVE OF DREAD CRASHED OVER ME. THE FLOOR UNDER MY FEET seemed to give way, and I clung to the balustrade for fear that I would fall and be shattered on the tiles below the landing. Rapid gasps drained the breath from me as Captain Innes's commands echoed in my ears. I thought I would die—and well I might have, but the Queen and Prince Consort emerged from the nursery, and I was forced to compose myself.

Her Majesty said, "We shall see you in the morning, Miss Brontë."

Clutching the laudanum vial hidden in my hand, I slunk past her and the Prince Consort, not daring to look them in the eyes lest they read in mine what had transpired. I felt a powerful impulse to confess, but Kuan's threat held my tongue. I slipped into the nursery.

Vicky, Bertie, and Alfred lay asleep in their beds. I put out the lamp, then crumpled into a chair. Moonlight silvered their fair heads as I listened to their quiet, steady breathing. Mortal sickness permeated me. Kuan had decreed that I must choose between sacrificing these innocents or my own beloved kin. An involuntary sob rose in my throat. What was I to do?

Sometimes, in the midst of trouble, the mind conceives ideas that it never would on saner occasions. I began to think that perhaps Kuan could be appeased, and his goals attained, without harm to anyone. Sometime during the long, wakeful night, I conceived an audacious plan.

The next morning, accompanied by the children and myself, and other members of their entourage, the Queen and Prince Consort strolled down the riverside terraces. The flowerbeds and shrubbery of the formal gardens had run together in a weedy, unkempt tangle. It was a fine day, the sky blue, the bright sun dappling the overgrown paths we trod beneath the mountain ash and weeping birch trees. Around us rose the lofty peaks; below, the river sparkled through the foliage that rustled in the fresh Highland wind. The Prince walked with the children, pointing out birds and squirrels to them. The entourage scattered. I glimpsed Mr. Slade among the guards, but I avoided him. I took my courage in hand and approached the Queen.

"Your Majesty?" I said timidly.

She fixed a cold, reproving eye upon me. "What is it?"

I fell into step beside her, aware that I was taking advantage of an intimacy with Her Majesty that most subjects could never claim. She clearly objected to my presence, but I couldn't afford to care. "Might I please have a word with you?"

The Queen hesitated, then yielded to the curiosity I saw on her face. "Very well."

I trembled with dread because the favor I wanted of her was far beyond my right to ask. Were I to have any chance of getting it, I must be circumspect. "Your Majesty has much influence over the affairs of the world," I began.

"The sovereign of a great nation exercises power abroad as well as at home," she agreed, with suspicion as well as pride.

"And Your Majesty has unsurpassed ability to use this influence for the good of mankind." My voice quavered and my heart pounded.

"Naturally," the Queen said in a tone that forbade me to attribute anything but the noblest motives to her. "Now please get to the point of this conversation."

"Yes, Your Majesty." I steeled my waning courage. "I wish to discuss the opium trade."

"The opium trade!" Surprise inflected her voice: She would

never have expected me to raise this subject. Apparently no one had explained to her the story behind Kuan's crimes.

"Yes," I said, as meekly and agreeably as possible. "I wish to broach the subject of its problems with your majesty."

"Its problems?" She narrowed her eyes in offense. "Opium is produced by colonial plantations in India. It is prized for its unparalleled medicinal properties, which have hitherto been unmatched by those of any other plant and have allowed for enormous advances in medical science. It is the principal commodity sold abroad by British merchants. It produces some three million pounds in annual revenue for the Crown. The money earned recoups the fortune spent by Britain on tea, silks, and spices in the Far East."

This was news to me. Kuan had spoken only of the evils of the opium trade. The Queen knew only the good. I ventured cautiously, "But there are terrible ills associated with opium." I saw her bristle. However little I wished to affront her, I must continue, for the sake of her children and my family. "Opium enslaves the people who use it. It saps their bodily strength and their moral character. It weakens their will to do anything but obtain more opium and sink themselves deeper in vice." My need to enlighten the Queen impassioned my speech. "People have stolen, murdered, suffered, and died for opium. It does far more evil than good."

Distrust darkened the Queen's expression. I realized that even if she knew these facts, she was bound to protect the trade that financed such a large portion of her Empire's activities. She said, "Perhaps you would tell me how you derived these notions of its evils?"

I couldn't admit that I had learned them from Kuan; I didn't want her to think that I was in league with him in any way. "My brother is a slave to opium. I have personally witnessed his destruction."

The Queen made a disdainful sound. "Some people whose minds are weak overindulge in opium; some overindulge in liquor. It is the overindulgence that causes their troubles. Opium is wholesome when used in moderation; it is perfectly legal and respectable. In fact, it is a good sedative for infants. I've used it on my own children."

My hope of altering her opinion faded; yet I persisted: "One may decide to use opium oneself, for better or worse." I grew reckless in my desperation. "But should opium be forced upon people who don't want it, who have enacted laws to prohibit it in their land? Britain is forcing opium on China and waging war there in order to perpetuate the trade which brings suffering to multitudes." Halting on the path, I faced the Queen; I clasped my hands in ardent entreaty. "I beg Your Majesty to put an end to the trade!"

I thought that if it ceased, Kuan would be satisfied enough to give up his desire for revenge against Britain. I hoped that if I helped him thus, he would release me. I would not have spoken so boldly to the Queen had I not considered it my only chance to save both my family and hers.

She drew back from me, repulsed by my vehemence. Her cheeks flushed scarlet. "Miss Brontë, you have gone too far," she said with great indignation. "Your outburst hardly deserves the courtesy of an answer. But answer I will, if only to correct your deplorable misconceptions and rebuke your flagrant disrespect. In the first place, no one is forcing opium on anyone. Should there be people who do not want it, they may refuse to buy it. In the second place, the Crown would never have waged war against China had China not mistreated British merchants, destroyed valuable opium stores that belonged to them, and insulted British honor. Britain has rightfully exacted compensation for these offenses and protected British commerce in the Far East. The issues of warfare and international trade are far more complex than a humble governess untutored in the arts of statesmanship could ever grasp."

Her words dashed my hopes. In my sad humiliation I realized that from the Queen's perspective, the greatest good would necessarily always lie in what best served Britain. The Queen had no reason to take the part of distant foreigners over that of her own country.

"Furthermore, Miss Brontë," the Queen said, "your presumption at questioning your Queen's judgment about what is best for

Britain borders on treason." She waved an imperious hand at me. "Go. Vex me no more."

I slunk away like a whipped animal. All around me was bright; all within me, black with misery. As I stumbled down a flight of stone stairs cut into the terraces, someone called my name. It was Mr. Slade. He was the last person I wanted to see. In my haste to elude him, I tripped on the rough stairs; he caught up with me and steadied me.

"Are you all right?" he said.

"Yes."

"No, you're as pale as death. You're trembling. Something has happened. What is it?"

How I longed to blurt it out! Such a temptation I felt to share the burden of my knowledge with Mr. Slade in the hope that he could help me! But even as my tongue quivered on the brink of confession, I glimpsed a figure below us, on the terrace nearest the wide, sparkling river. It was Captain Innes. He waved cheerily at us and winked at me. My heart sank at his reminder that my family would die if I breathed a word of what he'd said to me last night. I looked at Mr. Slade, and although he stood close enough for me to touch, he seemed as remote as the other side of the world.

"Nothing has happened," I mumbled, turning away from Mr. Slade. "If you'll excuse me, I must go back to the children."

I felt Mr. Slade—and Captain Innes—watching me as I hurried up the stairs. On an upper terrace I found Vicky, Bertie, and little Alfred rambling about with the Prince Consort and the Duchess of Norfolk. The Queen was absent, to my relief.

"Ah, there you are, Miss Brontë," the Duchess said with a welcoming smile. "Come join us."

I did, grateful for her friendliness. The rest of that morning, her blithe conversation enlivened the party. The children were fond of her; Bertie behaved with more decorum while in her presence; even the somber Prince Consort cheered up. That afternoon, when the Queen and Prince Consort went driving in a pony cart, the Duchess helped me tend the children. I was glad to have her company, for I noticed Mr. Slade and Captain Innes loitering nearby, and her presence kept them both away from me.

But I couldn't stop thinking about the vial of opium hidden in my room. I couldn't deny that the next day I would have to deliver the children into Kuan's hands or condemn my own family to a terrible death. As the hours passed, I became certain that I could do neither.

>←

My apprehension increased during dinner and the musical entertainment afterward. By the time I retired to my chamber, my heart agitated within my ribs like a bird beating its wings against the bars of a cage. I paced the floor while the clock ticked a cadence of doom. At three in the morning, unable to sleep or sit still or bear the waiting any longer, I flung my cloak over my shoulders and raced out of the castle.

The freezing Highland wind gusted at me, stirring the dark forests. The moon and stars shone icy silver radiance upon the castle's turrets and the snow-peaked mountains. The vast, dark landscape seemed haunted by ancient Scottish ghosts; wolves howled. I ran through the night, as if by running I could escape from Kuan. While I ran, I wept. I stumbled through woods, over rocks and fallen branches, caring naught that I didn't know where I was going.

Suddenly I struck an obstacle that emerged from the shadows. It was neither tree nor stone, but flesh and blood. Strong hands seized me, arresting my flight. I cried out in terror and fought wildly until I heard Mr. Slade exclaim, "Miss Brontë! What are you doing?"

He released me. I sank to my knees, sobbing while I panted with exertion. I remembered how little Mr. Slade slept at night; he had probably come out of his lodgings for a walk in the fresh air. Some instinctive impulse must have guided me to him.

"Help me," I cried. The words I'd held in all day burst from me like water through a dam weakened by its pressure. "Please—you must save them!"

"Who?" Mr. Slade said, perplexed.

"Papa. Anne. Emily. Branwell." Gasps punctuated the names I spoke. "They're in terrible danger!"

Mr. Slade crouched before me and peered into my face, trying to make sense of me. "What kind of danger?"

"They've been taken prisoner," I said.

"How do you know this?"

"At the parsonage," I babbled through my sobs. "He'll kill them unless I—"

"Who? What?" Then enlightenment cleared the confusion from Mr. Slade's eyes. "It's Kuan, isn't it? His accomplice has approached you. Kuan has taken your family hostage to force your cooperation in the kidnapping." Mr. Slade grasped my shoulders. "Who is the accomplice? When and how is the kidnapping to take place?"

"I can't tell you." I rose, pulled free of Mr. Slade, and fled before he could press me for answers.

"Miss Brontë!" Mr. Slade called. "Wait!"

I rushed headlong into the forest. Branches leapt out of the darkness and raked my face. I crashed into trees, groped around them. The wind howled past me and the earth sloped steeply downward beneath my feet. I lost my balance and tumbled head over heels down a hill, screaming as rocks battered me all the way to the bottom. Dizzy and sore, I stood up but was too exhausted to run any farther. Mr. Slade barreled down the hill and skidded to a stop near me.

"Leave me alone," I cried, raising my hand to forestall more questions.

His arms locked around me. "I want to help you, and I promise I will, but first you must tell me everything."

We were in a clearing in the forest. Trees held the moon in their foliage. I could see Mr. Slade's eyes intent on me, feel the rhythm of his breathing. My need to confide shattered my will to resist.

"Captain Innes is the accomplice," I said in a small, forlorn voice. "The kidnapping is set for tomorrow night. Captain Innes has instructed me to drug the children with laudanum. Then we shall deliver them to Kuan. He'll free my family afterward." I felt relief at unburdening myself, but a terrible dread because I had disobeyed Kuan. "Unless I do as he wishes, he'll kill them."

"Good God," Mr. Slade said. He clasped me to him; I wept unabashedly against his shoulder. "I should have known Kuan would do something like this. I should have known he would try to use your family against you. This is my fault."

"No," I said. "The fault is mine. I didn't tell you everything that went on between Kuan and me in Cornwall. If I had, then perhaps we both would have foreseen what he would do and prevented it." At the thought of my family captive, frightened, and helpless, a fresh spate of sobs erupted from me. "I can't let them die. But I can't hurt those children!"

"You won't," Mr. Slade assured me.

"But what is to be done?"

"I'll send agents to Haworth at once to rescue your family. In the meantime . . ." He related a plan that seemed a good means of thwarting the kidnapping and capturing Kuan. "Can you do what is required of you?"

"Yes," I said fervently. "I'll do whatever you say."

I wept tears of joy that there was some hope for our success and for my family's salvation. I felt immense gratitude towards Mr. Slade, who had released me from terror and despair. But in the wake of those strong, departing emotions, other emotions rushed in. I became suddenly conscious of Mr. Slade holding me, the warmth from his chest against my cheek, his hard, muscular arms, his trousers touching my skirts, of the fact that we were far from anyone else. Suddenly there surged through me the torrent of desire that I had tried to suppress for so long. My breath caught. I heard Mr. Slade's catch at the same moment. His arms tightened around me. Slowly I raised my face. Mr. Slade was gazing at me, his features lit by the moon yet dark with serious thoughts. He inhaled a deep breath, like a man preparing to dive into the ocean, then bent his head towards me.

Our lips met, his warm and firm upon mine, in the kiss that I had longed for all my life. My eyes closed as powerful sensations of pleasure and mortal fear spread through my entire self. I was falling through darkness. Images flashed through my mind—the curate William Weightman, Monsieur Heger. My feelings for them had been nothing compared to this hunger for Mr. Slade. My lips involuntarily parted. His tongue entered and found mine. Oh, the shocking, wet, intimate, thrilling contact! It seemed that our souls and thoughts fused. I saw the visage of a beautiful woman— his deceased wife. I felt in him the desire unsatisfied during seven years of mourning.

We kissed again and again, each kiss deeper and more fevered. Mr. Slade moved his hands up from my waist; he clasped my bosom. I allowed it, even though I knew I shouldn't. So intoxicating were my sensations that they shattered all vestiges of self-control, all thoughts of propriety. Mr. Slade drew me to the ground—or I drew him; I know not which. We lay together on the soft bed of fallen leaves. The trees vaulted like a cathedral ceiling above us. The moonlight shone down on us, white and pure. As Mr. Slade kissed and caressed me, the heavy layers of my clothing seemed to vanish, and I felt each caress as though upon my bare skin. Need overcame inhibition. I dared to touch Mr. Slade in a place where I'd thought I would never touch a man. Through his trousers I felt, for the first time in my life, masculine arousal. A profound awe moved me. My desire quickened to an unbearable frenzy. I clutched at Mr. Slade, pulling him atop me.

"Please," I cried.

Mr. Slade hesitated, gasping. On his face I saw lust reined in by apprehension: He knew the risk that an illicit carnal union posed for a woman, and although I was beyond caring about it, he was cautious on my behalf. Not one garment of mine or his did he remove or disarrange. He did not ravish me as I would gladly have allowed. Instead he lowered himself onto me, and we moved together. My body arched against his. As the rhythm of our movements accelerated, my pleasure rose towards heights I had never imagined possible. A terrifying, wonderful alchemy turned everything in me to molten fire. The most incredible rapture I had ever experienced pulsed through me. I exclaimed in joy and amazement. *This* was the ecstasy hinted at but never actually described in love stories I'd read. *This* was what I had unknowingly yearned for during lonely nights spent indulging in secret fantasies.

I clung to Mr. Slade. His breaths came faster as he thrust himself harder and more insistently at me. Suddenly he flung back his head; he uttered a groan. I felt him shudder with the pleasure of his release. Then a sigh eased the tension from him. My own ecstasy yielded to quiet bliss. We lay side by side, embracing. It seemed that we floated together in some private universe high above the world.

"Forgive me," Mr. Slade said, his voice filled with guilt and regret. "I should not have let this happen."

I kissed away his apology. "There's nothing to forgive," I said, for I was as much to blame as he, and I had no regrets. At that moment, my love for him justified all sins.

Slade caressed my hair. "I must confess that I've been wanting you ever since that day on the moors."

Delighted I was to learn that my feelings had not been unrequited. Although the forest was cold, I wished we could stay there forever. But a lightening of the sky presaged dawn. We disengaged, rose, and walked, hand in hand, until we reached the edge of the forest and Balmoral Castle was in sight.

"I'll see you soon. Don't worry," Mr. Slade said, "all will be well."

We kissed one last time, then he headed back towards his lodgings, while I hurried into the castle. I was giddy with excitement and happiness. It was not until later that I began to think clearly on what had happened between Mr. Slade and me. It was not until morning that our plans foundered terribly.

37

OO OFTEN OUR PLANS FAIL NOT
BECAUSE THEY LACK MERIT OR
because we mishandle their execution. Sometimes they go awry
due to the folly of another person whose motives run counter to
ours. Alas, I experienced this hard lesson at the worst possible time.

Two mornings after Captain Innes approached me with Kuan's
orders, a solemn gathering took place in the Balmoral Castle drawing room. The Queen and Prince Consort sat on a chintz-covered
sofa. Mr. Slade and I, and Foreign Office agents armed with rifles,
stood against walls hung with faded floral wallpaper. Beyond the
open French doors, the children played in the sunny garden. Lord
Unwin posed dramatically in the center of the room.

"Your Majesty, Your Highness," he said in his most pompous
manner, "I am pleased to announce that I have discovered the identity of Mr. Kuan's accomplice."

Last night Mr. Slade had informed Lord Unwin about
Captain Innes. Thereafter, Lord Unwin had insisted upon taking
full charge and breaking the news to the Queen. Now she and
her husband leaned forward in surprise.

"Well?" she said. "Who is it?"

"It is Captain Innes," Lord Unwin said.

Mr. Slade looked unhappy, although not because Lord Unwin
was taking credit for the discovery. He didn't trust Lord Unwin to

handle the matters that remained. I was so worried about my family that I could barely stand still. Knowing that Mr. Slade's men were on the way to their rescue gave me little comfort, for Haworth was far from Scotland.

"Surely Captain Innes cannot be the accomplice to the kidnapping!" the Queen cried in disbelief.

"He has been in my wife's service since she took the throne," said the Prince Consort. "He has always been devoted to her."

Other worries further disturbed me. Even while such momentous events were taking place, I could not cease thinking about what had transpired between Mr. Slade and me last night. By yielding myself to Mr. Slade, by compromising my chastity, I had pledged him my heart all the more, but what did our lovemaking mean to him?

"Captain Innes has betrayed Your Majesty's trust." Lord Unwin smiled: He enjoyed the attention he was finally getting. "He revealed himself to Miss Brontë last night."

Lord Unwin described the events I had related to Mr. Slade and displayed the opium vial the captain had given me. The Queen shook her head, incredulous. The Prince Consort said to me, "Is that an accurate account?"

I could tell that he didn't trust Lord Unwin either. "It is, Your Highness."

The Queen clutched her bosom. "That I trusted him when he had evil designs against us! This is a shocking revelation." Crimson anger suffused her face; her luminous eyes shot sparks. She spoke in a voice resonant with dire portent: "Where is Captain Innes?"

"He's under arrest in his lodgings," said Lord Unwin. "My men are guarding him." He had refused to allow Mr. Slade to speak to Captain Innes; he had interrogated the prisoner himself. Puffed up with conceit and heroism, he said, "The old scoundrel can't hurt the children now."

"But his master is still at liberty somewhere." The Prince Consort gestured outside, where Bertie, Vicky, and little Alfred were playing a noisy game of tag with the ladies-in-waiting. "Is he not still dangerous?"

"What do you propose to do about him?" the Queen demanded.

"I've devised a scheme to capture Mr. Kuan," Lord Unwin said, then presented Mr. Slade's idea: "Captain Innes and Miss Brontë will pretend to carry out the kidnapping. They'll take bundles wrapped in blankets, which resemble sleeping children, out of the castle. They'll go to the rendezvous place from which Kuan's other henchmen are supposed to take Miss Brontë and the children to him. My agents will follow. They'll arrest the henchmen, then force them to reveal the location of the next rendezvous place and the identity of the other henchmen stationed there. They'll work their way up Kuan's chain of command until they find him."

"That sounds a reasonable plan," the Queen said.

I prayed that all would go as planned, and that Kuan would be caught and my family rescued before he found out that I'd sabotaged him and he could retaliate.

"Will Captain Innes cooperate with you?" the Prince Consort said.

"Oh, indeed he will," Lord Unwin said. "But let us allow him to tell you himself." Turning to Mr. Slade, he said, "Go fetch Captain Innes."

He clearly relished this chance to order Mr. Slade about in front of everyone. Mr. Slade's expression was stoic, but I could tell he disliked the idea of parading Captain Innes before the Queen like a trophy from a hunt. I myself didn't want to see the man again.

"Yes, my lord," Mr. Slade said, and departed.

Soon he returned with two soldiers escorting Captain Innes. I was shocked at the change in Innes. He shambled into the drawing room like a lame old man. His hair was disheveled, his shirt blood-stained, his face bruised: Lord Unwin's men had apparently rough-handled him during the interrogation. His eyes were wild, crazed.

"Ah. Greetings, Captain Innes," Lord Unwin said, his manner filled with contempt. "Face up to the sovereign you swore to serve and then betrayed."

As the Queen and Prince Consort stared at him, Captain Innes shrank from them. "No," he muttered. "Please. I can't!" But the soldiers pushed him onto his knees before the Queen.

She beheld him with as much hurt as hatred. "I trusted you, and you deceived me. How could you?"

Captain Innes broke into loud, shuddering sobs. "I had no choice! Please forgive me, Your Majesty." He proffered his clasped, trembling hands to her. I could almost pity him. "Please let me make up for what I've done!"

The Queen's glowering silence refused his entreaty. Lord Unwin said, "You certainly shall make up for your betrayal of your Queen. Tonight you will help us capture Mr. Kuan."

"No!" Terror shone in Captain Innes's streaming eyes. "I told you I won't. I can't!"

I felt a shock that I saw mirrored on Mr. Slade's face. Lord Unwin had given us to understand that he had persuaded Captain Innes to cooperate. Now we realized that he had not.

"Don't be obstreperous, man," Lord Unwin snapped. Perhaps he had hoped that bringing Captain Innes before the Queen would break his resistance. "It's the least you can do to restore your honor before you're executed."

"I beg you to have mercy!" Captain Innes cried, lurching to his feet. "If I betray Kuan, he'll punish my family. Kuan is invincible. You'll never get him, no matter what. Do as you wish to me, but please spare my wife and children!"

I saw that the captain feared Kuan more than he did the law; he cared more for his kin than repentance. Although I could hardly blame him, dismay filled me. What would we do if he refused to cooperate? I thought he'd been promised that his family would be protected; that had been part of Mr. Slade's plan. Lord Unwin had obviously neglected to execute that part, whether out of arrogance or sheer stupidity.

Consternation registered on Lord Unwin's face. I saw his fear that he would disgrace himself in front of the Queen. "You will help us whether you like it or not."

"No!" Captain Innes cried.

Panic-stricken, he bolted. Mr. Slade and the agents lunged to grab him, but he was quicker than I would have imagined a man his age, in his condition, could be. He hurtled across the drawing room past the Queen and Prince Consort, who uttered sounds of alarm.

"Stop him!" Lord Unwin shouted.

Captain Innes burst through the French doors with Mr. Slade and the agents in pursuit. He ran straight towards the children as they laughed and chased one another on the sunlit grass.

"Vicky! Bertie! Alfred!" the Queen cried.

She and her husband hurried to the doors. "My God!" exclaimed the Prince Consort. "Don't let him near them!"

Their voices rang across the garden. The children and ladies turned; they caught sight of Captain Innes fleeing Mr. Slade and the agents. The children's laughter gave way to frightened shrieks as they realized that something was amiss. Panic scattered them and the ladies.

Lord Unwin was on the terrace. He ordered the agents, "Draw your weapons!"

They halted and shouldered their rifles. "Captain Innes! Stop or they'll shoot!" Lord Unwin called, as the Queen, Prince, and I looked on in speechless horror.

Captain Innes kept running. Bertie, crying and confused, veered into his path. The Queen screamed.

Lord Unwin shouted, "Fire!"

Mr. Slade shouted, "No!" as he ran. He was almost within reach of Captain Innes.

Gunshots boomed. Captain Innes jerked; he gave a yowl of pain. His gait faltered and he crashed facedown on the grass. All was suddenly still. Everyone stood paralyzed—the Queen, Prince, and I at the doors; Lord Unwin on the terrace; Mr. Slade, the agents, the children, and ladies-in-waiting ranged around the lawn. At the center of the tableau lay Captain Innes's prone figure. Blood from bullet wounds in his back spread crimson patches across his shirt.

The Queen let out a moan. She and her husband rushed across the garden and gathered the children into their arms. Bertie began shrieking hysterically. A lady-in-waiting fainted; the others ran to her aid. Mr. Slade, Lord Unwin, the agents, and I clustered around

Captain Innes. The agents trained their rifles on him in case he should move—but he did not.

Mr. Slade crouched, felt Captain Innes's pulse, and spoke to Lord Unwin in a tone sharp with accusation: "He's dead."

The agents lowered their rifles. "Well," Lord Unwin said, sounding dazed by the course of events and taken aback by Mr. Slade's manner.

I'd never before seen a man gunned down like a rampant beast. My mind noted his hand curled limp on the grass, his eye already glazed, his body reduced to soulless flesh. My emotions were many, but foremost was a sense that things had just progressed from bad to much worse.

"You shouldn't have given the order to fire," Mr. Slade said as he stood and faced Lord Unwin. "You should not have killed him."

"You dare to criticize me? Who do you think you are?" Lord Unwin's pale eyes blazed. "What should I have done? The man was a menace. He might have hurt the Crown Prince." Lord Unwin gestured towards Bertie, whose cries shrilled loud while the Queen tried to soothe him. "He might have gotten away."

"I almost had him," Mr. Slade pointed out, matching Lord Unwin's fury. "We should have taken him alive."

All the animosity between the men had risen to the surface. I wanted to berate Lord Unwin myself; I wanted Mr. Slade to thrash him, for I now understood the terrible consequences of Lord Unwin's quest for glory.

Lord Unwin was too indignant to think of anything other than justifying his actions. "Captain Innes was a traitor to the Crown. He deserved to die."

"Even a bloody imbecile like you should be able to see what his death has cost us," Mr. Slade retorted. "Whatever Innes knew of Kuan's plans, his whereabouts, or his other henchmen, he'll take to his grave."

38

THE DEATH OF CAPTAIN INNES HAD IMMEDIATE AND SERIOUS repercussions. Lord Unwin confined Mr. Slade to his quarters, and I to mine, while he notified the local authorities about the incident and they removed Captain Innes's body. I spent many distressful hours wondering what would happen next. At midday Lord Unwin gathered Mr. Slade and me in the cottage where they were lodged. Mr. Slade and I sat in hard wooden chairs in front of the cold hearth, while Lord Unwin stood before us, severe and formal. Outside, rain began to fall, pelting the thatched roof; mist cloaked the forested hills.

"John Slade," said Lord Unwin, "you are hereby dismissed from the employ of the Foreign Office."

"What?" Mr. Slade exclaimed, leaping up from his chair. "Why?"

"Sit down," Lord Unwin said.

Mr. Slade remained standing face to face with Lord Unwin. "Is it because I pointed out that you made a mistake by giving the order to fire on Captain Innes?"

"It is not," Lord Unwin said, but annoyance twitched his mouth, and I knew that Mr. Slade had deduced at least part of the reason for the dismissal. "Rather, your actions have led to the death of an important witness in an official investigation."

Enlightenment and dismay struck me at the same moment they became apparent in Mr. Slade's expression. "Ah. I see. You intend for me to take the blame for your mistake." His eyes flashed with anger. "You're seizing on the death of Captain Innes as an excuse to get rid of me."

Lord Unwin puffed with satisfaction. "Think what you wish. Tomorrow morning you will take the train to London, where you will settle your affairs at the Foreign Office."

"You can't do this!" Mr. Slade clenched his fists and took a step towards Lord Unwin. "Kuan has still to be captured. My mission is not yet finished!"

"The mission is yours no longer," Lord Unwin said spitefully. "I am assuming charge of the hunt for Mr. Kuan."

"I've brought the hunt this far," Mr. Slade said, loud with indignation. "And for the sake of the kingdom, you had better let me finish it. You couldn't catch a fish in a barrel by yourself!"

I wholeheartedly agreed; yet my opinion would count for nothing with Lord Unwin. His face reddened with ire at Mr. Slade's insult; he spoke with haughty derision: "Save your breath. My decision is final. Here ends your career in the service of the Crown."

Mr. Slade's indignation subsided into defeat. Humiliation sagged his posture and quenched the rage in his eyes. I felt deep sympathy for him, but he wouldn't look at me.

"As for you, Miss Brontë," said Lord Unwin, "Her Majesty has decided that she no longer wishes you to serve as governess to the children. The Prince Consort agrees." Here ended my brush with royalty. I bowed my head in shame at the ignominious dismissal. "The Foreign Office also has no further need of your services. You will join Mr. Slade on his journey to London and thereafter proceed to your home."

"You're dismissing Miss Brontë?" Mr. Slade stared as though he couldn't believe it. "But she's the only connection you have to Kuan. Now that his accomplice is dead, you need her more than ever."

"Her assistance has produced little result beyond a wild goose chase across the kingdom and continent, and at considerable expense, I might add," Lord Unwin said. "The pursuit of Mr. Kuan will be carried out according to my own plans."

What those were, I could not imagine, and I would have wagered that Lord Unwin didn't know, either. In his haste to be rid of Mr. Slade and me, he strode to the door and opened it. Outside, the cold rain poured.

"Goodbye, Mr. Slade," he said. "Goodbye, Miss Brontë."

>✦<

My belongings took only moments to pack, and I had nothing else to do for the rest of that day. The Queen and Prince Consort kept the children away from me, the ladies-in-waiting shunned me, and servants brought my meals to my room. I felt like an outcast. To my further distress, Mr. Slade also avoided me. I supposed that he was preoccupied with the loss of his profession and his honor. What had happened last night might as well have never been. I had hoped we might at least talk over what had happened and devise some plan to counter Lord Unwin, but our only communication was a letter from Mr. Slade that said he'd had no word from the agents he'd sent to Haworth. Such fear I suffered for my family! Now that I could never accomplish the task Kuan had set me, were they all doomed? My despair increased with each passing hour.

I did not expect to sleep that night, but I was so exhausted that I dropped into a black well of slumber the moment my head touched the pillow. Much later I was roused by someone shaking my shoulder. I blinked in the moonlight. Startled and confused, I uttered a cry. A hand clapped over my mouth.

"Quiet!" an urgent voice hissed.

It was the Duchess of Norfolk, leaning over me, dressed in black, her fair hair covered by a hat with a veil. She removed her hand from my mouth, then raised a finger that cautioned me to be still. I came fully alert and put on my spectacles, and saw that her expression was as fearful as I suddenly felt.

"What do you want?" I said.

"Get up, Miss Brontë," she said. "Dress yourself. You're coming with me."

"Why?" I said, more confused than ever. Somewhere in the castle a clock struck two. "Where are we going at this hour?"

"To kidnap the children."

Shock caught my breath. Horror rendered me inarticulate; I could only stammer.

"Hurry," the Duchess ordered, her own voice shaky with nerves. "Mr. Kuan doesn't like to be kept waiting."

I had assumed that the death of Captain Innes had rid the royal household of Kuan's accomplice; so had Mr. Slade and Lord Unwin. But we had underestimated Kuan. He had arranged a second accomplice in case the captain failed him.

"No," I declared, furious as well as amazed. "I won't go. You must know why." What had happened, and my role as a spy, could be no secret.

But the Duchess hardly seemed to listen, let alone care. She took from her handbag a pistol, which she aimed straight at me. "Do as I say."

The pistol trembled in her hand. Although fear clenched my heart, I couldn't believe she had the courage to use the gun. "Go ahead and shoot me," I said. "The noise will awaken everyone. They'll come running. They'll find me dead and catch you. You'll be hanged for murder."

"Don't argue!" the Duchess hissed, ramming the gun against my temple.

The cold, hard steel jolted a whimper from me, and I realized that she was crazed enough to kill me unless I obeyed her. She said, "Mr. Kuan warned me that if you should ruin his plans for the kidnapping, then I must kill you, and the children too. And I swear I will if you don't get up right this moment!"

Even while terror overwhelmed my thoughts, I said, "Why must you do this? What has Mr. Kuan promised you in exchange, or threatened upon you if you refuse?"

The Duchess made an impatient sound. "That is not your business, Miss Brontë."

Whatever hold Kuan had upon her was a strong one. I felt a desperate wish to live, and a duty to protect the children. I had to cooperate with the Duchess and hope that some opportunity to save them and myself would later arise.

"Very well," I said.

She kept the gun aimed at me as I quickly dressed. When I had finished, she hurried me through the door that led from my room to the nursery. Two royal guardsmen were standing near the beds in which Bertie, Vicky, and Alfred slept.

"Wrap them up," the Duchess whispered to the guards, "and let us be gone."

These guards were also in Kuan's employ! How many other accomplices might there be in the royal household? I asked the Duchess, "Why don't you and the guardsmen kidnap the children yourself? Why not spare me?"

"We all have roles to play for Mr. Kuan," she said. "Yours is to take the children. Ours is to stay behind."

I now understood that Kuan intended that his minions remain inside the royal household, in the event he should need them again. Such foresight he had! I watched helplessly as the guards drew back the covers from Vicky and Bertie. The children neither stirred nor made a noise.

"I slipped laudanum into their cocoa," the Duchess said. "They'll not waken for quite some time."

The sight of the men bundling the two frail, pliable children into blankets pained my heart. I forgave Bertie his mischief. When the men reached for little Alfred, protest rose in me. "Please don't take him!" I cried. "He's just a baby."

"Be quiet!" The Duchess eyed the door as if fearing someone would burst in upon us.

Heedless of her gun, I tried to pull Alfred away from the guards. As we tussled, the boy mewled.

"Leave him," the Duchess said urgently to the guards. "We can't take the risk that he'll make more noise and wake people. The others will have to suffice."

I had at least saved one child. The Duchess opened the nursery door. The guardsmen slipped through, one carrying Vicky, the other Bertie. The Duchess pushed me after them. We filed along the dark corridor and descended the stairs. The castle was as silent and deserted as a crypt. The guards who'd once patrolled Balmoral had vanished; the Queen and her retinue slept peacefully in the mistaken belief that the children were safe. Our furtive procession continued outdoors, through the forest that had sheltered Mr. Slade and me last night but now seemed a godforsaken wilderness. Predatory birds shrieked above trees whose branches groaned and creaked. My heart ran a race with fear. I was so weak from it that I could not have walked except for the gun at my back. At last we emerged onto a moonlit road. There we met a carriage. Two men jumped down from the box. One helped the guards stow the sleeping children inside the carriage. The other man approached me.

"We meet again, Miss Brontë," he said.

I recognized his gallant, mocking voice; the moon shone on his blond hair. It was Mr. Hitchman. "Good evening," I stammered while my fear scaled new heights. The man had never quite trusted me. I recalled his threatening to kill me if I should betray his partner.

"Please get in the carriage," Hitchman said.

While I reluctantly obeyed, I cast an anxious glance towards the Duchess, who knew I had turned in Kuan's other accomplice and tried to prevent the kidnapping. If she should tell Hitchman . . . But she was gone. She and the guards had slipped away into the forest. They probably hated Kuan as much as they feared him, and they cared not if they sent an enemy into his camp.

Hitchman proffered me a vial. "If you would be so kind as to drink this laudanum, Miss Brontë? It will relax you and spare me the trouble of worrying about you during our trip."

I was reluctant to lull the wits that I needed to plot my escape; nor did I wish to leave the children alone at Hitchman's mercy. But I feared Hitchman as much as ever. I must give the appearance that I was a willing ally to him and Kuan. I therefore accepted the vial and downed the bitter draught.

"Excellent," Hitchman said.

He closed the carriage door on me. The bolt clanged into place. I heard him jump up on the box beside the driver; I heard the whip crack. The carriage sped down the road in a storm of rattling wheels and hooves. I hugged the sleeping, blanket-swathed Vicky and Bertie, whose innocent lives depended on me. I could not fail them.

As the carriage sped onward, I fought down my rising hysteria. I told myself that Mr. Slade would soon find me gone from Balmoral and rescue me and the children. My last thought, as I drifted into black oblivion, was a disturbing question: Once Kuan had Vicky and Bertie in his hands, what further use would he have for me?

39

⇥⇤

DRUGGED AND ASLEEP WHILE I RODE TOWARDS AN UNKNOWN destination, I was unaware of the other events associated with Kuan's scheme. I cannot describe with precision the scene the next morning when the Queen discovered that her children were gone, for she and I never spoke of it. But in my mind's eye I see the Queen opening the nursery door and her puzzlement at the sight of the two vacant beds in which she had tucked Vicky and Bertie the previous night. Little Alfred sits up in his crib and calls to her. As she takes him in her arms, she asks where his brother and sister are. She enters my room, sees that it is empty, and rushes to her husband, crying, "Bertie, Vicky, and the governess are gone!"

The Prince Consort summons their attendants and mounts a search of the castle and grounds, but we are nowhere to be found. The Queen inspects my room, where she discovers my outdoor clothes missing. There is but one terrible conclusion for her to draw.

I do know what happened next, because Mr. Slade later told me. He and Lord Unwin came riding up to the castle in a carriage intended to take Mr. Slade and me to the train station. Lord Unwin meant to go along and ensure that we departed. The Queen and Prince Consort rushed outside to meet them.

"Miss Brontë has kidnapped Bertie and Vicky!" the Queen announced in distraught rage.

"That cannot be!" Mr. Slade said.

"She and the children are gone," said the Prince Consort. "What else are we to believe?"

"This is all your doing," the Queen fumed at Mr. Slade and Lord Unwin. "Had you not convinced me to go along with your outrageous scheme and bring Miss Brontë here, this would never have occurred!"

As she burst into hysterical tears and the Prince Consort tried to calm her, Lord Unwin hastened to say, "It was Mr. Slade's idea."

"Miss Brontë is a woman of good moral character," Mr. Slade said. "She would never harm the children."

I know Mr. Slade was sorely vexed by Lord Unwin's attempt to put all the blame on him, and even more upset on my account. Did he wonder if Kuan had suborned me into carrying out the kidnapping after all?

"I never trusted Miss Brontë," said Lord Unwin. "Now she's proven herself a criminal."

"Well, I don't give a damn which of you is at fault!" the Queen shouted. "I order you to get my children back. And find Miss Brontë, that I may have her hanged for treason!"

Lord Unwin turned to Mr. Slade. "You'd best hurry up."

"You discharged me yesterday," Mr. Slade reminded him.

"You're reinstated," Lord Unwin said grudgingly.

>←

As to events that transpired farther afield, I learned them from another source. Into my tale I insert pages from a letter written by Branwell to Francis Grundy, an engineer he had met while working for the Leeds and Manchester Railway, a letter he never sent.

My dear Francis,

Since we last met, I have had a most astounding, incredible experience. I hesitate to write of it, for fear that you will not believe me.

As you know, I have been in quite a bad state. Daily I grow weaker and more wretched. I must drink liquor and laudanum or suffer the worst, blackest despair. When their blessed sedative effects wear off, then come the chills, the trembling, the nauseous stomach, the pounding headache, the intolerable bodily misery. Worst of all, I am plagued by regrets for what I might have been—a great artist, writer, and hero in my own life story. That was my condition on what I believe was 10 September, when I found myself without a drop of either remedy at hand. Nearly insane with desire for relief, I ransacked the room and oh! Good fortune smiled upon me, villain that I was! I found money in Father's drawer!

I hastened to the village and bought a vial of laudanum, which I tucked in my pocket; I then stumbled into the Black Bull Inn. A boxing match was in progress. Two country lads were throwing fists at each other. Spectators roared, laughed, drank their pints, and flung down coins. They welcomed me, and soon the wine was flowing like fire through my veins. I felt like a candle burned down to its end, the wick sputtering in a pool of wax. My head whirled. I remember nothing of the hours that ensued, until I awoke in an upstairs room. A maid from the inn came and told me I'd slept all day and it was time to go home.

Dizzy and nauseated, I staggered through the village. It was the dead of night; the streets were deserted. Stars shone like evil eyes in the black sky. The wind howled from the moors. Having laboriously scaled the hill, I fell against the door of the parsonage. It was locked. I banged loudly, calling for someone to let me in. It was opened by a big, brutish man I'd never seen before.

"Who are you?" the stranger said.

Surprised and disturbed, I said, "I am Branwell Brontë. I live here. What are you doing in my house?"

He hauled me inside, then slammed and bolted the door. I fell to my knees. Terror kindled in me, for even though my senses were still befuddled by drink, I knew something was seriously wrong.

"Where are my father and sisters?" I said. "What have you done with them?"

Two more men materialized in the hall. I blinked, unsure if they were real or my vision had multiplied the image of the first man. He said, "It's the son. I couldn't leave him outside to make noise and attract attention. What should we do with him?"

Another of the men said, "Put him down with the others."

The third man opened the cellar door. They forced me towards the stairs. How I shrieked and fought! Since childhood I have always been afraid of the cellar; I cannot shake my notion that it is haunted by goblins. But I was too feeble to resist. I tumbled down the stairs into the black pit. The door slammed and locked. The cold miasma of the grave enclosed me.

"Let me out!" I shrieked in terror. "I beg of you!"

I tried to crawl up the stairs, but I was trembling so violently that my efforts failed. Whimpering, I curled up on the floor. I heard whispers and rustling movements.

"No!" I cried, thinking that the goblins were coming to pull me down into hell. "Go away!"

"Branwell, is that you?" said a voice near me.

"Leave me alone!" I pleaded.

Cold fingers touched my cheek. I screamed and writhed until the being that I'd taken for a goblin said, "It's Anne."

Now I recognized her voice, and the murmuring voices of Emily and my father. Such relief overwhelmed me that I wept. We embraced in the darkness. "What has happened?" I asked her. "Why are those men holding us prisoners?"

Anne told me a fantastic tale of murders, of Charlotte and a Foreign Office spy and the Queen, and a pursuit of a villainous madman. I did not understand most of it; nor could I believe it. But the fact remained that we were locked in the cellar, at the mercy of strangers.

"What are we going to do?" I asked.

Father said, "We must trust in God to deliver us."

Anne clasped my hand. "Help will come," she said.

I was suddenly overcome by sickness. My stomach convulsed and heaved as if there were a wild beast inside me trying to get out. I vomited time and again, while tremors wracked me. Oh, what pain, what mortal suffering!

"O, death, take me now!" I begged. "Release me from this misery!"

Anne stroked my forehead and spoke soothing words. Emily said, "Enough! You're only making things worse for the rest of us!"

With such scorn and hatred did she speak! It stabbed me to the heart. I began to sob. But Emily cared not for my feelings. She said, "If you were the man you should be, you wouldn't have let those men throw you into the cellar. You would have fought them and rescued us. At the very least, you could have run for help."

She berated me with accusations that I was weak, wretched, selfish, stupid. I knew she was right. Such woeful shame did I feel! Such a poor excuse for a brother and son was I!

"You're no good to anyone including yourself," Emily said in a tone so cruel that it withered my spirit. "You might as well die."

But though I prayed for an end to my sorrows and humiliations, there leapt within me a contradictory desire almost as strong. Emily's harsh words had awakened some long-dormant part of me that wanted to *live*. It urged me to rise up and prove her criticism undeserved, to fend off the shadow of death that encroached upon me. I realized that I might have but one more chance to atone for my evils, to show some small degree of the heroism I had craved all my life, before I died. Beneath my sickness and tremors, a force hardened like a steel tendon inside me. It was my *will*, which I had thought long gone.

"I'm going to save us all," I declared.

But my voice was as weak as my body. Anne and Papa said nothing; Emily uttered a disdainful laugh and said, "Just how shall you do that?"

40

✦

A RHYTHMIC CREAKING NOISE PIERCED THE VEIL OF SLEEP THAT enshrouded me. I became aware of the hard surface upon which I lay, a rocking motion, and a sensation of nausea. My head ached; my tongue felt furry inside my parched mouth. Rough, thick fabric covered my body, which was stiff and sore. I heard splashing noises. Above me was the night sky, filled with stars that wheeled, like lanterns on a carousel, around a full moon. A cold, reviving breeze swept my face; I inhaled the scent of the ocean. My memory was a blank. More puzzled than afraid, I sat up, and the world rocked; my stomach slid to and fro inside me. I saw that I was in a boat—a small, open craft. A man sat not far from me, rowing. His oars splashed in the ocean, which spread all around us, its black waves shimmering with reflections from the moon and stars. For one frightful moment I imagined that I had died and that the man was Charon, ferrying me along the River Styx. Then I recognized him. It was Nick, the mute servant of Kuan.

"Good evening, Miss Brontë," said Hitchman's voice.

I turned and saw him seated behind me in the boat. Eerie lights from the sea played across his face, which wore its familiar, sardonic smile.

Terror surged within me. "Where are the children?"

"Right next to you," Hitchman said.

Now I became conscious of warm, solid weight pressed against me. Vicky and Bertie lay under the blanket that covered us. Their delicate faces were pale in the moonlight. Vicky's eyelids fluttered; Bertie whimpered. I felt them stirring.

"How long have I been asleep?" I said, trying to speak calmly and hide my fear lest it rouse his suspicion.

"Long enough," came the reply.

My heart plunged, for I calculated that I must have slept through an entire day. By now the Queen must have discovered that the children and I were gone, and Mr. Slade must have begun a search, but still no one had rescued us.

"Where are we?" I said.

"On the North Sea," Hitchman said.

I looked backward as Nick rowed and our boat cut across the water. Lights twinkled on a distant shoreline. My hope that Mr. Slade would come for me waned further.

"Where are we going?" I said.

"To meet Kuan."

Ahead loomed the dark form of a steamship floating at anchor. I deduced it to be the vessel that Kuan had stolen from the opium traders and that had brought him to England. Lanterns burned on its deck. Skeletal masts supported weather-beaten sails on rigging that was like the web of a giant spider. The huge, curved wheel-houses bulged with latent power. The funnel rose tall enough to impale the heavens. Nick brought our boat alongside the ship. A ladder was mounted on its hull.

"Up you go, Miss Brontë," Hitchman ordered.

Still weak and sick from the laudanum, and trembling with fright, I climbed the ladder. The ship's hull was scarred from long journeys, infested with barnacles, algae, and wormholes. Two Chinese sailors hauled me aboard. Their narrow, hostile eyes stared at me; they wore pistols and daggers at their waists. More Chinamen loitered around the deck. I felt as though I'd stepped onto foreign territory. I despaired, knowing that Mr. Slade would never find me there.

Hitchman, Nick, and the sailors brought Vicky and Bertie and the dinghy onto the ship. Hitchman said, "Come, Miss Brontë, I'll show you where you'll live during our voyage to China."

China! I felt a stab of horror. I never imagined events would reach this point. Hitchman and Nick carried the children down a flight of stairs below deck. My responsibility towards Vicky and Bertie outweighed my fears for myself: Whatever happened, I could not allow harm to come to them. I followed them into a narrow passage that smelled of coal smoke, tar, and fish as well as those odors produced by humans living in close, unsanitary quarters. We entered a tiny chamber that had four bunks mounted on the walls, a washstand, and a porthole window.

"See to the children," Hitchman said as he and Nick laid them on the two lower bunks. By now they were restless and yawning. "Make sure they behave themselves. Nick will bring you food and water. You'll find everything else you need in the cupboards under the bunks."

The men departed. I unwrapped Vicky and Bertie. They had wet themselves while asleep, and their nightclothes were soaked. In the cupboards I found children's garments, and some that would fit me. Those were of much better quality than I usually wore. Kuan had provided well for us. This dismayed rather than pleased me: It seemed the final confirmation that I would indeed be going on this journey. Nick brought bread, cheese, cold meat, and a water jug. I cleaned the children and dressed them.

"Miss Brontë," Vicky murmured. "Where are we?"

I felt a terrible pity for her, and a guilt even more terrible. "On a ship."

"What are we doing here?" Vicky sat up, rubbing her eyes. "I don't feel good. Where are we going?"

I hadn't the heart to tell her.

"Where's Mama?" Bertie demanded. I tried to put shoes on him, but he kicked at me. "Go away! I want Mama!"

"I'm sorry, but your mama isn't here." Wondering how in the world I would manage him, I resorted to an outright lie: "Be a good boy, and you'll see her soon."

Bertie began to cry and wail, "Mama! Papa!"

When I tried to soothe him, he pushed me away and wailed louder. Vicky sat silent on her bunk, prim as ever; but her chin trembled.

"You must be hungry and thirsty," I said in an attempt to distract the children from their woe.

Vicky drank some water, but she refused the food. "No thank you, Miss Brontë," she said politely. "I don't think I can eat."

Bertie said, "I'm going to find Mama," and scrambled out the door.

I followed, calling, "Bertie! Come back here at once!"

He ran down the passage, but Nick stood blocking the stairs. Nick picked up Bertie, who shrieked and fought, carried him into our chamber, and dumped him on the bunk. Bertie lay there squalling. Nick gave me a look that warned me to keep Bertie inside, then left. The rolling of the ship churned my stomach. I wanted to vomit up my sickness and terror, to weep with despair. But I had to hold myself together for the sake of the children. It was up to me to save them from Kuan. I sat beside Vicky and took her cold little hand in mine.

"Can you keep a secret?" I whispered.

She gave me a somber, questioning look. Then she nodded.

"Some bad men have kidnapped us," I whispered. "I promise I'll take you and Bertie back to your mama and papa." Somehow, God willing, I would. "But I need you to promise to help me. Can you?"

I couldn't explain to a child the terrible specifics of what might transpire, but Vicky seemed to understand at once that we were in danger and must band together. She said, "Yes, Miss Brontë. What do you want me to do?"

"You must try not to make those men angry," I said. "Should there arise a chance for us to escape, be ready to do whatever I tell you." She nodded solemnly. "And if you can calm your brother, please do it right now."

Vicky hopped down from her bunk and addressed Bertie: "Shame on you, Prince Albert Edward. That's no way for the future King of England to carry on. Be quiet!" She cuffed the sobbing boy on the head. "Show some courage!"

At that moment she sounded just like her mother. Bertie ceased his tantrum and pouted. I gave Vicky a look of thanks, which she acknowledged with a gracious nod.

Hitchman appeared at the door. "Mr. Kuan would like to see you," he told me.

He locked the children in the room. Apprehension gripped me as we went up on the deck. Kuan stood gazing eastward out to sea. He had shed his European garb and now wore the coat, trousers, cap, and slippers of a mandarin. He looked altogether foreign, and even more sinister than before.

"Greetings again, Miss Brontë," he said.

He motioned for Hitchman to leave us and extended his hand to me. The Chinese crew loitered nearby, armed and wary. I gave Kuan my hand, which he pressed to his lips. I stifled a tremor of revulsion. No matter that I could still sympathize with his cause, Kuan was the devil incarnate. I avoided his gaze, lest mine reveal my thoughts.

"A thousand thanks for delivering the royal children to me," Kuan said. "You have performed admirably."

Despite his extensive network of informants and virtual omniscience, he seemed unaware that I had betrayed Captain Innes and that the man was dead. Nothing in his manner indicated that he suspected me of collaborating with his enemies. I silently thanked God.

"It was my pleasure to serve you," I said, eager to keep his trust, the better to find a way to escape.

"I regret holding your family hostage," Kuan said. "It was but a necessary precaution. Before we set sail for China, I will send word to my men to release them. I hope I haven't caused them any inconvenience."

He spoke as if imprisoning my family were so trivial that I wouldn't mind. I swallowed my anger and said, "When do we sail?"

"Tomorrow," he said, "when the rest of my men arrive. They will bring the gold we need to journey around the world and carry out my plans in China."

My spirits lifted momentarily, thinking I'd been granted a

reprieve; then it dawned that I had but one day to save the children. And how could I, when we were on this ship, so far from shore? If only Slade would find us!

Kuan said, "How are the children?"

"They're a bit shaken," I said, "but otherwise unharmed."

"Very good," Kuan said. "I need them alive. Your duty is to keep them in good health."

That answered my question regarding what else he wanted from me. The voyage to China might take as long as a year, depending on the seas, the winds, and the vicissitudes that travelers face. And Kuan's crewmen were obviously ill qualified to serve as nursemaids.

"Once we get to China, I will issue an ultimatum," Kuan went on. "Either the British must leave my kingdom, or their Queen's children will die. The secret arsenal of weapons that I've sent to my accomplices in Canton over the years is waiting for me. With the gold that my men are bringing, I will raise an army. I will ban foreigners from China forever and restore Chinese honor."

Clever though his plan was, I couldn't share his confidence that he would succeed. Would the Queen surrender to him because he held her children hostage? More likely, she would send the army to rescue them and crush him.

"The emperor will reward me as a hero," Kuan said. Visions of glory swirled in his eyes, and I realized that he was no longer the genius who had previously laid so many remarkable entrapments. His quest for revenge and power had driven him to near insanity. "I will resume my status as an imperial official. You will live in my estate, where you will want for nothing."

But I predicted that Kuan and his country would face more war, and suffer even greater defeat and humiliation than before. What then would become of Vicky and Bertie? Would Kuan kill them after they had outlived their usefulness to him? Would they die during a war between England and China? What terrible fate awaited me unless we escaped?

Hitchman and T'ing-nan joined Kuan and me. "Ah, Miss Brontë, here is your former pupil," Kuan said.

T'ing-nan gave me a baleful look: He was no gladder to renew our acquaintance than was I.

"When China is purged of foreign influence and peace is restored, my son will study for the civil service exam," Kuan said. "He must work hard to make up for the education he has missed while we've been abroad." He gave T'ing-nan a warning look. "You must practice self-discipline instead of lazing about as you have become accustomed to do."

T'ing-nan slouched against the railing; a sneer twisted his mouth.

"What's the matter?" Hitchman said, irritated by the boy's surliness. "You've been longing to go back to China. Aren't you pleased that you finally are going?"

"We no go China," T'ing-nan said. "I never get home again."

"Discontent has become a habit for you," Kuan rebuked him. "You would rather complain than appreciate your good fortune."

T'ing-nan pushed himself away from the railing and glared at Kuan. "You think you know everything. But you not as smart as you think." A cunning, malevolent smile stole across his face. "You a fool to think you can take children to China and drive out British." He thumped his fist against his chest. "I know better."

Hitchman's expression derided him; but the conviction in T'ing-nan's manner made me wonder if he wasn't just baiting his father. I saw Kuan narrow his eyes as the same thought struck him. "Why do you say that?" Kuan asked T'ing-nan.

The young man's eyes glinted with mischief. "You trust her," he said, pointing at me. "You think she help you. But she no good. She trick you."

Hitchman and Kuan turned on me. The suspicion I had often seen in Hitchman's eyes was now reflected in Kuan's. Dismayed, I looked at T'ing-nan, who grinned. We both knew he'd spoken the truth, but how had he found me out?

"Explain," Kuan ordered his son.

"The night I run away," T'ing-nan said, "I hide outside house. I see her come out while you and Nick and Hitchman looking for me. She run off. I follow her."

Now I remembered my feeling of being watched by someone. It had been T'ing-nan, spying on me. Horror crept into my bones.

"She go to house in village. There she meet man. She tell him all about you." T'ing-nan regarded his father with triumph. "She not work for you—she work for him. She try help him catch you, punish you."

He'd seen me with Mr. Slade and overheard us through the open window. Now T'ing-nan's triumphant smile included me. He had said he would make me pay for refusing to hide him from Kuan. Now he'd fulfilled his threat.

"Is this true, Miss Brontë?" demanded Kuan.

"No!" I cried with all the conviction I could feign. "I don't know what T'ing-nan is talking about."

But I instinctively backed away from him, and I could no longer hide my terror. Kuan's gaze pierced straight through it to the truth. A storm of rage gathered in his eyes. "Who is this man?" His voice was a quiet, menacing hiss.

"There was no man," I faltered. "I never—"

Hitchman seized me by my shoulders. "Who is he?"

His fingers dug painfully into my flesh. His face was so close to mine that I could see the sharp edges of his teeth and smell his sulfurous breath. I shrank from him.

"Answer me!" Hitchman struck my cheek a hard slap.

My head snapped backward. Pain reverberated through my skull. My ears rang; the lights on the deck shattered into bright fragments. I had never been struck with such deliberate, calculated violence. The blow was as shocking and intimate as it was hurtful. It diminished me to a puny, hapless creature. How I wish I could have insisted on my innocence and persuaded Kuan that his son was lying! But my cowardly impulse was to obey Hitchman and avoid another blow.

"His name is John Slade," I said even as shame filled me. "He's an agent with the Foreign Office."

"A spy for the Crown." Hitchman spoke to Kuan in a tone of revelation and disgust while tightening his hold on me. "I warned you against taking Miss Brontë on. I never quite trusted her myself.

But I never suspected that she had such dangerous connections." He regarded me with amazement. "Well, well—the demure little governess has turned out to be a spy for a spy."

The rage in Kuan's eyes turned murderous. His mouth thinned; his nostrils flared. Behind him the Chinese crew was watching, avid to see how he would punish me. T'ing-nan was grinning with childlike joy at my plight. So spiteful was he that he didn't care that he had jeopardized his own hope of returning to China by not telling his father about me sooner.

"When did you and this agent Slade join forces against me, Miss Brontë?" Kuan asked.

I hesitated, but Hitchman raised his fist to strike me again. Cringing, I blurted, "It was after your henchman stole Isabel White's book from my home and almost killed my brother."

"A man purporting to be your cousin accompanied you to Belgium," Kuan said. "Was he in fact Mr. Slade?"

"Yes," I said. Hitchman's fist remained poised above me.

"Did he also accompany you to Balmoral Castle?" Kuan asked. "Did you tell him of my plan to kidnap the children?"

Weak with terror and shame, I nodded. Kuan suddenly reached towards me. Panic exploded in my heart, for I thought he meant to rip it out of my chest. My back was pressed against the railing; Hitchman's grasp imprisoned me. But Kuan's fingers merely grazed my cheek in a caress almost tender.

"Miss Brontë, I am most disappointed in you," he said. His voice was reproving yet gentle, his gaze almost affectionate. "Your deceit is unforgivable. I regret that you will not enjoy the good fortune that I offered you. Instead, you will reap your punishment for betraying my cause as well as myself. So will your family suffer on your account. I will send my men to execute them rather than set them free."

"Please don't hurt them!" I knew not what I was babbling. So eager was I to save my family, myself, and the children that I would have said anything. "I'm sorry for what I did. I've learned my lesson. I promise I'll be loyal to you from now on. Have mercy!" I pleaded.

"No more lies, Miss Brontë," Hitchman said scornfully.

He closed his hands around my throat. I clawed at them, trying in vain to tear them away. "Help!" I screamed.

My voice drifted across empty ocean. T'ing-nan giggled. The crew waited, immobile. In my mind arose an image of the stone tablets inside Haworth Church that bore the names of my mother and my sisters Maria and Elizabeth. Never would I rest beside them. Never would Papa, Emily, Anne, Branwell, or Mr. Slade know my fate. After Hitchman strangled me, I would simply vanish beneath the waves.

Then Kuan said, "No. Wait."

Hitchman paused, although his hands still encircled my throat. "We can't let her live," he said. "She could have destroyed you. She'll try again."

"She is no danger to me here," Kuan said. "She cannot get away. Nor can she communicate with her confederates."

The reprieve gave me hope. I held my breath and silently prayed for deliverance.

"We've no use for her," Hitchman said.

All along I had feared Hitchman; now he was eroding Kuan's favor towards me, and my chances of survival.

"I do indeed have further use for Miss Brontë," Kuan said. "I need her to care for my hostages."

I started to expel my breath in a sob of relief. Then Kuan said, "We shall wait until we're far from England, near some foreign port where we can engage a nursemaid to tend the children." He smiled at me—a dreadful smile that anticipated revenge. "Then we'll dispatch Miss Brontë to the hell reserved for traitors."

41

✥

THAT NIGHT I DID MY BEST TO HIDE OUR GRAVE PREDICAMENT FROM the children and keep them quiet, but they were restless. Vicky asked me time after time what was going to happen to us. I didn't know what to tell her. Bertie sulked and roamed the cabin like a caged animal. I tried the door and discovered that although the lock was strong iron, the door itself was loose in its frame. I searched the room for any instrument I could use as a lever to pry it open. The bunks were built of wooden rails, and after considerable effort, I managed to wrest one free—but even if I could force the door, how would I get the children off the ship and across the ocean to safety?

I hid the rail under my mattress in the vain hope of later making use of it. The motion of the ship made me so ill that I lay on my bunk while the children fretted and I wondered what was happening at Balmoral. I imagined Mr. Slade and the Queen's soldiers riding the roads, searching the forests and villages, and finding no trace of us. Later, I learned that that was indeed how Slade had spent the hours after our disappearance. I worried that his agents wouldn't reach Haworth in time to free my family before Kuan's henchmen arrived to kill them. What I never imagined were the events taking place at the parsonage. Here shall Branwell's letter to Francis Grundy continue and explain:

The hours that I passed in the cellar were the worst I'd ever known. Nausea, tremors, fever, and chills tortured me. I lay helpless on the floor, which was wet and foul from my effluvium. The dark pressed in on me like the death I welcomed yet dreaded. Anne did her best to nurse me, holding my head in her lap, stroking my brow. Emily uttered frequent, disgusted exclamations. Father prayed to the God who had forsaken us.

After an eternity, the sickness departed. It left me exhausted, but my mind was miraculously lucid. For ages it had been so obsessed with thoughts of my dear, lost Lydia, my own misery, and my craving for liquor and laudanum that there was no capacity for anything else. Not a single line of verse, not a single new idea, had occurred to me in all that time. But lo, the voice of Inspiration now spoke to me! It told me how I might deliver us from this hellish nightmare.

I pushed myself upright. Anne said, "What's wrong?"

Oh, the powerful temptation to lie down and allow whatever would happen to happen! But the voice whispered, *This is your last chance:* "Help me get up," I said, gasping as I struggled to rise.

"What for?" Emily said. "There's nowhere to go. And there's certainly nothing you can do." I could feel her bitter scorn towards me, like poisonous fumes in the darkness.

"Be still and rest," Anne said.

But I clambered to my hands and knees. I crawled across the cellar, groping my way. A wall suddenly materialized before me and slammed against my head. I yelped in pain.

"What are you doing?" Father said, puzzled and anxious.

I felt along the cold, rough stones embedded in the earthen surface of the wall. "Looking for the bottle of whisky that I just remembered I hid."

There was silence, during which I sensed them thinking that they'd believed they'd disposed of all the liquor I'd squirreled away in the house but I had outwitted them.

Some months ago, desperate to secure the bottle in case of urgent need, I had forced myself to venture into the cellar. My family, knowing I was afraid of it, hadn't thought to look here.

"Trust you to find a drink, even at a time like this," Emily said with a sneer in her voice.

"I'm not going to drink the whisky," I said.

Blind luck favored me. My hands found the large, square stone I remembered. I tugged it loose and dropped it to the floor. I reached into the void that I'd dug and that the stone had concealed.

"Then why do you want it?" Anne said.

My fingers touched smooth, cool glass. I pulled out the bottle and shook it. The whisky sloshed inside. "To buy our freedom."

This provoked exclamations of surprise and confusion. Father said, "What are you talking about?"

"Pay him no mind," Emily said. "He has gone completely insane at last."

Clutching the bottle, I staggered around the cellar, bumping into walls, until I stubbed my foot against the stairs. I crawled slowly, laboriously, up them.

"What are you doing?" Anne said.

If I told them my intentions, they would surely try to dissuade me; coward that I am, I would just as surely let them. Upon reaching the top of the stairs, I thumped on the door and called loudly, "Hello! May I please speak with you gentlemen?"

Father and Anne tried to hush me for fear that I would make the men angry. Emily said, "It's no use. They won't let us out."

But I kept calling and thumping. After some time I heard footsteps in the passage outside. "Be quiet!" called a man's irate voice.

"Forgive me for annoying you, good sir, but I've got something that I think you would like to have," I said in the polite, ingratiating tone that I'd often used to wheedle my way into company and out of trouble.

No immediate reply came, but I felt the man's presence still on the other side of the door. Would his curiosity work in my favor? At last he said, "What is it?"

"Open the door," I said, "and I'll show you."

I felt him hesitate. I hoped he was bored with sitting in the parsonage and wanted diversion. To my delight, I heard him unbolt the door, which then opened a few inches. I saw the man, his figure lit from the lamps in the passage behind him. I hastily backed down a few stairs, out of his reach.

"Well?" he demanded. "What have you got?"

From my vantage point I could discern little about him except that he was much bigger than myself. Fortunately, my plan did not require brute strength of me as much as cunning. I held up the bottle so that the lamplight glinted on it.

"This is the finest-quality Irish whisky," I said. "May I offer you a taste?"

The man opened the door wider. Two other men appeared behind him. The light was now sufficient that I got a good view of them. The man who'd answered my call had narrow, hostile eyes deep-set in a fleshy face, and a complexion like raw meat.

"What do you think you're doing?" demanded the man at his right, who looked enough like him to be his brother.

The other man ordered, "Shut that door." He was fair of hair and sharp-featured. Although he and his comrades all wore dark coats and trousers, his looked tailored to fit him. His speech suggested higher society than theirs. Surely he was their leader.

"But he's got whisky," said the first man.

A person recognizes in others the desires that he himself possesses. I could sense their thirst for the liquor; I could see it in the way they looked at the bottle. The leader thrust his hand through the doorway and said, "Give me that."

I held it out of his reach. My family made not a sound; yet I felt them waiting fearfully. "If you let me come up," I said, "I'll serve you all a drink."

He and his comrades studied me. On their faces I read suspicion mixed with disgust at my decrepit appearance. Once I would have been ashamed that my fellow humans beheld me thus, but now their low opinion of me was to my advantage. I smiled at them, striving for the charm that had won me many friends and lovers in my youth. Their faces assumed another expression that I'd seen too often of late. It said, *Here's a harmless buffoon who can help us while away the time.* They shrugged and grinned at one another.

"Come on, then," the leader invited me.

Up the stairs I scrambled. I felt like a soul risen from the depths of hell. But Father, Emily, and Anne were still trapped in abysmal darkness below me. The men barred the cellar door. They hovered around me as I faltered into the dining room. Playing cards lay strewn across the table amidst burning candles, and tobacco smoke tainted the air. The windows were dark with night, and the wind keened outside. I estimated that I'd spent some twenty-four hours in the cellar, but how much longer these men had held Father, Anne, and Emily captive, I knew not. If anyone had come to the parsonage to see us, they must have gone away believing we were not home. The men must have kept themselves well hidden so as not to arouse suspicion. No rescue would come from outside quarters. All was up to me. My legs quaked under the burden of responsibility.

But I hid my thoughts behind an idiotic smile as I fetched four glasses. My hands shook as I poured whisky. I said, "A toast to new friends!"

The men raised their glasses and drank. I only pretended to follow suit, for although I desperately craved the whisky, I must keep sober. There was a slackening of tension in the atmosphere, and the men's faces relaxed; already the liquor was doing its work. Now I cast about for a way to keep my companions occupied for as long as I needed.

I said, "May I join your game?"

"How much money have you?" the leader asked, his eyes alight at the prospect of enriching himself at a fool's expense.

"None, alas," I said, "but for every hand I lose, I'll recite you a verse."

"That suits me," said one of the leader's comrades.

"What better fun have we got?" said the other.

We sat down and played, and I lost every round. While I recited poetry, my captors cheered and egged me on. I felt myself once again to be the Branwell Brontë who had entertained audiences in taverns all over England. That I refilled the men's glasses time after time probably accounted for their enjoyment of my verse. If only I had ever won such an enthusiastic reception from publishers! But never had my poetry served such a serious purpose as now. Soon we were on first-name terms. The leader was Cecil; the two brothers, Jim and Bill. Soon they were quite tipsy.

"Tell me," I said, "what brought you here?"

"We were sent by the chap we work for," Cecil answered. "He's kidnapping the Queen's children. Your sister's supposed to help him. We're here to make sure she does. She's been told that if she doesn't, her family will die."

He uttered this astounding explanation in a tone as matter-of-fact as if he were talking about the weather. My first reaction was shock; the second, disbelief. Had my fevered brain dreamed up these men? But they seemed as real as I. Their story explained why Charlotte was absent and seemed as creditable a reason as any for the imprisonment of our family.

"When is this kidnapping to take place?" I said.

"It should have happened yesterday," Cecil said while Jim dealt the cards again. "We're waiting for word."

"What are your employer and Charlotte going to do with the children?" I asked as casually as I could.

"Take them to China," came the reply. "They should be aboard his ship off the coast of Aberdeen as we speak."

Horror seized me as I realized that whatever was really going on, these men would never free my family and myself. Surely they knew that as soon as they did, we would set the police after them and their employer. They must have orders from him to murder us and thereby ensure our silence. Cecil didn't care if I knew about this kidnapping because I would be dead and unable to interfere.

Sweat broke out on my forehead and tremors shivered through me, but I hid my terror behind loud, careless laughter, as though I thought kidnapping and treason to be the best prank in the world. "Let's have another drink!"

I took the glasses to the sideboard and poured out the last of the whisky. While the men were busy looking at their cards, I dipped my hand into my pocket and brought out the vial of laudanum that I'd bought before I came home, before my drunken revel at the Black Bull Inn an eternity ago. For a moment I held it in my fist, resisting my desire for it. Then I quickly apportioned the laudanum among three glasses. I pocketed the empty vial and set the glasses before the men. They drank without noticing that I abstained. I sat down, endured another game, and waited.

Eventually they began to yawn as the combined effects of whisky and laudanum took hold. Jim canted backward in his chair and dozed off. Bill dropped his head onto the table and fell asleep amidst the cards. Cecil stared at me, the only person still alert. Suspicion and anger battled drowsiness in his gaze as it moved to his empty glass then back to me.

"What did you put in that last drink?" he demanded.

Rising clumsily from his chair, he lurched towards me. His knees buckled; his eyes rolled up inside his head. He crashed to the floor and lay unconscious. Never had any venture of mine succeeded so brilliantly. I staggered to the cellar door, unbarred it, and flung it open.

"Father! Anne! Emily!" I cried.

Thus ends Branwell's letter. His writing is shaky and almost illegible on the last page, as though he'd lost the strength to write. Let an extract from Emily's diary complete his story.

The Journal of Emily Brontë

I sat on the cold floor of the dark cellar, deep in despair. A great distance seemed to separate me from Father and Anne, who prayed in low voices together. I was silently pining for sunlight, for the fresh wind on the moors, when I heard someone calling.

"Come upstairs! Hurry!" Branwell shouted.

Light shone at the top of the stairs. In it stood Branwell's thin, frail figure. Sobs of joy erupted from me as I bounded up the stairs. Anne and Father were close behind me. We burst into the passage.

"What has happened?" Papa asked Branwell.

"Where are those men?" Anne said.

"I gave them whisky and laudanum," Branwell said, breathless with excitement. "They're out cold."

We all hurried to the dining room. There, two men slumbered at the table; the third lay sprawled asleep on the floor.

"Help me tie them up," Branwell said.

Anne fetched a ball of stout twine and a knife. She and Papa bound the sleeping men's wrists and ankles. Papa said, "I'll fetch the constable."

"Wait," Branwell said urgently.

"But we must have these criminals arrested," Anne said.

"Charlotte is in trouble," Branwell said. "These men told me that she has been forced into kidnapping the Queen's children. She's been taken with them aboard a ship that's soon leaving for China." Anne and Father exclaimed in horror. "The ship is presently anchored off the coast of Aberdeen. Before we do anything else, we must rescue her."

"We must tell Mr. Slade," Papa said. "He'll know what to do."

"But Mr. Slade is at Balmoral Castle in Scotland," Anne said. "We can't travel so far in time for him to save Charlotte and the children."

"We need only get as far as the railway station at Ludden-den Foot," Branwell said. "It has a telegraph. My friend Francis Grundy can communicate instantaneously with any other station in the kingdom."

"The telegraph is truly a modern miracle," Papa proclaimed.

"We'll ask Mr. Grundy to send an urgent message to the station nearest Balmoral," Anne said.

"Let's be on our way," Branwell said, but a violent fit of coughing sank him to his knees.

Papa knelt beside him and held him close. "My son, you have demonstrated great courage tonight," Papa said, his voice roughened by emotion. "Your actions have more than atoned for all your sins."

"It was the courage of the damned, Father," Branwell rasped. "I had nothing to lose."

"You could have lost your life trying to save us," Papa said.

"My life is almost done. It was but a small stake to gamble." Branwell laughed weakly. "At least perhaps I'll die a hero even if I never lived as one."

Papa and Anne were both weeping. Anne said to Branwell, "You've done your part. Now you must stay home and rest."

"But who will go to Luddenden Foot?" Branwell said.

I spoke aloud: "I'll go."

Papa, Anne and Branwell regarded me with surprise.

Papa said, "Very well, Emily; but I will go with you. On our way we'll send the constable to rid us of these criminals. Anne, you stay and help Branwell guard them." He fetched his pistol and put it in her hands, then said, "Let us make haste, Emily."

"I may be gone when you return. Let me bid you good-bye now," Branwell said.

42

❯❮

THE WIND QUICKENED, SLAPPING WAVES HIGHER AGAINST THE SHIP, which rocked fitfully and nauseously; I heard the masts and rigging creaking, and the sails flapping, all through the night. When at last the rising sun spread a crimson sheen across the ocean, I wondered how many more mornings I would live to see.

The children and I spent an awful day together. Hitchman brought us food that none of us had the appetite to eat. Bertie alternately raged and pouted. Vicky said, "It's going to be all right, isn't it, Miss Brontë?" I did my best to calm her growing anxiety, even though I was loath to give her false hope.

Afternoon had lapsed into a cloudy, blustery twilight when there began a commotion above us. Voices called in English and Chinese. We heard thuds and scrambling noises as cargo and persons came aboard. With much consternation I deduced that the rest of Kuan's retinue had arrived by boat. Next there was a cacophonous metallic racket of the anchor being hauled up from the water. A loud rumbling began in the depths of the ship. I smelled smoke and heard steam hissing. The engine roared to life; its mighty pulse throbbed. The ship began to move.

Bertie shouted, "No!"

He pounded and kicked the door; he sobbed with rage. Vicky uttered not a sound, but tears trickled down her face. The ship gathered speed, its great wheels churning the water. I experienced the wrenching sensation of being torn from all that was familiar and dear. An invisible, impenetrable barrier slammed down behind me, sealing me off from my past life, its joys and woes. Papa, Emily, Anne, Branwell, and Mr. Slade were lost to me, as were all dreams for the future. My unfinished book would remain unfinished; I would never write another. The voice that I had labored to make heard by the world would be silenced forever.

Vicky huddled tight against my side. When Bertie realized that his hysterics were futile, he quieted and came to sit by me. I put my arms around the children and mutely prayed for the ship to reach China safely even with myself no longer on it. I beseeched God to let the Crown negotiate the return of Vicky and Bertie even if I perished. They embodied not only generations of royal ancestry; they, like all children, represented mankind's hope for the future. That they should die for offenses committed by their elder was a sin most grievous.

The sea and the horizon flowed past our window, their emptiness relieved only by occasional, faraway ships, until darkness fell. I knew not how many miles we traveled. Silver lights from the moon and stars flecked the choppy waves. The engine roared and the wheels churned without cessation. I had the opportunity to realize that there was even more to be lost than I'd initially thought.

The family Brontë had never had much in the way of worldly possessions or status. But we had taken a quiet pride in knowing that our name was respectable. Our personal honor had conferred upon us a sense of value. But when the world learned that I had been party to the kidnapping, I would be forever reviled. Even if my family survived their imprisonment, they would forever be tainted by their association with me, the name Brontë ruined. They would live out their lives beneath a cloud of shame. Furthermore, they were not the only ones who would suffer on my account. With myself dead and beyond punishment, Mr. Slade would take the blame for our mission's disastrous conclusion. He, whom I also loved, would surely hang.

Suddenly Vicky tensed beside me and said, "What's that sound?"

"I don't hear anything," I said.

But Vicky's face brightened with hope. "I hear ships."

"So do I!" Bertie said. "They're coming for us."

Now I heard what their acute young ears had discerned first: a distant thunder carrying across the ocean. We grouped around the window. Clusters of lights came into view. As they neared, they became four steamships lit by lanterns, puffing smoke. Their noise grew louder. Shouts erupted on our ship's upper deck: The crew had sighted the fleet. The engine roared louder and throbbed harder; the paddlewheels plowed a bumpy, accelerating swath across the water, but our pursuers gradually gained on us. Our ship tilted off course, throwing me and the children sideways. Again and again this happened while Kuan tried to maneuver away from the fleet. My stomach lurched with every roll. Vicky and Bertie shrieked as we tumbled onto the floor. For an instant I thought the ship might keel over and sink.

The engine's noise dwindled; the ship slowed, regaining balance. The racket from the wheels stopped. We glided to a halt, rocking and tossing upon the waves. The children and I peered out the window. Two ships were standing afloat near us. Their idle engines rumbled like tigers ready to pounce. Armed soldiers stood on their decks; guns protruded from their hulls. Banners fluttering on their masts bore the insignia of the Royal Navy.

"Mama and Papa have sent them to rescue us!" Vicky cried.

Tears of relief pricked my eyes. I breathed a prayer of fervent thanks, even as I wondered how this miracle had come to be.

A voice thundered from one of the ships: "Attention, Mr. Kuan! In the name of the British Crown, I order you to surrender!"

I recognized that voice. It belonged to Mr. Slade! Now I spotted him on a naval ship amidst the soldiers. Jubilation swelled my heart. With his keen, determined features lit by the lanterns and his black hair wild in the wind, he looked to me like a Spartan warrior come to rescue Helen of Troy.

"I will not surrender," came Kuan's voice, his tone fearless and adamant. "Let me pass."

"You cannot escape," Mr. Slade called. "You're surrounded. We're coming aboard to take the children and Miss Brontë. I advise you to cooperate."

The ship on which he stood rumbled its engine louder and approached nearer to us, huffing steam and smoke. Kuan said, "Come no closer, or I'll open fire."

From above me I heard the scrape and creak of mechanical devices moving and heavy wheels rolling: Kuan's crew was opening the gun ports and positioning cannon. I heard Mr. Slade reply, "You would be a fool to attack us. We have far greater fire power than you do."

"You would be a fool to attack me while I hold your royal prince and princess captive," Kuan said. "How unfortunate for you if they should be killed in a battle."

"We'll not allow you to take them to China," Mr. Slade said. Although I knew he must fear for the children, his voice remained calm; his determination matched Kuan's. "We're coming to fetch them and Miss Brontë."

"I'll kill them first," Kuan said.

Vicky gasped. "He isn't really going to hurt us, is he, Miss Brontë?"

"He can't," Bertie declared.

But Kuan was doomed to die for his crimes whether or not he surrendered, whether or not he spared us. He had nothing to lose by resisting. Furthermore, his pride would never allow him to surrender, and he would take us down with him to spite his enemies.

The ship on which Mr. Slade stood advanced on ours. Sudden, thunderous booms jarred my bones, deafening my ears, and I smelled acrid gunpowder. Vicky and Bertie screamed and hugged me. The floor below us shook with each explosion. Kuan had fired his cannons. Smoke wafted from Mr. Slade's ship, where troops scrambled about the deck. I heard them shouting as volleys of gunshots filled the night. I could no longer see Mr. Slade, who was lost in the chaos. On the other naval ship visible to me, men floundered beneath a fallen mast. Sparks flared from rifles as the navy troops' bullets cracked against our ship, and I gathered the children as far from the window as possible. During an instant's lull in the din, I heard Kuan call, "Bring up the hostages."

If there ever was a time for me to act, it was now. I could not wait out the battle in the vain hope that Providence would favor us. Our rescuers were themselves in peril, and Kuan might kill us before they could board his ship. Determined to keep us out of his hands, I grabbed the rod I had hidden under my bunk. Inserting it between the door and the frame, I pried. The gunshots and cannon fire continued. Footsteps hastened down the staircase towards us.

"They're coming. Hurry up!" shouted Bertie.

"Exert yourself, Miss Brontë," Vicky pleaded.

Although I strained mightily, the door did not budge. Someone was working the lock. I sprang backward, the rod still gripped in my hands, shielding the children behind me. The door flew open, and a Chinese crewman burst into the cabin. His face was savage; he held a pistol. Vicky and Bertie screamed. Compelled by a sudden swift, primitive instinct, I swung the rod at the man and struck him hard across the face. I felt the sensation of flesh yielding, bones breaking. Blood poured from his nose, and his eyes went blank as he crashed to the floor.

Never before had I struck down anyone, but I had no time to marvel at my deed, for Nick appeared at the threshold. Mute and menacing, he stepped towards us over the inert Chinaman. I swung the rod, but he caught it, wrenched it from my hands, and tossed it away. He reached for me, when suddenly Bertie hurled himself at Nick. The boy pummeled Nick while screeching at the top of his lungs. When Nick tried to push him away, Bertie sank his teeth into Nick's calf. Nick yowled—the first sound I'd ever heard from him. He punched Bertie and pulled at his hair, but Bertie growled and hung on, like a dog gnawing a bone. He and Nick fell down together. Vicky snatched up the rod. She beat Nick soundly about the head until he lay motionless. Bertie sprung up, Nick's blood trickling from his mouth. He and Vicky cheered in triumph. No king among their ancestors could have fought a battle more valiantly.

"We must hurry," I said, urging them towards the door.

I took the pistol from the fallen Chinaman. A weapon might prove useful, although I'd never fired a gun and it felt heavy and awkward. I put it gingerly in my pocket, afraid I might somehow shoot myself. I hurried the children along the vacant passage, then up the stairs. Through the open hatch I heard the shooting. Our way was lit by red-orange firelight; screams of agony from men struck by bullets greeted us as we climbed. We paused at the top of the stairs and peered out through the hatch.

On the deck, bodies lay in puddles of blood while sailors manned the cannons or hunched at the railings and fired rifles. Our ship quaked as the guns below deck roared. In the distance loomed a naval ship engulfed by flames. Smoke billowed to the turbulent sky. I couldn't know whether the ship was Mr. Slade's. I suppressed the terrible thought that he had died in his attempt to rescue us. That the navy had not destroyed our vessel was due only to its fear of harming the children. I didn't see Kuan, Hitchman, or T'ing-nan, but I could not assume they were among the dead. My only hope was to get Vicky, Bertie, and myself out of their reach. But how? As I frantically looked about for inspiration, I spied T'ing-nan shambling down the deck. He caught sight of us, and his eyes filled with murderous rage.

"This your fault," he shouted, pointing his finger at me. "We all die because of you!"

He rushed towards us. Vicky and Bertie squealed, cowering against me. Suddenly T'ing-nan cried out, his body jerked, and the rage on his face turned to shock. Blood gushed from a wound in his neck, where a bullet had struck him. He fell and lay still. I experienced an ache of pity for the boy whose life had been destroyed by his father's evil.

A hailstorm of bullets battered the cabin wall very near us. If I couldn't get the children off the ship, I must find them shelter. Holding hands, we raced past the cabin while bullets impinged its walls. The deck pitched with the sea's motion; we skidded on boards slick with blood. Fortunately, the crew was too busy returning fire to notice us. I hurried them through a door in the cabin, into a dim space that contained barrels, ropes, and other equipment. The battle sounds were muted, and I heard voices from an adjacent room whose door stood ajar. Inside it, Kuan and Hitchman were engaged in an argument. I turned to flee with the children, but I saw Nick outside on the deck, crouching below the barrage of gunfire. What a pity that Vicky's blows hadn't killed him! His head was bruised and bloody, his eyes searching for us. Trapped between him and Kuan, we hid ourselves behind the barrels.

Hitchman said, "You must face the truth, Kuan. It's over."

"It is not over until I decide it is," came Kuan's cold, firm reply.

"Half our crew is dead," Hitchman said. I heard panic and urgency in his voice. "The rest of them can't hold off the navy forever."

"Justice is on our side," Kuan said with a calmness that seemed eerie under the circumstances. "We will prevail."

Hitchman uttered a humorless laugh. "No doubt our adversaries think the same of themselves. And they are far better equipped than we are."

"As long as I am alive, I shall not give up." Kuan's face blazed with ferocious determination.

He still clung to his hope of forcing Britain out of China and halting the opium trade. But Hitchman said, "Your plans are done for. I say we hand over the children and surrender."

"Are you mad?" Kuan stared at Hitchman in disbelief. "If we let them capture us, we'll be executed."

"If we let them capture us, at least we won't die tonight," Hitchman said. I knew then that he had never been truly committed to carrying out Kuan's scheme, and his personal devotion to Kuan was waning fast.

"We'll live only for as long as it takes us to be sent to the gallows," Kuan said.

"I was lucky enough to escape death once before when things looked hopeless," Hitchman said. "I'm willing to bet I'll be lucky again."

The gunfire continued, but there seemed to be more shots

coming in our direction than going towards the navy. "You were lucky only because I saved you in China," Kuan said, harsh and unyielding. "We must stand together."

"Sorry, old friend," Hitchman said, "but this is where we part ways. I'm going to hand over the children and the Brontë woman and bargain for leniency."

As he turned to walk out the door, the children and I shrank behind the barrels. I didn't trust him to do right by us, and if Kuan should find us, he would never let us go.

Kuan blocked Hitchman's exit. "I forbid you!" Outraged that Hitchman would defy him, he shouted, "You owe me your life. You will not betray me now!"

"I've more than repaid my debt to you," Hitchman said. "Move out of my way."

Just then Nick hurried in to them. He said in urgent, stilted, guttural speech: "Woman and children—gone!"

Kuan and Hitchman turned to him in consternation. I seized the children by their hands and fled with them. On our way out of the cabin, I bumped some object, which toppled with a loud clang. I heard Hitchman say, "There they are!"

We ran down the deck. They pounded after us as we swerved around dead bodies, past troops loading cannons.

"Stop them!" Kuan shouted.

Chinese crewmen joined the pursuit. Vicky moaned in fright while Bertie whooped as if this chase were a game of tag. The ship rocked; we zigzagged back and forth amidst flying bullets. Reaching the stern, we veered around the cabin. Hitchman and Nick came racing at us from the opposite direction, while Kuan and his crewmen caught up with us. Trapped and out of breath, we backed towards the railing. The battle and noise faded to the periphery of my awareness as I faced Kuan.

"You are even more clever than I thought, Miss Brontë." Kuan's smile expressed both admiration and annoyance. "What a pity that you and I are on opposite sides. Together we might have accomplished great things."

Flames from the burning navy ship rose behind him; his eyes

shone with their own, mad light. "But you won't get off this vessel. You might as well give up." He beckoned to me.

I felt the strange lassitude, the weakening of my will, that he always induced. How tempted I was to surrender! How much easier that would be! "No," I said, shaking my head in an effort to throw off Kuan's spell. "Let us go!"

"Negotiate with the navy," Hitchman urged Kuan. "Offer to hand over the hostages in exchange for our lives."

Kuan gestured to Nick, who pulled Hitchman away and held on to him. As Kuan stepped closer to me, I fumbled the pistol I'd stolen from the Chinaman out of my pocket. I held it in both hands, aimed at him.

"Stop," I said in a voice that trembled with panic. "Get away from us."

Kuan froze, startled for a moment before he recovered his poise. "Don't be ridiculous. Give me the gun, Miss Brontë."

He held out his hand. His eyes compelled my obedience; they drew me into their fiery depths. "Don't come any closer," I quavered as the heavy pistol wobbled in my grip.

"You will not shoot me." Confidence and scorn broadened Kuan's smile. "You cannot."

I feared he was right, for I had never killed and my very soul reviled the thought of taking a human life, even his. The lassitude encroached as my determination crumbled. Kuan now stood close enough to touch me, his face inches from the gun, his eyes intent on mine. The gun's weight exerted a vast downward pull on my muscles, my spirit.

"Let us go," I stammered, "or—or—"

"Or we'll jump off the ship!" Bertie climbed up on the railing. "Come on, Vicky!"

Frightened out of her wits, she followed suit. She and Bertie sat perched atop the railing, their backs towards the roiling ocean. Horrified, I said, "Get down this instant!"

There was an abrupt pause in the shooting from the navy: The troops had spied the children and ceased fire. I saw alarm on Kuan's face as he realized that Bertie was reckless enough to jump overboard with Vicky.

"If you jump, you'll drown," he told Bertie in a voice sharp with his fear of losing his hostages. "Now get off the railing."

"All right, I will!" Bertie flung his arms around Vicky and toppled overboard. They disappeared from view. I heard a high-pitched scream from Vicky, then a splash.

"No!"

Kuan's cry of rage echoed to the horizons. Leaning over the rail, he peered at the water, as did I. Below us, the children thrashed in the waves. We turned on each other in mutual fury. I thrust the gun at his face. An instant passed during which he stared down the barrel and I felt my anger towards him break his hold on me. I pulled the trigger.

Instead of a deafening boom, there came a harmless click. But even as Kuan laughed in derision, I dropped the gun, clambered up on the rail, and threw myself overboard. I heard him curse, felt him grab my skirt. It tore. I plummeted, screaming and waving my arms in a vain, instinctive attempt to fly. The ocean heaved up to claim me. I hit the water with a smack that knocked me breathless. Far into the freezing black depths I plunged.

My experience at swimming consisted of one occasion, on a trip to the shore with Ellen. We'd hired a bathing machine—a horse-drawn carriage in which we donned our bathing dresses and rode into the sea. We'd paddled about in the shallows, careful not to wet our hair. Now a cry of terror burbled from me. I flailed in blind panic until I surged to the surface. My head broke through to blessed air. I gulped a breath, but waves washed over me; I swallowed briny sea, choked, and spat. More waves tossed me. I treaded water, hampered by the clothing that billowed around me. Somehow my spectacles had stayed on my face, and I peered, through lenses streaming with water, in desperate search for the children.

At first I saw nothing but empty ocean, and my heart almost died. Then I spotted two heads, bobbing close together nearby. I paddled towards them. Vicky and Bertie gasped and sobbed, tiny flotsam on the swells.

"Hold onto me," I said.

They obeyed, and I began to swim, albeit incompetently, towards the navy ship. But their weight held me back, as did the crashing waves. The ship seemed as far away as the moon. I glanced back at Kuan's vessel and saw, to my horror, a boat that contained four Chinese crewmen rowing towards us. I kicked and paddled frantically. As my strength waned, Kuan's crew sped closer, and I feared we would perish. I saw another boat coming from the direction of the navy ship.

"Miss Brontë!" Mr. Slade shouted from the bow where he sat in front of two officers armed with rifles while two others manned the oars.

Such relief filled me as his boat neared me and Mr. Slade leaned over the side, extending his hand. I heard Kuan shout, "Stop them!"

Gunshots rang. Bullets pelted the water around us. While Mr. Slade lifted Vicky, his officers returned fire. One dropped his rifle and slumped lifeless. Mr. Slade hauled Vicky into the boat, but as he reached for Bertie, he faltered. He clutched his right arm; pain contorted his face: He'd been shot. He grabbed Bertie with his left hand. Kuan's rowboat closed in on us. One of Mr. Slade's oarsmen collapsed dead. I pushed Bertie upward. My strength, combined with Mr. Slade's, propelled Bertie into the boat. I clung to its side, straining to climb in. Mr. Slade grasped my collar; his injured arm dangled, bleeding. The boat dipped low under my weight. The surviving oarsman rose to help Mr. Slade, but the gunfire tumbled him overboard. I scrambled into the boat, streaming water, moaning in gratitude.

But now Kuan's rowboat was upon us. Its crew seized hold of our boat. We rocked and pitched in tandem while the Chinamen reached for the children. Vicky and Bertie squealed. Mr. Slade punched one man in the jaw, another in the stomach, and sent both falling into the sea. They tried to climb into our boat. I snatched up an oar and beat them. One of their comrades aimed a rifle at Mr. Slade. The other seized Bertie. The boy screamed, bit, and kicked. I swung my oar and struck the rifle a hard blow that knocked it sideways. It fired, missing Mr. Slade. Kuan's man lost his balance and splashed into the ocean. Mr. Slade lurched towards the

Chinaman who was tussling with Bertie and kicked him in the ribs. The man howled, loosing his grasp on Bertie. I hit him with the oar, and Mr. Slade shoved him overboard. Mr. Slade sat down and grabbed the other oar.

"Row!" he commanded me.

I obeyed, clumsily because I'd never rowed a boat before. Mr. Slade winced in pain as he wielded his oar. We rolled and buffeted over the waves towards the navy ship.

"Do not let them get away alive!" Kuan shouted. Muzzles spewed bursts of light and a din of shots at us. Bullets hit our boat and cannonballs splashed into the water around us.

"Lie down!" Mr. Slade shouted to Vicky and Bertie.

They flattened their shivering bodies on the boat's floor. The navy ship loomed huge above us. Officers flung down a rope ladder. I urged Bertie and Vicky up the ladder and followed while shots thudded the ship's hull. The officers hauled us aboard, then Mr. Slade. The ship blasted Kuan's with round after round of rifle and cannon fire. Navy men hurried the children into the shelter of the cabin. Exhausted, wet, and shivering on the cold deck, I wept for the joy of salvation. Mr. Slade caught me in a fierce, warm embrace as we watched Kuan's ship come steaming across the water towards us.

Its masts had fallen; its damaged wheels ground an uneven course. Flames erupted and smoke plumed from within it. Kuan stood alone on a platform in the bow, his face monstrous with rage, hatred, and madness. He shook his fist and ranted words inaudible over the navy's continuing barrage. Just when I thought his ship would ram ours in a last, futile effort to destroy us, the navy ships launched a concerted onslaught of cannon fire. Great booms resounded to the heavens. Missiles shattered Kuan's ship. Kuan struggled to keep his balance on his platform. His gaze met mine, and I felt his wrath leap across the narrow distance between us as his crippled vessel slowed and teetered. His lips formed my name; his voice in my head damned me. I saw and heard, as though in a vision we shared, the wartorn city of Canton and the screams of his wife and children as they died victims of a murder that he would never avenge. Mr. Slade held me tight while my sympathy for Kuan and my abhorrence of his evils fought one last battle within me.

Kuan raised his fists in a gesture of defiance, then dove into the ocean. His ship exploded in a pyre of flames and began to sink. Triumphant cheers arose from navy troops. Mr. Slade and I rushed to the railing and peered overboard. Kuan had vanished.

I turned to Mr. Slade, who gazed intently into my eyes. "My dearest Charlotte," he said in such a low voice that I could barely hear him above the noise of the troops rushing and shouting around us. His hand cupped my face. I felt its warmth, its trembling. The ardor in his expression rendered me breathless.

"I've always believed that some thoughts are better left unspoken," Mr. Slade said. "But this experience has made me realize that by remaining silent, one risks losing the opportunity to say what one needs most to say. If you had died, God forbid—" He shook his head, as though too horrified by the thought to complete it. "Here is what I need to say, and consequences be damned: Please allow me to tell you how deeply I am in love with you."

His voice dropped to a whisper that reverberated through me more powerfully than cannon fire. I felt a sweet, soaring bliss that I had never known. For the first time in my life, my love was returned by its object. For this I would gladly relive every terror I had experienced.

Mr. Slade frowned at me. "Have you nothing to say?" A look that verged on disappointment stole into his eyes. "I thought—I hoped—that you shared my feelings. Was I wrong?"

"You were not," I whispered, alight inside with a fire brighter than the flames that still leapt and blazed on the water. "I do."

He smiled; he bent his head to mine. As our lips met, I closed my eyes while the bliss soared higher and sweeter inside me. Here, in Mr. Slade's kiss, was the tenderness that our urgent coupling in the forest had lacked. Here was the moment I had awaited all my life and wished I could savor forever.

43

❊

MY STORY SHOULD HAVE ENDED THERE. IT WOULD HAVE allowed you, Reader, to believe that I lived happily ever after, like a princess in a fairy tale. But reality intrudes on the best occasions in life, which are as fleeting as the worst.

That kiss was the last private moment I was to spend with Mr. Slade for quite some time. We were interrupted by a navy officer, who informed me that the children required my care. I hurried to Vicky and Bertie, took off their wet clothes, wrapped them in blankets, fed them hot broth, and tucked them in bed. They fell asleep while I dried my own waterlogged self and the navy searched for Kuan and survivors from his ship. Hitchman was taken prisoner. Nick, the crew, and T'ing-nan's body had gone down with the wreck. No trace of Kuan was ever found.

I was summoned by Lord Unwin, who'd been aboard the navy ship all along, hiding during the battle. He commanded me to give him a full account of the kidnapping. Afraid that I would be blamed for it, I hastened to explain how the Duchess had threatened me at gunpoint. Lord Unwin replied that soon after the Queen had discovered the children missing, he had suspected that Kuan must have another accomplice besides Captain Innes. He'd searched Balmoral Castle and found a pistol and an empty laudanum vial in the Duchess's room. When he confronted her, she admitted her deed and named the royal guards who had helped her. She also confessed that Kuan had kidnapped her beloved niece to force her to participate in his scheme. I took that to mean that *Mr. Slade* had suspected, searched, confronted, and obtained the confession. But in any case, I was exonerated; the Duchess and her confederates were to hang.

It was Lord Unwin who explained to me how the children and I had been located: Mr. Slade had received a telegram from Papa, which said that Kuan had taken us aboard a ship anchored off Aberdeen. How Papa had known this was, at that time, a mystery. The Foreign Office had then joined forces with the navy to find the ship. Lord Unwin swore me to secrecy in regards to the kidnapping and all related events. It was in the best interest of the kingdom that as few persons as possible should know how vulnerable the Crown was, he said, lest Kuan's example inspire other such attacks. He ordered me to swear my family to secrecy as well. And until the time of this writing, as I relate these details in this document that shall perhaps go unread, I have kept my vow.

I watched over the children while the ship steamed back to port. Mr. Slade was recuperating from his wound, then occupied with business, and I didn't see him for some time. At sunrise we reached Aberdeen, where the Queen and Prince Consort joyously greeted Vicky and Bertie and took them away. Me they ignored. Lord Unwin hurried after the royal procession, I assumed to take credit for the rescue and to curry favor. Mr. Slade, reinstated to his post, accompanied Lord Unwin. I was given over to the care of a kindly Scottish officer, whose wife lent me clean, dry clothes, fed me, and gave me a room in which to sleep that night. Longing to see my family, I traveled home by train on the morrow, and reached Haworth the day after that.

The village that I had once wished to escape now seemed like Paradise. Never had the September sun shone brighter from a bluer sky; never had the moors seemed more magnificent nor the parsonage more inviting. Anne, Emily, and Papa welcomed me with glad exclamations and tears. The company of my kin brought me much more joy than the brilliant society I'd hoped to find when I'd gone to London. We eagerly shared the tales of our experiences.

"But how were you able to tell Mr. Slade where to find me?" I asked. "And how did you happen to send the news by telegraph?"

"It was Branwell's doing," Emily said with grudging admiration.

When she explained, I could hardly believe that Branwell had outwitted the men who had imprisoned them in the cellar, obtained the vital information, and thought up the means to convey it. That my wretched brother had ultimately brought about Kuan's downfall was amazing indeed. "Where is Branwell?" I said, eager to thank him.

My father's and sisters' expressions grew somber. Papa said, "We don't know."

Anne sighed. "Unfortunately, he has resumed his old ways."

Six days after my return, Branwell fainted while walking to the Black Bull Inn. The next day he was unable to get up from his bed, and his condition rapidly declined. We sent for Dr. Wheelright, who examined Branwell and declared that he was close to death. What a profound shock! Branwell's health had worsened so gradually that none of us had noticed; he'd been threatening to die for so long that we had failed to take him seriously. Not until now did I learn he was suffering from consumption, the same disease that had taken Maria and Elizabeth.

Branwell lay, his wasted frame shrunken to the size of a child's, under the coverlet. His red, unkempt hair straggled around his gaunt face. His features were yellow and sunken, his thin, white lips shaking. While Anne, Emily, and I wept around his bed, Papa knelt beside Branwell and clasped his hand.

"Oh, Father, I am dying," Branwell cried. "I have misspent my youth and utterly, miserably disgraced myself. In all my past life I have done none of the great things I intended."

"But you have," I said. "You saved all our lives and proved yourself a hero."

Throughout that day and night, my sisters and I sat vigil with Branwell; Papa prayed for his soul. Gradually, Branwell came to repent of his vices. He appeared to forget the Robinson woman;

indeed, he seemed unaware that he'd ever loved anyone but his family. Towards us he expressed a tender affection that gladdened, yet broke, our hearts. The next morning—Sunday, 24 September— we watched his life draw to an end. He grew calm and remained alert; to the last prayer which Papa offered up at his bedside, Branwell whispered, "Amen." After a sudden, brief convulsion, he departed us in his thirty-first year.

I felt as I had never felt before that there would be peace and forgiveness for him in Heaven. Every wrong Branwell had done, every pain he'd caused, vanished. I regretted that none but a few could know how brilliantly he'd risen to the last challenge of his life. I sank into a terrible state of grief, compounded by a delayed reaction to my harrowing experiences. Headache, bilious fever, and weakness kept me abed while Papa, Emily, and Anne made preparations for Branwell's funeral.

When it was done, our household regained harmony, even though a pall of sadness hung over it. Papa went about his business in the parish with his usual dedication. Anne seemed at peace while she did her chores. I believe her efforts in the investigation had satisfied her need for accomplishment. Emily scribbled industriously on what looked to be a new novel. It seemed that our adventures had helped her break through the mental barrier that prevented her from writing and inspired her creative force. I believe she is destined for greatness, for immortality.

Only I was discontented.

I received a letter from George Smith, in which he said he looked forward to publishing my next novel and hoped I would visit him again soon. But he seemed part of another life, and I could not settle down to writing. I could feel no sense of resolution until I saw Mr. Slade again.

He sent me a note, from the Foreign Office in London. It said that he had interrogated Hitchman, who had revealed names and locations of Kuan's confederates in the kingdom and abroad, in exchange for a sentence of life in prison instead of death by firing squad. Mr. Slade and his associates were presently occupied with arresting those criminals and purging corrupt officials from the government. The Charity School had been closed, the Reverend and Mrs. Grimshaw arrested, and the pupils sent to better institutions. Mr. Slade said he would call on me as soon as he could, but there was no renewal of the declarations he had made before we parted; I could not discern his sentiments between the lines. Had he changed his mind? Had I dreamed the words he'd said to me? When I composed my reply, I withheld the questions I longed to ask; I invited Mr. Slade to visit, and I shared our sad news of Branwell's passing.

I also wrote to Isabel White's mother, informing her that the man responsible for the murder of her daughter had been delivered to justice. My vow of secrecy forbade me to give her the specifics, but I hoped she would feel some satisfaction.

Then I waited.

October came, bringing cold weather. Two weeks after Branwell's funeral, I donned my cloak and bonnet, intending to walk the moors, but instead I found myself in the graveyard beside the church. The wind blew around the grey stone slabs that marked the graves. Misty drizzle fell from the dark afternoon sky. As I strolled upon sodden grass, a funeral party dressed in black gathered around a new grave. My heart was as melancholy as the scene, until I heard a horse's hooves pounding and saw a man riding up the lane. My spirits rocketed into joy.

"Mr. Slade!" I called.

He dismounted outside the graveyard. As he approached me, the dreary day brightened. I ran to meet him, then faltered because his serious expression inhibited my inclination to fling myself into his arms. All during our acquaintance we had advanced towards, then retreated from, each other; now he was in a phase of retreat.

"I was sorry to hear about your brother," Mr. Slade said, his manner coolly formal. "My condolences to you and your family."

I murmured my thanks. We avoided each other's gazes as we strolled together through the graveyard. My heart lapsed into a familiar state of painful, unrequited longing. Mr. Slade must have spoken insincerely on the ship, perhaps carried away by the excitement of the moment. Now he wished to forget what had passed between us. I could think of nothing to say except, "How is your wounded arm?"

"It's healing," Mr. Slade said.

"How are the Queen and the children?"

"They are well," Mr. Slade said. "Her Majesty sends you her best regards. Vicky and Bertie told her how valiantly you fought to save them, and she says that if you should ever need her services in return, you have only to ask."

"I am glad to be in Her Majesty's good graces."

"Regarding Lord Unwin," said Mr. Slade, "he has received a promotion."

"After the trouble he caused?" I said, dismayed.

A hint of a smile lifted Mr. Slade's mouth. "Lord Palmerston has sent him to join the colonial administration in India. The climate and tropical fevers should make quick work of him."

We had a stilted conversation about the ongoing effort to dismantle Kuan's criminal empire. I then said, "What will you do next?"

"The Foreign Office is sending me on a new assignment, to Russia. I expect to leave very soon. I cannot be certain when I'll return to England."

I heard in his voice that he was happy to go. He had no regret that we should soon part. Anguish stabbed me, yet I felt an unexpected rage. Throughout my life I had fallen in love with men and meekly accepted their rejection of me, but this time was different. I would not suffer in silence. My experiences had given me the courage to speak my mind.

"I understand what you are about," I said, turning upon Mr. Slade. "You've come to bid me a perfunctory goodbye. You dallied with me in Scotland, you played at romancing me on the ship, and now you think you can act as if it never happened and we can go back to being strangers." Offended beyond courtesy, I smote him on the chest. "You, sir, are the worst kind of cad!"

Mr. Slade beheld me as if astounded. "That isn't why I came. What are you talking about?"

"You said you were in love with me, but I should have known better." I didn't care that my voice rose loud and now the funeral party was watching us. "Especially since you told me that you require beauty and vivacity in a woman and could never form an attachment to one who lacks them."

"What nonsense is this?" Mr. Slade demanded in confusion. "When did I say that?"

"On the train to London," I said, "when we were discussing *Jane Eyre*."

Mr. Slade looked flabbergasted by recollection. "I was speaking of the characters in the book, not of you and myself." He uttered a laugh. "Women be damned! They're always taking personally the things men say, reading into them meanings that were never intended. They never forget the most casual passing remark that we might make. You fool, I meant every word I said to you on that ship."

As I stared, blank and speechless, Mr. Slade grasped my shoulders. "And I'm not here to tell you goodbye." His gaze was intense with passion. "I'm here to ask you to come to Russia with me—as my wife."

It was my turn to be flabbergasted. He wasn't brushing me off; he was proposing marriage! He, who had spurned romantic attachments since his wife's death, now sought to attach himself to me! Our experiences together had swept away the past and turned him towards the future, which he wanted us to share.

"Well? Do you accept my offer?" The beginnings of disappointment contended with hope on Mr. Slade's face. "Or am I to find out that *you* were playing at romance with *me*?"

I understood why he'd acted so coolly towards me at first: He'd been working himself up to this proposal and hiding his fear that I might refuse. Now my spirits soared on the sweet euphoria I'd felt when he'd kissed me. I thought back to the time when we first met, in the National Gallery, and the shock of recognition we'd felt. Our instincts must have sensed that we would one day be husband and wife.

"Good God, don't keep me in suspense!" Mr. Slade said. "Is your answer yes or no?"

With all my heart I cried, "Yes!"

I thought I'd wept all my tears when Branwell died, but now they flowed anew, from the same radiant gladness that I saw on Mr. Slade's face. He drew me close, but as he bent to kiss me and seal our pledge, I felt a misgiving so powerful that I stiffened in his embrace.

"What is it?" Mr. Slade said, drawing back from me in concern. "You're not having doubts about marrying me?"

Amazingly, I was. Here I had gained what I'd thought all my life was the ultimate prize—a marriage proposal from a man I loved, and who loved me. But I felt as if I had opened a beautiful gift package only to discover that its contents, although exactly what I'd wished for, were somehow wrong.

"Not about marrying you," I said, "but perhaps about what would happen afterward. We would live in Russia for the foreseeable future?"

"Yes." Mr. Slade's eyes shone with his relish of exploring new, foreign territory.

I had a vague notion of czars, Cossacks, and frozen steppes. Three months ago this would have stirred a pleasant thrill in me, but now . . . "Russia is so far away."

"Well, yes," Mr. Slade said, chastened by my hesitation. "But wouldn't you like to see the world?" When I nodded, he said, "Here's our chance to see it together."

But I felt a strong resistance to leaving Papa, Emily, and Anne. My remaining kin were dearer to me than ever now. I also felt a strong attachment to Haworth, small and isolated though it be. This was the center of my universe, the haven to which I must always return, the thought of which had sustained me during my wanderings.

"I don't know the Russian language," I said.

"I'll teach you," said Mr. Slade.

Still I hesitated. "I don't know anyone in Russia. I would be all alone while you're busy working. What would I do?"

"You can write more books."

But my books had deep roots in my own history. If I pulled up those roots, inspiration would vanish. My writing anchored me to

Haworth as strongly as did my kin. My unfinished book, and other books yet to be written, had a claim on me stronger than Mr. Slade's. Sorrowful wisdom filled my heart. I withdrew from Mr. Slade and leaned on a stone tomb.

"I cannot marry you," I said, though tearful with regret and desolation.

"Why not?" Mr. Slade said. When I explained my reasons, he waved them away. "There are difficulties, to be sure, but together we can overcome them."

I had once believed that love conquered all, but I knew the nature of his profession, and I knew we would be more apart than together if we married. I pictured myself alone and idle, waiting for him to come home, and affection turning to resentment because I'd given up everything for him. Once, everything I had in life had seemed so little, but now I recognized that it was too precious to lose—and that what I would lose upon sacrificing it was myself.

"No," I said sadly. "We belong to different worlds. This is mine." I gestured at the parsonage, the church, the village, and the moors. "Anywhere else, I would be lost."

"Then I'll quit the Foreign Office," Mr. Slade said. "We'll live here in Yorkshire."

He renounced his profession with the rash impulse of a man in love. For only a moment was I tempted to allow it. I could see that his eyes were focused on distant horizons even as they watched me; I felt the restlessness in him that required the whole world to roam. His spirit, and his love for me, would die in the confines of my life here.

"I cannot accept such a sacrifice," I said.

We argued long and fervently, he trying to sway me and I standing solid even while I ached with love for him. There was some talk of marrying even though I would remain at home while he went abroad, but a marriage in which we might never see each other seemed pointless to us both. At last Mr. Slade conceded.

"It seems I've come to say goodbye after all," he said, his head bowed, his countenance shattered by despair.

I already regretted my decision, even though I knew it was right. My tears streamed as the funeral party filed past us. I thought Mr. Slade wept too, but I couldn't be certain.

"If I should return to England," he said in an unsteady voice, "may I call on you?"

"Yes," I said, gladdened by the possibility, even as the thought of many years without him gave me pain.

"Then farewell," Mr. Slade said.

He kissed me tenderly, and I clung to him. I memorized the taste and the warmth of him, the power of our desire; I didn't care who saw. Then we released each other. After one last, longing look passed between us, Mr. Slade turned from me. Rain began to fall, and even as I watched him walk out of the graveyard, I sobbed. Mr. Slade paused at the gate. His gaze searched me. What an overwhelming urge I fought to call him back! Mr. Slade's expression grew resigned. He mounted his horse. A desolate peace came over me: If I had to be alone, it was at least by my own choice.

Mr. Slade rode off. I watched until he disappeared from sight.

Reader, I let him go.

EPILOGUE

A YEAR HAS PASSED SINCE THE DAY I RECEIVED THE LETTER THAT sent me to London and launched me into the adventures described herein. I have finished writing my account of them, and all that remains to be told is their aftermath.

The black chariot of death soon visited my family again following Branwell's demise. Consumption took Emily on 19 December 1848, and Anne followed her shortly afterward, on 28 May 1849. Their suffering, and mine, do not bear description. Let my tears that fall on this page suffice. Now Papa and I are the sole survivors of the family Brontë. Light shines from his study where he sits working on a sermon. I am writing alone at the table where Emily, Anne, and I once read and discussed our manuscripts. The house is silent but for the crackling of the fire in the grate; outside, the wind gusts and rain lashes the windows. Tonight, as on many other nights, my mind reflects upon the happier past and ponders questions unresolved.

Was the joy of knowing Mr. Slade worth the sorrow I felt at his absence? Had I been able to predict that this terrible, empty solitude would be my lot, would I have married him and gone with him to Russia? Would my misgivings have been overcome had I known that I would soon lose my beloved companions and long for a husband to love in their place?

Reason tells me that I would have stayed. That I did allowed me to spend Anne's and Emily's final hours with them; I was able to comfort Papa. I would not have willingly given up those privileges.

Yet I cannot help imagining how much richer and happier my life would have been as Mr. Slade's wife. Nor can I dismiss the superstitious notion that if one thing in the past had turned out differently, so might everything else. If I had married Mr. Slade, would Anne and Emily be alive now? My imagination fills the room with voices, laughter, and warmth. Anne and Emily sit across the table, Mr. Slade beside me—he and I are home on a respite from our world-wandering. I add Branwell to the picture; miraculously restored to life and health, he entertains us with poems. The firelight glows on our happy faces.

But reality cannot be altered. The apparitions of my dear departed fade away; the room is again quiet. The pages of this manuscript are my testament to the valor of Emily, Anne, and Branwell. Someday may it be read and their heroics known. In the meantime, blank pages wait ready for me to fill with other tales. My writing is my comfort, as it has been in the past. And although I have had neither sight nor word of Mr. Slade, and my yearning for him pains me yet, I would not have forgone that which we shared. Somewhere in the world, he walks and breathes, and I feel in my heart that fortune will someday bring us together again.

God speed him to me.

Farewell.

AUTHOR'S NOTE

>‹‹

*T*HE *SECRET ADVENTURES OF CHARLOTTE BRONTË* IS A FANTASY built around actual persons and historical events. Charlotte, Emily, Anne, Branwell, and the Reverend Patrick Brontë were real people. Other real characters whose names and personal details I have borrowed for this novel are Martha Brown, Ellen Nussey, George Smith and his family, Arthur Bell Nicholls, Constantin Heger, Lord Russell, Lord Palmerston, and Queen Victoria, Prince Albert, and their children. Charlotte and Anne did visit London in 1848. Political revolutions did erupt in Europe during that year, and the Chartist movement did sweep across England. However, the plot of this novel and all the scenes dramatized herein are purely fictional. The first Opium War between China and Britain, the events leading up to it, and the political consequences for China are a matter of record; so are the serious problems that opium addiction caused in China. Kuan is a fictional character, whose grievances and motives are arguably justified even if his actions are not. I have tried to be true to history in my portrayal, but all other aspects of the novel are products of my imagination.

READERS GROUP GUIDE

The Secret Adventures of Charlotte Brontë

LAURA JOH ROWLAND

For more information, a Q&A with Laura Joh Rowland, and an expanded reader's guide, please visit our Web site at www.overlookpress.com.

A NOTE FROM LAURA JOH ROWLAND ABOUT THE WRITING OF *The Secret Adventures of Charlotte Brontë*:

She was a Victorian parson's daughter, from a remote English village, who wrote a best selling, notorious, and beloved novel. That's what many people know about Charlotte Brontë, author of *Jane Eyre*. Not as many are aware that she lived a life as rich in adventure, romance, and tragedy as her famous novel.

I happened upon her story years ago, by sheer accident. I was a premed student at the University of Michigan, struggling to keep my head above water in my chemistry, biology, and physics courses. My favorite study break was browsing the shelves in the library and reading books about subjects far removed from science. One day I picked up a biography of Charlotte Brontë. I was enthralled by her experience at a grim Victorian boarding school, her extraordinary siblings, her dramatic rise to literary fame, her late in life marriage, and her early, tragic death.

Life intervened. I never went to med school. (The fact that I preferred reading for pleasure to studying science probably had something to do with it.) Inspired at least in part by Charlotte, I eventually became a writer, although of books as unrelated to her as one could imagine. But I never forgot her. What particularly stuck in my mind was the thought that no matter how much adventure she'd experienced, she always craved more. She was the ultimate yearning, romantic, creative spirit. Many years into my career as an author, I decided that Charlotte would make the perfect heroine for a historical suspense novel. Thus was born *The Secret Adventures of Charlotte Brontë*.

There are definite parallels between Charlotte and Jane. Both had a lot of passion. They were ambitious—they had the fire to be something more than they were. Like the classic heroine, they wanted to go places. Charlotte cared what people thought of her, but she did what she wanted to do and took the hits. She triumphed over the everyday things that circumscribed her life.

As I wrote the book, I combined the rich material of her life with the political and sexual intrigue beneath the prim morality of Victorian England. I tried to give Charlotte the adventure she craved. In the Victorian era, things were changing fast. The world was opening up through technology. It was a time of high propriety and moralism with a dirty underbelly—a sex trade that flourished amid great poverty, for example. It was hard to come up with a plot that took advantage of that fascinating time. I didn't want to write a small and limited village mystery. I had to learn all of European history of the period to send Charlotte on her adventures. England in the Victorian era had a finger in every pie in the world Charlotte was passionately interested in politics and the world around her. I couldn't have her limited to her own life in Haworth—she wanted to do more.

The Secret Adventures of Charlotte Brontë is my heartfelt tribute to one of the greatest authors of all time.

➤✦◄

Discussion Questions

1. Do you think the narrative style reflects a nineteenth-century woman writer? What aspects of the prose contribute to the notion that Charlotte Brontë actually wrote the story?

2. Victorian England is known for its strict sense of propriety and tradition. How did the characters in the story either abide by or diverge from these customs? Discuss the relationships between these characters: George White and Charlotte; John Slade and Charlotte; Monsieur Heger and Charlotte; Isabel White and Kuan Tzu-chan; Kuan Tzu-chan and Charlotte; Queen Victoria and Prince Consort; Branwell and his sisters.

3. The novel also addresses the clearly defined social hierarchy in Victorian England. What different social classes are represented in the novel? Which characters fall into those categories? How do the characters' social positions affect their role in the action of the novel? Consider the Brontë family, the relationship between John Slade and Lord Unwin, the Royal family, Isabel White, and the girls at the Charity School.

4. Women in Victorian England had very few opportunities for employment. Their need to work in Victorian society depended on their social status. What does the Brontë sisters' employment as governesses say about their social status?

5. Charlotte, Anne, and especially Emily have many arguments about revealing their true identities to the public. Many women authors used male pen names so that readers would take their books more seriously. What are some other reasons the sisters may have had for not wanting to reveal themselves as authors?

6. Since the novel is written from Charlotte's point of view in first person, in order to describe scenes in which Charlotte was not present, she rewrites entries from other people's journals or letters that people wrote. Because of this, we are aware of occurrences in the plot that Charlotte herself does not know until after her story ends. For example, we know Emily's experiences at the Charity School as it fits into the story, but Charlotte only learns of them after Emily's death. How do these points of view shift and change the narrative? How do they affect your reading experience, and the way you identify with Charlotte?

7. We do not learn the significance of the dramatic scene in the prologue describing Beautiful Jade's murder until almost the end of the novel. How did this opening affect your expectations for the rest of the novel? If this scene had appeared later, when Kuan describes his life to Charlotte, how would it have changed your reading experience?

8. When Kuan first begins telling Charlotte about his life, Charlotte marvels at how foreign his life in China is from England society. During the nineteenth century, many Western countries separated themselves from Eastern cultures, categorizing them as exotic and foreign. In many novels written during the Victorian era, authors describe the Far East less as civilized than England. Charlotte admits that she had always "preferred to believe that people in the Far East were savage, ignorant heathens, and if they only knew better, they would understand that we wanted what was best for everyone. We, after all, were more advanced in science and philosophy; we were Christians, with God to justify our actions" (p. 261). Is Charlotte's realization that these assumptions may not be justified something that an average Victorian reader would think? Why or why not? How do you approach these kinds of beliefs from a contemporary standpoint?

9. Many issues, such as sexuality, gender, class, and political corruption that plagued Victorian England persist in society today. Discuss any characters

that relate to current events or issues in our time. Consider Lord John Russell's corruption, Isabel White's prostitution, Charlotte's suppressed sexuality, and any others you can think of.

10. During the nineteenth century, England was a formidable power that ruled colonies all over the world. Kuan almost convinces Charlotte of his reasoning for his crimes by describing the terrible situation opium created in China. Do you think Charlotte was convinced only because of Kuan's alluring nature, or did Kuan have legitimate reasons for his actions? Later, Queen Victoria argues the other side of the issue—in favor of England. Charlotte realizes that the Queen of England will understandably argue for whatever helps England, but the Queen also makes some legitimate points. Does Charlotte ultimately believe in John Slade and their mission, or does she see Kuan's point of view to the end? How does Branwell's addiction to opium affect her views?

11. The novel centers itself in a widely studied time and place in history—the Victorian era. How well does the novel describe the society of that time to a reader who has never studied or read Victorian literature? Does biographical information about Charlotte Brontë and her family come through clearly in the midst of the fictional plot?

12. Throughout the story, Charlotte references her popular novel, *Jane Eyre*, as a loose parallel to her life—a life of adventure and love that she had always yearned to experience. How does the ending of this novel compare to the ending of *Jane Eyre*? Even though Charlotte has adventures that exceed her heroine's, she does not share the same fate in love as Jane Eyre. Why doesn't Charlotte marry John Slade? Discuss her reasoning for refusing along with what would have happened if the novel did end with their marriage.